In his essay, "On Faerie Stories," J. R. Tolkien speaks of a great cauldron of myth into which all writers dip. This metaphor comes from witch mythology. The goddess is frequently depicted with a cauldron. For the Welsh, this is the Cauldron of Ceridwen, which holds great power for life and death. For the Norse, this cauldron belongs to Mimir and contains the magic of story-telling. For Shakespeare, the cauldron is presided over by three witches and contains "eye of newt and toe of bat"—and prophetic vision.

HECATE'S CAULDRON contains thirteen modern versions of our fascination with witchcraft. Look at these stories as thirteen different spells. You may laugh, you may shiver, or even want to weep, but if the spells work, you will be enchanted.

—S.M.S.

**SUSAN M. SHWARTZ** received her B.A. from Mount Holyoke College and her M.A. and Ph.D. from Harvard University. She writes: "As a reader, writer, scholar, I am extremely interested in witches. My academic training is in medieval literature, especially Arthurian romance which boasts one major wizard and, in the persons of the Ladies of the Lake, many witches and one great sorcerous antagonist to Camelot, Morgan le Fay. Because of my background in romance studies and my experience in teaching fantasy, I can organize an anthology and write on the subject of witches. Because of my own fiction—a story published in *The Keeper's Price*, another forthcoming in *Analog*, and others circulating—I can make *Hecate's Cauldron* even more entertaining."

# *Hecate's Cauldron*

*Edited by*

Susan M. Shwartz

**DAW Books, Inc.**

DONALD A. WOLLHEIM, PUBLISHER

1633 Broadway, New York, NY 10019

PUBLISHED BY
THE NEW AMERICAN LIBRARY
OF CANADA LIMITED

Cover art by Michael Whelan.

(For color prints of this and other Michael Whelan cover paintings, please contact: Glass Onion Graphics, 172 Candlewood Lake Road, Brookfield, CT 06804.)



FIRST PRINTING, FEBRUARY 1982

2 3 4 5 6 7 8 9

PRINTED IN CANADA
COVER PRINTED IN U.S.A.

# CONTENTS

**TO MERLIN**

**and to all good familiars everywhere.**

*Introduction*

# SEASONS OF THE WITCH

## *by Susan M. Shwartz*

Pumpkins, black cats, and children in pointed hats at Halloween . . . hysterical girls and stern Puritan judges in Salem . . . in a clearing, a house made all of gingerbread . . . thirteen skyclad figures dancing in a ring . . . a woman tied to a stake. Who says there are no such things as witches?

Lovers of fantasy have always known that witches exist. Maybe their first exposure to witches was the Wicked Witch in "Sleeping Beauty" or "Rapunzel," or perhaps Glinda the Good in *The Wizard of Oz.* Or perhaps they learned to chant, "double, double, toil and trouble" with the Three Witches in *Macbeth* or became fascinated with the sorceresses who dominate Andre Norton's Witch World—or with the Witch-king in E.R. Eddison's *The Worm Ourobouros* who battles Demons and Goblins in Zimiamvia.

*When* was the first witch? Some historians speak of a Mother Goddess whose generative powers, allied with the earth and the cycles of the moon, were reflected in women's ability to bear children. When people learned that men too played a role in the creation of children, the goddess was dethroned and her power was transformed from something beneficent into something fearsome, mysterious, and bloody. Like the Furies of Greek drama, the goddess went underground. As one of Marion Zimmer Bradley's most unsympathetic characters in *Two To Conquer* (DAW, 1980) says, "it had always been death to spy on women's mysteries and for that reason all sensible societies had always outlawed women's mysteries." But they could not eradicate them. The mysteries simply went underground, anthropologists say, and from them emerge the witch stories as well. Thus the goddess of fertility can turn into something fearsome. The goddess of love too has her dark side. Most important in the study of goddess-worship is Diana, the virgin goddess of the hunt. The Romans called her Diana Trivia because she had three aspects. As Diana, she was a huntress with a savage as well as a gentle nature. She might favor a hunter like Hippolytus or a runner like Atalanta, but she could also turn ferociously upon Acteon, who saw her bathing, or Callisto, a woman sworn to her who became pregnant. As Selene, Diana ruled the changes of the moon and governed beauty—and lunacy as well. Finally, as Hecate, Diana stood at the crossroads at midnight and was the patroness of dark sorcery. Diana is simply one name for the Triple Goddess—Maiden, Mother, Crone—whose images pervade modern fantasy and whose consort hunts at her side.

Several of the stories in this anthology—C.J. Cherryh's "Willow" and Jayge Carr's "Reunion"—reveal these various aspects of the goddess. In "Willow," for example, Maiden and Mother attract the protagonist; the Crone, however, terrifies him by hinting at punishment. In "Reunion" Venus appears both as a coquettish vampire/witch and the patroness of lovers. And Diana Paxson's "Riddle of Hekaitë" shows the goddess as mistress of fates.

The figure of the witch, like that of the goddess, is profoundly ambivalent. For most of us, the associations of "witch" call to mind demented Puritans, fanatical witchburning monks, or Walt Disney's animated version of "Night on Bald Mountain" in *Fantasia.* These are the dark aspects of witchery. But we can match every hag-witch in fantasy with a good witch. Glinda protects Oz and Dorothy against the Wicked Witch of the West. Galadriel, whom the people of Gondor regard as a witch, guards them from Saruman and Sauron. The Lady of the Lake's gift of a magic sword helps defend Arthur against Morgan le Fay. Sometimes, in fact, the conflict between good and evil so central to satisfying fantasy is contained in the witch herself.

Take some of our earliest recorded witches, Circe from the *Odyssey*, her niece Medea, from the *Argonautica* of Apollonius of Rhodes. Descended from Helios the sun-god, these two witch-women can be identified by their more than mortal sunning and the glints of gold in their dark eyes. Circe, it is true, changes men into swine, but when Odysseus forces her to restore them to their original form, they emerge younger and more handsome from the experience. And she tells Odysseus how to descend to the underworld . . . and how to return. She appears menacing; but she is ultimately helpful. Medea is able to restore people to life and youth, or kill them swiftly with potions. Only Jason's abandonment of her turns her toward grisly vengeance.

Why is the witch ambivalent? According to psychologist Bruno Bettelheim in *The Uses of Enchantment*, the witch in fantasy represents either the totally good mother who satisfies all our desires or the evil stepmother who rejects and destroys. This power to satisfy or kill makes witches as dangerous as they appear in fantasy stories. "Do not meddle," say Tolkien's elves, "in the affairs of wizards, for they are subtle, and quick to anger." That goes double for witches.

The opposition of good witch and bad witch may be seen in Arthurian stories. Merlin, the wise mage, allies with Arthur; his own sister Morgan le Fay hates him and, as Sir Thomas Malory writes, "sets the land on fire with ladies that were enchantresses." While this might seem the same archetype of good male wizard/bad female witch that Ursula LeGuin uses in *The Wizard of Earthsea,* sorcery in Arthurian romance is actually more complicated. At the last, Merlin (allegedly of diabolical origin) is betrayed by his own power in the hands of a sorceress, who then helps Arthur's knights and even marries one of them, Sir Pelleas. And finally, when Arthur must be carried to Avalon for the healing of his wounds, even Morgan le Fay helps get him there. That the witch allies with the warrior for the good of the realm seems to be the pattern here as in modern fantasies like the Witch World series.

The Middle Ages, which created Merlin and Morgan, were especially odd in their attitudes toward witches. On one hand, sorcerers, alchemists, clairvoyants, and astrologers were commonly associated with the households of great lords. These, however, were primarily men. At the same time, what psychiatrist Thomas Szasz calls "marginal" and "socially expendable" people—the old, the eccentric, the mentally ill, or surplus women—were tormented and executed as witches and heretics. "Thou shalt not suffer a witch to live," proclaimed Exodus 22:18, and medieval clergy obeyed it with a vengeance. A witch could be anything—lunatic, heretic, worker in the Craft, or merely someone who was in the way.

Consider the case of Dame Alice Kyteler of County Kilkenny, Ireland. Dame Alice was a wealthy woman who had had four husbands and enjoyed a very active life indeed. Unfortunately, she antagonized the children of her first marriages by bequeathing all her property to her youngest children. So in 1324 Dame Alice's children claimed that she had renounced Christ and the Church to obtain magic. She sacrificed animals to demons, they said. Moreover, she had a familiar—and demon lover—named Robin, one of the first familiars in the history of witchcraft to bear a name. Robin would appear to Dame Alice (when they weren't making love) as a cat, a dog, or a black man accompanied by comrades. At night, Dame Alice's scandalized children claimed, their mother would blow out the candles, cry "Fi, fi, fi, amen!" and join in an orgy with other witches.

Although Dame Alice herself escaped punishment (and, one hopes, lived to a ripe and rowdy old age), some of the people implicated in her children's testimony were indeed executed.

This case includes several interesting features of later witch stereotypes: the named familiar (cats, dogs, and strangers are most common), the intercourse with a demon lover, the band of associates—generally twelve—around a leader, and the emphasis on renunciation of the Church. It also shows how the cry of "Witch, witch!" could be used to persecute someone who simply did not fit in. Apparently Dame Alice's refusal to resign control of her life and property made her singular. Brought up in a misogynist tradition as well as in an atmosphere of folktales, her children resorted predictably to accusations of witchcraft to attempt to control a mother who refused to retire into senile powerlessness. This is the same thing that Joisan in Norton's *Crystal Gryphon* (published 648 years later) describes when she says that a woman who opposes custom runs the risk of being accused, even by close kin, of striking a bargain with dark powers.

Despite modern prejudices against the Middle Ages, the most vicious persecutions of witches came during the allegedly civilized Renaissance and Reformation. In 1484 Pope

Innocent VIII deplored the outbreak of witchery in Germany and sent two Dominican inquisitors to stamp it out. Their publication in 1486 of the *Malleus Maleficarum* (Hammer of Witches) proclaimed to all Europe that open season on witches had started. In a way, it is ironic that movable type, which was such a force for civilization, enabled the *Malleus Maleficarum* to be distributed so widely. Thus began the wave of witch persecutions that is sometimes called the Burning Times.

The witch craze moved out from the Alps and the Pyrenees—isolated, mountainous regions where people preserved old traditions—to touch other rural cultures like that of Essex in England or all the mountain cultures where, as historian H. Trevor-Roper points out, the thin air creates hallucinations, vertigo, and fear while the avalanches and glaciers make it easy for people to believe that powers hostile to mankind exist. Thousands of men and women died, while clergymen made their reputations as witch-finders or witchburners. And if monks brought witch-hunts into the Spanish possessions in the New World, the Puritans also had their witch trials. So, for that matter, did the native Americans whom they were to decimate.

In England at this time, Henry VIII was divorcing his second queen, Anne Boleyn. Among the charges against her were adultery, incest, and witchcraft.

Shakespeare's three witches date from the century following Henry. *Macbeth*, first performed in 1616, was first published in 1623 during the reign of James I, one of the most neurotic and superstitious kings who ever ruled England. He was also a witchhunter who wrote a treatise against sorcery. So in *Macbeth* are "black and malignant hags" and a malevolent Hecate (helped along by an anonymous rhyming hack) who represent the worst imagining of the witchfinders. Even though they predict the coming of James himself, the witches had to be hateful.

And witches in literature stayed hateful until the nineteenth-century revival of the *Märchen*, or fairy tales, by people like the brothers Grimm and Hans Christian Andersen. If they gave us the wicked witch of "Hansel and Gretel," they also gave us the beautiful Snow Queen whom Joan Vinge's 1979 novel transformed into an incarnation of the goddess and took out among the stars. Writers once again were becoming interested in witches as something more than a convenient subject for sermons.

Today loremasters and writers of fantasy (often the same people) will tell you that "witch" does not come from the Old English word "witan" that means "to know." Instead it comes from the words "wicce" and "wicca," or male and female witches. Some modern fantasists call male witches warlocks, but this, in fact, is a misnomer. The warlock (Old English *Waerloga*) actually is an oathbreaker and outlaw.

Still other writers—notably Andre Norton—will concentrate on the woman as witch and stress the fact that her role was "one of the few which an intelligent and knowledge-seeking woman could find in the past to supply her need for intellectual growth." It is little reason, then, that a majority of writers of stories about witches are women.

In this anthology, many writers explore non-Western systems of magic. Jessica Amanda Salmonson presents the *kami*, the Japanese spirits; Charles Saunders tells a fearsome tale of African sorcery involving twins, whom some tribes consider to be accursed. Writers like Jacqueline Lichtenberg and Jean Lorrah take advantage of the twentieth century's fascination with the occult to bring it into the lives of characters whom one might meet in a supermarket. Katherine Kurtz explains witchcraft genetically while Diana Paxson and Diana Wynne Jones make their characters switch times and universes. We should not think that this is strange. There are as many myths of witches as there are cultures, or minds to perceive them, and hearts to respond to them.

In his essay "On Faerie Stories," J.R.R. Tolkien speaks of a great cauldron of myth, or story, into which all writers dip. This metaphor too comes from witch mythology. The goddess is frequently depicted with a cauldron. For the Welsh, this is the Cauldron of Cerridwen, which holds great power for life and death. For the Norse, this cauldron belongs to Mimir and contains the magic of story-telling. For Shakespeare, the cauldron is presided over by three witches and contains "eye of newt and toe of bat"—and prophetic vision.

*Hecate's Cauldron* contains thirteen modern versions of our own fascination with witchcraft. (The number, of course, has been chosen deliberately.) Look at these stories as thirteen different spells. You may laugh, you may shiver, or even want to weep, but if the spells work, you will be enchanted.

# BORIS CHERNEVSKY'S HANDS

## by Jane Yolen

*When I contacted Jane Yolen, I was delighted to receive her answer, "How about Baba Yaga?" This Russian witch, whose house perches on chicken legs, has long been a favorite of mine. And Jane's taking the story out into some future world of a spacefaring, Yiddish-speaking carnival only makes this story's background richer and more comic.*

*Jane Yolen was the 1974 Golden Kite Award winner for her book* The Girl Who Cried Flowers, *which was also a finalist for the National Book Award. This is but one of her many prize-winning books. In the past five years she has begun to publish in the fantasy and science fiction magazines; and their worlds are brighter places thanks to her polished writing, her compassion, and her own personal magic. A full-time writer and occasional composer of songs, she lives with her family in western Massachusetts, entirely too close to Northampton where Puritan minister Jonathan Edwards preached in the tradition of the Salem witch-hunters.*

*Jane's style is more subtle. As a writer of children's books as well as of adult fiction (and where the cut-off comes, nobody knows) Jane Yolen blends message with humor. Her stories are what Ursula LeGuin calls psychomyths—carefully crafted tales that appeal to readers on two levels—as stories and as evocations of their inner needs. "Boris Chernevsky's Hands" is such a story.*

Boris Chernevsky, son of the famous Flying Chernevskys and nephew to the galaxy's second greatest juggler, woke up unevenly. That is to say, his left foot and right hand lagged behind in the morning rituals.

Feet over the side of the bed, wiggling the recalcitrant left toes and moving the sluggish right shoulder, Boris thought about his previous night's performance.

"Inept" had been Uncle Misha's kindest criticism. In fact, most of what he had yelled was untranslatable and Boris was glad that his own Russian was as fumbling as his fingers. It had not been a happy evening. He ran his slow hands through his thick blond hair and sighed, wondering—and not for the first time—if he had been adopted as an infant or exchanged *in utero* for a scholar's clone. How else to explain his general awkwardness?

He stood slowly, balancing gingerly because his left foot was now asleep, and practiced a few passes with imaginary *na* clubs. He had made his way to eight in the air and was starting an over-the-shoulder pass, when the clubs slipped and clattered to the floor. Even in his imagination he was a klutz.

His Uncle Misha said it was eye and ear coordination, that the sound of the clubs and the rhythm of their passing were what made the fine juggler. And his father said the same about flying: that one had to hear the trapeze and calculate its swing by both eye and ear. But Boris was not convinced.

"It's in the hands," he said disgustedly, looking down at his five-fingered disasters. They were big-knuckled and grained like wood. He flexed them and could feel the right moving just a fraction slower than the left. "It's all in the hands What I wouldn't give for a better pair."

"And what *would* you give, Boris Chernevsky?" The accent was Russian, or rather Georgian. Boris looked up, expecting to see his uncle.

There was no one in the trailer.

Boris turned around twice and looked under his bed.

Sometimes the circus little people played tricks, hiding in closets and making sounds like old clothes, singing. Their minds moved in strange ways, and Boris was one of their favorite gulls. He was so easily fooled.

"Would you, for example, give your soul?" The voice was less Georgian, more Siberian now. A touch of Tartar, but low and musical.

"What's a soul?" Boris asked, thinking that adopted children or clones probably weren't allowed any anyway.

"Two centuries ago," the voice said and sighed with what sounded like a Muscovite gurgle, "everyone had a soul and no one wanted to sell. Today everyone is willing to sell, only no one seems to have one."

By this time, Boris had walked completely around the inside of the trailer, examining the underside of chairs, lifting the samovar lid. He was convinced he was beginning to go crazy. "From dropping so many imaginary *na* clubs on my head," he told himself out loud. He sat down on one of the chairs and breathed heavily, his chin resting on his left hand. He didn't yet completely trust his right. After all, he had only been awake and moving for ten minutes.

Something materialized across the table from him. It was a tall, gaunt old woman whose hair looked as if birds might be nesting in it. Nasty birds. With razored talons and beaks permanently stained with blood. He thought he spotted guano in her bushy eyebrows.

"So," the apparition said to him, "*hands* are the topic of our discussion." Her voice, now that she was visible, was no longer melodic but grating, on the edge of a scold.

"Aren't you a bit old for such tricks, Baba?" asked Boris, trying to be both polite and steady at once. His grandmother, may she rest in pieces on the meteorite that had broken up her circus flight to a rim world, had taught him to address old women with respect. "After all, a grandmother should be. . . ."

"Home tending the fire and the children, I suppose." The old woman spat into the corner, raising dust devils. "The centuries roll on and on but the Russian remains the same. The Soviets did wonders to free women up as long as they were young. Old women, we still have the fire and the grandchildren." Her voice began to get louder and higher. *Peh*, she spat again. "Well, I for one, have solved the grandchildren problem."

Boris hastened to reach out and soothe her. All he needed now, on top of last evening's disastrous performance, was to have a screaming battle with some crazy old lady when his Uncle Misha and his parents, the Famous Flying, were asleep in the small rooms on either side of the trailer. "Shh, shhh," he cautioned.

She grabbed at his reaching right hand and held it in an incredibly strong grip. Vised between her two claws, his hand could not move at all. "This, then," she asked rhetorically, "is the offending member?"

He pulled back with all his strength, embarassment lending him muscles, and managed to snag the hand back. He held it under the table and tried to knead feeling back into the fingers. When he looked up at her, she was smiling at him. It was not a pretty smile.

"Yes," he admitted.

She scraped at a wen on her chin with a long, dirty fingernail. "It *seems* an ordinary-enough hand," she said. "Large knuckles. Strong veins. I've known peasants and tsars that would have envied you that hand."

*"Ordinary,"* Boris began in a hoarse whisper and stopped. Then, forcing himself to speak, he began again. "Ordinary is the trouble. A juggler has to have *extraordinary* hands. A juggler's hands must be spider web strong, bird's wing quick." He smiled at his metaphors. Perhaps he was a poet-clone.

The old woman leaned back in her chair and stared at a spot somewhat over Boris's head. Her watery blue eyes never wavered. She mumbled something under her breath, then sat forward again. "Come," she said. "I have a closet-full. All you have to do is choose."

"Choose what?" asked Boris.

*"Hands!"* screeched the old woman. "Hands, you idiot. Isn't that what you want?"

*"Boris,"* came his uncle's familiar voice through the thin walls. *"Boris,* I need my sleep."

"I'll come. I'll come," whispered Boris, just to get rid of the hag. He shooed her out the door with a movement of his hands. As usual, the right was a beat behind the left, even after half a morning.

He hadn't actually meant to go anywhere with her, just

maneuver her out of the trailer, but when she leaped down the steps with surprising speed and climbed into a vehicle that looked like a mug with a large china steering rudder sticking out of the middle, his feet stepped forward of their own accord.

He fell down the stairs.

"Perhaps you could use a new pair of feet, too," said the old woman.

Boris stood up and automatically brushed off his clothes, a gesture his hands knew without prompting.

The old woman touched the rudder and the mug moved closer to Boris.

He looked on both sides and under the mug for evidence of its motor. It moved away from him as soundlessly as a hovercraft, but when he stuck his foot under it cautiously, he could feel no telltale movement of the air.

"How do you *do* that?" he asked.

"Do what?"

"The mug," he said.

"Magic." She made a strange gesture with her hands. "After all, I am Baba Yaga."

The name did not seem to impress Boris who was now on his hands and knees peering under the vehicle.

"Baba *Yaga*," the old woman repeated as if the name itself were a charm.

"How do you do," Boris murmured, more to the ground than to her.

"You know . . . the witch . . . Russia . . . magic. . . ." Her voice trailed off. When Boris made no response, she made another motion with her hands, but this time it was an Italian gesture, and not at all nice.

Boris saw the gesture and stood up. After all, the circus was his life. He knew that magic was not real, only a matter of quick hands. "Sure," he said, imitating her last gesture. His right hand clipped his left bicep. He winced.

*"Get in!"* the old woman shouted.

Boris shrugged. But his politeness was complicated by curiosity. He wanted to see the inside anyway. There had to be an engine somewhere. He hoped she would let him look at it. He was good with circuitry and micro-chips. In a free world, he could have chosen his occupation. Perhaps he might even have been a computer programmer. But as he was a member of the Famous Flying Chernevsky family, he had no choice. He climbed over the lip of the mug and, to his chagrin, got stuck. The old woman had to pull him the rest of the way.

"You really are a klutz," she said. "Are you sure all you want is hands?"

But Boris was not listening. He was searching the inside of the giant mug. He had just made his third trip around when it took off into the air. In less than a minute, the circus and its ring of bright trailers was only a squiggle on the horizon.

They passed quickly over the metroplexes that jigsawed across the continent and hovered over one of the twenty forest preserves. Baba Yaga pulled on the china rudder, and the mug dropped straight down. Boris fell sideways and clung desperately to the mug's rim. Only a foot above the treetops the mug slowed, wove its way through a complicated pattern of branches, and finally landed in a small clearing.

The old woman hopped nimbly from the flier. Boris followed more slowly.

A large presence loomed to one side of the forest clearing. It seemed to be moving toward them. An enormous bird. Boris thought. He had the impression of talons. Then he looked again. It was not a bird, but a hut, and it was walking.

Boris pointed at it. "Magic?" he asked, his mouth barely shaping the syllables.

"Feet," she answered.

"Feet?" He looked down at his feet, properly encased in naugahyde. He looked at hers, in pointed lizard leather. Then he looked again at the house. It was lumbering toward him on two scaley legs that ended in claws. They looked like giant replicas of the chicken feet that always floated nails-up in his mother's chicken soup. When she wasn't practicing being a Famous Flying, she made her great great grandmother's recipes. He preferred her in the air. "Feet," Boris said again, this time feeling slightly sick.

"But the subject is hands," Baba Yaga said. Then she turned from him and strolled over to the hut. They met halfway across the clearing. She greeted it and it gave a half bob as if curtsying, then squatted down. The old woman opened the door and went in.

Boris followed. One part of him was impressed with the special effects, the slow part of him. The fast part was already convinced it was magic.

The house inside was even more unusual than the house outside. It was one big cupboard. Doors and shelves lined every inch of wall space. And each door and cupboard carried a hand-lettered sign. The calligraphics differed from door to door, drawer to drawer, and it took a few minutes before Boris could make out the pattern. But he recognized the lettering from the days when he had helped his Uncle Boris script broadsides for their act. There was irony in the fact that he had always had a good calligraphic hand.

In Roman Bold were "Newts, eye of," "Adder, tongue of," and similar biological ingredients. Then there were botanical drawers in Carolingian Italic: "Thornapple juice," "Amanita," and the like. Along one wall, however, marked in basic Foundational Bold were five large cupboards marked simply: Heads, Hands, Feet, Ears, Eyes.

The old woman walked up to that wall and threw open the door marked "Hands."

"There," she said.

Inside, on small wooden stands, were hundreds of pairs of hands. When the light fell on them, they waved dead-white fingers as supple and mindless as worms.

"Which pair do you want to try?" Baba Yaga asked.

Boris stared. "But . . ." he managed at last, "they're miniatures."

"One size fits all," Baba Yaga said. "That's something I learned in the twentieth century." She dragged a pair out of the closet on the tiny stand. Plucking the hands from the stand, she held them in her palm. The hands began to stretch and grow, inching their way to normal size. They remained the color of custard scum.

Boris read the script on the stand to himself. "Lover's hands." He hesitated.

"Try them," the old woman said again, thrusting them at him. Her voice was compelling.

Boris took the left hand between his thumb and forefinger. The hand was as slippery as rubber, and wrinkled as a prune. He pulled it on his left hand, repelled at the feel. Slowly the hand molded itself to his, rearranging its skin over his bones. As Boris watched, the left hand took on the color of new cream, then quickly tanned to a fine, overall, healthy-looking beige. He flexed the fingers and the left hand reached over and stroked his right. At the touch, he felt a stirring of desire that seemed to move sluggishly up his arm, across his shoulder, down his back and grip his loins. Then the left hand reached over and picked up its mate. Without waiting for a signal from him, it lovingly pulled the right hand on, fitting each finger with infinite care.

As soon as both hands were the same tanned tone, the strong, tapered polished nails with the quarter moons winking up at him, Boris looked over at the witch.

He was surprised to see that she was no longer old but, in fact, only slightly mature with fine bones under a translucent skin. Her blue eyes seemed to appraise him, then offer an invitation. She smiled, her mouth thinned down with desire. His hands preceded him to her side, and then she was in his arms. The hands stroked her wind-tossed hair.

"You have," she breathed into his ear, "a lover's hands."

"Hands!" He suddenly remembered, and with his teeth ripped the right hand off. Underneath were his own remembered big knuckles. He flexed them experimentally. They were wonderfully slow in responding.

The old woman in his arms cackled and repeated, "A lover's hands."

His slow right hand fought with the left, but managed at last to scratch off the outer layer. His left hand felt raw, dry, but comfortingly familiar.

The old woman was still smiling an invitation. She had crooked teeth and large pores. There was a dark moustache on her upper lip.

Boris picked up the discarded hands by the tips of the fingers and held them up before the witch's watery blue eyes. "Not *these* hands," he said.

She was already reaching into the closet for another pair.

Boris pulled the hands on quickly, glancing only briefly at the label. "Surgeon's hands." They were supple-fingered and moved nervously in the air as if searching for something to do. Finally they hovered over Baba Yaga's forehead. Boris felt as if he had eyes in his fingertips, and suddenly saw the old woman's skin as a map stretched taut across a landscape of muscle and bone. He could sense the subtle traceries of veins and read the directions of the bloodlines. His right hand moved down the bridge of her nose, turned left at the cheek, and descended to her chin. The second finger tapped her wen, and he could hear the faint echo of his knock.

"I could remove that easily," he found himself saying.

The witch pulled the surgeon's hands from him herself. "Leave me my wen. Leave me my own face," she said angrily. "It is the stage setting for my magic. Surgeon's hands indeed."

Remembering the clowns in their make-up, the wire-walkers in their sequined leotards, the ringmaster in his tie and tails, costumes that had not changed over the centuries of circus, Boris had to agree. He looked down again at his own hands. He moved the fingers. The right were still laggards. But for the first time he heard and saw how they moved. He dropped his hands to his sides and beat a tattoo on his outer thighs. Three against two went the rhythm, the left hitting the faster beat. He increased it to seven against five, and smiled. The right would always be slower, he knew that now.

"It's not in the hands," he said.

Baba Yaga looked at him quizzically. Running a hand through her bird's-nest hair and fluffing up her eyebrows, she spoke. But it was Uncle Boris's voice that emerged between her crooked teeth: "Hands are the daughters of the eye and ear."

"How do you *do* that?" Boris asked.

"Magic," she answered, smiling. She moved her fingers mysteriously, then turned and closed the cupboard doors.

Boris smiled at her back, and moved his own fingers in imitation. Then he went out the door of the house and fell down the steps.

"Maybe you'd like a new pair of feet," the witch called after him. "I have Fred Astaire's. I have John Travolta's. I have Mohammed Ali's." She came out of the house, caught up with Boris, and pulled him to a standing position.

"Were they jugglers?" asked Boris.

"No," Baba Yaga said, shaking her head. "No. But they had soul."

Boris didn't answer. Instead he climbed into the mug and gazed fondly at his hands as the mug took off and headed toward the horizon and home.

# Mirage and Magia

## *by Tanith Lee*

*In 1975 Tanith Lee's* The Birthgrave *appeared on bookstands, and I knew that here was one of the major new talents for the seventies and the eighties. The tale of Karrakaz held me obsessed all the while I should have been looking out over the deserts of Arizona and New Mexico during a summer vacation. Subsequent books such as* Companions on the Road, Volkhavaar, Quest For The White Witch, *and* Death's Master*—to name a few—show her preoccupation with magic of all kinds. When Tanith writes, however, she has a magic all her own. Werewolves prowl chateaux, vampires neurotically roam New Mars, and magnificent djinns scout out the earth for new temptations. You can always tell a Tanith Lee story by its texture—shadowy, sinister, and bejeweled, the sort of work Aubrey Beardsley would have loved to illustrate.*

*But Tanith's work consists of more than style and sorcery. Her characters are always on quests for their identity, for love, or for their hearts' desires. So, in the City of Qon Oshen, which never existed except in the glittering imagination of one of our finest fantasists, comes yet another witch to try to achieve her quest.*

During the Ninth Dynasty of the Jat Calendar, Taisia-Tua lived at the town of Qon Oshen, in a mansion of masks and mirrors.

At that time, being far inland, and unlinked by road or bridge to any of the great seaports of the Western Peninsula, Qon Oshen was an obscure and fulminating area. Its riches, born of itself and turned back like radiations upon itself, had made it both exotic and psychologically impenetrable to most of those foreigners who very occasionally entered it. Generally, it was come on by air, almost by accident, by riders of galvanic silver and crimson balloon-ships. Held in a clasp of pointed, platinum-colored hills, in which one break only poured to the shore of an iridium lake, Qon Oshen presented latticed towers, phantasmal soaring bridgeways, a game board of square plazas and circular trafficuli. Sometimes, gauzelike clouds, attracted to the chemical and auric emanations of the town, would hang low over it, foaming the tower tops. In a similar manner, the reputation of Taisia-Tua hung over the streets, insubstantial, dreamlike, menacing.

She had come from the north, riding in a high white grasshopper carriage, which strode on fragile legs seven feet in the air. The date of her coming varied depending on who recounted it. Seventeen years ago, ten, the year when Saturo, the demon-god, sent fire, and the cinnamon harvest was lost. Her purpose for arrival was equally elusive. She chose for her dwelling a mansion of rose-red tilework, spiraled about with thin stone balustrades on which squatted antimony toads and jade cats, and enclosed by gates of wrought iron, five yards high. Dark green deciduous, and pale-grey fan-shaped pines spread around the mansion, as if to shield it. After sunset, its windows of stained glass turned slotted eyes of purple, magenta, blue, emerald, and gold upon the town. Within the masking trees and behind the masking windows, the Magia—for everyone had known at once she was an enchantress—paced out the dance moves of her strange and insular life.

One thing was always remembered. On the morning or noon or evening or midnight of her arrival, someone had snatched a glimpse inside the grasshopper carriage. This someone, (a fool, for who but a fool would risk such a glimpse?) had told how there were no windows but that, opposite the seat of lush plum silk, the wall above the driver's keys was all one polished mirror. The only view Taisia-Tua had apparently had, all the way from the north to Qon Oshen, was that of her own self.

"Is she beautiful, then?"

"Most beautiful."

"Not at all beautiful."

"*Ugly.*"

"*Gorgeous.*"

"One cannot be sure. Whenever she passes through the town she is always partly masked or veiled. Nor has anyone ever seen her in the same gown twice, or the same wig (she is always wigged). Even her slippers and her jewelry are ephemeral."

It was usually agreed this diversity might be due to such powers of illusion as an enchantress would possess. Or simply to enormous wealth and extravagance—each of which qualities the town was prepared to admire. Certainly, in whatever clothing or guise, Taisia-Tua Magia was never mistaken for another.

At Midsummer of her first year, whenever that was, at Qon Oshen, she perpetrated her first magic. There were scores of witnesses.

A round moon, yellow as wine, hung over the town, and all the towers and bridgeways seemed to reach and stretch to catch its light. The scent of a thousand peach trees, apricot gardens, lily pools and jasmin pergolas filled the darkness. Gently feverish with the drunkenness of summer, men and women stole from the inns and the temples—on such nights, even the demon-god might be worshipped—and wandered abroad everywhere. And into Seventh Plaza Taisia-Tua walked with slow measured steps, a moment or so behind the midnight bell. Her gown was black and sewn with peacocks' eyes. Her hair was deepest blue. Her face was white, rouged the softest, most transparent of vermilions at cheekbones and lips, and like violet smoulder along the eyelids. This face itself was like a mask, but an extra mask of stiff silver hid her forehead, brows, and the hollows under the painted eyes. Her nails were silver, too, and each of them four inches in length, which presumably indicated these also were unreal. Her feet were gloved in silk mounted on golden soles which went *chink-chink-chink* as she moved. She was unaccompanied, save by her supposed reputation. The crowd in the plaza fell back, muttered, and carefully observed. Instinctively, it seemed, they had always guessed this creature boded them no particular good. But her exoticism was so suitable to the mode, they had as yet no wish to censure.

For some while, the Magia walked about, very slowly, gazing this way and that. She took her time, glancing where she would, paying no apparent heed to any who gazed or glanced at her. She was, naturally, protected by her masks, and perhaps by the tiny looking-glass that hung on a chain from her belt, and which, now and then, she raised, gazing also at herself.

At length, she crossed the plaza to the spot where the three-tiered fountain played, turning now indigo, now orchid. Here a young man was standing, with his friends. He was of the Linla family, one of the highest, richest houses in the town, and his name was Iye. Not merely an aristocrat and rich, either, but exceedingly handsome and popular. To this person the enchantress proceeded, and he, caught in mid-sentence and mid-thought, paused, watching her wide-eyed. When she was some few feet from him, Taisia-Tua halted. She spoke, in a still, curious, lifeless little voice.

"*Follow* me."

Iye Linla turned to his friends, laughing, looking for their support, but they did not laugh at all.

"Magia," said Iye, after a moment, staring her out and faltering, for it was hard to stare out a mask and two masked unblinking eyes. "Magia, I do not follow any one without good reason. Excuse me, but I have business here."

Taisia-Tua made a very slight gesture, which spread her wide sleeves like the wings of some macabre night butterfly. That was all. Then she turned, and her golden soles went *chink-chink-chink* as she walked away.

One of Iye's friends caught his shoulder. "On no account go after her."

"I? Go after that hag—more likely I would go with demoniac Saturo—"

But already he had taken a step in her direction. Shocked, Iye attempted to secure himself to the ground. Presently, finding he could not, he gripped the wrists and clothing of his companions. But an uncanny bodily motivation possessed him. Like one who is drowning, he slipped inexorably from their grasp. There was no longer any conversation. With expressions of dismay and horror, the friends of Iye Linla beheld him walk after the enchantress, at first reluctantly, soon with a steady, unrelenting stride. Like her dog, it seemed, he would pursue her all the way home. They broke abruptly from their stupor, and ran to summon Iye's father, the Linla kindred and guards. But by the time such forces had been marshalled and brought to the mansion of rose-red tile, the gates were shut, nor did any answer the shouts and knocking, the threats and imprecations, while on their pedestals, the ghostly toads and greenish cats grinned at the sinking moon.

Only one old uncle of the Linla house was heard to remark that a night in bed with a mage-lady might do young Iye no harm at all. He was shortly to repent these words, and half a year later the old man ritually stabbed himself before the family altar because of his ill-omened utterance. For the night passed, and the dawn began to surface like a great shoal of luminous fishes in the east. And a second or so after the sunrise bell, a slim carved door opened in the mansion, and then closed again behind the form of Iye Linla. A second more, and a pair of ironwork gates parted in their turn, but Iye Linla advanced no further than the courtyard. Soon, some of his kindred hastened into the court, others standing by the gates to keep them wide, and hurried the young man from the witch's yard.

On the street, they slapped his cheeks and hands, forced wine between his lips, implored him, cursed him. To no avail. His open eyes were opaque, seldom blinking, indicating blindness. They led him home, where the most eminent physicians and psychologists were called, but none of these made an iota of progress with him. Eventually, Iye's official courtesan stole in to visit him, prepared to try such remedies as her sensual arts had taught her. She had been in the chamber scarcely two minutes when her single piercing shriek brought half the household into the apartment, demanding what new thing was amiss.

Iye's courtesan stood in a rain of her own burnished hair, and of her own weeping, and she said, "His eyes—his eyes—Oh, I looked into his eyes—Saturo has eaten his soul."

"The woman is mad," was the common consensus, but one of the physicians, ignoring this, went to Iye, and himself peered between the young man's lids. This physician then spoke in a hushed and awful manner that brought quiet and terror on the whole room.

"The courtesan is clever. Some strange spell has been worked here, and any may see it that will look. It is usual, when glancing into the eyes of another, to see pictured there, since these lenses are reflective, a minute image of oneself. But in the eyes of Iye Linla I perceive only this: The minute image of Iye Linla himself, and, what is more, I perceive him from the back."

Fear was, in this event, mightier than speculation.

By noon, most of Qon Oshen knew of Iye's peculiar fate, and brooded on it. A re-emergence of the enchantress was expected with misgiving. However, Taisia-Tua did not walk in the town again for several weeks. In her stead, there began to be seen about, in the high skies of twilight or early morning, a mysterious silvery kite, across whose elongated tail were inscribed these words:

IS THERE A GREATER MAGICIAN THAN I?

In Qon Oshen, not one man asked another to whom this kite belonged.

It may be supposed, though such deeds were performed in secret, that the Linla family sent to the enchantress's house various embassies, pleas and warnings, not to mention coffers full of bribes. But the spell, such as it was, was not removed from Iye. He, the hope of his house, remained thereafter like an idiot, who must be tended and fed and laid down to sleep and roused up again, exercised like a beast, and nursed like a baby. Sallow death banners were hung from the Linla gates about the time the kite manifested in the sky. By the autumn's end, another two houses of Qon Oshen were mourning in similar fashion.

At the Chrysanthemum Festival, Taisia-Tua, in a gown like fire, hair like burning coals, wings of cinnabar concealing cheeks and chin, scratched with a turquoise nail-tip the sleeve of a young priest, an acolyte of the Ninth Temple. He was devout and handsome, an intellectual, moreover a son of the aristocratic house of Kli-Sra. Yet he went after the Magia just as Iye Linla had done. And came forth from her mansion after the sunrise bell also just as Iye Linla did, so that in his eyes men beheld the young priest's own image, reversed, and to be seen only from the back.

A month later, (only a month), when the toasted leaves were falling and sailing on the oval ponds and inconsequently rushing along the narrow marble lanes of Qon Oshen, an artist of great fame and genius turned from his scroll, the gilded pen in his hand, and found the Magia behind him, her lower face hidden by a veil of ivory plaques, her clothes embroidered by praying mantises.

"Spare me," the artist said to her, "from whatever fate it is you put on those others you summoned. For the sake of the creative force which is in me, if not from pity because I am a human man."

But—"*Follow* me," she said, and moved away from him. This time the soles on her gloved feet were of wood, and they made a noise like fans snapping shut. The artist crushed the gilded pen in his hand. The nib pierced his palm and his blood fell on the scroll. The pattern it made, such was his talent, was as fair as the considered lines any other might have devised. Yet he had no choice but to obey the witch, and when the morning rose from the lake, he was like the others who had done so.

Sometimes the Magia's kite blew in the skies, sometimes not. Sometimes some swore they had seen it, while others denied it had been visible, but all knew the frightful challenge of its writing:

IS THERE A GREATER MAGICIAN THAN I?

Sometimes a man would vanish from his home, and they would say: "*She* has taken him." This was not always the case. Yet she *did* take. In the pure blue days of winter, when all the town was a miracle of ice, each pinnacle like glass, and to step on the streets seemed likely to break every vista in a myriad pieces, then she would come and go, and men would follow her, and men would return—no longer sensible or living, though alive. And in the spring when the blossoms bubbled over and splashed and cascaded from every wall and walk, then, too, she would work her magic. And in the green, fermenting bottle of summer, in its simmering days and restless nights, and in autumn when the world of the town fell upward through a downfalling of purple and amber leaves—then. Randomly, persistently, seemingly without excuse. Unavoidably, despite war being made against her by the nobility of the place, despite intrigues and jurisdiction, despite the employment of other magicians, whose spells to hers were, as it turned out, like blades of grass standing before the curtain of the cyclone. Despite sorties and attacks of a physical nature. Despite the lunacy of firing a missile from a nearby hill in a reaction of fury and madness of the family Mhey, which had lost to her three of its sons. The rocket exploded by night against the roof of the rose tile mansion with a clap like forty thunders, a rose itself of flame and smoke, to wake most of the town with screams and cries. But running to the spot there were discovered only huge hills of clinker and cooling cinders in the street. The mansion was unscathed, its metals and stones untwisted, its jewelry windows unsmashed, its beasts of antimony and jade leering now downward at those who had come to see.

"Her powers are alarming. Why does she work evil against us?"

"What are her reasons?"

"What is the method of the dreadful spell?"

Qon Oshen prayed for her destruction. They prayed for one to come who would destroy her.

But she preyed upon them like a leopard, and they did not know how, or why.

There was a thief in Qon Oshen who was named Locust. Locust was hideous, and very cunning, and partly insane with the insanity of the wise. He slipped in among a gathering of respected rich men, flung off his official-seeming cloak, and laughed at their surprise. Although he was a thief, and had stolen from each of them, and each surmised it, Locust fitted within the oblique ethics of the town, for he was a lord of his trade and admired for the artistry of his evil-doing. If he were ever caught at his work, he knew well they had vowed to condemn him to the Eight Agonizing Deaths. But while he eluded justice, sourly they reveled in his theatrical deeds against their neighbors and bore perforce with those nearer home.

"I, Locust, knowing how well you love me, for a certain sum, will perform a useful task for you."

The rich men turned to glance at each other. Their quick minds had already telepathically received the impression of his next words.

"Excellently deduced, your excellencies. I will pierce into the Magia's mansion, and presently come tell you what goes on there."

Some hours after, when the bow of the moon was raising its eyebrow at him, Locust, lord of thieves, penetrated, by means of burglars' skills and certain sorceries he himself was adept in, the mansion of rose-red tiling. Penetrated and watched, played hide and seek with shades and with more than shades, and escaped to report his news. Though from that hour of revelation, he reckoned himself—in indefinable, subtle, sinister ways—altered. And when, years later, he faltered in his profession, was snatched by the law, and—humiliatingly—pardoned, he claimed he had contracted emanations of the witch's house like a virus, and the ailment had gradually eroded his confidence in himself.

"It was a trick of leaping to get over the gate—my secret. Entering then by a window too small to admit even a cat—for I can occasionally condense and twist my bones in a fashion unnormal, possibly uncivilized, I dealt with such uncanny safeguards as seemed extant by invoking my demon patron, Saturo; we are great friends. I then dropped down into a lobby."

It was afterward remarked how curious it was that a thief might breach the defenses of the mansion which a fire missile could not destroy.

But Locust, then full of his cleverness, did not remark it. He went on to speak of the bewildering aspect the mansion had come, internally, to display. A bewilderment due mainly to the labyrinthine and accumulative and mirage-making and virtually hallucinatory effects that resulted from a multitude of mirrors, set everywhere and overlapping like scales. Mirrors, too, of all shapes, sizes, constructions and substances, from those of sheerest and most reflective glass, to those of polished copper and bronze, to those formed by sheets of water held bizarrely in stasis over underlying sheets of black onyx. A fearful confusion, even madness, might have overcome another, finding himself unguided in the midst of such phenomena. For of course the mirrors did not merely reflect, they reflected into each other. Image rebounded upon image like a hail of crystal bullets fired into infinity. Many times, Locust lost himself, fell to his knees, grew cold, grew heated, grew nauseous, passed near to fainting or screaming, but his own pragmatism saved him. From room to unconscionable room he wended, and with him went thousands of replicas of himself (but, accustomed to his own unbeauty, he did not pay these companions much heed). Here and there an article of science or aesthetics might arrest him, but mostly he was bemused, until hesitating to examine a long-stemmed rose of a singular purple-crimson, he was startled into a yell. Without warning, the flower commenced to spin, and as it spun to peal off glowing droplets, as if it wept fire. A moment more and the door of the mansion, far away through the forest of mirrors, opened with a mysterious sigh. Locust hastily withdrew behind a mirror resembling an enormous eye.

In twenty seconds the Magia came gliding in, lavender-haired and clad in a gown like a wave drawn down from the moon. And behind her stumbled the handsome fourth son of the house of Uqet.

And so Locust the thief came to be the only intimate witness to the spell the Magia wove about her victims.

Firstly she seated herself on a pillow of silk. Then she folded her hands upon her lap, and raised her face, which on that day was masked across eyes and forehead in the plumage of a bird of prey. It seemed she sat and gazed at her visitor as if to attract his attention, gazed with her plumaged eyes, her very porcelain skin, her strawberry mouth, even her long, long nails seemed to gaze at him. She was, Locust explained, an object to rivet the awareness, had it not been for the quantities of mirrors, which plainly distracted the young man, so he did not look at Taisia-Tua the enchantress, but around and around, now into this image of himself, now into that. And soon he began to fumble about the room, peering into his own face in crystal, in platinum, in water, jade and brass. For perhaps two hours this went on, or maybe it was longer, or less long. But the son of Uqet wavered from looking glass to looking glass, at each snagging upon his own reflection, adhering to it, and his countenance grew stranger and stranger and more wild and—oddly—more fixed, until at last all expression faded from it. And all the while, saying nothing, doing nothing, Taisia-Tua Magia sat at the room's center on the pillow of silk.

Finally the son of Uqet came to stare down into the mirror paving under his feet, and there he ceased to move. Until, after several minutes, he fell abruptly to his knees, and so to his face. And there he lay, breathing mist against his own reflected mouth, and the witch came to her feet and stepped straight out of the chamber. But as she went by him, Locust heard her say aloud: "You are all the same. All the same as he who was before you. Is there no answer?"

This puzzled Locust so much, he left it out of his report.

At the witch's exit, it did occur to the thief to attempt reviving the young man from his trance, but when a few pinches and shakings had failed to cause awakening, Locust abandoned Uqet and used his wits instead to gain departure before the enchantress should locate him.

This story thereafter recited (or most of it), earned much low-voiced meditation from his listeners.

"But did she summon no demon?"

"Did she utter no malody?"

"Did she not employ wand or ring, or other device?"

"No."

Uqet was found in the morning, lying in Taisia-Tua's yard: Locust's proof. Uqet's eyes were now a familiar sightless sight.

Immediately a whole tribe of fresh magicians was sent for. Their powers to hers were like wisps of foam blowing before the tidal wave. Not the strongest nor the shrewdest could destroy the horror of her enchantment, nor break a single mirror in her mansion. Houses of antique lineage removed themselves from the vicinity. Some remained, but refused to allow their heirs ever to walk abroad.

They prayed for her destruction. For one to come who would destroy her.

The kite inquired of heaven and earth:

IS THERE A GREATER MAGICIAN THAN I?

In a confusion of datelessness, the years shriveled and fell like the leaves. . . .

But though the date of her arrival was uncertain, the date of his arrival was exactly remembered.

It was in the year of the Scorpion, on the day of the blooming of the ancient acacia tree in Thirty-Third Plaza, that only put forth flowers once in every twenty-sixth decade. As the sun began to shine over the towers and bridges, he appeared under the glistening branches of this acacia, seated cross-legged on the ground. The fretwork of light and shadow, and the mothlike blooms of the tree, made it hard to be sure of what he was, or even if he was substantially there. He was indeed discernible first by an unearthly metallic music that sewed a way out through the foliage and ran down the plaza like streams of water, till a crowd began to gather to discover the source.

The music came from a pipe of bone which was linked, as if by an umbilical cord of silver tubing, to a small tablet of lacquer keys. Having observed the reason for the pipe's curious tone, the crowd moved its attention to the piper. Nor was his tone at all usual. The colors of his garments were of blood and sky, the shades, conceivably, of pain and hope. Around his bowed face and over his pale hands as he played hung a cloud of hair dark red as mahogany, but to which the sun rendered its own edging of blood and sky-blue rainbows.

When the music ceased, the crowd would have thrown him cash, but at that moment he raised his head, and revealed he was masked, that a face of alabaster covered his own, a formless blank of face that conveyed only the most innocent wickedness. Although through the long slits of the eyes, something was just detectable, some flicker of life, like two blue ghosts dwelling behind a wall. Then, before the crowd had scarcely formed a thought, he set the instruments of music aside and came to his feet, (which were bare), rose straight and tall and pliant as smoke rising from a fire. He held up one hand and a scarlet bird soared out of his palm. He opened the other hand and an azure bird soared out of that. The two birds dashed together, merged, fell apart in a shattering of gems, rubies, garnets, sapphires, aquamarines, that dewed the pavement for yards around. With involuntary cries of delight and avarice, men bent to pick them up and found peonies and hyacinths instead had rooted in the tiles.

"Then stars spun through the air, and he juggled them—ten stars or twenty."

"Stars by day—day-stars? They were fires he juggled from hand to hand."

"He seemed clothed in fire. All but the white face, like a bowl of white thoughts."

"Then he walked on his hands and made the children laugh."

"A vast throng of people had congregated when he removed several golden fish from the acacia tree. These spread their fins and flew away."

"He turned three somersaults backwards, one after another with no pause."

"The light changed where he was standing."

"Where did he come from?"

"That is speculation. But to our chagrin, many of us saw where he proceeded."

Into the crowd, like the probing of a narrow spear, the presence of the enchantress had pressed its way. They became aware of her as they would become aware of a sudden lowering of the temperature, and, not even looking to see what they had no need or wish to see, they slid from her like water from a blade. She wore violet sewn with beads the color of green ice. All her face, save only the eyes, was caged in an openwork visor of five thin curving horizontal bars of gold. Her hair today was the tint of tarnished orichalc.

She stood within the vortex the crowd had made for her, she stood and watched the magician-musician. She watched him produce silver rings from the air, fling them together to represent atoms or universes, and cast them into space in order to balance upside down on his head, catching the rings with his toes. Certainly, she had had some inkling of the array of mages who had been called to Qon Oshen against her. If it struck her that this was like some parody of their arts, some game played with the concept of witchcraft, she did not demonstrate. But that she considered him, contemplated him, was very evident. The crowd duly grew grim and silent, hanging on the edges of her almost tangible concentration as if from spikes. Then, with a hundred muffled exclamations, it beheld the Magia turn without a word and go away again, having approached no one, having failed to issue that foreboding commandment: *Follow* me.

But it seemed this once she had had no necessity to say the ritual aloud. For, taking up the pipe and the tablet of keys, leaving seven or eight phantasms to dissolve on the air, five or six realities—gilded apples, paper animals—to flutter into the hands of waiting children, the masked, red-headed man walked from under the acacia tree, and followed her *without* being requested.

A few cried out to him, warning or plea. Most hugged their silence, and as he passed them, the nerves tingled in their spines. While long after he had disappeared from view, they heard the dim, clear notes of the pipe start up along the delicate arteries of the town, like new blood running there in the body of Qon Oshen. It seemed he woke music for her as he pursued her and what must be his destruction.

Men lingered in Thirty-Third Plaza. At last, one of the Mhey household spoke out in a tone of fearful satisfaction:

"Whatever else, I think on this occasion she has summoned up a devil to go with her."

"It is Saturo," responded a priest in the crowd, "the demon-god of darkness and fire. Her evil genius come to devour her."

In alarm and excitement, the people gazed about them, wondering if the town would perish in such a confrontation.

She never once looked back, and never once, as those persons attested which saw him go by, did he falter, or the long sheaves and rills of notes falter, that issued from the pipe and the tablet of lacquer keys.

Taisia-Tua reached her mansion gates, and they swung shut behind her. Next, a carved door parted and she drew herself inside the house as a hand is drawn into a glove, and the door, too, shut itself firmly. In the space of half a minute the demon, if such he was, Saturo, if so he was called, had reached the iron gates. Whole families and their guards had been unable to breach these gates, just as the rocket had been unable to disunify the architecture. Locust the thief had wriggled in by tricks and incantations, but the law of Balance in magic may have decreed just such a ludicrous loophole should be woven in the fabric of the Magia's safeguards. Or she may have had some need for one at least to spy the sole enchantment she dealt inside her rose-red walls.

He who was supposed to be, and might have been, Saturo, the demon-god of flame and shade, poised then at one of the gates. Even through the blank white mask, any who were near could have heard his soft, unmistakable voice say to the gate:

"Why shut me out, when you wish me to come in?"

And at these words the gate opened itself and he went through it.

And at the carved door he said: "Unless you unlock yourself, how am I to enter?"

The door swung the slender slice of itself inward, and the demon entered the mansion of the witch.

The mirrors hung and burned, and fleered and sheered all about him then, scaled over each other, winking, shifting, promising worlds that were not. Saturo paid no attention to any of them. He walked straight as a panther through the house, and the myriad straight and savage images of him, sky and snow, and the drowning redness of his hair, walked with him—but he never glanced at them.

So he arrived quickly in the room where the rose spun and threw off its fiery tears. And here the enchantress had already seated herself on the pillow of silk. Her face, in its golden cage, was raised to his. Her eyelids were rouged a soft, dull purple, the paint on her skin—a second skin—dazzled. Each of her terrible clawlike nails crossed over another. Her eyes, whose hue and character were obscured, stared. She looked merciless. Or simply devoid of anything, which must, therefore, include mercy.

Saturo the demon advanced to within two feet of her, and seated himself on the patterned floor in front of her. So they stared at each other, like two masked dolls, and neither moved for a very long while.

At length, after this very long while had dripped and melted from the chamber like wax, Taisia-Tua spoke to the demon.

"Can it be you alone are immune to my wonderful magery?"

There was no reply, only the stare of the mask continuing unalleviated, the suspicion of two eyes behind the mask, unblinking. Another season of time went by, and Taisia-Tua said:

"Will you not look about you? See, you are everywhere. Twenty to one hundred replicas of yourself are to be found on every wall, the floor, the ceiling. Why gaze at me, when you might gaze at yourself? Or can it be you are as hideous as that other who broke in here, and like him do not wish to be shown to your own eyes? Remove your mask, let me see to which family of the demons you belong."

"Are you not afraid," said Saturo, "of what kind of face a demon keeps behind a mask?"

"A face of black shadow and formlessness, or of blazing fire. The prayers of the town to be delivered from me have obviously drawn you here. But I am not afraid."

"Then, Taisia-Tua Magia, you yourself may pluck away the mask."

Having said this, he leaned toward her, so close his dark red hair brushed her suddenly uplifted hands, which she had raised as if to ward him off. And as if she could not help herself then, the edges of her monstrous nails met the white mask's edges, and it fell, like half an eggshell, to the floor. It was no face of dark or flame which appeared. But pale and still, and barely human in its beauty, the face looked back at her and the somber pallor of the eyes, that were indeed like two blue ghosts haunting it. It was a cruel face, and kind, compassionate and pitiless, and the antithesis of all masks. And the moment she saw it, never having seen it before, she recognized it, as she had recognized him under the acacia tree. But she said hastily and coldly, as if it were sensible and a protection to say such things to such a creature: "You are more handsome than all the rest. Look into the mirrors. Look into the mirrors and see yourself."

"I would rather," said Saturo, who maybe was not Saturo, "look at you."

"Fool," said the enchantress, in a voice smaller than the smallest bead on her gown. "If you will not surrender to your vanity, how is my magic to work on you?"

"Your magic has worked. Not the magic of your spells. Your own magic."

"Liar," said the witch. "But I see you are bemused, as no other was, by fashion." At this, she pulled the gold cage from her face, and the orichalc wig from her hair—which flew up fine and electric about her head. "See, I am less than you thought," said Taisia-Tua. "Surely you would rather look at yourself?" And she smeared the paint from her face and wiped it clean and pale as paper. "Surely you would rather look at yourself?" And she threw off her jewels, and the nails, and the outer robe of violet, and sat there in the plain undergown. "Surely you would rather look at yourself?" And uncolored and unmasked she sat there and lowered her eyes, which was now the only way she could hide herself. "Surely, surely," she muttered, "you would rather look at yourself."

"Who," said he, quieter than quietness, and much deeper than depth, "hurt you so in the north that you came to this place to revenge yourself forever? Who wounded you so you must plunge knives into others, which certainly remained the same knife, plunged again and again into your own heart? Why did the heart break that now enables these mirrors not to break? Who loved himself so much more than you that you believed you also must learn to love only your own image, since no other could love you, or choose to gaze on you rather than on himself? True of most, which you have proven. Not true of all. What silly game have you been playing, with pain turned into sorcery and vanity turned into a spell? And have you never once laughed, young woman, not even at yourself?"

Her head still bowed, the enchantress whispered, "How do you know these things?"

"Any would know it, that knew you. Perhaps I came in answer to praying, not theirs, but yours. Your prayers of glass and live-dead men."

Then taking her hand he stood up and made her stand with him.

"Look," he said, and now he leaned close enough she could gaze into the two mirrors of his eyes. And there she saw, not another man staring in forever at himself, but, for the first time, her own face gazing back at her—for this is what he saw. And finding this, Taisia-Tua, not the rose, wept, and as everyone of her tears fell from her eyes, there was the sound of mirror-glass breaking somewhere in the house.

While, here and there about Qon Oshen, as the mirrors splintered, inverted images crumbled inside the eyes of young men, and were gone.

Iye Linla yawned and cursed, and called for food. The sons of Mhey came back to themselves and rolled in a riotous heap like inebriated puppies. A priest bellowed, an aristocrat frowned, at discovering themselves propped up like invalids, their relatives bobbing, sobbing, about the bed. Each returned and made vocal his return. In Twenty-First Plaza, an artist rushed from his house, shouting for the parchment with the bloodstain of his genius upon it.

By dusk, when the stars cast their own bright broken glass across the sky, the general opinion was that the witch was dead. And decidedly, none saw that wigged and masked nightmare lady again.

For her own hair was light and fine, and her skin paler yet, and her eyes were grey as the iridium lake. She was much less beautiful, and much more beautiful than all her masks. And in this disguise, her own self, she went away unknown from Qon Oshen, leaving all behind her, missing none of it, for he had said to her: "*Follow* me."

A month of plots and uneasiness later, men burst in the doors of the vacant mansion, hurling themselves beneath the grinning toads and the frigid cats of greenish jade, as if afraid to be spat on. But inside they found only the webs of spiders and the shards of exploded mirrors. Not a gem remained, or had ever existed, to appease them. No treasure and no hoard of magery. Her power, by which she had pinned them so dreadfully, was plainly merely their own power, those energies of self-love and curiosity and fear turned back, (ever mirror-fashion), on themselves. Like the reflection of a moon, she had waned, and the mirage sunk away, but not until a year was gone did they sigh with nostalgia for her empire of uncertainty and terror forever lost to them. "When the Magia ruled us, and we trembled," they would boastfully say. They even boasted of the mocking kite, until one evening a sightseer, roaming the witch's mansion—now a feature of great interest in Qon Oshen—came on a scrap of silk, and on the silk a line of writing.

Then Qon Oshen was briefly ashamed of Taisia-Tua Magia. For the writing read: LOVE, LOVE, LOVE THE MAGICIAN IS GREATER, FAR GREATER, THAN I.

# WILLOW

## *by C.J. Cherryh*

*"Read* Gate of Ivrel," *Andre Norton told me several years ago. I've been reading C.J. Cherryh's novels and short stories ever since. A winner of the John Campbell Award for best new writer, C.J. Cherryh generally sets her stories of hives, mri mercenaries, or iduve predators and starship captains in the far future.*

*But in stories like "The Dreamstone"* (Amazons!, DAW) *and in the fantasy-oriented books about Vanye and Morgaine, warrior, schemer, and questing heroine, C.J. Cherryh presents women who have fought and who continue to fight with archaic weapons, but who are tired. In "Willow" she now tells the story of a man whom too-long warfare and bad leadership have worn out physically and morally. After any war, what happens to such men? How can they go home and take off their armor if they have no home left?*

*Such men take several roads. They can turn rogue, they can wander aimlessly, hoping just to eke out the rest of their lives, or they can find healing. In "Willow" Dubhan is just such a man. He kills a man who might have offered him a place at his fireside, and rides off fast. And then he meets a mad child and comes to a ruined keep, a welcome, and a Lady . . . all of which show that a subtle writer can reveal more about a man's nature by brief hints than by piling horror upon horror.*

*Cherryh says that "Willow" is set in the mists of*

*a place like medieval Cornwall, a land of keeps and quarrels and of a magic as powerful as it is unobtrusive. As in Diana Paxson's story, here in "Willow," you will see . . . but let C.J. Cherryh tell you instead.*

Seven days he had been riding, up from the valley and the smoke of burned fields, and down again with the mountain wall at his back, a winding trail of barren crags and eagles' perches, gray sere brush and struggling juniper. The horse he rode plodded in sullen misery, gaunt and galled. His armor was scarred with use and wanted repair he neglected to give it; that was the way he traveled, outward from the war, from his youth which he had lost there and his service which he had left.

Dubhan was his name, and far across the land in front of him was his home, but the way looked different than it had looked ten years ago. He remembered fields and villages and the sun on the mountains when he rode up to them, when the horse was young, his colors bright and his armor gleaming as he rode up to the duke's service—but now when the winding trail afforded sometime glimpses of the plains, they seemed colorless. It was the season, perhaps; he had come in a springtime. He rode out in a summer's ending, and that might be the reason, or the color might have been in his eyes once, when he had been easily deceived, before the old duke had taught him the world, and the lord he served changed lords, and knights who had defended the land drifted into plunder of it, and the towns fell, and the smokes went up and the fields were sown with bones and iron, and the birds hunted carrion in roofless cottages. Maybe the war had spilled beyond the mountains; maybe it had covered all the world and stripped it bare. It had taken him this long to remember what sunlit green he had seen here once, but no longer seeing it did not surprise him, as worse sights had ceased to surprise him. There were scars on him which had not been there that springtime ten years gone. He ached where the mail bore down on old wounds; pains settled knife-pointed into joints in nighttime cold and made him know what pains years ahead held, lordless and landless and looking—late—for another lord, another place, and some more hopeful war while there was something left of vigor in his arm, some strength to trade on to put a roof over his head before he was too old, and too broken, and finally without hope. Bread to eat, a place to sleep, a little wine for the pains when it rained: that was what he rode out to find.

At one cut and another the nearer land lay spread below the rocks, dull tapestry of the tops of trees where the trail turned and some slide had taken away the curtaining scrub. The trees came nearer, and stretched farther as the trail wound down the mountainside, more of forest than he recalled. At such vantages he looked out and down, marking what he could of the road to come, all curtained below in trees and gray bush.

So he saw the birds start up, and drew in the horse so sharply that the old head came up and muscles tensed. A black beating of wings rose above the woods below, and hovered a time before settling back into that rough patterning of treetops elsewhere. He marked where, and moved the horse on, and got his battered shield out of its leather casing. He thought about his armor, regretting mending not done, and took his helmet from where it hung on his saddle, and kept toward the inside of the road whenever he came near some other open place, fearing some movement, some show of metal might betray him—prudence not of cowardice, but of cold purpose.

That was also the way of the war he had waged, that no one met friends on the road. He rode carefully, and thought about the sound of the horse's hooves and kept off bare stone where he could. He stalked that rememberd location in the woods below with wolfish hope—of provisions, of which he was scant, and whatever else he could lay hand to. If they were many he would try to ride by; if one man—that was another matter.

The sun was sinking when he came to that lower ground. The woods held no color but a taint of bloody light beyond the dull leaves. The trees which had seemed small from above arched above the way, gnarled and dark and rustling with the wind. Something had disturbed the leaves and the brush which intruded onto the roadway: a broken branch gleamed white splinters in the twilight. He kept on the way, came on the fresh droppings of a horse, some beast better fed than his, from some other trail than he had followed.

A thin, high sound disturbed the air, a voice, a woman's—sudden silence. He reined close in, fixed the direction of the sound and rode farther. There was someone in the dark ahead who took no account of the noise she made; and someone there was who did. He drew his sword from its sheath with the softest whisper of metal, kneed the horse further, and it walked warily, ears pricked now, head thrust forward.

The trail forked sideways, and the leafy carpet was disturbed there, ruffled by some passage. He kneed the horse onto it, kept it walking. Fire gleamed, a bright point through the branches. Again the voice, female and distraught; a man's low laughter . . . and Dubhan's mouth stretched back from his teeth, a little harder breathing, a little grin which had something of humor and something of lust. His heart beat harder, drowning the soft whisper of the horse's moving through the brush—jolted at the sudden rise of a black figure before the light in front of him.

Two of them, or more. He spurred the horse, broke through the brush into the light, swung the sword and hacked the standing figure, saw one more start up from the woman's white body and wheeled the horse on him, rode him down and reined the horse about the circuit of the camp as two horses broke their picket and crashed off through the brush. The first man, wounded, came at him with a sword; he rode on him again and this time his blade bit between neck and shoulder, tumbled the armorless man into the dead leaves.

The woman ran, white flashing of limbs in the firelight. He jerked the horse's head over and spurred after, grinning for breath and for anticipation, reined in when she darted into the brush and the rocks—he vaulted down from the saddle and labored after, armor-burdened, in and out among the brush and the branches, with one thought now—some woman of the towns, some prize worth the keeping while she lasted, or something they had gotten hereabouts from the farms. He saw her ahead of him, naked among the rocks, trying to climb the shoulder of the mountain where it thrust out into the forest, white flesh and cloud of shadow-hair, shifting from one to the other foothold and level among the black stones. "Come down," he mocked her. "Come down."

She turned where she stood above him, and looked at him with her pale fingers clutching the rock on her right, her hair blowing about her body. Looked up again, where the rocks became an upward thrust, a wall, unclimbable. "Come down to me," he called again. "I'm all the choice you have."

She made a sign at him, an ancient one. The fingers let go the rock—a blur of white through shadow, a cry, a body striking the rocks. She sprawled broken and open-eyed close by him, and moisture was on his face and his hands. He wiped at his mouth and stood shuddering an instant, swore and stalked off, blood cooled, blood chilled, a sickness moiling at his gut.

Waste. A sorry waste. No one to see it, no one to know, no one that cared for a trifle like that, to be dead over it, and useless. A little warmth, a little comfort; there was not even that.

He found his horse, bewildered and lost in the brush, took its reins and led it back to the fire where he hoped for something of value, where two dead men lay in their blood; but the horses had run off in the dark and the woods.

There was food, at least; he found that in the saddlebags by the fire, and chewed dried beef while he searched further. There were ordinary oddments, bits of leather and cord and a pot of salve; and wrapped in a scrap of dirty cloth—gold.

His hands trembled on the heavy chalice-shape in unveiling it, trembled; and he laughed and thought about his luck which had been wrong all his life until now. Gold. He rummaged the other saddlebags, hefting them and feeling the weight with his heart pounding in his chest. Out of one came a second object wrapped in cloth, which glittered in the firelight, and weighed heavy in his hands. A cross. Church plunder. They had gotten to that in the last stages.

He let it down with a wiping of his hands on his thighs, gnawed his lip and gathered it up again, shoved it into one bag. Then he snatched another bit of the beef, swallowing the last . . . found a wine flask by the fire and washed it down. He knelt there staring thoughtfully at the dead face of the first man, which lay at an odd angle on a severed neck. Familiarity tugged at him . . . someone he had seen before;

but in ten years he had seen many a man on both sides, and bearded, dead and dirty faces tended to look much alike. He drank deeply, warmed the death from his own belly, got up to tend his horse and paused by the other corpse, the one the horse had trod down.

Then familiarity did come home to him . . . long, long years, that he had known this man. Bryaut, his name was, Bryaut Dain's-son; young with him; afraid with him in his first battle; wounded in another . . . ways parted in the war and came together again here, tonight. Of a sudden the wine was sour in his mouth. He could have ridden in on the camp and Bryaut would have welcomed him. Not many men would, in these days; but this man would have. If there had been friends in his service—this was one, a long time ago, and mostly forgotten; but there was the face, no older than his, and blond, and with that scar down the brow he had gotten at Lugdan, when he himself had gotten the one on his jaw, where the beard would not grow.

He swore, and was ashamed in front of that dead face with its eyes looking sideways toward the fire, as if it had stopped paying attention. There was a time they had talked about winning honor for themselves, he and this young man no longer young, wealth and honor. And then he laughed a sickly laugh, thinking of the church-robbing and the woman and what an end it had come to, the war and the things they had planned and the reasons they had had for going to it at all. Bright treasure and fine armor and a station close to a king; and it came all to this. Church gold and a cold woman. He tipped up the wine flask and drank and walked away, thinking with a wolf's wariness that there had been too much noise and too much firelight and that it was time to go.

He was wiser than Bryaut, and maybe soberer. He packed the gold and the food and the things he wanted onto his horse and climbed into the saddle with the flask in his hand . . . rode off slowly, leaving the fire to die on its own, with the dead eyes staring on it. When he slept finally it was in the saddle, with the flask empty; and the horse staggered to a stop and stood there till he mustered the strength to climb down and shelter in the brush.

There he slept again in his armor, his sword naked across his knees—dreamed, of towns burning and of dead faces and naked white limbs plunging past him; waked with an outcry, and shuddered to sleep again.

Dreamed of a church, and fire, and a priest nailed to his own chapel door.

Lugdan and the mindless push of bodies, the battering, hours-long thunder of metal and human voices; and the silence after—the empty, feelingless silence—

A stone-walled room with candles burning, a gleam of gold on the altar, the chalice brimming full, the solemn sweet chanting of voices echoing out of his youth. The Lady Chapel, the blue-robed statue with painted eyes, hands offering blessings for all who came . . . The silence fell here too, taking away the voices, and the candles went out in the wind.

The stones became jumbled, and the wind blew, scattering smoke-black hair across pale features. The silence shrilled asunder, the shriek of the woman, the white limbs falling. . . .

He cried out, and the horse started and shied off through the thicket, stopped when the brush stopped it and he scrambled after it cursing, still dazed with sleep and dreams, scratched by brush across his face and hands.

Daylight had pierced the canopy of leaves. He retrieved his sword and sheathed it, checked the girth, dragged himself back into the saddle and rode on, on a trail narrower than he recalled. A bird sang, incongruous in the shadow where he traveled, under the arch of branches, some bird sitting where the sun touched the tops of the trees, some bird seeing something other than the dead brush and old leaves and the contorted trunks; and he hated it. He spurred the horse at times where the road was wider, pushed it until the froth flew back on his knees and its bony sides heaved when he let it walk. He spurred it again when he saw daylight beyond, and it ran from dark to light, slowed again, panting, under the sun, where the forest gave way to open grass and brush, and the road met another road from the west.

It was not the way that he remembered. He traveled with the sun on his back, warming now until sweat ran under the armor and prickled in the hollows of his body and stuck his padding to his sides and arms and thighs. By afternoon the way led downward again, into yet another valley, and by now he knew himself lost. There were signs of man, a boundary stone, a mark of sometime wheels on the narrow road, which wended two ways from a certain point—one which tended, wheel-rutted, west, and one which tended easterly, overgrown with grass, snaking toward a distant rim of woods.

He had no heart now for meetings, for braving alone the farmers who would have feared him if he had come with comrades. A knight alone might have his throat cut and worse if the peasants had their chance at him. He had seen the like. It was the eastward way he chose, away from humankind and homes, only wanting to go through the land and to find himself somewhere the war had never been, where no one had heard of it or suffered of it, where he could melt down his gold and pass it off bit by bit, find a haven and a comfort for the rest of his years.

Sometimes he would sleep as he rode, his head sinking forward on his chest while his hand, the reins wrapped about his fingers, rested behind the high bow. The horse plodded its way along, stole mouthfuls from brush along the track, dipped its head now and again to snatch at the grass, which pitching movements woke him, and he would straighten his back at waking, and feel relieved at the daylight still about him. He dreamed of fire and burnings; those had been his dreams for months. He no longer started awake out of them, only shivered in the sweat-prickling sun and listened to the ordinary sounds of leather and metal moving, and the whisper of the grass and the cadence of the hooves. He tried not to sleep, not for dread of the dreams, but because of the road and the danger; but the sounds kept up, and the insects sang in the late summer sun, and try as he would his head began to nod, and his eyes to close, not for long, for a little time: the horse was only waiting its chance for thefts, and it would wake him.

A downward step jolted him, a sudden sinking of the horse's right shoulder, a splash of water about the hooves at every move. He lifted his head in the twilight haze and saw green slim leaves about him, weeping branches and watery waste closely hemmed with trees and brush. Mud sucked, and the horse lurched across the low place, wandered onto firmer grass.

Dubhan turned in the saddle, looking for the path, but the brush was solid behind, and the place looked no different in that direction, closed off with trees trailing their branches into the scummed water, mazed with heaps of brush and old logs and pitted with deeper pools. Willow fingers trailed over him as the horse kept its mindless course—he faced about and fended the trailers with his arm, and the horse never slowed, never hesitated, as if it had gone mad in its exhaustion, one step and the other through the sucking mud and the shallow pools. The light was going; the sky above the willow tangle was bloodied cream, the gloom stealing through the thickets and taking the color from willow and water bit by bit, fading everything to one deadly deceptive flatness. He tugged at the reins and stopped the horse, but no sooner did he let the reins slack than the horse tugged for more rein and started moving again its same slow way, never faltering but for footing in the marsh, patient in its slow self-destruction. Frogs sang a numbing song. The water gurgled and splashed about the hooves and a reek of corruption went up from the mud, cloying. The water wept, a strange liquid sound. He pulled again at the reins, and the horse—instantly responsive in battle—ignored the bit and tugged back, going madly on. He wrapped his hand the tighter in the rein and hauled back with his strength against it, forcing the beast's head back against its chest, and then he could stop it . . . but whenever he let the rein loosen, it took its head again, and bent its head this way and that against the force he brought to bear; he hauled its head aside and faced it about to confuse it from its course, but it kept turning full circle, feet sliding in the mire, and came back again to force a few steps more. He cursed it, he cajoled it, the old horse he had ridden young to the war, he reminded it of days past and the time to come, some better land, some warm shelter against the winter, no more of fighting, no more of sleeping cold. But the horse kept moving in the colorless twilight, with the sky gone now to lowering gray, and the water weeping and splashing in the silence.

Something touched his eyes, like cobweb, crawled on his face and hands. He waved his hand, and the cloud came about him, midges started up from the reeds and the water; they crawled over his skin, buzzed about his ears, investigated the crack of his lips and settled into his eyes and his ears and were sucked up his nose. The horse snorted and threw its head, moved faster now, and Dubhan flailed about him with his free hand, wiped his eyes and blew and spat, blinded, inhaling them, clinging to the horse as the horse lashed its tail and shook itself and pitched into a lurching run. Branches whipped past, raked at Dubhan, and he tucked down as much as he could, clung to reins and saddle and clenched his hand into the war-horse's shorn mane, shorn so no enemy could hold; and now he could not, and reeled stunned and bruised when a branch hit his shoulder and jolted him back against the cantle and the girth. The horse staggered and slid in the mud, recovered itself, feet wide-braced, head down.

Then the head came up and the legs heaved and the horse waded fetlock deep, slowly, on its winding course, while the sobbing sounded clearer than before. Dubhan clung, wiped at his eyes with one hand, body moving to the relentless moving of the beast he rode. He crossed himself with that hand, and remembered what he had in the saddlebags—a memory too of painted eyes, and fire and darkness, voices silenced. Fear gathered in his gut and settled lower and sent up coils that knotted about his heart. His hand no longer fought the reins . . . no hope now of going back, in that mad course he had no idea which way they had turned, or how far they had come. He had faith now only in the horse's madness, that terror might be driving it, that his brave horse which had charged at the king's iron lines might be running now, and it might in its madness get him through this place if only it could walk the night through and not leave him afoot here and lost. He talked to it, he patted its gaunt neck, he pleaded; but it changed its going not at all, neither faster nor slower, though the breath came hollow from its mouth and its shoulders were lathered with sweat.

They passed into deeper shadow, under aged willows, through curtains of branches which trailed cutting caresses and kept night under their canopies, back into twilight and into night again, and the sobbing grew more human, prickling the hairs at Dubhan's nape and freezing the life from his hands and feet. It became like a child's weeping, some lost soul complaining in the night; it came from left and right and behind him, from above, in the trees, and from before. There was no sound but that; it wrapped him about. And suddenly in a prickling of apprehension he turned in the saddle and jerked free the saddlebag, tore it open and flung out the cup and the cross, which spun with a cold gleaming through the curtain of willow branches and struck the black water with a deep sound, swallowed up. The horse never ceased to move. He turned about again in time to fend the branches, sweating and cold at once. The gold was gone. It bought him nothing;

the sobbing was before him now, and above, a gleam of pallor in the gnarled willow-limbs of the next tree, a shadow-fall of hair. He saw a ghost, and drove spurs into the horse.

The beast flinched, and stopped, panting bellowslike between his legs, head sinking. He looked up into the branches and the gleam of flesh was gone—looked down and beside him and a white figure with shadow-hair moved the willow branches aside—all naked she was, and small . . . and came toward him with hands held out, a piquant face with vast dark eyes, a veil of hair that moved like smoke about white skin. The eyes swam with tears in the halflight of the night. The hands pleaded. The limbs were thin . . . a child's stature, a child's face. He dug the spurs at the horse to ride past as he had ridden past the war's abandoned waifs: it was their eyes he saw, their pleading hands, their gaunt ribs and matted hair and swollen bellies naked to the cold; but the horse stayed and the small hands clutched at his stirrup and the face which looked up to him was fair.

"Take me home," she asked of him. "I'm cold."

He kicked the stirrup to shake her fingers loose. She started back and stood there, her hair for a veil about her breasts if she had any, her body white and touched with shadow between the thighs like another whiteness in the dark, among the rocks; but these eyes were live and they stared, bruised and dark with fear.

"Was it you," he asked, "crying?"

"I gathered flowers," she said. "And men came." She began to cry again, tiny sobs. "I was running home."

His belief caught at that kind of story, held onto it double-fisted, an ugly thing and the kind of thing the world was, that made of the girl only a girl and the marsh only a river's sink and some homely place of safety not far from here. Slowly his hand reached out for her. She came and took it, her fingers cold and weak in his big hand; he gained his power to move and caught her frail wrist with the other hand, hauled her up before him—no weight at all for his arms. The horse began to move before she was settled; he adjusted the reins, tucked her up against him and her head burrowed against his shoulder, her arms going about his neck. His hand about her ribs felt not bone but softness swelling beneath his fingers, smooth skin; his eyes looking down saw a dark head and a flood of shadowy hair, and the rising moon played shadow-tricks on the childish body, rounded a naked hip, lengthened thighs and cast shadow between. Her body grew warm. She shifted and moved her legs, her arms hugging him the tighter, and the blood in him grew warm. Willow branches trailed over them with the horse's wandering and he no more than noticed, obsessed with his hands which might shift and not find objection to their exploring, with a thin body the mail kept from him, kept him from feeling with his.

It was a child's clinging, a child's fear; he kept the hands still where they were, on naked back and under naked knees, and patted her and soothed her, with a quieter warming in his blood that came from another human body in the night, a child's arms that expected no harm of him; and he gave none—should not be carrying double on the horse, his numbed wits recollected. He ought to get down and lead, the child sitting in the saddle, but the horse moved steadily and she seemed no weight at all on him, slept now, as it seemed, one arm falling from his neck to lie in her lap, delicate fingers upturned in the moonlight like some rare waterflower. Moonlight lay bright beyond the branches; the horse walked now on solid ground. The branches parted on a road, flat and broad, and he blinked in sleep-dulled amazement, not remembering how that had started or when they had come on it.

Hills shadowed against the night sky, a darkness against the stars: a mass of stone hove up before that, on the very roadside, placed like some wayside inn, but warlike, blockish, tall, a jumble of planes and shadow, far other than the woodcutter's cottage he had imagined.

"Child," he whispered. "Child. Is this your home?"

She stirred in his arms, another shifting of softness against his fingers, looked out into the dark between the horse's ears. "Yes," she breathed.

"There are no lights."

"They must be abed."

"With you lost?" A servant's child, perhaps, no one of consequence to the lords of the place; but then a lord who cared little for his people—he had served such a lord, and fought one, and lost himself. Apprehension settled back at his shoulders, but the horse plodded forward and the stone shadow loomed nearer in the moonlight, not nearly so large as it had seemed a moment ago, a tower, a mere tower, and badly ruined. Some woodcutter after all, it might be, some peasant borrowing a former greatness, settling himself in a tower's shell. The child's arms went again about his neck. He gathered the small body close to him for his own comfort. Exhaustion hazed his wits. The keep seemed now large again, and close. He had no memory of the horse's steps which had carried them into the looming shadow of the place, up to the man-sized stones, up to the solid wooden door.

He hugged the child against him, and then as she stirred, set her off, himself got down from the saddle, his knees buckling under his own mailed weight. She sought his hand with both of hers, and in her timid trust he grew braver. He walked up the steps leading her and slammed his fist against the ironbound oak, angered by their sleeping carelessness inside, that owed a lost child shelter and owed her rescuer—something, some reward. The blows thundered. He expected a stir, a flare of lights, a hailing from inside, even the rush of men to arms.

But the door gave back suddenly, swinging inward, unbarred or never barred. He thrust the child loose from his hand in sudden dread, drew his sword, seeing the gleam of light in the crack as he pushed the door with his shoulder, sending the massive weight farther ajar. A night fire burned in the hearth of a great fireplace, the only light, flaring in the sudden draft. He felt behind him for the child, half fearing to find her gone, felt a naked shoulder. The horse snorted, a soft, weary explosion in the dark at his back, ordinary and unalarmed. He walked in. The child followed and slipped free, pushed the door to with a straining of her slight body. "I'll find Mother," she said. "She'll be sleeping."

"No longer." He struck with his naked sword at a kettle hanging from a chain against the wall; it clattered down and rolled across the flags with a horrid racket. "Wake! Where are the parents of this child?"

"Child," the echoes answered. "Child, child, child."

"Mother?" the girl cried. He reached too late to stop her. She darted for the stairs which wound up and out of sight, built crazily toward the closed end of the high ceiling. "Girl," he called after her, and those echoes mingled with those of "Mother?" and likewise died, leaving him alone.

He retreated toward the door, shifted his grip on the swordhilt to pull the door open again and look outside, wary of ambushes, of a mind now to be away from this place. His horse still stood, cropping the grass in the moonlight.

Footsteps creaked on the stairs. The child came running down again as he whirled about, the naked body clothed now in a white shift. She came to him, caught his hand with hers. "Mother says you must stay," she said, wide dark eyes looking up into his. "She was afraid. We're all alone here, mother and I. She was afraid to let it seem anyone lived here. The bandits might come. Please stay; please be careful of my mother, please."

"Child?" he asked, but the hands broke from his and she ran, a flitting of white limbs and white shift in the dim firelight, vanishing up the stairs. He pushed the door gently, felt it close and looked back toward the fire—drew in his breath, bewildered. His exhausted senses had played him tricks again. About him the hall stretched farther than he had realized. The shadows and the fire's glare had masked a farther hall, which could not have appeared from the road. A table stood there, set with silver. Arms hung on the walls of that chamber, fighting weapons, not show.

A light flickered in the corner of his eye; he looked and saw a glow moving down the wall of the stairs . . . a woman came into his view, carrying a taper in her hand, and his heart lurched, for the child's beauty was nothing to hers. The woman's hair was a midnight cloud about her in her white shift and robe, her face in the candle's glow as translucent and pure as the wax gleaming in the heat, her body parting the strands of her hair with the full curves of breast and hip. Barefoot she walked down the wooden steps, her eyes wide with apprehension.

"You brought Willow home."

He nodded agreement and faint courtesy, the sword still naked in his hand. The woman came off the last step and walked to him, a vision in the candlelight, which shone reflected in her eyes with a great sadness.

"Willow's mad," she said in a voice to match her eyes. "Did you realize, sir? She runs out into the woods . . . I can't hold her at such times. Thank you for bringing her safe home again." Lashes swept, a soft glance up at him. "Please, I'll help you with your horse, sir, and give you a place to sleep in the hall."

"Forgive me," he said, remembering the drawn sword. He

reached for the sheath and ran it in, looked again at the lady. Food, shelter, the warmth of the hall. . . . *We're all alone,* the child had said. He looked at wide dark eyes and woman's body and delicate hands which clasped anxiously together about the candle—like Willow's hands, fine-boned and frail. He was staring. Heat rose to his face, a warmth all over. "I'll tend my horse," he said. "But I'd be glad of a meal and shelter, lady."

"There's a pen in back," she said. "We have a cow for milk. There's hay."

"Lady," he said, his brain still singing with warmth as if bees had lodged there and buzzed along his veins. He bowed, went out, into the dark, to take the reins of his horse and lead the poor animal around the curve of the tower—it *was* extended on the far side: he could see that now, from this new vantage. A byre was built against the wall, several pens, a sleepy cow who lurched to her feet in the moonlight and stood staring with dark bovine eyes. He led the horse in, gently unsaddled it, rubbed its galled and sweaty back with hands full of clean straw while the cow watched. He did his best for the horse, though his bones ached with the weight of armor and the ride. He hugged its gaunt neck when he was done, patted it, remembering a glossier feel to its coat, a day when bones had not lain so close to the skin. It bowed its head and nosed his ribs as it had done in gentler days before wars, before the hooves were shod with iron. It lipped his hand. The wide-eyed cow lowed in the dark, the moonlight on her crescent horns, and he pitchforked hay for them both, farmer's work, armored as he was, and made sure that there was water, then walked out the gate and latched it, walked around the curving stone wall, up the steps, opened the yielding door.

The fire inside was bright and red, the board in the recessed hall spread with bread and cold roast on silver plates and set with jugs of wine. He rubbed at his face, stopped, numb in the loss of time. He had dallied in the yard and the lady—the lady stood behind the table, spread her white-sleeved arms to welcome him to all that she had done.

He came and sat down in the tall chair, too hungry even to unburden himself of the armor, seized up a cup of dry red wine and drank, filled his mouth with fresh bread and honey and with the other hand worked at the straps at his side.

Strength flooded back into him with a few mouthfuls. He looked up from his piggishness and saw her at the other end of the table with her dark eyes laughing at him, not unkindly.

Such manners he had gained in the wars. He had aspired to better, once. He stood up and rid himself of belt and sword, hung the weapon over the chair's tall finial, and she rose and moved to help him shed the heavy mail. That weight and heat passed from him and he breathed a great free breath, shed the sweat-soaked haqueton, down to shirt and breeches, fell into the chair again and ate his fill, off silver plates, drank of a jeweled cup—and paused, heart thumping as he turned it within his hand: the shape the same, the very same. . . .

But silver, not gold. He drained it, gazed into dark and lovely eyes beyond the candleglow. "Is there," he asked thickly, "no lord in this hall . . . no servant, no one—but you and the child?"

"The war," she said with that same sadness in her eyes. "I had a servant, but he stole most all the coin and ran away. The villagers beyond the hills . . . they'll not come here. Willow frightens them; and I'm frightened of them—for Willow's sake, you see."

"What of your lord?"

"The war," she said. "He's not come home."

"His name?"

"Bryaut."

His breath stopped in him. He looked about the hall beyond her shoulders for some crest, some device—there was none. "Not Dain's-son—"

"You know him? You have news of him?"

"Dead," he said harshly. The lovely eyes filled with tears. The mouth trembled. "In the war," he said.

"Bravely?"

She asked that much. He stared past her, saw the trampled, half-naked man on the ground, the eyes slid unseeingly uninterested toward the campfire. Saw the boy he had known at Lugdan ford, the rain and the silence and the heaps of dead, raindrops falling in the bloody water. Men puking from exhaustion. A horse screaming, worse than any man. The fire again, and the forest, and rape. "Bravely," he said. "In battle. I saw him fall. His face toward the enemy. Five of them he took down; and they kept coming. We pushed them back too late for him. But he saved that day."

Tears fell. She pulled a handkerchief from her sleeve and blotted at her eyes. "You were his friend," she said.

"I knew him."

A second time she wiped at her eyes, and put on a smile greatly forced and sad. "You're twice kind."

"You'll be alone."

"Willow and I."

"I might stay a time."

She rose from table. He got up from his place. "Please," she said. "I'll make you a bed." Her voice trembled. "You'll sleep the night and go your way in the morning."

"Lady—"

"In the morning." She turned away, toward the stairs, her unbound hair a cloud about her bowed head and shoulders. She turned back and looked at him where he stood staring after her. "Come."

She took a candle from its sconce, paused by the stairs. He unrooted his feet from where he stood and came after, cold inside from remembering Bryaut, bones crushed beneath the horse's hooves, and white flesh, Bryaut's possession; Bryaut, who had died half-naked and in such a moment—before or after? Dubhan wondered morbidly—to die like that and to be cheated too. . . .

He followed her, up the narrow stairs designed for the tower's last defense, so narrow a wooden winding that his shoulders nearly filled the way side to side, and she must bend double to pass the doorway at the top, the candle before her. The light cast her body into relief, the shadow of a breast, of slim legs against the white linen, and he found his breathing harder than the climbing warranted—followed after into a hall where they could both stand upright, a wooden raftering, a maze among the timbers where the candle chased shadows, doors on either side.

She opened the first door and brought him within a room, touched her candle to another's stub—another flaring, another shadow through the loose linen gown—doubling the light, upon a pleasant wide bed with flowers on the table beside it. The linens were rumpled, the down mattress bearing the imprint of a body. "Mine," she said. "I'll make up the room next door for myself tonight. Rest. I'll bring you water for washing."

She came back to the doorway to pass him and leave, glanced down at such close quarters, denying him her eyes. "Lady," he said so that she would look up, and she did, close to him, almost touching body to body, and kept looking. He reached out his hand to the black cloud of her hair and stroked it because it was female and beautiful. The wine he had drunk sang in him, laid a haze on all else but her. He took her hand up, blew out the candle it held, rested both hands on her shoulders, on thin linen which eased downward, on smoothness and curving softness. "No," she said, and a weak hand pushed at him. He put his arms about her and drew her to the bed and sank down on the feathers and her gentle softness. "No," she said a second time, struggling under him, and he stopped her mouth with his, kissed her eyes, her smooth flesh. "*No,*" she wept, screaming, and of a sudden the heat froze in him. He felt her heaving sobs and heard her, and saw that other, pale figure in the dark, the hurtling rush of limbs, dead eyes staring at the moon. He did not move for the moment. Her hands made pathetic gestures toward covering her nakedness. She pushed at him to be free. He got off her and drew her shift up about her, smoothed her hair. It in no wise mended the wanting; but the doing—

"You are my *guest,*" she said. "In my hall. Let me go."

Her eyes glistened, dark and bright. He had lost, he thought, lost everything with his rashness. Might take, still; her, the tower, the wealth downstairs. He might live here, with Willow's madness. Might have her too. He was strong and they could do nothing; could never drive him out. They would fear too much to lift a hand to him, and they would understand they were better off with him. No cold winters, no death on the road. Every evening she would serve him food on silver plates; and every night they would lie here where the linens smelled of rosemary and the bed was soft. He would ride into that village she named, gather men to build a gate and wall, levy taxes, fear nothing. . . .

"Let me go," she said. Not pleading. Not fearfully. Just like that—asking.

"Some man," he said, "will come down this road . . . and take it all from you. Your lord's not coming back. Think how it will be."

"Do you intend to take it from me?"

His hand lifted toward her hair. He touched it compulsively and stopped it short of her breast, drew it away. "I'd see you were safe."

"From you?"

"I'd not force you. Go out of here. Talk to me tomorrow. Will you do that?"

"If you wish. But if I say no?"

"Think of me. Think that I wish you well. Good *night*, lady."

She rose and slipped away, her white robe trailing past him, across the floor, toward the door, and closed it after. He got up, drew a great breath, drove his fist against the wooden wall and clutched it to him, eyes shut from the pain, from the madness, but the blood welled up there and in his arm and diminished that elsewhere, and he worked his bruised hand and paced the creaking floor until his heart had stopped pounding.

He washed then, in water she had used. The cool water from her bedside bowl smelled of lilies and numbed the pain of his hand, numbed the ache of his shoulders and his ribs and left him shivering. He stripped, and used the linen towels and found the chamberpot beneath the bed, crawled at last between the rosemary-smelling sheets marvelously clean and comforted, leaned out to blow out the candle and blinked in a dark which, accustomed as he was to the stars at night and the moon, seemed fearsomely dark indeed. But his eyes closed a time, and a smile settled on him as he rolled and settled amid the scented sheets, until he had found just that hollow which suited him, and rest closer than he would have thought a while ago.

A step creaked in the hall, outside: the boards were old. The Lady? he wondered, dreaming dreams; the door opened, and the blackness was such that even lifting his head and looking, he could see nothing at all. A step crossed the boards, their creaking alone betraying its bare softness. A rustling of cloth attended it. "Who is it?" he asked, not entirely liking this dark and the visiting. A weight sank onto the foot of his bed and he jerked his foot from its vicinity realizing in one rush that sword and armor were downstairs, the cautions of a lifetime wine-muddled, woman-hazed. "Who? Lady?"

He moved to sit up all in a rush, but a gentle touch stole

up his sheeted leg, a whisper of cloth leaned forward, and a woman's perfume reached him. "Lady?" he said again, beginning to have different thoughts. And then another, colder: "Or is it Willow?"

"We are three," the whisper came to him. "Mother, Maid—and *me.*"

He thrust himself for the bedside. A grip caught his arm, a band like ice, burning chill that would not yield. He reached for that grip and met a hand soft-fleshed as age itself, frail-seeming, and strong. A like grip closed on the other arm, and the cold went inward, numbing breath, numbing heart, which beat in painful flutterings.

*"Man,"* the voice whispered, a breath of ice across his face, driving him backward and down. *"Man* . . . that you did not touch Willow in the marsh; well done; that you did not force my daughter: again well done; but that you forced a kiss of my daughter . . . now I repay: what's for one . . . is for all, like and like, Mother, Maid, and me."

He was drowning . . . felt a touch on his lips, an embrace about his limbs, and it was ice stealing inward. "No," he said, despairing. The white face came back to him, that despair, that flung itself from the rocks, cursing him. "No," he said again, colder still—Willow's face, and the starving children, the hollow-eyed, hollow-hearted children the war had made. A third time: *"No."* It was the lady crying out, her outrage at a world that took no regard of her, where force alone availed; and himself, his, that comrades met and killed each other, and no force could mend what was and what had been. He had no strength now, none, only the anger and the grief, alone.

His shoulders struck the wooden floor; he sprawled, his senses beginning to leave him as his sight had done, and tears were freezing on his lashes, the moisture freezing on his lips so that he could open neither, sightless, speechless in the dark, void of all protest. Sense went last. He was not aware for what might have been a long time; and then he felt again, wood beneath his naked back, perceived a light through his lids, but still he could not open his eyes. A shadow bent above him, breath stirred across his face; soft lips kissed one eyelid and then the other, and lastly his mouth.

He looked on Willow, who crouched by him in her shift, holding a lighted candle, her arm about her knees.

"It's day," said Willow. "There's just no window here."

He dared no words. He rolled over and got up, ashamed in his nakedness, drew his clothing on under Willow's silent, dark-eyed stare. She had stood up. He walked for the door, turned the remembered way in haste down the creaking hall, through the low doorway and down the windings of the stairs in the dark—down into the main room of the keep, where wood mouldered silver gray and cobwebs hung, the nests of spiders, fine spinnings in the daylight which sifted in through broken beams. His armor lay in the dust. He put it on, hands trembling, worked into the mail and did the buckles.

A step creaked on the stairs. He looked about. It was Willow coming down. He seized up the sword and belted it about him, and looked again, where the Lady stood in Willow's place.

The outside door gaped; the wood was gone. He ran for it, for the sunlight, around to the pen behind, where his horse cropped the green grass alone in a ramshackle enclosure, and his saddle and gear lay on the dewy ground. He saddled the horse in haste, climbed into the saddle and rode carefully past the keep, hearing the lowing of a cow at his back. That ceased. He blinked and Willow sat on a stone of the ruined wall, swinging her bare feet and waving at him. He spurred the horse past, reined back again with the feeling of something at his back. He looked to the doorway. The Lady stood there. She had a lily in her hair and her feet were bare. "Good journey," she wished him. "Farewell, sir knight."

He snapped the reins and rode quickly onto the road. A black, bent figure stood among the trees and brush on the far side of it, robed and hooded. The horse shied, trembling. Dubhan could see nothing but the robes, hoped for all the life that was in him that it would not look up, would not fling back the hood.

"Not yet," the voice came like the sighings of leaves. "You have years yet, sir knight."

He cracked the reins and rode. The sunlight warmed him finally, and the birds sang, until the chill melted from his gut where it had lain. He looked back, and there was only the forest.

When he had ridden a day there was a village. He watered his horse there, and the townsfolk came shyly round him and asked the news. He told them about the war; and the king dead, and the duke; but they had never heard of either, and blinked and wondered among themselves. They gave him bread and ale, and grain for his horse, and he thanked them and rode away.

On that day he hung the sword from his saddle and carried it no more.

On the next he took off the armor and stowed it away, let the breeze to his skin, and rode through lands widely farmed, where villages lay across the road, open and unfearing.

They saw the weapons, the children of these villages, and asked him tales.

He made up dragons, and unicorns. The children smiled.

In time, so did he.

# MOON MIRROR

## by André Norton

*For me as for so many of us, Andre Norton was one of the first writers whose books had a lasting impact. And she was definitely the first one with whom I corresponded, starting in 1973, when I was still in graduate school. Her thoughtfulness—and her stories about her cats—buoyed me up throughout my graduate program and beyond. When I first outlined the idea of an anthology of stories about witches, she was the first writer to say, "Count me in!" I began to realize that perhaps* Hecate's Cauldron *might be more than illusion after all.*

*Andre Norton's Witch World has probably had as least as much influence on the treatment of the supernatural in modern fantasy as any other major series. In the Witch World, the Power touches all lives—in the Dales, in Arvon, or in Estcarp where women surrender their names in return for the jewels of witchdom. Women rule Estcarp, but their control is often assailed by enemies without—and loneliness within.*

*In "Moon Mirror," Andre Norton's character Alathi too must battle to use her powers and gain what she needs to lead a rewarding life. Though Alathi is not a woman of Estcarp, as "Moon Mirror" is* not *a Witch World story, it combines many elements of the Witch World—a brooding sense of ancient power, the magical quest, the evocation of ancient deities—with features from her many other books—strange new worlds, the fascination with animals, and, above all, her sympathy with young people who have been deprived of a home, yet who find one within themselves to share with people they care about. Alathi is a worthy sister to Jaelithe of Estcarp. She begins alone and finishes content. So will the reader.*

Alathi edged farther into the brush where she had left her backpack. The provisions within it she had added to during the past five days by judicious thievery while she had dogged the caravan. Now she held a last such trophy in one hand, the claw knife of her people in the other. The cape hood of her jerkin hid her silky blue-gray hair and formed a half mask covering her face near to the chin, so that in this dawn hour she was a gray-brown shadow well able to fade into the desolate countryside.

This leather wallet, which she had filched from the tent of the master trader himself, was plump, the most promising she could find. Only, since she had crept away from the camp a new uneasiness had arisen in her, leading the furlike hair on the nape of her neck to twitch. Thus she did not hurry to plunder her prize, rather sat cross-legged, running her fingers back and forth across its worn leather.

Yes, there was something. . . .

The wallet was old. She could trace only by touch a design cut into its surface. The fringe across its bottom seam protruded like the stubs of broken teeth. She fingered those.

Her hand jerked. She raised her fingers to her lips as if they had been thrust into flames and she must so lick them cool. There was also a taste—acrid, almost as if she crunched ashes.

With her knife she worried the stitches, sawing through tight strands. This seam was wider than it looked to be. What it contained had been so long hidden that she had to use knife point to loosen it from embedding leather.

A narrow thread-ribbon of metal lay as limber across her palm as if it were a chain, save that it was one piece, not linked. It was silver, untarnished, and across it played flashes of color. The two ends were thicker, one forming a loop, the other a hook, so that they might be joined.

Though Alathi had never seen its like before, her inner sense told her this was a thing of power. As a hunting cat could fix upon prey, so could her race recognize such. They told tales of these things among themselves. Perhaps those were no tales in truth, rather fragments of history of a people who had once been rulers. That day was far past. "Hill Cats" had been prey for lowland hunters for years. Still they had not lost their pride nor command of special senses. Alathi knew the worth of what she held now as if it were shouted aloud at a Fire Feast. Its touch made her flesh tingle, the skin of her whole arm roughen. Her hand closed into a fist as she shivered at her roused feelings.

Then she dared to hook it about her throat where it lay as snug as if fashioned for her alone. She pulled her jerkin higher, laced the breast thongs tight to hide it. Its purpose she had yet to learn, but she was certain now she had been guided to its hiding place.

There was no food in the wallet pouch, rather a thick wad of folded parchment. Alathi freed this. Did she hold the same map she had watched the Merchant Coultar refer to yesterday when his wains had set up camp?

The Merchant Coultar—her green-yellow eyes narrowed. Why had this man among all those who had sheltered in the inn she had spied upon drawn her interest enough that she had chosen to skulk in his wake? He was taller than most lowlanders, fair of hair and skin, where they were loweringly dark. Born of a different people she had guessed—perhaps from across the salt sea where few now voyaged since the world had been rift and burnt by the long war. He was no lordling by his dress—but his manner, that was something else. Both his own men and the guard of blankshields he had with him jumped to his word, though he never raised his voice. And see where he had boldly led them. . . .

Anatray!

Alathi hunched her shoulders, refusing to look westward. If Coultar had come seeking what stood there he was suntouched, or ghost-ridden! She had thought to prey on these travelers long enough to get back to the hills, out of this war-riven land which had been drowned in blood so long. But she had not thought that *these* were the hills that company sought.

They made a black fringe across the sky; did he propose to win beyond their barrier, set up a trade flag for the nomads? That was folly upon folly, for there were too many blood feuds between herdsmen and coast dwellers.

No, he had made camp, a well planned one, Alathi thought critically—probably protected against any except a "Hill Cat." Still it was in short distance of that one peak ahead—that shaped by spirits for an emphatic warn-off. The spire formed an unmistakable fist, thumb curled into palm, fore and small fingers pointed skyward. Just so did prudent men gesture against ill luck and dark omens.

There were legends of the Fist, chiefly that it marked Anatray—a treasure site which might be anything from a forgotten temple to the tomb of a world ruler. Men had sought it out—there were always greedy fools. None had returned. Even those who camped nearby suffered from plague or wind-earth storms. Those who survived raved of unseen things which rode the wind.

How could Coultar have recruited men to follow him here? The wain men might be long oath-bound to his service, and the blankshields without hope of another lord, but they were all good at their jobs. She had had to exert herself these past days to keep up with them and evade their scouts.

Alathi's growing curiosity was like an itch tormenting some place she could not reach to scratch. Thus she had stayed with them past the point of prudence. Not only wanting to know where they went—but because this man Coultar teased her with a strong desire to learn more of him.

Her people continued to live only because they used well their eyes, their ears, any other inborn talent. She could prowl that camp by night, sending forth sooth-thoughts to the horses, eluding any sentry. But in all her skulking she had learned nothing of the merchant's plans.

No "Hill Cat" could trust one of another race, especially one plainsborn. Still she observed the merchant with care. He appeared to walk as softly as one of her own kind, never raising his voice (still men jumped at his bidding), his eyelids half lowered lazily, sometimes a faint half smile about his lips, as if he found in life some secret jest. He was unlike any other merchant she had observed. His power, she had decided, came not out of his purse, but was a part of him.

Now she studied the parchment, crossed by straggling lines, pricked here and there by symbols which she could not read. There was a strange odor wafting up out of its creases—as if it had lain as a covering for spices. She gnawed upon her lower lip. Perhaps her choice of the wallet had been a sorry mistake—it might be quickly missed.

As she looked from it to the land about, she found it hard to decide whether this was a representation of what she saw. Unconsciously her hand went to her throat where the band felt warm. That find had been so long hidden perhaps even Coultar had not known of it.

There was a stir in the camp. Coultar and the guard commander were mounting horses. Five of the other men also led out mounts. The girl stuffed the map back into the wallet, shoved that into her backpack, before she transformed her thin body into a misshapen outline by shrugging on the pack itself.

The horsemen trotted out, heading for the Fist. Alathi watched for a moment. If she did have Coultar's map, he had not missed it. However, he seemed entirely confident of his way. If she were wise she would stay where she was. However, that itch of curiosity would not allow her that safety.

She eyed every possible cover before her, knowing she must let them get well ahead before she followed. Last night they had unloaded some of the boxes in the wains, moving them with such ease as to suggest those were empty. If Coultar had not carried goods—then he was prepared to find such here. The fabled treasure of Anatray?

Alathi was returning to the home hills with nothing. Her people had been harried for years by the lowlanders. Suppose she let this merchant take the risk of looting the unknown and then help herself, as she was confident she was able to do, from what he garnered? She had nothing left save her skill and perhaps—again her fingers sought that throat band—that was not so poor a heritage that she would not profit.

She could not push from her mind the fantasy that, in some manner, she was linked with Coultar; that his good fortune might be turned to her use also. Every time she watched the man she had felt the harnessed power in him, recognized that he was one who would be master not servant in fortune's train.

So what if he rode now into demon-haunted land? After all, death had brushed her times without number during the past years. She must have long ago used up the number of "lives" which had been sung at her birthing. If she were to die, what would it matter? She was alone, and that stark loneliness strode always at her side, set upon her a weariness beyond the power of banishing. It slept with her, matched steps, haunted the night hours when she could not sleep.

Alathi flung up her head, the pride of her people rising hot in her. Legends sometimes possessed a core of truth. If there was aught ahead for the bold to seize she would take it. If it was for ill . . . that she was well accustomed to.

Sure that the goal of the riders was the Fist, Alathi made flitting rushes from one bit of cover to the next, watching the men rather than the demon spire. She had patience, freezing into the land whenever one of them looked about.

Now she struck north, away from their track, intending to come down from a different direction. The party had reached the Fist, three men remaining with the mounts, the rest, with Coultar, disappearing around its base.

Alathi lay belly down behind an outcrop of rock. The horse guards were alert, crossbows to hand. They were patrolling, but they made no attempt to go beyond the Fist. She still had a chance to retreat, but she also knew that she would never take it.

There was a promising line of shadow along the foot of the hills. She headed for that. Her breast heaving, she crouched low, waiting to hear a shout, even the whistle of a dart. No sound. Heartened, she scuttled on.

The ridge she followed broke; here was a cut which might hold a roadway. She sped ahead and now the Fist itself was between her and the guards. A pavement, but of a different stone than that which formed the bones of this land, had been set by purpose to form a path into the hills. It led through a dark canyon, along the shadowed throat where Coultar and his men already moved.

Their pace was slow, as suited those scouting the unknown, the men glancing from side to side, bare steel or crossbows ready. Yet Coultar marched as one who knew where he would go, looking only at something which he cupped in the palm of his hand, an object too small to be a map.

Alathi sidled along the wall of that half-hidden road. So intent was she upon following undetected, she had no preparation for what came. Her head jerked forward with such force she toppled to her knees, her hand clawing at her throat where that band had tightened, setting her gasping for air, black fear blotting out the world—everything except the need to loosen that choking thread of metal.

She tore with frantic fingers at the constriction, striving to slide the hook from the loop. Then she felt an urgency—a need. Only it was not *her* need—not now—for the loop loosened of itself, as if its sharp attack had come only to establish control over her, as if some presence that could reach her neither by voice nor gesture so claimed her full attention.

Gasping, rubbing her neck, she was filled with a new fear; she could not understand from whence this power came or what use it sought to make of her.

Blackness walled her. Yet she feebly struggled against the void that would use her for its own purpose. She was blind, voiceless, still she held desperately to an inner core of self, stubborn even in the face of what might be death.

Only dimly did she sense that she had regained her feet, was lurching from side to side as she ran, that something within urged her to ever greater effort, blotting out caution. She mouthed words which she heard, though they arose from no thought or will of her own:

"Ye Lords of the Four Watchtowers, ye are called upon. Rise to bear witness, arm to guard! The Great One who comes is the beauty and the bounty of the green earth. Her crown is the white moon among the spinning stars. From Her all things proceed, and have proceeded, from the birth of the world. To Her all things, in due time, return. She is the beginning and the ending. In Her hands lie strength, power, compassion, honor, humility, mirth and awe.

"Those who seek Her shall do so in vain if they know not the mysteries, nor call upon Her with the names of power. If they do not find such knowledge within, then it shall be closed to them without.

"Blessed are the eyes which can indeed behold Her in Her glory, mark Her path to follow. Blessed is the mouth which sings Her praise. Blessed be the body which is fruitful in Her service, blessed the feet walking in Her ways.

"Her names are many among the living, thus those who do Her honor call upon Her in diverse ways. She is Isis, and Astarte, Bast, Curwen, Diana, Skula, Freya, Ya-ling, Britta. . . .

"Blessed be!"

The blindness had lifted, she could clearly see the men ahead. As one they had turned to stare. One of the crossbows raised, a dart lay ready to fire. Still she could only run helplessly on.

Coultar's hand swung out, knocked down that bow. He strode forward, as if to meet her, his eyes now wide open, a strange look on his face. He might be seeing the very treasure that he had come seeking. But it was not the merchant she must meet—no. The force that drew her lay beyond—the Inner Place which belonged to *Her*, the Shining One!

Helplessly possessed, Alathi prepared to dodge, running more swiftly and surely, while that within assured greater control of her body. She was now only a tool—or a weapon—for another's use!

As she passed Coultar, avoiding his grasp, she saw his face fully alive. He had dropped some mask which had shielded him. There was avid eagerness in his wide eyes, his lips parted hungrily. He flung up his hand in the hollow of which rested a silvery disc. From that burst a thin flash of light.

Alathi pawed at the neck of her jerkin. The band about her throat was heating again. Words once more came to her even as she passed him by:

"*She* is the Great One whom no *man* dares name, though Her names are as many as there are nations, clans, and kin. She holds life in one hand, in the other the sword of death, maintaining the balance of the world. She welcomes the fall of seed into the waiting furrow, the growth that arises from the seed, the reaping of it when it ripens. She faces, unfearing, the coming of cold and of the winter sleep. For this is the pattern—"

One of the men against the wall put out his hand swiftly, then shrank back. Perhaps the force that dwelt in her now had shown itself in some way—perhaps even Coultar had signed some order. Alathi slid between them as if they were not there.

More words spilled from her jerkily as she ran. These were different, clicking, guttural, so unlike her own speech that the very sound terrified her. She could not stop uttering them—they seemed to arise from a mind portion where not even memory still lay.

Before her now was only the narrowing ancient road, down which she must go, helplessly. Nor did she fall into silence, for she singsonged, croaked, sometimes repeated phrases which made some sense, until her mouth dried and her throat ached. Nor could she rest while that inner one remained in command.

The walls, formed by the heights, drew together; now she was in a tunnel, a dark way. At its entrance had shimmered a haze curtain across which colors crossed, even as such had swept across the neckband's silver surface.

"Lord of the Watch Tower of the West—" She was once more speaking sense. "I am summoned. Speed you my way, For to this summoning there must be no hindrance—"

Through the haze she burst, feeling a flash of intense cold, as if she had broken a skim of ice across a winter prisoned pond. The way was no longer dark, the haze encased her.

Now the fear which had struck at the beginning of this wild and unaccountable action ebbed, not to rise again. In its place welled excitement akin to that she had felt days earlier when she had first seen Coultar.

"By the Lady. . . ." Those words she had willed herself. "By the favor of the Lady. . . ."

The haze swirled faster about her, its colors like jewels whirled about on cords—blazing into fantastic brilliance. She came forth from the tunnel.

Abruptly whatever had driven her withdrew, even as a man might snap his fingers. Alathi swayed, now aware of a sharp pain in her side, her aching feet, the dryness of her mouth. But those were of the body—they meant little or nothing in this place.

Here were no rocks, no earth. Rather there lay a mirror of silver water in a round basin filling all the space between straight cliffs, those as smooth as if they had been deliberately chiseled so that none might find footing upon them. Across the mirror once more played those flashes of vivid color, rippling as might the waves of the salt sea.

The surface of the pool (or lake, for it extended for a far

distance) was opaque. One could not see below. Around it ran a curbing near as tall as her waist. She staggered toward that, energy seeping out of her, not only weak and trembling, but bereft, as one whose treasure has been snatched by an enemy.

She fell to her knees behind the curbing, her hand steadying her. As Alathi clung there, near to the edge of consciousness, she saw the other wonder of this stretch of water. The sun shone down, well on its westward journey. Only the brilliance of that was not mirrored below.

Rather there rested on the surface a disc, growing outward from the heart of the lake. No shadow broke the pale, perfect round. Still there appeared upon it certain changes of color. Alathi, marking those, first dully and then with awakening recognition, knew what it resembled. Just as the moon was so clouded here and there so did the same patterns appear.

She wailed, voicing the low, keening cry uttered by the women of her own people as they leapt and danced beneath silver rays in the ancient rites of their sex. Alathi's body twitched as if she would dance—as if—

She pulled herself up, shrugged off her backpack, not caring where it might fall. From her thigh sheath she drew her long sword knife; from her belt her "claw"—such must not be worn here.

Straight she stood, watching that disc on the water grow ever more distinct, as if it were solid. Deep in her throat Alathi voiced a sound which was very old, reaching back into the first beginnings of her people, beginnings which even legends could not touch. She took a high step, to balance on the top of the curb, her eyes only for the moon shape.

Then—

Pain!

So sharp that it split through her skull like the blade of an axe. She wailed, writhed, fell back into a darkness which she thought fleetingly was death. No fear—just loss, a loss which was also pain—then nothing at all.

Distant sounds broke through the envelope of the dark. She strove to hold the dark intact. It promised safety and rest from troubling. Flashes of memory followed, too fleeting to be held.

"—Hill Cat! Best cut her throat, lord. They're as treacherous as a bal-serpent and nearly as deadly. Do they not dance evil down from the moon and spread it abroad in the dark of night?"

"Stand away! This one has in her what I have long sought. If you fear, Damstiff, then back with you. She is indeed a holder of power past your guessing!"

Alathi felt the band of fire about her throat. Only it did not burn, rather from it she drew strength, urging her out of the safety she had sought in the dark. She was aware of her body though she did not yet open her eyes, lay limp in another's hold.

Those voices used the hated click-click of lowland speech. Fragments wheeled through her mind in broken pictures. She could not hold onto them long enough to gain meaning—

"Ahhhhh!"

A scream rang in her ears, pierced through her head. She had been lifted, was being carried—No! The pool—they would take her from the pool!

The clash of steel, a smell . . . she had scented that before. The map . . . an old map and from its creases this same spicy odor. He who held her was moving. Did she have a chance to wriggle free? A second scream choked off in the midpoint as if a throat could no longer give it passage.

Alathi opened her eyes and, at the same moment, made her bid for freedom, twisting her body sharply. Coultar held her, but his head was half turned away as if his attention were drawn elsewhere. She was free of his hold, tumbling, to bring up, back against an earth wall—in the tunnel.

One of the guardsmen staggered by her, his hands to his face, weaving from side to side as if blind. Another, his mouth twisted by fear, leaned against the wall opposite her, seeking to aim, in spite of trembling hands, his crossbow. Then he screamed, a high cry like a woman's, hurled the weapon from him. Out of it, as it crashed on the pavement, curled a feather of pale smoke, then white flames leaped.

He whose weapon that was screamed again, pulled himself away from the wall, still staring at the crossbow, his features a mask of terror passing the bounds of sanity.

Alathi looked to Coultar. He held no steel—perhaps he had dropped weapons when he had taken her captive. Swinging nearly completely around, his face that of a sentry alert to attack, he looked back to the pool. Both of his hands were now heart high, and in the right one was that disc.

Those with him had all fled. Knowing that she had nothing now to fear from them the girl straightened. Strength came flowing back. She willed it to her as she might at the end of a training bout. Her breath no longer came in ragged gasps, rather smoothly as a precious draught of water in the desert. With herself once more under control she became more and more aware of a force which filled this narrow way. It was so strong that she believed she might put forth a hand and gather up its substance.

It was not aimed at her. Coultar's face grew more tense, he began to breathe faster. His lips were forced back against his teeth in a half snarl of effort as he visibly fought for speech:

"By Curwen, by Thethera, by Skula, by the oak, the ash, the red thorn, by the waxing moon—the moon that is full—that which wanes. By—"

He passed into another language, one in which the sounds began low in his throat, ascending note by note to a higher pitch than she could believe any man might naturally utter.

The disc he held was no longer that. Rather he cupped a length of white flame. His fingers writhed, blistered before her eyes, still he held it, and stood, rock firm.

"By the Law of the Worlds, and that which lies between them, by those who walk still our paths, and those who have gone before," he dropped into intelligible speech again. "In the name of Herne, Thoth, Abyis, Lord of Light, by Suth, and Korn, also the Watch Lords of the East, West, North, and South, do I stand here. Two things that have contact—" he held the flame a fraction higher—"will come together. A power strengthens a power. O, *She* who—"

The flame in his hand leaped free. To Alathi it sped. He wheeled to face the girl as that flame struck against the latched hoop at her throat, clung, changed. She felt no fire, from this uniting came no harm to her.

Alathi raised hands to the disc once more formed, then she stretched out the right slowly to the man who had held it earlier. A wall might have fallen—she saw. He was no merchant—rather a seeker—one who was a stranger, still closer than any kin.

She gasped, for his body seemed to flow, to change. This was not the man she had followed secretly across the waste of Ghritz. Though something of that one remained. Only more had been revealed.

"Who are you!" she asked.

"There is the Lady." There was a weight in his words as if he were one of more authority than she had ever met. "There is also He who comes with the winter—into whose hands *She* passes the Sword, that He may complete that circle which balances the world—Life and birth, death and sleep, before life comes anew. I am one who is vowed to that Lord of Winter. He has been lost from the time and people of my birth world; thus I must journey into another time and place to call upon him again for the sake of my own kind.

"Evoe, Evoe, Pan! Evoe, Herne! Evoe, Thoth!" He threw back his head. His voice came as a great shout which seemed to rock the very world under and about them.

Again he changed. Here stood a dark-skinned man who wore the spotted skin of some beast about him over a white kilt; another with a head of close-curled hair, his body bare save for a small strip of hide, the badge of kinship with the world of beasts; a man in armor; one in a long robe across which ran runes in scarlet, to glow and fade. He was all these, yet also the Coultar of the here and now.

"I swear by the wide and fruitful womb of my mother, by my honor among men, by the blood shed in the Circle—" He spoke softly, as if he sought some answer from her. Though her ears still rang from his shouts, she could hear.

Alathi answered, knowing, even as she spoke, that she had said the words before many times. When and in what places? That did not matter now—this was the time, the place, to which she had been led so that she might say them again and so enter into what waited.

"I swear by my hope of the Great Glory beyond, by my past lives, my hope of future ones yet to come—"

At last their hands might meet. Around them surged the power. Not driven by it, but a part of it, they went back—Hill Cat and merchant no longer. What they were now they must learn.

They came out to the pool. Alathi understood. In each life there waits a door to the Innerworld ready. Some never found it. That she had was as fair a fortune as the stuff of dreams.

"Blessed Lady, I am thy child—"

"—thy child," he echoed her.

Together they climbed upon the curbing; together they

leaped, hand in hand, out into the great waiting moon mirror. It closed about them, drew them in. However, their search had only begun, their feet but touched upon the first steps of the widest and straightest road of all.

# THE SAGE OF THEARE

## *by Diana Wynne Jones*

*"Medicine men, witch doctors, shamans, devils, enchanters?" asks a character in Diana Wynne Jones's* Charmed Life *(Pocket, 1977). "Hags, fakirs, sorcerers? Are they thick on the ground, too?"*

*"Hag is rude," she is told.*

*This exchange describes the particular charm of Diana Wynne Jones's writing. Set in a pre-World War I England on another Earth,* Charmed Life *is a magic world of tea, vicars, muslins—and wizards, witches, and sorcerers, regulated (if you please) by the British Civil Service. Chief among its specialists in magic is Chrestomanci the enchanter. His job is not just to keep all the witches in order; he must also police all the known worlds and make sure that the magic in them does not get out of balance.*

*When I first wrote to Diana Wynne Jones about this anthology, my letter was forwarded to her as "a letter from an unknown person." That, she says, started her thinking about what became "The Sage of Theare," and her newest story about Chrestomanci.*

*In "The Sage of Theare," Chrestomanci saunters in characteristically absentminded grandeur between the worlds—and up to the gods—in order to set the balance of magic straight once more. In so doing, he gives gods the sniffles and helps a little boy get a start in life. Chrestomanci, you see, has more than magic. He has style. So does Diana Wynne Jones.*

There was a world called Theare in which Heaven was very well organized. Everything was so precisely worked out that every god knew his or her exact duties, correct prayers, right times for business, utterly exact character and unmistakable place above or below other gods. This was the case from great Zond, the King of the Gods, through every god, godlet, deity, minor deity and numen, down to the most immaterial nymph. Even the invisible dragons that lived in the rivers had their invisible lines of demarcation. The universe ran like clockwork. Mankind was not always so regular, but the gods were there to set him right. It had been like this for centuries.

So it was a breach in the very nature of things when, in the middle of the yearly Festival of Water, at which only watery deities were entitled to be present, Great Zond looked up to see Imperion, god of the sun, storming toward him down the halls of Heaven.

"Go away!" cried Zond, aghast.

But Imperion swept on, causing the watery deities gathered there to steam and hiss, and arrived in a wave of heat and warm water at the foot of Zond's high throne.

"Father!" Imperion cried urgently.

A high god like Imperion was entitled to call Zond Father. Zond did not recall whether or not he was actually Imperion's father. The origins of the gods were not quite so orderly as their present existence. But Zond knew that, son of his or not, Imperion had breached all the rules. "Abase yourself," Zond said sternly.

Imperion ignored this command too. Perhaps this was just as well, since the floor of Heaven was awash already, and steaming. Imperion kept his flaming gaze on Zond. "Father! The Sage of Dissolution has been born!"

Zond shuddered in the clouds of hot vapor and tried to feel resigned. "It is written," he said, "a Sage shall be born who shall question everything. His questions shall bring down the exquisite order of heaven and cast all the gods into disorder. It is also written—" Here Zond realized that Imperion had made him break the rules too. The correct procedure was for Zond to summon the god of prophecy and have that god consult the Book of Heaven. Then he realized that Imperion *was* the god of prophecy. It was one of his precisely allocated duties. Zond rounded on Imperion. "What do you mean coming and telling me? You're god of prophecy! Go and look in the Book of Heaven!"

"I already have, Father," said Imperion. "I find I prophesied the coming of the Sage of Dissolution when the gods first began. It is written that the Sage shall be born and that I shall not know."

"Then," said Zond, scoring a point, "how is it you're here telling me he *has* been born?"

"The mere fact," Imperion said, "that I can come here and interrupt the Water Festival, shows that the Sage has been born. Our Dissolution has obviously begun."

There was a splash of consternation among the watery gods. They were gathered down the hall as far as they could get from Imperion, but they had all heard. Zond tried to gather his wits. What with the steam raised by Imperion and the spume of dismay thrown out by the rest, the halls of Heaven were in a state nearer chaos than he had known for millennia. Any more of this, and there would be no need for the Sage to ask questions. "Leave us," Zond said to the watery gods. "Events even beyond my control cause this Festival to be stopped. You will be informed later of any decision I make." To Zond's dismay, the watery ones hesitated —further evidence of Dissolution. "I promise," he said.

The watery ones made up their minds. They left in waves, all except one. This one was Ock, god of all oceans. Ock was equal in status to Imperion and heat did not threaten him. He stayed where he was.

Zond was not pleased. Ock, it always seemed to him, was the least orderly of the gods. He did not know his place. He was as restless and unfathomable as mankind. But, with Dissolution already begun, what could Zond do? "You have our permission to stay," he said graciously to Ock, and to Imperion: "Well, how did you know the Sage was born?"

"I was consulting the Book of Heaven on another matter," said Impérion, "and the page opened at my prophecy concerning the Sage of Dissolution. Since it said that I would not know the day and hour when the Sage was born, it followed that he has already been born, or I would not have known. The rest of the prophecy was commendably precise, however. Twenty years from now, he will start questioning Heaven. What shall we do to stop him?"

"I don't see what we can do," Zond said hopelessly. "A prophecy is a prophecy."

"But we must do something!" blazed Imperion. "I insist! I am a god of order, even more than you are. Think what would happen if the sun went inaccurate! This means more to me than anyone. I want the Sage of Dissolution found and killed before he can ask questions."

Zond was shocked. "I can't do that! If the prophecy says he has to ask questions, then he has to ask them."

Here Ock approached. "Every prophecy has a loophole," he said.

"Of course," snapped Imperion. "I can see the loophole as well as you. I'm taking advantage of the disorder caused by the birth of the Sage to ask Great Zond to kill him and overthrow the prophecy. Thus restoring order."

"Logic-chopping is not what I meant," said Ock.

The two gods faced one another. Steam from Ock suffused Imperion and then rained back on Ock, as regularly as breathing. "What did you mean, then?" said Imperion.

"The prophecy," said Ock, "does not appear to say which world the Sage will ask his questions in. There are many other worlds. Mankind calls them if-worlds, meaning that they were once the same world as Theare, but split off and went their own ways after each doubtful event in history. Each if-world has its own Heaven. There must be one world in which the gods are not as orderly as we are here. Let the Sage be put in that world. Let him ask his predestined questions there."

"Good idea!" Zond clapped his hands in relief, causing untoward tempests in all Theare. "Agreed, Imperion?"

"Yes," said Imperion. He flamed with relief. And, being unguarded, he at once became prophetic. "But I must warn you," he said, "that strange things happen when destiny is tampered with."

"Strange things maybe, but never disorderly," Zond asserted. He called the watery gods back and, with them, every god in Theare. He told them that an infant had just been born who was destined to spread Dissolution, and he ordered each one of them to search the ends of the earth for this child. ("The ends of the earth" was a legal formula. Zond did not believe that Theare was flat. But the expression had been unchanged for centuries, just like the rest of Heaven. It meant "Look everywhere.")

The whole of Heaven looked high and low. Nymphs and godlets scanned mountains, caves and woods. Household gods peered into cradles. Watery gods searched beaches, banks and margins. The goddess of love went deeply into her records, to find who the Sage's parents might be. The invisible dragons swam to look inside barges and houseboats. Since there was a god for everything in Theare, nowhere was missed, nothing was omitted. Imperion searched harder than any, blazing into every nook and crevice on one side of the world, and exhorting the moon goddess to do the same on the other side.

And nobody found the Sage. There were one or two false alarms, such as when a household goddess reported an infant that never stopped crying. This baby, she said, was driving her up the walls and, if this was not Dissolution, she would like to know what was. There were also several reports of infants born with teeth, or six fingers, or suchlike strangeness. But, in each case, Zond was able to prove that the child had nothing to do with Dissolution. After a month, it became clear that the infant Sage was not going to be found.

Imperion was in despair, for, as he had told Zond, order meant more to him than to any other god. He became so worried that he was actually causing the sun to lose heat. At length, the goddess of love advised him to go off and relax with a mortal woman before he brought about Dissolution himself. Imperion saw she was right. He went down to visit the human woman he had loved for some years. It was established custom for gods to love mortals. Some visited their loves in all sorts of fanciful shapes, and some had many loves at once. But Imperion was both honest and faithful. He never visited Nestara as anything but a handsome man, and he loved her devotedly. Three years ago, she had borne him a son, whom Imperion loved almost as much as he loved Nestara. Before the Sage was born to trouble him, Imperion had been trying to bend the rules of Heaven a little, to get his son approved as a god too.

The child's name was Thasper. As Imperion descended to

earth, he could see Thasper digging in some sand outside Nestara's house—a beautiful child, fair-haired and blue-eyed. Imperion wondered fondly if Thasper was talking properly yet. Nestara had been worried about how slow he was learning to speak.

Imperion alighted beside his son. "Hallo, Thasper. What are you digging so busily?"

Instead of answering, Thasper raised his golden head and shouted. "Mum!" he yelled. "Why does it go bright when Dad comes?"

All Imperion's pleasure vanished. Of course no one could ask questions until he had learned to speak. But it would be too cruel if his own son turned out to be the Sage of Dissolution. "Why shouldn't it go bright?" he asked defensively.

Thasper scowled up at him. "I want to know. *Why* does it?"

"Perhaps because you feel happy to see me," Imperion suggested.

"I'm not happy," Thasper said. His lower lip came out. Tears filled his big blue eyes. "Why does it go bright? I want to *know*. Mum! I'm not happy!"

Nestara came racing out of the house, almost too concerned to smile at Imperion. "Thasper love, what's the matter?"

"I want to *know!*" wailed Thasper.

"What do you want to know? I've never known such an inquiring mind," Nestara said proudly to Imperion, as she picked Thasper up. "That's why he was so slow talking. He wouldn't speak until he'd found out how to ask questions. And if you don't give him an exact answer, he'll cry for hours."

"When did he first start asking questions?" Imperion inquired tensely.

"About a month ago," said Nestara.

This made Imperion truly miserable, but he concealed it. It was clear to him that Thasper was indeed the Sage of Dissolution and he was going to have to take him away to another world. He smiled and said, "My love, I have wonderful news for you. Thasper has been accepted as a god. Great Zond himself will have him as cupbearer."

"Oh not now!" cried Nestara. "He's so little!"

She made numerous other objections too. But, in the end,

she let Imperion take Thasper. After all, what better future could there be for a child? She put Thasper into Imperion's arms with all sorts of anxious advice about what he ate and when he went to bed. Imperion kissed her good-bye, heavy-hearted. He was not a god of deception. He knew he dared not see her again for fear he told her the truth.

Then, with Thasper in his arms, Imperion went up to the middle-regions below Heaven, to look for another world.

Thasper looked down with interest at the great blue curve of the world. "Why—?" he began.

Imperion hastily enclosed him in a sphere of forgetfulness. He could not afford to let Thasper ask things here. Questions that spread Dissolution on earth would have an even more powerful effect in the middle-region. The sphere was a silver globe, neither transparent nor opaque. In it, Thasper would stay seemingly asleep, not moving and not growing, until the sphere was opened. With the child thus safe, Imperion hung the sphere from one shoulder and stepped into the next-door world.

He went from world to world. He was pleased to find there were an almost infinite number of them, for the choice proved supremely difficult. Some worlds were so disorderly that he shrank from leaving Thasper in them. In some, the gods resented Imperion's intrusion and shouted at him to be off. In others, it was mankind that was resentful. One world he came to was so rational that, to his horror, he found the gods were dead. There were many others he thought might do, until he let the spirit of prophecy blow through him, and in each case this told him that harm would come to Thasper here. But at last he found a good world. It seemed calm and elegant. The few gods there seemed civilized but casual. Indeed, Imperion was a little puzzled to find that these gods seemed to share quite a lot of their power with mankind. But mankind did not seem to abuse this power, and the spirit of prophecy assured him that, if he left Thasper here inside his sphere of forgetfulness, it would be opened by someone who would treat the boy well.

Imperion put the sphere down in a wood and sped back to Theare, heartily relieved. There, he reported what he had done to Zond, and all Heaven rejoiced. Imperion made sure that Nestara married a very rich man who gave her not only wealth and happiness but plenty of children to replace Thasper. Then, a little sadly, he went back to the ordered life of Heaven. The exquisite organization of Theare went on untroubled by Dissolution.

Seven years passed.

All that while, Thasper knew nothing and remained three years old. Then one day, the sphere of forgetfulness fell in two halves and he blinked in sunlight somewhat less golden than he had known.

"So that's what was causing all the disturbance," a tall man murmured.

"Poor little soul!" said a lady.

There was a wood around Thasper, and people standing in it looking at him, but, as far as Thasper knew, nothing had happened since he soared to the middle-region with his father. He went on with the question he had been in the middle of asking. "Why is the world round?" he said.

"Interesting question," said the tall man. "The answer usually given is because the corners wore off spinning around the sun. But it could be designed to make us end where we began."

"Sir, you'll muddle him, talking like that," said another lady. "He's only little."

"No, he's interested," said another man. "Look at him."

Thasper was indeed interested. He approved of the tall man. He was a little puzzled about where he had come from, but he supposed the tall man must have been put there because he answered questions better than Imperion. He wondered where Imperion had got to. "Why aren't you my Dad?" he asked the tall man.

"Another most penetrating question," said the tall man. "Because, as far as we can find out, your father lives in another world. Tell me your name."

This was another point in the tall man's favor. Thasper never answered questions: he only asked them. But this was a command. The tall man understood Thasper. "Thasper," Thasper answered obediently.

"He's sweet!" said the first lady. "I want to adopt him." To which the other ladies gathered around most heartily agreed.

"Impossible," said the tall man. His tone was mild as milk and rock firm. The ladies were reduced to begging to be able to look after Thasper for a day, then. An hour. "No," the tall man said mildly. "He must go back at once." At which all the ladies cried out that Thasper might be in great danger in his own home. The tall man said, "I shall take care of that, of course." Then he stretched out a hand and pulled Thasper up. "Come along, Thasper."

As soon as Thasper was out of it, the two halves of the sphere vanished. One of the ladies took his other hand and he was led away, first on a jiggly ride, which he much enjoyed, and then into a huge house, where there was a very perplexing room. In this room, Thasper sat in a five-pointed star and pictures kept appearing around him. People kept shaking their heads. "No, not that world either." The tall man answered all Thasper's questions, and Thasper was too interested even to be annoyed when they would not allow him anything to eat.

"Why not?" he said.

"Because, just by being here, you are causing the world to jolt about," the tall man explained. "If you put food inside you, food is a heavy part of this world, and it might jolt you to pieces."

Soon after that, a new picture appeared. Everyone said "Ah!" and the tall man said. "So it's Theare!" He looked at Thasper in a surprised way. "You must have struck someone as disorderly," he said. Then he looked at the picture again, in a lazy, careful kind of way. "No disorder," he said. "No danger. Come with me."

He took Thasper's hand again and led him into the picture. As he did so, Thasper's hair turned much darker. "A simple precaution," the tall man murmured, a little apologetically, but Thasper did not even notice. He was not aware what color his hair had been to start with, and besides, he was taken up with surprise at how fast they were going. They whizzed into a city, and stopped abruptly. It was a good house, just on the edge of a poorer district. "Here is someone who will do," the tall man said, and he knocked at the door.

A sad-looking lady opened the door.

"I beg your pardon, madam," said the tall man. "Have you by any chance lost a small boy?"

"Yes," said the lady. "But this isn't—" She blinked. "Yes it *is!*" she cried out. "Oh Thasper! How could you run off like that? Thank you so much, sir." But the tall man had gone.

The lady's name was Alina Altun, and she was so convinced that she was Thasper's mother that Thasper was soon convinced too. He settled in happily with her and her husband, who was a doctor, hard-working but not very rich. Thasper soon forgot the tall man, Imperion and Nestara. Sometimes it did puzzle him—and his new mother too—that when she showed him off to her friends she always felt bound to say, "This is Badien, but we always call him Thasper." Thanks to the tall man, none of them ever knew that the real Badien had wandered away the day Thasper came and fell in the river, where an invisible dragon ate him.

If Thasper had remembered the tall man, he might also have wondered why his arrival seemed to start Dr. Altun on the road to prosperity. The people in the poorer district nearby suddenly discovered what a good doctor Dr. Altun was, and how little he charged. Alina was shortly able to afford to send Thasper to a very good school, where Thasper often exasperated his teachers by his many questions. He had, as his new mother often proudly said, a most inquiring mind. Although he learned quicker than most the Ten First Lessons and the Nine Graces of Childhood, his teachers were nevertheless often annoyed enough to snap, "Oh, go and ask an invisible dragon!" which is what people in Theare often said when they thought they were being pestered.

Thasper did, with difficulty, gradually cure himself of his habit of never answering questions. But he always preferred asking to answering. At home, he asked questions all the time: "Why does the kitchen god go and report to Heaven once a year? Is it so I can steal biscuits? Why are invisible dragons? Is there a god for everything? Why is there a god for everything? If the gods make people ill, how can Dad cure them? Why must I have a baby brother or sister?"

Alina Altun was a good mother. She most diligently answered all these questions, including the last. She told Thasper how babies were made, ending her account with, "Then, if the gods bless my womb, a baby will come." She was a devout person.

"I don't want you to be blessed!" Thasper said, resorting to a statement, which he only did when he was strongly moved.

He seemed to have no choice in the matter. By the time he was ten years old, the gods had thought fit to bless him with two brothers and two sisters. In Thasper's opinion, they were, as blessings, very low grade. They were just too young to be any use. "Why can't they be the same age as me?" he demanded, many times. He began to bear the gods a small but definite grudge about this.

Dr. Altun continued to prosper and his earnings more than kept pace with his family. Alina employed a nursemaid, a cook, and a number of rather impermanent houseboys. It was one of these houseboys who, when Thasper was eleven, shyly presented Thasper with a folded square of paper. Wondering, Thasper unfolded it. It gave him a curious feeling to touch, as if the paper was vibrating a little in his fingers. It also gave out a very strong warning that he was not to mention it to anybody. It said:

> Dear Thasper,
>
> Your situation is an odd one. Make sure that you call me at the moment when you come face to face with yourself. I shall be watching and I will come at once.
>
> Yrs,
> Chrestomanci

Since Thasper by now had not the slightest recollection of his early life, this letter puzzled him extremely. He knew he was not supposed to tell anyone about it, but he also knew that this did not include the houseboy. With the letter in his hand, he hurried after the houseboy to the kitchen.

He was stopped at the head of the kitchen stairs by a tremendous smashing of china from below. This was followed immediately by the cook's voice raised in nonstop abuse. Thasper knew it was no good trying to go into the kitchen. The houseboy—who went by the odd name of Cat—was in the process of getting fired, like all the other houseboys before him. He had better go out and wait for Cat outside the back door. Thasper looked at the letter in his hand. As he did so, his fingers tingled. The letter vanished.

"It's gone!" he exclaimed, showing by this statement how astonished he was. He never could account for what he did next. Instead of going to wait for the houseboy, he ran to the living room, intending to tell his mother about it, in spite of the warning. "Do you know what?" he began. He had invented this meaningless question so that he could tell people things and still make it into an inquiry. "Do you know what?" Alina looked up. Thasper, though he fully intended to tell her about the mysterious letter, found himself saying, "The cook's just sacked the new houseboy."

"Oh bother!" said Alina. "I shall have to find another one now."

Annoyed with himself, Thasper tried to tell her again. "Do you know what? I'm surprised the cook doesn't sack the kitchen god too."

"Hush dear. Don't talk about the gods that way!" said the devout lady.

By this time, the houseboy had left and Thasper lost the urge to tell anyone about the letter. It remained with him as his own personal exciting secret. He thought of it as The Letter From A Person Unknown. He sometimes whispered the strange name of The Person Unknown to himself when no one could hear. But nothing ever happened, even when he said the name out loud. He gave up doing that after a while. He had other things to think about. He became fascinated by Rules, Laws and Systems.

Rules and Systems were an important part of the life of mankind in Theare. It stood to reason, with Heaven so well organized. People codified all behavior into things like the Seven Subtle Politenesses, or The Hundred Roads To Godliness. Thasper had been taught these things from the time he was three years old. He was accustomed to hearing Alina argue the niceties of the Seventy-Two Household Laws with her friends. Now Thasper suddenly discovered for himself that all Rules made a magnificent framework for one's mind to clamber about in. He made lists of rules, and refinements on rules, and possible ways of doing the opposite of what the rules said while still keeping the rules. He invented new codes of rules. He filled books and made charts. He invented games with huge and complicated rules, and played them with his friends. Onlookers found these games both rough and muddled, but Thasper and his friends revelled in them. The best moment in any game was when somebody stopped playing and shouted, "I've thought of a new rule!"

This obsession with rules lasted until Thasper was fifteen. He was walking home from school one day, thinking over a list of rules for Twenty Fashionable Hair Styles. From this, it will be seen that Thasper was noticing girls, though none of the girls had so far seemed to notice him. And he was thinking which girl should wear which hair style, when his attention was caught by words chalked on a wall.

IF RULES MAKE A FRAMEWORK FOR THE MIND TO CLIMB ABOUT IN, WHY SHOULD THE MIND NOT CLIMB RIGHT OUT, SAYS THE SAGE OF DISSOLUTION.

That same day, there was consternation again in Heaven. Zond summoned all the high gods to his throne. "The Sage of Dissolution has started to preach," he announced direfully. "Imperion, I thought you got rid of him."

"I thought I did," Imperion said. He was even more appalled than Zond. If the Sage had started to preach, it meant that Imperion had got rid of Thasper and deprived himself of Nestara quite unnecessarily. "I must have been mistaken," he admitted.

Here Ock spoke up, steaming gently. "Father Zond," he said, "may I respectfully suggest that you deal with the Sage yourself, so that there will be no mistake this time?"

"That was just what I was about to suggest," Zond said gratefully. "Are you all agreed?"

All the gods agreed. They were too used to order to do otherwise.

As for Thasper, he was staring at the chalked words, shivering to the soles of his sandals. What was this? Who was using his own private thoughts about rules? Who was this Sage of Dissolution? Thasper was shamed. He, who was so good at asking questions, had never thought of asking this one. Why should one's mind not climb right out of the rules, after all?

He went home and asked his parents about the Sage of Dissolution. He fully expected them to know. He was quite agitated when they did not. But they had a neighbor, who sent Thasper to another neighbor, who had a friend, who, when Thasper finally found his house, said he had heard that the Sage was a clever young man who made a living by mocking the gods.

The next day, someone had washed the words off. But the day after that, a badly printed poster appeared on the same wall. THE SAGE OF DISSOLUTION ASKS BY WHOSE ORDER IS ORDER ANYWAY?? COME TO SMALL UNCTION SUBLIME CONCERT HALL TONITE 6:30.

At 6:20, Thasper was having supper. At 6:24, he made up his mind and left the table. At 6:32, he arrived panting at Small Unction Hall. It proved to be a small shabby building quite near where he lived. Nobody was there. As far as Thasper could gather from the grumpy caretaker, the meeting had been the night before. Thasper turned away, deeply disappointed. Who ordered the order was a question he now longed to know the answer to. It was deep. He had a notion that the man who called himself the Sage of Dissolution was truly brilliant.

By way of feeding his own disappointment, he went to school the next day by a route which took him past the Small Unction Concert Hall. It had burnt down in the night. There were only blackened brick walls left. When he got to school, a number of people were talking about it. They said it had burst into flames just before 7:00 the night before.

"Did you know," Thasper said, "that the Sage of Dissolution was there the day before yesterday?"

That was how he discovered he was not the only one interested in the Sage. Half his class were admirers of Dissolution. That, too, was when the girls deigned to notice him. "He's amazing about the gods," one girl told him. "His questions are really keen!" another girl told him. "No one ever asked questions like that before." Most of the class, however, girls and boys alike, only knew a little more than Thasper, and most of what they knew was second-hand. But a boy showed him a carefully cut-out newspaper article in which a well-known scholar discussed what he called "The so-called Doctrine of Dissolution." It said, long-windedly, that the Sage and his followers were rude to the gods and against all the rules. It did not tell Thasper much, but it was something. He saw, rather ruefully, that his obsession with rules had been quite wrong-headed and had, into the bargain, caused him to fall behind the rest of his class in learning of this wonderful new Doctrine. He became a Disciple of Dissolution on the spot. He joined the rest of his class in finding out all they could about the Sage. He went round with them, writing up on walls DISSOLUTION RULES OK.

For a long while after that, the only thing any of Thasper's class could learn of the Sage were scraps of questions chalked on walls and quickly rubbed out. WHAT NEED OF PRAYER? WHY SHOULD THERE BE A HUNDRED ROADS TO GODLINESS, NOT

MORE OR LESS? DO WE CLIMB ANYWHERE ON THE STEPS TO HEAVEN? WHAT IS PERFECTION: A PROCESS OR A STATE? WHEN WE CLIMB TO PERFECTION IS THIS A MATTER FOR THE GODS?

Thasper obsessively wrote all these sayings down. He was obsessed again, he admitted, but this time it was in a new way. He was thinking, thinking. At first, he thought simply of clever questions to ask the Sage. He strained to find questions no one had asked before. But in the process, his mind seemed to loosen, and shortly he was thinking of how the Sage might answer his questions. He considered order and rules and Heaven, and it came to him that there was a reason behind all the brilliant questions the Sage asked. He felt light-headed with thinking.

The reason behind the Sage's questions came to him the morning he was shaving for the first time. He thought *The gods need human beings in order to be gods!* Blinded with this revelation, Thasper stared into the mirror at his own face half covered with white foam. Without humans believing in them, gods were nothing! The order of Heaven, the rules and codes of earth, were all only there because of people! It was transcendent. As Thasper stared, the letter from the Unknown came into his mind. "Is this being face to face with myself?" he said. But he was not sure. And he became sure that when that time came, he would not have to wonder.

Then it came to him that the Unknown Chrestomanci he was to call then was almost certainly the Sage himself. He was thrilled. The Sage was taking a special mysterious interest in one teenage boy, Thasper Altun. The vanishing letter exactly fit the elusive Sage.

The Sage continued elusive. The next firm news of him was a newspaper report of the Celestial Gallery being struck by lightning. The roof of the building collapsed, said the report, "only seconds after the young man known as the Sage of Dissolution had delivered another of his anquished and self-doubting homilies and left the building with his disciples."

"He's not self-doubting," Thasper said to himself. "He knows about the gods. If *I* know, then *he* certainly does."

He and his classmates went on a pilgrimage to the ruined gallery. It was a better building than Small Unction Hall. It seemed the Sage was going up in the world.

Then there was enormous excitement. One of the girls

found a small advertisement in a paper. The Sage was to deliver another lecture, in the huge Kingdom of Splendor Hall. He had gone up in the world again. Thasper and his friends dressed in their best and went there in a body. But it seemed as if the time for the lecture had been printed wrong. The lecture was just over. People were streaming away from the Hall, looking disappointed.

Thasper and his friends were still in the street when the Hall blew up. They were lucky not to be hurt. The Police said it was a bomb. Thasper and his friends helped drag injured people clear of the blazing Hall. It was exciting, but it was not the Sage.

By now, Thasper knew he would never be happy until he had found the Sage. He told himself that he had to know if the reason behind the Sage's questions was the one he thought. But it was more than that. Thasper was convinced that his fate was linked to the Sage's. He was certain the Sage *wanted* Thasper to find him.

But there was now a strong rumor in school and around town that the Sage had had enough of lectures and bomb attacks. He had retired to write a book. It was to be called *Questions of Dissolution*. Rumor also had it that the Sage was in lodgings somewhere near the Road of the Four Lions.

Thasper went to the Road of the Four Lions. There he was shameless. He knocked on doors and questioned passersby. He was told several times to go ask an invisible dragon, but he took no notice. He went on asking until someone told him that Mrs. Tunap at 403 might know. Thasper knocked at 403, with his heart thumping.

Mrs. Tunap was a rather prim lady in a green turban. "I'm afraid not, dear," she said. "I'm new here." But before Thasper's heart could sink too far, she added, "But the people before me had a lodger. A very quiet gentleman. He left just before I came."

"Did he leave an address?" Thasper asked, holding his breath.

Mrs. Tunap consulted an old envelope pinned to the wall in her hall. "It says here, 'Lodger gone to Golden Heart Square,' dear."

But in Golden Heart Square, a young gentleman who might have been the Sage had only looked at a room and gone. After that, Thasper had to go home. The Altuns were not used to teenagers and they worried about Thasper suddenly wanting to be out every evening.

Oddly enough, No 403 Road of the Four Lions burnt down that night.

Thasper saw clearly that assassins were after the Sage as well as he was. He became more obsessed with finding him than ever. He knew he could rescue the Sage if he caught him before the assassins did. He did not blame the Sage for moving about all the time.

Move about the Sage certainly did. Rumour had him next in Partridge Pleasaunce Street. When Thasper tracked him there, he found the Sage had moved to Fauntel Square. From Fauntel Square, the Sage seemed to move to Strong Wind Boulevard, and then to a poorer house in Station Street. There were many places after that. By this time, Thasper had developed a nose, a sixth sense, for where the Sage might be. A word, a mere hint about a quiet lodger, and Thasper was off, knocking on doors, questioning people, being told to ask an invisible dragon, and bewildering his parents by the way he kept rushing off every evening. But, no matter how quickly Thasper acted on the latest hint, the Sage had always just left. And Thasper, in most cases, was only just ahead of the assassins. Houses caught fire or blew up sometimes when he was still in the same street.

At last he was down to a very poor hint, which might or might not lead to New Unicorn Street. Thasper went there, wishing he did not have to spend all day at school. The Sage could move about as he pleased, and Thasper was tied down all day. No wonder he kept missing him. But he had high hopes of New Unicorn Street. It was the poor kind of place that the Sage had been favoring lately.

Alas for his hopes. The fat woman who opened the door laughed rudely in Thasper's face. "Don't bother me, son! Go and ask an invisible dragon!" And she slammed the door again.

Thasper stood in the street, keenly humiliated. And not even a hint of where to look next. Awful suspicions rose in his mind: he was making a fool of himself; he had set himself a wild goose chase; the Sage did not exist. In order not to think of these things, he gave way to anger. "All right!" he shouted at the shut door. "I *will* ask an invisible dragon! So there!" And, carried by his anger, he ran down to the river and out across the nearest bridge.

He stopped in the middle of the bridge, leaning on the parapet, and knew he was making an utter fool of himself. There were no such things as invisible dragons. He was sure of that. But he was still in the grip of his obsession, and this was something he had set himself to do now. Even so, if there had been anyone about near the bridge, Thasper would have gone away. But it was deserted. Feeling an utter fool, he made the prayer-sign to Ock, Ruler of Oceans—for Ock was the god in charge of all things to do with water—but he made the sign secretly, down under the parapet, so there was no chance of anyone seeing. Then he said, almost in a whisper, "Is there an invisible dragon there? I've got something to ask you."

Drops of water whirled over him. Something wetly fanned his face. He heard the something whirring. He turned his face that way and saw three blots of wet in a line along the parapet, each about two feet apart and each the size of two of his hands spread out together. Odder still, water was dripping out of nowhere all along the parapet, for a distance about twice as long as Thasper was tall.

Thasper laughed uneasily. "I'm imagining a dragon," he said. "If there was a dragon, those splotches would be the places where its body rests. Water dragons have no feet. And the length of the wetness suggests I must be imagining it about eleven feet long."

"I am fourteen feet long," said a voice out of nowhere. It was rather too near Thasper's face for comfort and blew fog at him. He drew back. "Make haste, child-of-a-god," said the voice. "What did you want to ask me?"

"I—I—I—" stammered Thasper. It was not just that he was scared. This was a body-blow. It messed up utterly his notions about gods needing men to believe in them. But he pulled himself together. His voice only cracked a little as he said, "I'm looking for the Sage of Dissolution. Do you know where he is?"

The dragon laughed. It was a peculiar noise, like one of those water-warblers people make bird noises with. "I'm afraid I can't tell you precisely where the Sage is," the voice out of nowhere said. "You have to find him for yourself. Think about it, child-of-a-god. You must have noticed there's a pattern."

"Too right, there's a pattern!" Thasper said. "Everywhere he goes, I just miss him, and then the place catches fire!"

"That too," said the dragon. "But there's a pattern to his lodgings too. Look for it. That's all I can tell you, child-of-a-god. Any other questions?"

"No—for a wonder," Thasper said. "Thanks very much."

"You're welcome," said the invisible dragon. "People are always telling one another to ask us, and hardly anyone does. I'll see you again." Watery air whirled in Thasper's face. He leaned over the parapet and saw one prolonged clean splash in the river, and silver bubbles coming up. Then nothing. He was surprised to find his legs were shaking.

He steadied his knees and tramped home. He went to his room and, before he did anything else, he acted on a superstitious impulse he had not thought he had in him, and took down the household god Alina insisted he keep in a niche over his bed. He put it carefully outside in the passage. Then he got out a map of the town and some red stickers and plotted out all the places where he had just missed the Sage. The result had him dancing with excitement. The dragon was right. There was a pattern. The Sage had started in good lodgings at the better end of town. Then he had gradually moved to poorer places, but he had moved in a curve, down to the Station and back toward the better part again. Now, the Altun's house was just on the edge of the poorer part. The Sage was *coming this way!* New Unicorn Street had not been so far away. The next place should be nearer still. Thasper had only to look for a house on fire.

It was getting dark by then. Thasper threw his curtains back and leaned out of his window to look at the poorer streets. And there it was! There was a red and orange flicker to the left—in Harvest Moon Street, by the look of it. Thasper laughed aloud. He was actually grateful to the assassins!

He raced downstairs and out of the house. The anxious questions of parents and the yells of brothers and sisters followed him, but he slammed the door on them. Two minutes running brought him to the scene of the fire. The street was a mad flicker of dark figures. People were piling furniture in the road. Some more people were helping a dazed woman in a crooked brown turban into a singed armchair.

"Didn't you have a lodger as well?" someone asked her anxiously.

The woman kept trying to straighten her turban. It was all she could really think of. "He didn't stay," she said. "I think he may be down at the Half Moon now."

Thasper waited for no more. He went pelting down the street. The Half Moon was an inn on the corner of the same road. Most of the people who usually drank there must have been up the street, helping rescue furniture, but there was a dim light inside, enough to show a white notice in the window. ROOMS, it said.

Thasper burst inside. The barman was on a stool by the window craning to watch the house burn. He did not look at Thasper. "Where's your lodger?" gasped Thasper. "I've got a message. Urgent."

The barman did not turn round. "Upstairs, first on the left," he said. "The roof's caught. They'll have to act quick to save the house on either side."

Thasper heard him say this as he bounded upstairs. He turned left. He gave the briefest of knocks on the door there, flung it open, and rushed in.

The room was empty. The light was on, and it showed a stark bed, a stained table with an empty mug and some sheets of paper on it, and a fireplace with a mirror over it. Beside the fireplace, another door was just swinging shut. Obviously somebody had just that moment gone through it. Thasper bounded toward that door. But he was checked, for just a second, by seeing himself in the mirror over the fireplace. He had not meant to pause. But some trick of the mirror, which was old and brown and speckled, made his reflection look for a moment a great deal older. He looked easily over twenty. He looked—

He remembered the Letter from the Unknown. This was the time. He knew it was. He was about to meet the Sage. He had only to call him. Thasper went toward the still gently swinging door. He hesitated. The Letter had said call at once. Knowing the Sage was just beyond the door, Thasper pushed it open a fraction and held it so with his fingers. He was full of doubts. He thought, "Do I really believe the gods need people? Am I so sure? What shall I say to the Sage after all?" He let the door slip shut again.

"Chrestomanci," he said, miserably.

There was a *whoosh* of displaced air behind him. It buffeted Thasper half around. He stared. A tall man was standing by the stark bed. He was a most extraordinary figure in a long black robe, with what seemed to be yellow comets embroidered on it. The inside of the robe, swirling in the air, showed yellow, with black comets on it. The tall man had a very smooth dark head, very bright dark eyes and, on his body feet, what seemed to be red bedroom slippers.

"Thank goodness," said this outlandish person. "For a moment, I was afraid you would go through that door."

The voice brought memory back to Thasper. "You brought me home through a picture when I was little," he said. "Are you Chrestomanci?"

"Yes," said the tall outlandish man. "And you are Thasper. And now we must both leave before this building catches fire."

He took hold of Thasper's arm and towed him to the door which led to the stairs. As soon as he pushed the door open, thick smoke rolled in, filled with harsh crackling. It was clear that the inn was on fire already. Chrestomanci clapped the door shut again. The smoke set both of them coughing, Chrestomanci so violently that Thasper was afraid he would choke. He pulled both of them back into the middle of the room. By now, smoke was twining up between the bare boards of the floor, causing Chrestomanci to cough again.

"This would happen just as I had gone to bed with flu," he said, when he could speak. "Such is life. These orderly gods of yours leave us no choice." He crossed the smoking floor and pushed open the door by the fireplace.

It opened on to blank space. Thasper gave a yelp of horror.

"Precisely," coughed Chrestomanci. "You were intended to crash to your death."

"Can't we jump to the ground?" Thasper suggested.

Chrestomanci shook his smooth head. "Not after they've done this to it. No. We'll have to carry the fight to them and go and visit the gods instead. Will you be kind enough to lend me your turban before we go?" Thasper stared at this odd request. "I would like to use it as a belt," Chrestomanci croaked. "The way to Heaven may be a little cold, and I only have pajamas under my dressing-gown."

The striped undergarments Chrestomanci was wearing did look a little thin. Thasper slowly unwound his turban. To go before gods bareheaded was probably no worse than going in nightclothes, he supposed. Besides, he did not believe there were any gods. He handed the turban over. Chrestomanci tied the length of pale blue cloth around his black and yellow gown and seemed to feel more comfortable. "Now hang on to me," he said, "and you'll be all right." He took Thasper's arm again and walked up into the sky, dragging Thasper with him.

For a while, Thasper was too stunned to speak. He could only marvel at the way they were treading up the sky as if there were invisible stairs in it. Chrestomanci was doing it in the most matter of fact way, coughing from time to time, and shivering a little, but keeping very tight hold of Thasper nevertheless. In no time, the town was a clutter of prettily lit dollhouses below, with two red blots where two of them were burning. The stars were unwinding about them, above and below, as if they had already climbed above some of them.

"It's a long climb to Heaven," Chrestomanci observed. "Is there anything you'd like to know on the way?"

"Yes," said Thasper. "Did you say the gods are trying to kill me?"

"They are trying to eliminate the Sage of Dissolution," said Chrestomanci, "which they may not realize is the same thing. You see, you are the Sage."

"But I'm not!" Thasper insisted. "The Sage is a lot older than me, and he asks questions I never even thought of until I heard of him."

"Ah yes," said Chrestomanci. "I'm afraid there is an awful circularity to this. It's the fault of whoever tried to put you away as a small child. As far as I can work out, you stayed three years old for seven years—until you were making such a disturbance in our world that we had to find you and let you out. But in this world of Theare, highly organized and fixed as it is, the prophecy stated that you would begin preaching Dissolution at the age of twenty-three, or at least in this very year. Therefore the preaching had to begin this year. You did not need to appear. Did you ever speak to anyone who had actually heard the Sage preach?"

"No," said Thasper. "Come to think of it."

"Nobody did," said Chrestomanci. "You started in a small way anyway. First you wrote a book, which no one paid much heed to—"

"No, that's wrong," objected Thasper. "He—I—er, the Sage was writing a book *after* the preaching."

"But don't you see," said Chrestomanci, "because you were back in Theare by then, the facts had to try to catch you up. They did this by running backwards, until it was possible for you to arrive where you were supposed to be. Which was in that room in the inn there, at the start of your career. I suppose you are just old enough to start by now. And I suspect our celestial friends up here tumbled to this belatedly and tried to finish you off. It wouldn't have done them any good, as I shall shortly tell them." He began coughing again. They had climbed to where it was bitterly cold.

By this time, the world was a dark arch below them. Thasper could see the blush of the sun, beginning to show underneath the world. They climbed on. The light grew. The sun appeared, a huge brightness in the distance underneath. A dim memory came again to Thasper. He struggled to believe that none of this was true, and he did not succeed.

"How do you know all this?" he asked bluntly.

"Have you heard of a god called Ock?" Chrestomanci coughed. "He came to talk to me when you should have been the age you are now. He was worried—" He coughed again. "I shall have to save the rest of my breath for Heaven."

They climbed on, and the stars swam around them, until the stuff they were climbing changed and became solider. Soon they were climbing a dark ramp, which flushed pearly as they went upward. Here, Chrestomanci let go of Thasper's arm and blew his nose on a gold-edged handkerchief with an air of relief. The pearl of the ramp grew to silver and the silver to dazzling white. At length, they were walking on level whiteness, through hall after hall after hall.

The gods were gathered to meet them. None of them looked cordial.

"I fear we are not properly dressed," Chrestomanci murmured.

Thasper looked at the gods, and then at Chrestomanci, and squirmed with embarrassment. Fanciful and queer as Chrestomanci's garb was, it was still most obviously nightwear. The things on his feet were fur bedroom slippers. And there, looking like a piece of blue string around Chrestomanci's waist, was the turban Thasper should have been wearing. The gods were magnificent, in golden trousers and jeweled turbans, and got more so as they approached the greater gods. Thasper's eye was caught by a god in shining cloth of gold, who surprised him by beaming a friendly, almost anxious look at him. Opposite him was a huge liquid-looking figure draped in pearls and diamonds. This god swiftly, but quite definitely, winked. Thasper was too awed to react, but Chrestomanci calmly winked back.

At the end of the halls, upon a massive throne, towered the mighty figure of great Zond, clothed in white and purple, with a crown on his head. Chrestomanci looked up at Zond and thoughtfully blew his nose. It was hardly respectful.

"For what reason do two mortals trespass in our halls?" Zond thundered coldly.

Chrestomanci sneezed. "Because of your own folly," he said. "You gods of Theare have had everything so well worked out for so long that you can't see beyond your own routine."

"I shall blast you for that," Zond announced.

"Not if none of you wish to survive," Chrestomanci said.

There was a long murmur of protest from the other gods. They wished to survive. They were trying to work out what Chrestomanci meant. Zond saw it as a threat to his authority and thought he had better be cautious. "Proceed," he said.

"One of your most efficient features," Chrestomanci said, "is that your prophecies always come true. So why, when a prophecy is unpleasant to you, do you think you can alter it? That, my good gods, is rank folly. Besides, no one can halt his own Dissolution, least of all you gods of Theare. But you forgot. You forgot you had deprived both yourselves and mankind of any kind of free will, by organizing yourselves so precisely. You pushed Thasper, the Sage of Dissolution, into my world, forgetting that there is still chance in my world. By chance, Thasper was discovered after only seven years. Lucky for Theare that he was. I shudder to think what might have happened if Thasper had remained three years old for all his allotted lifetime."

"That was my fault!" cried Imperion. "I take the blame." He turned to Thasper. "Forgive me," he said. "You are my own son."

Was this, Thasper wondered, what Alina meant by the gods blessing her womb? He had not thought it was more than a figure of speech. He looked at Imperion, blinking a little in the god's dazzle. He was not wholly impressed. A fine god, and an honest one, but Thasper could see he had a limited outlook. "Of course I forgive you," he said politely.

"It is also lucky," Chrestomanci said, "that none of you succeeded in killing the Sage. Thasper is a god's son. That means there can only ever be one of him, and because of your prophecy he has to be alive to preach Dissolution. You could have destroyed Theare. As it is, you have caused it to blur into a mass of cracks. Theare is too well organized to divide into two alternative worlds, like my world would. Instead, events have had to happen which could not have happened. Theare has cracked and warped, and you have all but brought about your own Dissolution."

"What can we do?" Zond said, aghast.

"There's only one thing you can do," Chrestomanci told him. "Let Thasper be. Let him preach Dissolution and stop trying to blow him up. That will bring about free will and a free future. Then either Theare will heal, or it will split, cleanly and painlessly, into two healthy new worlds."

"So we bring about our own downfall?" Zond asked mournfully.

"It was always inevitable," said Chrestomanci.

Zond sighed. "Very well. Thasper, son of Imperion, I reluctantly give you my blessing to go forth and preach Dissolution. Go in peace."

Thasper bowed. Then he stood there silent a long time. He did not notice Imperion and Ock both trying to attract his attention. The newspaper report had talked of the Sage as full of anguish and self-doubt. Now he knew why. He looked at Chrestomanci, who was blowing his nose again. "How can I preach Dissolution?" he said. "How can I not believe in the gods when I have seen them for myself?"

"That's a question you certainly should be asking," Chrestomanci croaked. "Go down to Theare and ask it."

Thasper nodded and turned to go. Chrestomanci leaned toward him and said, from behind his handkerchief, "Ask yourself this too: Can the gods catch flu? I think I may have given it to all of them. Find out and let me know, there's a good chap."

# THE HARMONIOUS BATTLE

## *by Jessica Amanda Salmonson*

*DAW's "theme" anthologies like Gerry Page and Hank Reinhardt's* Heroic Fantasy *and Jessica Amanda Salmonson's* Amazons! *were really what started* Hecate's Cauldron *boiling. Consequently, I was delighted when "The Harmonious Battle" arrived in my mailbox—for two reasons. First: as I selected stories, I was definitely hoping for tales with non-Western backgrounds. This story's background is Japanese. Second: I was also looking for strongly plotted stories in which the magic is utterly central to the plot and to the characters. Once again, this story fills the bill. For warrior-woman Azo Hono-o, conquering the evil spell represents both a victory against magic and a victory against her own fears of being crippled.*

*In Jessica Amanda Salmonson's many publications in major anthologies, among them the* Berkley Showcase, *she creates strong female characters set in equally powerful cultures. Azo Hono-o, a minor character in* The Golden Naginata, *Jessica's forthcoming novel, is just such a woman.*

*A martial artist and editor of* Naginata, *a fanzine about women warriors, Jessica Salmonson consistently presents women in nontraditional occupations coping with natural and supernatural adversaries. Traditionally speaking, such women have always been called witches. Azo Hono-o is a warrior, not a sorceress, but her story is pure magic.*

Throughout her eight weeks recuperating at Emura Temple hot springs on Mount Awa, Azo Hono-o dwelt overlong on the loss of her left arm. Although she revealed none of these emotions, secretly she was consumed by self-pity. As *onna-bushi*, or woman warrior, she had excelled in the use of daito, a sword generally considered to be a two-handed weapon. There were one-handed styles which she could study, but there was no denying the handicap: her effectiveness was halved. How would the fame she had acquired in past encounters ever be maintained? Were she to strive exceptionally hard, she might achieve the strength of an average foot-soldier; but it did not seem possible to regain her previous abilities. It would take getting used to, the fact that none would comment any longer on the superiority of her fighting skill.

The shoulder had healed smoothly with the aid of ointments and the care provided by the priest of the temple. The hot springs were located on the mountainside overlooking Emura-ji. The view from the high pools had a curative effect of its own. Azo was well enough to be upon her way; but the self-pity and its attendant sense of ennui kept her lingering extra days.

She rested in the steaming waters, her head against a rock. Her one remaining arm reached out of the water like a lazy serpent. She turned her hand slowly to look at it from every angle. When she parted her fingers, she saw another woman coming down a mountain path. This was strange, for no one lived above the hot springs and only wild animals kept the paths clear of foliage. A pilgrim to the hotsprings ought to come from the temple below, not from the peaks above.

The woman was naked but for a towel around her hair. Azo's strong, serpentine arm withdrew into the water. She watched the graceful woman approaching.

The new arrival smiled pleasantly, bowed politely, then slipped into the farther side of the pool without creating the slightest ripple. The steam rose in ghostly veils between them.

Azo Hono-o ignored the other woman, closed her eyes, relaxed. In the next moment there was someone standing close to her, although Azo had not heard the woman walking through the pool.

"Did I frighten you, onna-bushi?" The woman's voice was sweet.

Azo Hono-o collected her wits and looked up at the woman standing in the shallow water. "It was impolite to come upon me without a sound!" she complained.

"It was impolite that you did not acknowledge my arrival," the woman countered. She squatted down until the water covered her breasts. Azo sat with water to her neck.

"I am here to recover from battle wounds," said Azo. Her hair drifted on the water's surface. "My mind is preoccupied with thoughts about my injury. I have forsaken many social amenities in order to regard my singular misfortune."

"I understand," the woman said, her tone forgiving. "In fact, that is why I have come."

"Ah!" said Azo. "The priest sends you to advise my departure?"

"No, onna-bushi! You are too sensitive to think so. I come because you seem so sad. There is no reason for it!"

Azo made a derisive sound. She lifted her head from the rock, sitting forward a bit so that part of her torso rose above the water. "You see?" said Azo, her armless shoulder evident. "There is cause indeed for melancholy."

"I would like to advise you," said the young woman with the towel upon her head.

"Advise me how?"

"Emura-ji hot springs has nothing more to offer you," she began. "I advise that you travel to Lake Miwa and seek there my two sisters. Tell them the witch of Awayama has sent you."

Azo sat upright and looked surprised. "Witch?"

"I am called that. I am also called spirit, fairy, devil." The woman unwrapped her hair. It was arranged in a beautiful style and was as white as the snow of Awayama's highest levels. The woman said, "I think of myself only as an ascetic."

The division between mortal and deity was a slender one; who to one person was an ordinary individual was, to another, someone profound and immortal. Azo Hono-o stirred immediately, getting to her knees and bowing ludicrously with her head in the water. When she lifted her face to the white-haired young woman, Azo said, "Kami of Mount Awa, please forgive my rude manners!"

"It is all right, onna-bushi. Only, go as I say to the lake called Beautiful Harmony. Its name, you'll find, is more ironic than descriptive. The trip will ease your troubled thoughts."

Azo said resignedly, "I will do as you instruct, Kami-awa. I will leave at once for Lake Miwa."

The promise received, the white-haired woman climbed from the hot pool and wrapped the towel around her waist. Momentarily, she vanished up the steep mountainside.

The priest of Emura-ji was surprised by the gloomy onna-bushi's sudden decision to leave. He insisted that she say what stirred her to activity, after pouting for so long. Azo told him. For a moment he only stared at her. Then he bowed full to the waist and blessed Hono-o's journey. She soon strode paths toward a mountain pass, clad in a split skirt called *hakama* and short kimono called *haori*, its left sleeve tied back. Through her cloth belt, or *obi*, she carried the longsword called daito and the shortsword called wakizashi.

It was many days to Lake Miwa.

Lake Miwa was a wild place, backed by sheer cliffs which vanished into white clouds. The forest was alive with small noises and continuously moving shadows. On the shores of the lake itself there was but one rude village, and the people there were reticent. Either they knew nothing or would not speak of what they knew regarding sister-ascetics in the region.

As she was a member of the *buké* or warrior caste, the people were required to feed Azo. In this they were generous. She made a little pack of food and then began the long trek around Lake Miwa's perimeters searching for a shrine or place where the Sisters might reside. In an area farthest from the village, halfway around the lake, she found the stone carving of a lantern. It sat on the far end of a small, rocky peninsula or jetty. Azo had seen no other sign of human presence, and even this site was not greatly suited to habitation.

It was impossible to travel farther, for the cliff walls met Lake Miwa at a point a little way on. The sky was darkening, so she would have to wait until morning to make the trip back to the village. Then she would wait for yet another morning before she began exploring the lake's shores in the other direction.

She made camp near the Peninsula of the Stone Lantern. When it was dark, the clouds parted for a while and Azo was able to see the Celestial River. It seemed to be a bridge from the cliff heights to the farther shore of Lake Miwa. Beneath this amazing arch Azo Hono-o slept with her arm drawn inside her haori for warmth.

While asleep Azo experienced a nightmare. In it she was being swept along a torrential river toward a black abyss. In her only hand she held a daito; but the sword could not slay the watery demons who clung to her clothing and sapped her of warmth and strength. Then she beheld salvation: a tree's limb reached out as though it were a generous hand. In order to take advantage of the limb, however, it would be necessary to drop the sword to the river bottom. The sword was her soul and she would not let it go. The river-demons babbled delightedly and bore her past the branch. The black abyss waited.

Before she fell from the brink, Azo awoke, chilled with sweat. She sat up abruptly and pushed her arm out of the sleeve of her haori. For a moment she was startled that her left arm did not slide out of its sleeve as well; reflexes were hard to unlearn. She remembered the dream with frightening clarity, remembered that she might have saved herself but for the lack of a second arm. She would have liked to curse the warrior whose sword had cleaved so neatly through flesh and bone; but Azo Hono-o respected her opponent too well to level curses at so late a date.

The night was moonless. Clouds sealed off the stars. There was only a feeble glow which came from within the stone lantern at the end of the peninsula. Had fireflies gathered there? Azo rose to her feet and gazed at the curious light. In a moment, she heard a faint sloshing which reminded her of waves slapping the hull of a boat. Something was coming across Lake Miwa, guided by the peninsula's strange beacon.

Mist clung to the water surface like fuzz on rotten plums. A round, luminescent boat appeared from those mists. The boat was made of mother-of-pearl with constantly shifting patterns of color. Two beautiful women reposed within. The hair of their heads was long and snowy white. Azo Hono-o ran a short way onto the narrow peninsula and shouted,

"Kami-miwa! I am sent by the Witch of Awayama!"

The glistening craft struck shore near the stone lantern. Fireflies scattered from the lantern and disappeared like sparks. The women were languid, deigning not to stand up or to leave their vessel. Their lazy eyes peered darkly at Azo Hono-o, and their voices said in harmony, "Long we have waited for one such as you. Priests and kings have ridden in our boat, but never onna-bushi."

Their musical voices were seductive. Azo Hono-o was almost drawn to the jetty's farthest reach, but she held back by force of will. "If it is a warrior you seek," said Azo, "I fear I must tell you that I have lost one arm and am thereby weakened."

"Our mountain sister would seem to disagree about your weakness," the voices sang as one. "Ride with us to the Secret Land. There you can test your merit and serve us by so doing."

Azo Hono-o could not resist the voices this time. She hurried to the boat. She was directed to the steerage at the rear and stood working a handle back and forth. The languid women continued to recline comfortably. Although Azo had become the tiny ship's source of power, she was confounded as to how it was kept on any special course. As it was round in design and had no actual prow, the boat ought to have traveled randomly about the lake.

Cliffs loomed to the left. It was nearly dawn when Azo Hono-o saw the gaping rent in those high stone walls. When she realized the boat was taking itself toward that frightful opening, it was Azo's strong desire to cease pumping the rear oar; but she was unable to conform to her own wish.

The barest moment before the sun was visible, the boat entered the inky gloom of the fissure. The waters were sluggish and thick so that the boat proceeded slowly. Azo worked hard at the oar, although she would have liked to stop. She could not see the walls in the darkness, but the echo of her own breath proved the narrowness of the passage.

Because of the boat's oily glisten, it was possible to see the white-haired women relaxing upon cushions. Their voices spoke together: "This is the longest part of our journey. To pass the time, we would like to hear stories of the outside world. We rarely have news."

It was more certain now than ever that Azo Hono-o was under some compulsion. She was in no mood for storytelling, yet could not resist the command. She could, at least, choose the story carefully.

"In the world today," said Azo, "there walks a Buddhist saint named Nichiren. He teaches the Lotus Sutra to all who will listen and wields sword against all who will not. Once, this martial priest was visited by a sly man who was a beggar. The beggar asked Nichiren if it was worth the smallest coin to hear Buddha speaking the Wonderful Law. Nichiren said, 'The largest coin would be too small an appreciation.' This reply made the sly beggar smile broadly. He sat on his knees and began to recite the Lotus Sutra, as though he were a follower of Nichiren. He shouted again and again at the top of his lungs: 'Namu-myo-ho-renge-kyo! Namu-myo-ho-renge-kyo!' As he shouted, the sound of his voice seemed strangely to fade away. In front of the beggar, or rather, between the beggar and Nichiren, there was manifested the apparent form of Amida Buddha. It was by then impossible to hear the beggar chant the sutra. Instead, Buddha said the words Himself: 'Namu-myo-ho-renge-kyo!' Nichiren was overcome with gladness and fell upon his face in thanksgiving. Then, slowly, the vision and the voice of Buddha faded away. The shouting of the beggar was heard once more. Tears slid down Nichiren's cheeks, for the sound and the appearance of Amida Buddha had been precisely as he had always imagined. He began to kiss the hands of the beggar. Those hands were held out for something other than kisses, however. 'What is it you require?' Nichiren asked, confused by the beggar's manner. 'Why, the coin you promised,' said the beggar. It was at that moment Nichiren realized he was the victim of *saimenjutsu*, the art of hypnotism. He stood from where he had knelt before the image of Buddha, the image which had been conjured from his own mind by the crafty beggar. 'How dare you mislead pious priests!' exclaimed Nichiren. He drew his sword at once and smote off the head of the beggar."

A light passed from eye to eye, back and forth between the reposing women. Eerie as that light was, and calculating, it yet alleviated some of the sense of darkness Azo thought she had seen within them.

"An interesting man is Nichiren," they said. "Perhaps someday he will come to us, as saints have done before. Do you subscribe to the law of the martial priest, onna-bushi?"

"I am a convert to the Lotus Sect," said Azo. "In this violent world, the edge of steel is the only religion that makes sense."

"If you were deceived," they asked together, "would you slay as swiftly as does Nichiren?"

"If I were," said Azo Hono-o.

"Then we had best erase illusions now," said the two women; and there was brilliant light all around. Azo Hono-o threw her arm across her face, shutting out the blinding light with the sleeve of her haori. When she lowered her arm, the women were gone, as was the boat. Azo Hono-o stood by a river which ran through the center of the hollow cliffs. There was blue sky above, for the high walls on four sides held clouds at bay. The land was dry except for the river. In the Secret Land, it never rained.

An acolyte was coming down the rocky hillside toward the woman. He was only eight or nine years of age. He carried a paper lantern, but the candle was not lit, for it was yet day.

"My master sends me to show you the way," said the head-shaven boy.

"Who is your master?" asked Azo Hono-o.

"He rules the Secret Land."

Azo Hono-o followed the boy through a maze of rocks and gulleys. She became hopelessly confused as to the direction of the river. It seemed as though they traveled in circles, but the acolyte was too sweet and young to doubt. The day was short but hot. The evening was long in the shadow of the high walls. Azo Hono-o became hungry, and offered to share the pack of food which she had brought in her sleeve's pocket.

"I am fasting," said the child. "I must not eat." So Azo ate by herself, still following the boy. Night fell upon the Secret Land. The boy removed flint and iron from his robe and with this fire kit lit the lantern's candle. Now the trip was eerier than before. Azo Hono-o felt as though she were following a pale ghost through the dark country. The acolyte held his lantern ever before and led Azo to nowhere.

"We must stop and rest!" Azo Hono-o suggested, for she had not slept well the night before.

"I am weary too," said the boy. "If I can travel, can't you?"

She supposed she could, when it was put that way. Eventually they came to a natural stone bridge which crossed the river. By this time Azo was indeed weary, though the boy seemed unaffected. At first Azo was glad to see the bridge, for it meant they had not been traveling in circles after all; or she would have seen the bridge before. Her mind was slow for need of sleep. But in a moment she realized she had indeed been led circuitously, for this was the river they had started from.

Though suspicious, Azo Hono-o kept silent. She followed the acolyte and watched the shadows carefully. The ground was dusty here. In the lantern's dim glow, Azo Hono-o could see that she was leaving obvious footprints. The acolyte, by contrast, left no track whatsoever.

Azo Hono-o withdrew her wakizashi, the shorter of two swords. She said, "I am sworn to slay illusion!" When she said this, the boy turned around and he was no longer sweet-faced. He had a demon's visage; and he began to grow. His white garments dissipated, revealing red, pockmarked skin. The lantern's stick was a sword in the demon's left hand. The candle became a flame upon the palm of his right hand. He was more than a head taller than Azo Hono-o, yet she did not hesitate. She advanced, but the demon had somehow come to be standing atop a boulder and she could not reach him.

"A one-armed woman cannot defeat Hidadité!" growled the demon. He had struck immediately at her one fear.

She backed away from the boulder, but said, "Leap down, then, and kill me."

The demon countered, "Climb up the rock and take my head!"

Azo Hono-o slipped her wakizashi back into its scabbard. Then she got down on her knees. She held her single hand in front of herself with the fingers together and pointed up. It was as near as she could come to the position for prayer. She began to shout the Lotus Sutra: "Namu-myo-ho-renge-kyo! Namu-myo-ho-renge-kyo!" When she had said it seven times, the demon vanished, loath to hear it the eighth. He had been illusion after all; and if he did truly live somewhere in the Secret Land, Azo Hono-o had yet to actually meet him.

When she slept, she dreamed again. This time she was running home as fast as she could go, for she knew that Hidadité intended to kill her mother and father and brothers and sisters. She came to a rise and saw her family's house at the bottom of the hill. Hidadité stood outside the house with his sword and flame, threatening to set the house on fire and slay everyone as they ran outside. He looked to the top of the hill and laughed at Azo Hono-o, for she was too far away to stop him. On the ground at her feet was a quiver of arrows and a longbow. With these, Azo Hono-o might have slain Hidadité and saved her family. But it took two hands to draw the bow; and that was why Hidadité left it there to torment her.

Azo Hono-o awoke, miserable but wiser. She knew that her own fears alone could defeat her. Her obsession with her lost arm weakened her far more than its actual loss; it pervaded even her dreams. To defeat her enemy, she must first defeat herself.

Toward noon, the parched country was unbearably warm, and Azo Hono-o could not find the river. She had eaten the last of the food she had brought along. Without food or drink, she perforce emboldened herself to spartan survival, traveling onward in search of Hidadité or the sister-ascetics who had abandoned her in the Secret Land.

She knew that she was being followed by as many as three or four pursuers, but doubted it would do any good to search for who they were. They would reveal themselves in good time, and she must be ready.

She loosened her haori to cool herself off and trudged onward, though she knew of no destination. When the sun had passed beyond the rim of the western wall, the long twilight began, and the Secret Land became cooler. Azo Hono-o came to a clearing surrounded by large stones. In the middle of the clearing was a drum tower or pagoda twice as tall as herself and made of granite.

Azo approached the drum tower cautiously and peered in one of its windows. There was a brightly painted box inside. The door to the drum tower was very small, so Azo had to crawl inside. Within, there was not room to stand. Azo knelt before the box. It had a lock, but the lock was undone. She was about to lift the lid when a chill ran up her spine. A dozen folk tales lept to mind, about boxes which, when opened, released misfortune. Yet Azo felt that there was something in the box of importance to herself. Why she felt this she did not know. Probably it was a feeling planted in her by the demon. Yet she felt the importance strongly. Something she needed was in the box. Something she had hidden from herself. With greatest difficulty, she turned away.

The woman warrior crawled out of the drum tower drenched in sweat and shaking. She felt as though she had just survived untold horrors.

A man stepped out from behind one of the rocks surrounding the clearing. He was a warrior. A second warrior stepped from behind another rock. Then a third appeared from his hiding place. The first one said, "I am Koji Nakashima. My associates are Bunzo Nomotashi and Rentaro Shimoda. We are the retainers of Hidadité, King of the Secret Land. We are sent to kill you."

Azo Hono-o did not reply, but bowed politely to her opponents. They charged at once, swords raised. Azo dropped to one knee. She drew her daito and with three quick gestures the three men were slain. They fell one in front and the others to each side of her. Azo Hono-o's quick sword slid neatly into its scabbard.

When she stood, the three corpses disappeared as though they had never been. Azo fled the place, not for fear of the vanished corpses, but for fear of the box inside the drum tower. She hurried through the shadowed country until she saw that three men blocked her path. They were Koji Nakashima, Bunzo Nomotashi and Rentaro Shimoda whom she had recently killed. They came at her again. Azo's sword licked out rapidly, but this time they knew her fighting style, and they were harder to kill; and yet she killed them, and their corpses vanished as before.

The third time they appeared she was less surprised. They attacked wordlessly. They fought even better than the previous two times. One of them succeeded in cutting a slit in the sleeve of her haori. It was the left sleeve. Had she had a left arm, it would have been wounded severely.

When they were dead and vanished, she hurried to find a place where the next encounter would give her an advantage. If they got better each time, they would eventually become too strong for her. She found a hump of ground with a boulder on top. Against that boulder she set her shoulders and waited. The three men appeared before her, and their leader laughed.

"It is because you have but one arm that you cannot defeat us!" said Koji Nakashima. "This time we will cut off your remaining arm, then hack it into pieces before your eyes!"

"It is true I cannot defeat you," she said. "But it is because you are already dead, not because my arm is missing. I will not duel with you again!" So saying, she fell upon her knees and held her hand in front of herself, chanting the Lotus Sutra.

"We were Buddhists in life!" said Koji Nakashima angrily. "The Lotus Sutra cannot frighten us away!" The three men rushed forward with their swords drawn. Azo Hono-o did not move. Three swords fell at once, stopping short of her right shoulder. She continued to recite the sutra and the swords could not touch her. At last she feared them no more and could stop chanting. She looked into the eyes of Koji Nakashima and told him.

"Tell your master he must fight with me himself. I will not duel weak assassins anymore."

Koji backed away, looking peevish. He motioned the other two to join him. Together they bowed to Azo with strained politeness. Then the three of them broke into a run, and disappeared into a solid wall of stone.

Azo Hono-o was afraid of sleep. Two nights in a row she had suffered nightmares. She would not suffer one tonight. As there was no likelihood of losing the way, inasmuch as she had no destination, Azo continued her explorations beneath the starry roof of the four walls. It was no surprise to see a fire in the distance. She had expected the demon Hidadité would show himself this night. He held the fire in his right hand and the sword in his left; and he sat in lotus position atop a three-sided, flat-topped boulder. He was humming a mantra to himself. Sitting thus, he looked like a war god. When he left off his mantra, it was because Azo Hono-o stood below him.

"Are you pious, onna-bushi?" the resonant, dreamy voice of Hidadité asked.

"I am pious," said Azo Hono-o.

"Have you come as a pilgrim to bow before me, onna-bushi?"

"No, Hidadité. I have come to slay a demon."

"Whose demon have you come to slay, onna-bushi?"

"I have come to slay you, Hidadité."

Hidadité smiled grimly. All his teeth were pointed. "To defeat me," he said, "you must first defeat yourself."

"I know it," said Azo Hono-o.

"How well do you know it?" the demon asked. "I think you do not know it very well. I think the sister-ascetics of Lake Miwa's Secret Land have tricked you, onna-bushi. Demons are not born on this earth; they are conjured. Did the Witches conjure Hidadité?"

"I do not know," said Azo. "Did they conjure you?"

"If so, it was their ill fortune, for I have proven myself stronger than them. They built the pagoda to appease me, but I was not appeased. After I have slain their champion, Azo Hono-o, I will slay the witches too. Then Hidadité will go from this place to terrorize the outside world. Only you, onna-bushi, with the ascetics, stand between me and absolute dominion of the mortal world!"

After saying these things, Hidadité stood up and flourished the sword in his left hand. His left-handedness would make him harder to defeat. Most fencers were right-handed, most especially Azo Hono-o who had only a right hand, and she was not so well-practiced at countering left-hand blows. Hadadité jumped from the boulder and a ferocious battle was begun.

There was something balanced and harmonious about the right-handed fighter versus the one left-handed. Again and again the demon struck at Azo. At least he, too, fought one-handed; for he would not put down the fire. Twice he tried to dash the fire into the woman's face, but she was too quick, and he nearly lost his hand those two times. It seemed as though they were evenly matched, for neither could break the other's guard. But slowly, Azo began to perceive a certain weakness in her opponent's style. He cut single-mindedly at her right shoulder, as though he believed it were her only vulnerable spot. Perhaps emotionally it *had* been her weak spot; but his three retainers had inadvertently cured her of the previous fear of losing her remaining arm. Azo Hono-o waited only for the right moment to take advantage of the demon's limited approach.

The moment came. Her sword sliced through his belly. But

the demon did not fall. He backed away and looked at his own bloodless rent. Then he laughed and threw his fire-hand outward in a sweeping gesture. Azo Hono-o was pressed away by the resultant heat. Fire-devils sprung from Hidadité's hand and came rushing at her. They were no higher than her knees, with pointed heads and huge flat feet. Her sword would not cut them so she was forced to retreat.

They chased her through darkness. When she looked over her shoulder, the brightness of the fire-devils made her night-blind when she looked ahead. As a result she ran headlong into the drum tower and knocked herself unconscious. Her last thought was that she would now be consumed by the fire-devils, or that the grandfather demon Hidadité would come and strike her with his sword.

She awoke in the clearing next to the pagoda in the bright of day. Many hours had passed, yet neither the devils of fire nor Hidadité had taken advantage. There was a large bump on her head which smarted at the touch. Her head swam when she tried to sit up.

"Do not trouble yourself," said the singing voice of the sister-ascetics. They had placed a rock under her head as pillow. They were sitting one to each side of her, serving as nurses. One of them held a quaint, small cup to Azo's lips and both of them said, "Drink only a little at first."

"Hidadité," Azo groaned. "I could not kill him."

"You hurt him more than he pretended," said the women. They helped Azo Hono-o to sit. She was distraught to see that the wooden chest had been dragged outside the pagoda. The sister-ascetics said, "Hidadité lives inside this box. He has returned to it until his wound heals; but no lock can hold him there when he is better. We are helpless to destroy him even in his weakened state, for he is your demon and not ours."

Azo's bruised head was still swimming. The words of the singing women made no sense to her. "How is he my demon? You are the witches who conjure devils! I am merely onna-bushi."

"Still is he your demon," they insisted. "We did not conjure him. You must know that 'hidadité' means 'left hand,' and he did not take his name from the fact that he is left-handed. Please open the box."

Azo obediently reached out and removed the loose lock with a shaky hand. When she raised the lid, she saw that a severed arm lay within. It was brown and dry and mummified.

"After the war between Yoshinaké and Yoritomo," said the white-haired women musically, "your arm came to the Secret Land, carried by the river. Cast onto these shores, it dried and hardened. Because your mind dwelt utterly upon your loss, the arm was given demonic life. If you cannot defeat your fear and anger and sorrow, Hidadité will rise again, more powerful than before."

Azo Hono-o looked at the mummified arm, but felt no horror of it. She had proven herself strong even one-armed. She no longer felt consumed with grief over her loss.

"I will put my arm to rest," said Azo Hono-o. "I will sit here for a day and a night reciting the Lotus Sutra, bowing to the box after each eighth chant. I will assure the arm that it is no longer hated and then I will build it a pyre. Do you think these things will appease its anger with me?"

Two voices sang: "With those acts, surely your poor arm's spirit will sleep easily."

Two nights later, Azo Hono-o returned to the rude village on Lake Miwa. Nobody saw the mother-of-pearl boat which brought her. She spoke to a priest about her adventure and she lingered several weeks in spite of the fact that the people had been unfriendly. In that space of time, Azo made a carving from a large, round piece of hardwood. The priest tutored her now and then, for she was not highly versed in the task she had undertaken and needed occasional instruction. When it was done, it was a lovely carving, for Azo Hono-o had put her heart into its making. Though it might seem crude compared to the work of a professional woodcarver, it yet captured excellently a general sense of beauty. It depicted the Witches of Lake Miwa reposed within a bowl.

Azo Hono-o carried the heavy carving on her back toward the Peninsula of the Stone Lantern; and she was surprised that a group of pilgrims joined her, for the villagers were instantly more friendly when they saw what she had made. The carving was situated in the middle of the stony peninsula with great ceremony. Then Azo Hono-o thanked the village's pilgrims. Everyone sat on their knees and bowed many times.

Several days later she had returned to Emura Temple hoping to meet the Witch of Awayama once more and express personal gratitude. At the Hour of the Ox on a night of a swollen moon, the woman warrior went up to the hot springs and lay quietly in the hot water. Kami-awa came down from her mountain peak and conversed with the warrior until morning. What they said, no one knows. But it was noted thereafter that the hair of Azo Hono-o began to turn prematurely white. It is common knowledge that people who dwell among ghosts become ghosts themselves; it is less well known that those who are favored by kami spirits become kami spirits also. Azo Hono-o lived many years and no one was really certain if she was immortal or not. It is said that she was defeated for the last time in a battle with another white-haired warrior, and that her grave was later moved to Emura-ji where you can find it today. Her grave is between three others: those of Koji Nakashima, Bunzo Nomotashi and Rentaro Shimoda, whose souls Azo Hono-o had seen to after fighting them in the Secret Land.

Many people who have lost one or both arms worship Azo Hono-o to this day at Emura-ji. And it is rumored that there are now two sister-ascetics on the top of Mount Awa, as there are two sisters on Lake Miwa. Sometimes people see Azo's three retainers on that mountain as well. These things are attested to by many pious individuals, but who is to say what is true?

# SCIENCE IS MAGIC SPELLED BACKWARDS

## *by Jacqueline Lichtenberg*

*Jacqueline Lichtenberg's fiction reveals a fascination both with mysticism and with the forms of classic science fiction. So a phrase like Robert Heinlein's "mad gods of nuclear physics" (in* Citizen of the Galaxy) *is bound, sooner or later, to have an effect on Jacqueline's writing. So is the growing controversy over nuclear energy. So here, set in a nuclear* fusion *plant of the near future, is a story that takes up where Lester Del Rey's classic "Nerves" left off—and then takes off in a bewitching new direction.*

*Jacqueline's first books, done in collaboration, on Star Trek gained her nationwide authority as a Trek expert. She has gone on to write* House of Zeor, Unto Zeor Forever, *and (in collaboration with Jean Lorrah)* First Channel *and* Channel's Destiny. *These are stories of the vampire-like Simes and the Gens to whom they are bound in a profoundly complicated symbiosis. They enable Jacqueline to use her training as a chemist and her fascination with the supernatural. Other books in this series are scheduled for release in coming years; Jacqueline, who regards millennia as mere eyeblinks, says that she is completely prepared to take the Simes and Gens out among the stars. A second series, which will begin with the book* Molt

Brother, *is planned. This one will combine aliens, archeology, and occult power.*

*As Marion Zimmer Bradley said in her introduction to* The Keeper's Price, *Jacqueline can seldom be persuaded to write less than 100,000 words at a time. I am delighted that she has chosen to fuse magic and high technology in this story—and done it all in 6400 words.*

"Mavrana," said my mother impatiently, "just give me one good reason why you won't join the coven!"

"Mama, are you trying to tell me I got my doctorate in nuclear plant management just because your—your—your *coven* performed certain stupid rituals?!"

"You don't suppose the good citizens of *this* town would have allowed that plant to be built here—just so you could have a job near home—*without* a little encouragement from us?!"

I jibbered and stuttered to a pressed silence. Her idea of scientific evidence had pushed my temper to the flashpoint and I had to get out of there before my brain melted down.

I stood and dumped my napkin into my soup bowl. "Mama, we're just talking past each other. I'll see you tomorrow."

Quickly, I whirled out of the kitchen, picking up my suitcase from where I had left it by the front door, and made for my car. Blinking away tears, I drove off without considering a destination. Homecoming, after eight years of university hopping, had not turned out as I'd dreamed it would. What to do now?

I had to report for work tomorrow morning, bright and cheerful and ready to take over the responsibility for the safety systems computer at the Sterling Bridge Nuclear Cycle Plant. It was a big chance for a new Ph.D. I knew I'd earned it. I knew I was ready. But I couldn't do it if I reported in with a crying jag hangover.

I found myself driving by the plant, located in what had been cow pasture and apple orchard back in the '90's when I was in high school. The humped buildings and thrusting towers silhouetted against the sunset sky took my breath away. My spirits lifted and I began to think again.

At the stoplight, I turned onto the new six-lane highway into town. The old town center was coughing itself clear of homebound traffic and rolling up the sidewalks.

I turned onto the two-lane street that had been the entire commercial district when I was a kid, before the shopping malls. The one- and two-story buildings looked tumbledown and dingy to my adult eyes, but I remembered the turns that put me into the parking lot of the Hotel Saginaw.

The clerks were all new. They didn't recognize me, or my name, when I checked in. Room 333. Third floor. That would have meant something profound to Mama, I'm sure.

I fidgeted around the single-bedded, bare room. It was no Lasergloss Inn. I thought of going to a movie, a bar—anything. Instead I took a bath—the plumbing rattled—and went to bed. But I couldn't sleep. No way could I banish my mother's face from my mind's eye. It was just like my freshman year in college all over again.

I flipped on the blurry, old television screen, promptly flicked it off, and instead counted the money in my wallet. What was I going to do? I'd counted on living at home, but that was obviously out of the question. Mama wasn't going to let me rest until I joined her group of whackos. I'd have to get an apartment. My salary would cover it—easily—but it would be a month until I got paid.

In all fairness, it did occur to me to wonder how it was that I'd been offered this marvelous job when the ink on my diploma wasn't even dry yet. *And*, of the ninety-two companies I'd applied to, this one, in my home town, was the only offer I'd gotten. Statistically, it was rather odd. Everyone else in the top ten of my class had gotten dozens of offers.

I lay awake the rest of the night, cataloguing all the lucky breaks I'd had for the last eight years—statistical anomalies all. And now I was boxed into a job which ought to have gone to someone with at least two years' experience. Oh, I was well prepared for it, but *they* didn't know that. So why was I hired?

I watched the dawn, and then grabbed a take-out breakfast

and ate on the way to the plant, keyed up as if for a final exam.

The personnel manager met me in the outer office, and before I could catch my breath, I'd been assigned an office, one quarter of a secretary, a security chip that opened some doors, and a whole list of things I was authorized to do. I was sitting at my absolutely bare and empty desk staring at a laserphoto of the plant that was the only decoration on the white walls, when a man walked in wearing a tag that said he was Alfred McCree.

He was about my own height, with medium brown hair, black eyes, a lovely straight nose, in a face which I estimated at perhaps thirty years old, and he *wasn't* wearing a wedding ring. The smile was dazzling, too. "Ms. Samchik? I'm supposed to train you for the hotseat—that's what we call your job around here."

"That's nice," I said as the room receded into a blur and he emerged with the blinding clarity of a laserphoto. "I mean," I said shaking myself, "I hadn't known I'd get any more than a manual to read."

He shrugged. "This plant is so new the manuals haven't been written yet! We went on-line just last year."

I liked his voice, too. "I know."

"But we have a new computer that's going to make this plant the safest in the country—maybe the world. And it's all yours from now on. Come, I'll show you!"

I followed him across the hall and learned that he had been in the hotseat when the plant opened, and now had been promoted. Within the hour, we had littered the desk, chairs, and most of the floors with opened binders, books, and magazines. Every screen in the room displayed one reference or another. Lunch was a cup of coffee, and an hour past quitting time I called a halt when I discovered I couldn't focus my eyes because of the hunger headache lurking behind them.

"Can I drive you home?" he asked.

I remembered how his masculinity had affected me when he'd first walked in. The effect had faded while we were working, but it was coming back. *Well*, I thought with a sigh, *it really isn't good to get too personal with your boss*. I shook my head. "I have my car."

"Can I offer you dinner to make up for keeping you so late?"

I thought fast. The offer was so tempting, considering my flat wallet, but I said, "No, thank you very much. I've got a lot to do—getting settled and all. I'll see you tomorrow." I couldn't afford to let him get the wrong idea about me.

That first month flashed by. I looked up the mother of my best friend from high school and rented a basement apartment in her house—on credit—and began to set up housekeeping. Mother insisted on feeding me dinners, and for that I could tolerate her lectures about how the energy problem was still an ongoing worldwide crisis due to an imbalance in psychic forces, which her coven was working to rebalance. She really believed that the commercial development of cleanburn nuclear fusion plants was due to the efforts of the hundreds of groups like hers, and therefore I should want to help them.

"Mavrana, this work is vital. We've already got the world convinced that fusion is as safe as any other energy source. If we don't convince the other half soon, there'll be another depression like there was in the nineties. With your magical talent, *why* won't you help us?"

"Mama, why won't you listen when I tell you there is no way—no way at all—that your prancing and dancing could have altered people's ideas!"

"What do I have to do," she protested, "trigger an earthquake under Sterling Bridge before you'll admit the obvious?"

"Oh, don't be ridiculous!" I shouted and stormed out.

But I kept coming back—because I liked to eat, and because she did shut up and listen quite often. I had nobody else to burble to about all the wonderful new toys I had to play with, and I wanted to share my success with her. I think I secretly felt that I might even convince her that science works—and magic doesn't. I owed her that much. She was, after all, my mother.

The second month, I worked on the simulator, drilling on every emergency in the book and half a dozen I was inspired to invent. I even presented the earthquake scenario mother had suggested, and though the administrative board thought it far-fetched, they encouraged me to set up procedures.

The third month, I was put to work for real. The hotbed as they affectionately termed the computer room where we controlled the safety systems, had one glass wall overlooking the pit where the main reactor lived. The other wall held the screens monitoring the rest of the plant. It took a crew of eleven to staff it, in three shifts, round the clock.

For the first two weeks, I was never left alone in the hotseat. Randomly, they hit me with every exotic drill they could imagine. But I never muffed it, and gradually I stopped worrying about whether it was a drill or real.

Then, one afternoon, McCree met me at shift change, and shook hands solemnly. "You're on your own, Ms. Samchik."

I had never known the meaning of pride before in my life. I wanted to scream for joy. Instead, I took a deep breath and ordered all stations to report. Ten all-clears snapped back to me, clean and crisp as could be. I was in charge of the whole fusion cycle plant.

For weeks it was all fresh and new, important and beautiful. I could sit in the hotseat, surrounded by my own controls and gaze out that majestic window at the pit, and know I'd achieved everything I envisioned as a kid.

But then I began thinking about McCree's new job. He was in charge of acquiring new computers for the plant, and he got to travel all over the world, keeping abreast of research in the field. Six months I'd been out of school, and I could feel my skills becoming outmoded. I began to drop into McCree's office, just to see what he was doing. But he took it for a personal interest.

"I've got two tickets to a Ravens concert for Friday night. Shame to let them go to waste. . . ."

The Ravens had given me my first glimpse of the romanticism behind nuclear fusion—man harnessing a piece of the sun—and often during difficult exam periods, their recordings had shored up my determination. But *I* hadn't been able to get a ticket to their concert. I gritted my teeth and said, "Fine. I'll take you out to dinner beforehand, okay?"

I *wish* I'd remembered I'd told my mother I wanted a ticket to this concert, and that I'd also mentioned McCree.

At the concert hall, I found he had front center balcony seats. The Ravens came on in feathered black capes and Amerind-style birdmasks which they tossed aside to sing their own songs in the soft, lyrical style they'd made famous. Their final number had been their first hit and reprised all the superstitions about the raven, and about how useful their mischief could be when tamed, ending, "So we'll fly to the sun and bring it down to you." Hearing that in person for the first time, I cried.

As we put on our coats, I said, "I'd really love to meet one of them, but the crowd backstage will be awful."

"I'm game if you are."

Our eyes met and we nodded. But as we inched up the aisle, I saw my mother, with all of those I thought belonged to the coven, seated in a block just above us. I maneuvered McCree's back to them and tried to hide both of us in the crowd. I don't know why. I'm sure Mama had been watching us the whole evening.

This new theatre had been designed to let crowds flow through backstage in neat autographing funnels. We joined the end of the line and waited. As the line began to move, McCree suddenly said, "I haven't got anything for them to autograph!"

"Neither have I!" We hadn't bought programs, and I'd lost the giveaway ad book in the ladies room. I searched my tiny formal handbag, came up with my wallet and a brainstorm. "I'll have them sign the back of my Plant ID card!" I pried it out of the holder.

He dug his out of an inside pocket. "It'll be worth a million some day!"

As the line crept forward, I began to feel foolish. What I really wanted was to *meet* these men, not this. When we got to the head of the line, the five Ravens were standing wrapped in black bathrobes, patiently autographing and smiling for pictures. I handed over my card mumbling about it being all I had with me to write on.

Phil Raven turned it over, saying, "What's this? Sterling Bridge Nuclear Cycle Plant? Hey, Art, come here!" The Raven on the end came around, looked at the pass, smiled and handed it back to Phil.

Meanwhile, McCree had handed his card to Dan Raven who was also examining it. Dan said, "Look, could you two step out around here for a few minutes? We'd like to talk to you."

McCree's eyebrow was climbing, but he said amiably, "Sure, I think we have some time."

We were drawn into the dressing room behind them. It was

a large suite with a sitting room from which eight small dressing rooms opened.

Soon, their manager cut off the flow of people and herded the five of them into the sitting room, pushing the door shut behind them. "You guys get dressed before you all catch cold!" he shouted at them.

"But," said Phil who seemed about to approach us.

The manager came over, waving a phone, "Get! Now!"

Phil said at us, "Five minutes," and let himself be crowded into one of the dressing rooms. The phones began ringing. Someone came in with a fistful of telegrams and a huge flower arrangement. Then several reporters were let in. In all, we waited an hour and a half, but finally Phil, Dan, and Art pulled us into one of the side rooms.

"I've always admired you people who could actually understand all that math. Science has always defeated me," said Dan. "I try to make up for it by writing songs that inspire kids to work hard at learning it."

"It worked," I said, and told them about struggling through college on their inspiration.

Phil smiled. "Well, now's a good time to pay the debt. Settle a bet for us, will you?"

I nodded, and Art said, "Ten percent of this grid's power comes from fusion, right? But Sterling Bridge is a fission plant."

Phil said, in that velvet bass voice I loved, "No, I remember distinctly when it was built. It's a fusion plant supplying thirty percent of this grid's power."

"No, that's the grid north of here!" protested Dan.

Art started to say something but McCree cut him off with a raised hand. "Sterling Bridge is the most advanced fusion plant on line now, but the grid has ten percent tidal, eight percent solar, sixty-five percent fission, and seventeen percent fusion, with Sterling Bridge providing half of that. That's approximately. There's still a coal plant on line, and some people are selling-back from windmills."

"And you're right, Dan," I added, "the grid north of here has a fusion plant supplying thirty percent of its power."

That settled the bet with no winners and no losers. They all laughed, and as I basked in the amiability of the three stars, I began to understand where their music came from. It only made me more hungry for their company, but now it was time to leave.

McCree's car was the last in the lot, but traffic was still clogging the intersections. We'd seen the Ravens piling into their long, black, chauffered limousine, still pursued by avid fans. They'd driven away in a different direction, so it was with some surprise that I heard Phil's velvet bass tones coming from a taxi sitting next to us at the traffic light. "I wonder how many of those fans are still following the limo?"

"Get your beak out of my ribs," complained Gordon, one of the Ravens we hadn't actually met.

"That's my elbow, dodo!" answered Art, laughing.

I stuck my head out of the window—McCree was driving—as the cars began to move. It was a very beat-up old taxi. Hardly where you'd expect to find *stars*. On a wild impulse, I called, "Mr. Raven?"

Two pale faces appeared at the taxi window. "Oh, what a relief!" To the others, Phil said, "It's not fans." And to me, again, he said, "Is the traffic always this bad on the airport road?"

"No, just when the theatre lets out. Are you trying to catch a plane?"

"No, we're staying over."

I had a marvelous idea. "If you'll be here tomorrow, come on out to the plant and we'll see you get the grand tour."

There was a hasty conference as the lines of cars began to separate, and he replied, "Would two o'clock be okay?"

"Fine," I shouted back, overjoyed.

"Look," Phil called over, "we're having some friends in for supper. Follow us, if you have time." And then he was out of range.

That night may go down as the high point of my life. The Ravens never sought us out, but they gave the impression to everyone else there that obviously we belonged. My one penetrating memory was of sitting on the floor with about ten others, listening to Phil and Dan reminiscing about the long string of miraculous breaks over the last twenty years—especially since their comeback some six years ago. Some of the scrapes they'd been through were hysterically funny, and some were just plain spooky.

When we left, the Ravens all waved to us, saying, "See you tomorrow!"

In the car, I shook off the starshock and said, "Alfred, do you have any idea what the odds were against this evening happening?"

"That's the first time you've called me Alfred."

"Yeah, but I'd really like to know what the odds were."

"I'll run it up for you tomorrow. Look, it happened, so it wasn't impossible."

But I couldn't help thinking about the hundreds of other Sterling Bridge employees who had been there and would have given anything for the evening we'd had. "If I hadn't lost my program, I wouldn't have thought of them signing the cards."

"So maybe you're psychic and knew about their bet?"

"You don't believe in ESP, do you?"

"I don't *believe* in it, but there *is* something about living things that sometimes affects chance, somehow, and bends it to our will. That's been experimentally established."

That was true, but I'd never believed those experiments. I lay awake all night wondering if McCree believed them, and if he did, then I began to wonder about the intensity of my original reaction to him. Why had Mama been at that concert, sitting just behind us? If she could control chance with her magic—at last I let the scary question surface: *What if she had caused the whole evening's sequence of improbable events?*

My mental model of the universe—acquired over eight long years in four colleges—had no room in it for the will of one person to affect the life of another. Such a power couldn't exist, therefore my mother didn't have it, therefore she was a charlatan or a fool.

I tried to force myself to face it but I only ended up crying wretchedly until sunrise. The anguished knot in my gut screamed out for some concrete proof, one way or the other. I didn't know how much longer I could live with this. "*I don't care what it costs,*" I finally said aloud, "*I've got to know.*"

I pasted myself together with stiff jolts of coffee and liberal applications of makeup—and made it to work on time. As I took over the hotseat, I even felt bright enough to trust myself with the job.

Later, I was sitting in a dim corner of the canteen during my coffee break when McCree showed up with a computer printout. He spread the sheets on my table. "Last Tuesday, when you couldn't get tickets, the odds against the Ravens inviting you to a private party were nine thousand five hundred fifty three to one—assuming you did something to attract their attention."

I scanned the printout, noting he had made the assumptions I would have made. I wanted to kiss him. No, I wanted him to kiss me. But I told my heart to shut up, and listened.

"The odds were still over a thousand to one after the concert," he said. "I guestimated the number of cars on the street and looked up the number of cabs working, then figured the mean-free-path of the two cars, and all the routes we could have chosen. It *could* have happened once, Mavrana, but if you make a habit of this sort of thing, the odds go up steeply. . . ."

His tentative ending was a probe. I don't know why I said it—I never seemed to be myself around McCree—but I blurted, "Yeah, it's the story of my life. My mother claims she's a witch, and she makes all these things happen to me!"

"Mavrana, be serious!"

"I am." He believed me, and his gaze changed subtly. Somehow, I had gone from fascinating woman to interesting experiment. "Look," I said, "I'm due back in the hotseat. I want to take this home and really read it." As I passed my office, I dumped the printout on my desk, wondering why I was fleeing McCree. He wasn't credulous—but he wasn't scornful either. That was chilling.

It was a singularly uneventful morning in the pit. I had made arrangements for the Ravens' visit that morning, when I arrived. At my two o'clock break, I made sure they were met at the gate and given our best tour guide. I couldn't show them around myself—the United Nations insurance law required me to be within two minutes of the hotseat at all times.

The guide was explaining that point just as he brought the Ravens into the hotbed. I relinquished my seat to my number two, and went to greet them. Phil scooped me into his arms and gave me a kiss on the cheek. So did the other Ravens, as if I were a long lost cousin, not a near stranger.

In the time it took me to recover, aware of the eyes on me, Art said, "This looks just like the auxiliary control room out on the edge."

He meant the backseat, so I said, "Yes, in case of ultimate disaster—a meltdown or major contamination—we could retreat past four more safety containments to the outer control room you saw on your way in. It's identical to this one in capability, except that their view of the pit is on screens. Here we have direct vision—a bit of a luxury."

They crowded around the window, and that's when it happened. A deep rumble, as if a truck were passing—but it grew to sound like a large freight train. Then the ceiling shook. With a loud report, a jagged crack appeared across the inner glass of the window and water began to leak from between the panes—radiation, too, no doubt. Another crack on the outer pane spurted water in a shower down into the pit, but you could barely see it for the billowing clouds of steam.

The Ravens tumbled back from the window, tangling with two of my desk men. Everyone was bewildered, paralyzed by the shock. I, however, had just come from the west coast. "Earthquake!" I shouted over the din and leaped into the hotseat, yelling, "Dan, bluephone for a complete shutdown. Max, yellowphone the Mayor an evacuation alert. Jill, redphone the grid we're going offline. Ken, what have you got?"

Ken flashed me his display, the flowchart for the whole plant. It showed line ruptures, valves opening to dump working fluids into containment, and other valves shutting down—but if those readings were correct, there wouldn't be any steam in the pit. My own monitors showed radiation rising in the hotbed. Fissionables had gotten loose. "Louanne, prepare to evacuate us to the backseat."

Frantically disciplined activity broke out as automatic commands seemed to issue themselves. Emotionally, I hadn't yet assimilated the fact that an earthquake—of better than five on the Richter scale—had just torn apart a plant on a seismically stable site.

Down in the pit ponderous machinery had begun to move along overhead tracks. The Pot was being shut down, but it would take hours to douse that sun, and we were losing coolant like crazy. The emergency crews were down there working, men and women paid to stand by on the off chance they'd have to risk—or give—their lives to contain an accident.

I picked up the orange phone as my colleagues began to

herd the Ravens out our emergency exit to the backseat. "This is an all-out Alert." I shoved my ID tag onto the plate and the phone glowed. Machinery was set in motion to bring every possible expert into our problem, either in person or on a conference line.

Then I called the President. And it was no drill.

I was the last one out of there. My radiation tag had taken on a sickly color, but I had no time to worry about it.

In the backseat, the readouts made more sense. Somehow, the firstline computer had been damaged. *God help us.*

As we completed our first emergency drills, the executive conference was convened in the deep bunker. I'd sent the Ravens to the infirmary because the Plant was now under strict quarantine. *Nothing* would leave until this was over.

I was the first to report. Standing up with all those hard eyes on me, I was more nervous than I'd been during my first solo in the hotseat. After me, damage control, Pot management, and power disbursement reported—and none of them was critical of my actions.

Doctor Howard Conwell, *the* ultimate authority in charge of the entire operation, said quietly, "Well done, all of you. So far, no stray radiation has been detected offsite. Our job now is to see that none ever is. Clear?"

We all nodded. I didn't envy Conwell his job. *He* would have to stand accountable for everything *we* had done. For the first time, I realized that *his* was the job I was ultimately aiming for. I wasn't too sure I wanted it anymore.

In the backseat, a tense hush had fallen. We had all changed into fresh hotsuits, and been treated by the duty physicians. I had reached my exposure limit, but was still safe.

What it came down to, three grueling hours later, was one tertiary backup valve. The two others that were supposed to do the job had been ruined by the quake. And the third one had not functioned. We didn't know why. Conwell had not yet ordered a suicide mission in there to ascertain why.

A quiet voice said at my elbow, "There's somebody here who insists on seeing you."

It was McCree. Behind him, flanked by Phil and Art Raven, stood my mother. She beamed pleasantly, "And look who I found!" she said gesturing to the Ravens. "Just when I needed them."

As I stared at the three of them, it all came into focus. The earthquake had produced the exact damage we had drilled to handle in my scenario. And I remembered mother saying, "*What do I have to do, trigger an earthquake under Sterling Bridge before you'll admit the obvious?*"

McCree said, "She had just been admitted at the main gate when the quake hit. Your 'all-out' sealed her in. I haven't had time to run a probability calculation on that one."

Mama said, "Mr. McCree has been nice enough to explain your problem to me. I want to help."

A bubble of hysterical laughter formed under my diaphragm.

McCree added, "If it might head off a dirty accident, I say it ought to be tried."

"Dirty" was absolutely the most powerful expletive in our jargon. "Do you have any idea what kind of help she's offering?" I asked tightly.

"I've explained the nature of my craft to him," answered Mama. She was in one of her distant-calm moods, as if not quite connected into reality. It wasn't drug induced; she never used mooders.

"I think we ought to discuss this in the conference room."

But McCree objected. "There's no time! Proceed on my personal authority."

"I can't! Redlaw is in effect now, and *I'm* in the hotseat. I can't—and won't—pass the buck."

"Look—what harm can it do?" asked McCree. "All she wants is a couple of square feet of space and a moment or two of silence."

I met Mama's eyes. McCree had the right attitude—scientific curiosity, not—fear. *God, I admire that man!* "All right," I said with a shrug. "But if the valve suddenly starts to work, it won't have proved anything."

"No," he agreed readily, "but it *would* be another wild improbability to add to the list. Besides, I'd like to see what's going to happen—wouldn't you?"

*No.* The feeling washed over me as I said, "Why not?" Somehow I knew what was going to happen. And if it did, then maybe I'd have to abandon my whole model of the universe.

I issued orders to clear a space in the middle of the floor. "Go ahead and do your thing," I said to my mother, "but don't be surprised if we have to interrupt you with reports. Our work can't be delayed."

"I do understand," she said. "Just show me which of these screens depicts the valve in question."

McCree pointed to the main monitor that replaced the window. "It's here," he said, touching the spot where colored lines crisscrossed. The valve marked ought to have dumped the hot coolant into containment and let cold fluid into the system. "If it doesn't respond within the next hour, Conwell is going to order the suicide crew in to fix it."

I glanced at the creeping temperature readouts. We might have an hour left at that—then again, we might not.

"And where is the control for that motor-valve system?" asked Mama.

My hand went to it automatically. McCree said, "Dan Ackers there has one, and Mavrana has the master control."

"Good. When I give the word, I want both of you to work your controls to signal the valve open. And the valve will open."

She was dressed in a dark blue business suit with a light yellow blouse. As she spoke, she took the jacket off, rolled up her sleeves and stepped out of her plain navy pumps. From her leather handbag, she took a silver ring and put it on her right index finger. Laying aside her glasses, she turned to the Ravens. "Now, as I explained before, give me an A-note."

Phil hummed the note, and Art joined, and the two of them took turns breathing to sustain the note.

Mother paced out her working space, then stood to face each of the cardinal compass points in turn, gesturing. Her face had smoothed to look ten years younger, and her eyes were half closed. In that state, she began to turn in place, her arms crooked outward at shoulder height. I knew it must hurt her arthritis.

As she turned, her body seemed to blur, as if she were surrounded by a transparent cape. I blinked the illusion aside, and scanned the instruments, tripping the valve switch again. But none of the indicators changed.

Everyone was staring fixedly at mother, abstract expressions on their faces. The Ravens had their heads together, eyes closed in concentration, oblivious to their surroundings. Mother spun like a corkscrew, also oblivious. Two minutes and thirty-five seconds had passed when mother began to sing. It was a word that sounded like all vowels, enunciated not with the mouth but with the gut. I felt my bones vibrating, and my brain tingling.

Then she was still, the ringed finger pointing at me. "Signal, and the valve will function."

I wanted to laugh it away, but McCree was staring at me intently. I tripped the valve control again, and mother jerked around to point at Dan. "Signal—now!"

His eyes had dilated, and he seemed to be staring at the end of her finger. But his hand moved to the control.

I was afraid to look at the main screen.

Mother moved to the Ravens, put one hand on a shoulder of each of them and brought them out of their trance, cutting off the A tone so suddenly everything changed.

McCree whispered reverently, "Dear God!"

On the main screen, the readout had shifted colors and symbols to show the valve was open. Coolant was moving.

I didn't believe it. It was just the computer readout. I flipped the displays until we were watching the pit. The plume of steam from the safety bleeder was waning. As we watched, it stopped. That had to mean the pressure was down and the coolant was being dumped—at last—into the pressure container designed to hold it.

In the awed silence, Jill said, "The temperature at the periphery has stopped rising."

At intervals during the next half hour, she reported as the other temperature monitors leveled off. It would be days until the actual pile temperature would go down, but we knew we'd won when the last of her monitors leveled.

The cheer was deafening.

At the executive conference that night, Conwell said, "You're all to be commended to the United Nations for preventing even a single death or injury during the worst fusion disaster in history." What he meant was that, because of our efficiency, his neck wasn't on the chopping block.

As soon as I could, I confronted Mama. "I'm still not convinced—so what are you going to do next time, bring a meteor down on top of us?"

She looked shocked. "Mavrana, you can't think that we *caused* the earthquake?"

"I recall that you *said* you would."

"That was just to plant the idea in your mind to drill them

for it. Our astrologer and three of our best psychics predicted it just after they built the plant, so our group has been working hard to prevent a real disaster."

Relieved and exasperated, I threw my hands up and walked away. Later, McCree brought me a printout of the probability estimates for this long chain of events. When I saw the actual figures in cold print, something snapped. In the scientific view of the universe, improbable events just do not happen in such long chains just for the convenience of man. There has to be some relationship between science and magic—and I'm going to find it.

The search will be quite a lot of fun since McCree has agreed to work with me, even after hours.

# AN ACT OF FAITH

## by Galad Elflandsson

*Because Exodus 12:18 ordered "Thou shalt not suffer a witch to live," and medieval monks took that with utter seriousness, the conflict between paganism and Christianity provides some of the most horrific stories in European history.*

*Galad Elflandsson's "An Act of Faith" is set, he tells us, during the life of the Norwegian Viking Olaf Tryggvason (born 948). As a child, Olaf was sent to kinsmen in Russia. While crossing the Baltic, his ship was attacked by Estonian vikings; Olaf and his mother were sold as slaves. In 958, Olaf's uncle saw him in a slave market and brought him to be fostered by King Valdemar until he was eighteen.*

*Then Olaf too went on viking. He was probably baptized around 994 as part of a bargain with Aethelraed Unraed, from whom he received tribute. He would convert and leave England alone; Aethelraed—who was indeed poorly advised, as his name suggests—would pay him Danegeld of 16,000 pounds of silver. In 995 Olaf returned to Norway and set to work. By 1000, Norway was Christian, made so by the sword of a man whom medievalist Gwyn Jones calls "Christ's best hatchet-man."*

*Galad Elflandsson, who is proud enough of his Viking ancestry to tackle the linguistic difficulties of Old Norse, uses his special knowledge to tell a story of horror that is not Ragnarok, the Twilight of the Norse Gods, but—for Astrid, former slave and trained seeress—might as well be. We know how certain loveless elements within the medieval church regarded pagans, and sometimes other Christians. Here, chillingly told, is the story of a pagan looking at the Scandinavian church.*

Learned I grew then, lore-wise,
Waxed and throve well:
Word from word gave words to me,
Deed from deed gave deeds to me.
—Hávamál 133

*In mid-morning she returned from Lang Vatn, from the house of a farmer whose wife had given birth to a son during the night. At her back the Skølen rose up into the pale sky, peaks yet crowned and clothed in deep snow though she knew spring thaw was not far off. Her boots of reindeer-hide whispered in the snow as she hurried along, hair long and flaxen blown about her shoulders by the first warm winds of the season. Her dress was of plain grey* vadmál *in all things save the whiteness of her woolen stockings and the bleached linen of her shift and apron. Upon her left hand she wore a ring of gold given by her lover; upon her breast lay a neck-chain of silver with emerald stones devised upon a triskell and the runes of her calling carved thereon, pledging her to Life and Love and the Lady. She was small and slender—not above middle height for a half-Saxon thrall now freed by her master—and though the birthing had gone well and swiftly, her face and eyes, the latter wide and deeply blue as a summer sky over Sjonafjord, were anxious, haunted by fear. House-welcome had been offered her by the grateful farmer; with mother and son resting quietly, she too had slept. In sleeping, she had dreamed.*

*Those who came to her for this philtre or another, or sought her counsel in the healing of a wound or a troubling of the heart, these folk knew her also to be the* draumspekingar, *the dream-wise. In her dream she had seen a crimson moon and red rain hissing upon the snow, and a lordling's table set for feasting, with blood sprinkled over the venison, thin ribbons of blood swirling in the ale cups. Ill omens all, they came to her in the long hours of the night, bidding her to rise and go homeward over the hills. In mid-morning she returned from Lang Vatn . . .*

1

At first glance Astrid could see nothing to lend credence to her vision of doom. At the foot of the low hill, nestled snugly in a stand of pine trees, her small cottage stood as placidly as ever—a thin spiral from yesterday's carefully banked fire still curled from the vent beneath the thatched roof; morning sunlight shimmered off the oiled membranes of the light-holes in the walls of squared pine and oak logs. She breathed a cautious sigh of relief, clutching the silver medallion on her breast and murmuring a brief word of thanks to the Lady as she started down the slope . . . stopping abruptly, startled, as a raucous cry reached her ears and a dark, fluttering shape arrowed from the sky to land on her shoulder, a riot of blue-black plumage and bright piercing eyes of jet.

"Grak. . . ." she said to the crow, smoothing his ruffled feathers in an attempt to quiet him. The question on her lips hung there, unspoken, as a high chittering joined itself to the bird's dismayed croaking. Frightened again, here eyes darted to where a fat grey squirrel bounced frantically in the snow atop the roof of the cottage.

"Nika . . ." she whispered, appalled by the sudden furious pounding of her heart. She began to run down the slope, snow spraying in all directions, hair whipping about her face in a silver-white cloud, blinding her. She stumbled, went sprawling into the snow even as a long, mournful howl echoed from the top of the ridge to the west. Dazedly, she lifted her head from the snow, brushing the hair from her eyes. Grak circled above her, croaking furiously; Nika chattered on the roof-beam; and Tosti howled again and again on the crest of the ridge, an earth-brown smudge of bear against a sky boiling with thick, black smoke.

2

She stared in disbelief, knowing the while that her dream

had not been false. Trembling, she struggled to her feet, snow-drenched, uncaring, moving stiff-legged across the wide bowl of the valley and up the ridge to where Tosti waited for her. Halfway, the bear lumbered down to meet her, making small moaning sounds in its throat. Astrid fell to her knees, burying her face in the thick ruff of fur around the little bear's neck.

"Hush, Tosti," she said soothingly, yet the sound of her voice was that of a stranger in her ears, already thick with grief. "Tosti, what has happened?"

The bear pulled away from her, taking her sleeve in his mouth and tugging gently, as if to lead her back the way he had come. Astrid nodded wordlessly, seeing the full reality of her half-formed sorrow in the animal's sad brown eyes. Tosti loosed her sleeve and she followed him, up over the ridge, closer to the monstrous black cloud that hung in the sky.

On the far side, the gently sloping uplands started to narrow steeply down to Sjonafjord, the hillsides dotted with solitary pines, outcroppings of rock and small patches of brier and gorse. She scanned the slopes fearfully, afraid to find whatever it was she was looking for. Grak's wingbeats boomed overhead and she saw bear and crow converge on a place beside a sharp jutting of granite. In the shadow of the stone Astrid saw the man-shape and then Tosti howled again, the sound tearing at her heart, making her gasp for breath as she rushed down the slope.

She remembered nothing of those first few moments, of how she came to him where he lay face down in the snow with his tangle of brown-gold hair clotted with blood . . . scarlet coat and breeches smudged and torn . . . splintered arrow-shafts jutting from thigh and between ribs . . . the charred, gaping ruin of his right eye. . . . She knew only that it was Baard—younger brother to Bjarne Arnesson who had been her master—and she wept for the pain of his wounds, holding him in her arms until her tears falling upon the still features of his face quickened them into life, and his one remaining eye quivered and opened.

"Astrid . . . ?" he said in a hoarse whisper. A froth of blood oozed from the corner of his mouth. "Tis you, sweet? Ah . . . the gods are good . . . kept you safe. . . ."

"Baard, what happened? Who did this to you? Baard . . . my Baard. . . ."

He lay unmoving, drinking in the image of her with what sight was left to him. "I knew they would come someday, Astrid. . . . At first you thought I meant to cast you off from me . . . building your cottage so far from the hall. . . . They gave us a choosing, but you . . . you they would have burned outright . . . the dogs . . . Loki spite them all . . . cowards. . . ." Baard choked on his words, chest heaving, red blood pouring from his lips as his face contorted with pain. "No more, love. You must go . . . north . . . my mother's brother keeps his high-seat on Glamfjord, tell him . . . tell him Tryggvasson comes . . . for all of us . . . that his sister's sons . . . all of their house . . . are slain by his word. . . ."

Astrid wiped the blood from his mouth with the hem of her apron, stroking his face. "Bjarne, too?" she asked dully.

"Aye, sweet," Baard groaned. "Would that you had never healed him of the spear-thrust he got a-viking . . . to die the death they gave him. . . ."

He convulsed in her arms, hand reaching to grasp her hand upon his face. "My love, Astrid . . . go quickly . . . with my love . . . always. . . ."

"No . . . Baard!" she screamed. "No. . . ."

Thereafter she seemed to lose sight of him and the world, falling into a deep shadow place devoid of all warmth or sensation. When she awoke it was to Tosti's unhappy mewling and his tongue wet on her face. Grak stood nearby, cawing sharply, beak stabbing at the long figure emerging from the thick pine woods at the foot of the ridge. She dared not look down at Baard, feeling the coldness which had crept from his body into her heart; the sun was high overhead, a nebulous circle of harsh light searing through the smoke-haze and into the empty well of her tears. The crow shrilled once, a cry of warning, and flapped away; Tosti shivered at her side. She turned her gaze to the woods below, dry-eyed, her sorrow becoming a cold and painful knot in the center of her being.

Silently, she watched him plodding up to her, stroking the dead face in her lap all the while, absently noting the sunglint on the cold iron collar around the stranger's neck, the look of anger on his face. In his right hand he carried a double-edged war-axe, bloodstained, and she wondered how a thrall came to be so armed. Then he stood before her, a broad man of middle years with flecks of grey in his beard and hair, and the smell of stale sweat about his singed woolen clothing . . . and blood . . . more blood . . . all over him. . . .

She realized it was Sigvat, the smith. They had been slaves together, before she had healed Bjarne of his wound and so earned the freedom to accept Baard's betrothal ring. Sigvat had always been kind to her, even when the other thralls had shunned her for the magic-seeming of her charms and healing. Sigvat had always been her friend.

"Can you . . . will you carry him . . . for me?" she asked quietly, without inflection.

Sigvat frowned, eyes narrowing under shaggy brows. "I'm no longer a slave, Astrid Arwensdottir," he growled bitterly. "I've been freed, though in such wise as I'd lief stayed in thrall. Aye! I'll carry him for ye. Out of love for him that was a good master, and out of love for you, I'll serve ye the once ere I get on with this glorious business o' bein' free."

3

She scarcely noticed the chill that had invaded the cottage in her absence. The sense of quiet peace that had filled her life was gone, and as she went about the task of cleansing the body of the man who was to have been her husband—removing the arrows, cutting away the soiled clothing, wiping the crusts of dried blood from his flesh, combing his hair and beard, and fashioning a soft leather patch for his ruined eye—an army of conflicting emotions made war on her soul until she fully expected her body to be shivered apart and carried away into dread Niflheim by a cold wind. After what seemed an eternity of time, she covered Baard with her own woolen blankets and stood over him, gazing down at his face.

*Don't leave me, Baard.* She begged in silence. *Wait for me, there is something that must be done. Whatever it is, let me do it.*

She turned away from him quickly, relieved to find neither Tosti nor Nika clamored for her attention. The little bear had crawled onto her bed, beside Baard, and fallen asleep; the grey squirrel was curled above her on a rafter, eyeing her guest with suspicion. Outside, on the roof, she heard the soft scratching of Grak's talons marching first one way and then the other along the ridge-pole. Faithful Grak, ever watchful. The thought almost made her smile. Almost.

"Astrid, ye must go away. They'll be hearin' of ye from those in the village soon enough . . . and then they'll come t'serve ye as they served us."

It was Sigvat's voice, as soft as a growl might be, not wishing to intrude upon her sorrow, yet urgent. Slowly, her consciousness re-focused on the things around her and she saw him, sitting motionless on a bench beside the dying embers of her house-fire, the bloody axe across his knees. Astrid shook her head abstractedly, her eyes wandering over the small loom in the corner, the sweet-smelling herbs that hung from the rafters, the sunlight streaming through the *skja* to make dust-dancing patterns across the rush-strewn earthen floor.

"You are not running away," she said accusingly.

Sigvat's smile was cold. "No," he said, "I'm not runnin' away. The blood o' my masters'll be avenged ere tis froze on the snow. There's no one else but me . . .

"I been a thrall for twice the turnin' o' seasons in your life, and Thor has ever been watchful on that account. But now I'm free t'seek a new master. Tonight, I go back with this," he grinned, patting the blade in his lap, "and win a place in Odin's hall."

"Baard said there was an uncle in Glamfjord—" she began, but Sigvat's snort of disdain cut her short.

"Aye," he growled scornfully, "an uncle who loves the sound of gold and the King's soft voice better than he loves the honor of his kinsmen."

"But what of the rest of my lord's house?"

The smith snarled. "There ain't no others. They burned us out. At false dawn they fired the steading and then they waited for us with spear and arrow." He looked at Baard's still figure on the cot. "I didn't even know he got away. . . ."

Astrid's eyes grew wide with horror. "Everyone?" she cried, disbelieving in spite of Sigvat's vehement assertion. She swayed dizzily on her feet, hands clutching at thin air for support until one came to rest on the thrall-smith's shoulder. For a moment her eyes went blank with the memory of her dream-seeing. She shivered once, then sat beside the smith.

"Tell me of it, Sigvat," she said in a low voice. "Everything, from the beginning. Baard said it was Tryggvasson coming . . . for all of us. Was't him?"

Sigvat bent his head, his brow creased as he sought to convert the images in his mind into words. His voice was a soft rumble when he began, vibrant with anger.

"Nay, 'twas not our good king Olaf in the flesh, Astrid," he muttered. "Was't one of his shaveling priests, fresh from the treachery at Hladir this Yuletide past. . . ."

She nodded, having heard the story from Baard's own lips—how the King had invited the foremost men of the Trondelag region to feast with him at Yuletide and then, having made them drunk with the best of his wines and ales, had called his soldiers about these men and given them a coward's choosing . . . either to die, or give up the old gods and embrace the southron god, Kristr. Sigvat had gone on, musing aloud.

". . . He came last evening, when my lords and all the house sat at board, and Bjarne gave him house-welcome, gave him a place of honor close by him on the high-seat, fed this dog of his own plate, feasting him like the best of men.

"When the meal was done, Bjarne asked him then his name and what it was brought him to Nordurheim, and the shaveling said he was called Frodi, son of Skeggi; that he was come to Halogaland on an errand for Olaf the King and that he bore the blessing of Sigurd, the King's bishop, upon his head.

"Then my lord Baard got up from his bench and made some pretty speech about this and that, welcoming the shaveling as though he were Olaf himself and asking whether or no there was aught he and Bjarne might do t'aid him with this errand. Then the dog of a priest smiled t'himself and he said, 'Tis the word and wish of Olaf, King of all Norway, that his subjects forswear the worship of the false elder gods and give rightful worship to the one God and His only son who is Jesus Christ.'

"And of a sudden things was very quiet in the hall, until Baard laughed a bit, saying, 'By Thor's Hammer, I am confused, god Frodi. Are we to worship the one God only . . . or his only son . . . or only his son and Loki take the father?' Then all laughed and clapped at Baard's jest, all save the priest who asked Bjarne if it pleased him to give insult to his house-guests.

"Thereupon, Bjarne put down his ale-cup and answered him, saying, 'Nay, Frodi, my brother meant thee no insult. For myself, I trow the old gods are as good as any new one; even better, for my father and his father before him served the High One and His Kin, and what gifts we have this day have been got from Them. You may tell your master that I am his good and loyal man in all things, yet I will have nothing to do with this Kristr or his father. As for those of my house, no man however great may direct the faith and beliefs of another's heart. I give them leave to choose for themselves.'

"Then the shaveling was very still, and he said nothing more as one by one, down t'the very meanest of us by the cook-fires, everyone in the hall swore aloud their faith to Odin and Thor and Freyr. And though he was all quiet smiles thereafter, 'twas seen that the priest was much wroth with my lords and their household, declining a bed for the night with the words that he must needs get himself back to Austurviken that very hour. . . ."

4

A brooding silence filled the cottage, deepening as the shadows deepened with the coming of night. The two sat upon the bench, Sigvat fingering the bloodstained filigrees of gold and silver on the axe-blades before him, Astrid nervously plucking at the scissors and bone-handled knife tucked into the sash about her waist. At length, she raised her head and looked at Baard, almost believing him to be asleep, half-expecting him to stir and raise himself from the bed, smiling at her as he had always smiled.

She had learned something of the race of men who had enslaved her mother, learned of them and their ways and also of the strange gods they worshipped; how these gods prized above all else the qualities of courage, honour and loyalty in those who acknowledged them. She had chosen Freyja, the Lady, as her especial patron and now she went to a darkened niche beside her bed and looked upon Her crudely carven image—a rough thing of wood, lovingly painted, faithfully served. Astrid stood before her goddess, hands clasping the silver circle at her breast.

"Lady," she began inwardly, speaking through the incredible aching weariness that filled her. "Lady, I have ever done as I felt in my heart you would have me do. I have kept the light of Life sacred, yet now I feel only Death around me and I am lost. . . ."

She looked down at what had been a kindly, albeit primitively fashioned face, and saw that a measure of sternness had crept into those features. She trembled, but only for a moment, as a soft sighing voice whispered through her mind.

*There are two sides to every coin, my daughter, yet is the coin any less a coin for the different-seeming of its sides? So it is with Life as well. You have ever served me faithfully; shall I leave thee in the time of your need? You have trodden the path which your heart has directed thee to take, yet my path has ever been twofold, and thou shalt never leave my service if now your heart bids thee take the second path. Two sides to every coin, my daughter, two sides to Life and Love and the Lady.*

Astrid nodded, returned slowly to the bench where Sigvat seemed to be a lifeless figure cut from stone. She wondered if he might already have begun his journey and now stood, precariously balanced, between one side of Life and the other. She touched his broad shoulder gently, calling him back.

"You have not finished the tale, Sigvat," she whispered to him.

The smith raised his head, looking up at her with glazed eyes. "There's nothin' t'tell that ye don't already know," he replied hoarsely, "and tis time the both of us was goin' our ways."

"I haven't yet chosen my way, Sigvat, and you have not finished the tale," she insisted harshly. Memory kindled bale-fire in his eyes, burning away the mists around his inner thoughts. His voice was like clanging iron in her ears.

"When they burned us from our beds the dog-priest and his soldiers was waitin', him howlin' aloud as they cut us down, yammerin' out the lies of Olaf's Hel-hound god that preaches us peace and goodness while his pups are cuttin' our throats t'make believers of us.

"So they pent us up like sheep—all of us, men, women and children—and we sent a good number screamin' down to Corpse Strand, but in the end there was nobody but me and my lords and I saw them go down and went mad with rage until there was no one willin' t'stand between me and the hills above Nordurheim steading. 'Twas from there I seen 'em take out Bjarne's eyes; twas from there I heard him laughin' till they cut out his tongue and cut off his head t'dress the point of a spear-shaft . . . and it was there I wept and cursed my-self into black sleep—"

Something stirred in Astrid's heart, something apart from the horror of Sigvat's tale, something strange and alien to her who had lived only Love that she might keep faith with the Lady. It was a rending and a tearing open, the groaning of a grave-mound gaping wide and the chill winds of Hel hissing into sunlight . . .

*What god could be so mean and hateful as to command faith with pain and fear of death . . . ?*

. . . the hissing of the wind growing to a roaring thunder . . .

*What god could demand one way of life of its followers and yet allow them to do elsewise in its name . . . ?*

. . . the thunder becoming the voice of the Lady, dark with passion . . .

*Two sides to every coin, my daughter, two sides to Life and Love.*

Suddenly she knew the path that she would walk, and the aching weariness within her melted, merged with the frozen core of hatred forming in her soul. Sigvat had risen from the bench, towering above her, and she smiled at him, blue eyes hard as a winter sky over Sjonafjord.

"You will die this night, Sigvat," she said to him, and he looked at her with awe and wonder in his own grey eyes.

"Aye, Lady," he nodded soberly, "tonight I will die. Tonight, when I rouse the *nithingur* from their beds with flame and blood and the name of the Allfather on my lips, tonight I will die as a true Norseman was meant to die—laughing in the teeth of cowards who would fright me from the heritage of my fathers."

His massive hands gripped the haft of his axe lovingly as he strode to the door of the cottage, footfalls shaking the earth. She halted him with a word and he looked back at her, a great shadow limned against the half-light of the open door.

"I will be with you, Sigvat."

Again, he nodded. "I know it, Lady," he answered grimly. "I will watch for you. Grey man and golden lady. It is good."

When he was gone, Astrid raised her head and spoke softly to the fat grey squirrel sitting nervously among the rafters.

"Go, Nika, back to the home that was yours ere you came

to share my home with me. The tale is almost told." More loudly, she called to Grak, outside on the ridge-pole. "Go, Grak, go to the Grey Man, for I name thee now 'Stormcrow' and you must call the gods to this reckoning that we do."

On the bed, Tosti raised his muzzle, blinking at her with sad inquiring eyes, and Astrid found that not all her tears were frozen within her. Eyes glistening, she went slowly to the bed, hugging the little bear round the neck as she had done that morning.

"You are right, Tosti," she sobbed into his fur, "there is no other home for you. You will come with Baard and me. I will try . . . I swear . . . you will have no pain. . . ."

For a time, the cottage was dark and silent as a grey squirrel chattered a soft farewell from a pine bough and a crow winged westward toward the town of Austurviken. Inside the cottage a corpse, a bear and a golden-haired woman lay sleeping.

## 5

She sat upon a platform fashioned of ash and oak and rowan boughs with the hot flames of a sacrificial fire sending waves of heat against her naked body, glinting upon the emerald-set circlet of silver between her breasts. In one hand a *gandr*, or staff, of rowan wood wove patterns in the lurid glow as her lips moved soundlessly, endlessly in cryptic strophes learned long ago under a gibbous moon.

Those who had come to her for this philtre or another, or sought her counsel in the healing of a wound or a troubling of the heart, these folk knew her to be dream-wise and well-versed in the arts of *galdr*, the singing magic of light and goodness. But the words that came now from her lips were not the liquid cadences of the *galdrismál*, the songs of white-magic; rather, they were the harsh and sharp gutturals she had learned from the small, dark woman who had lived high among the crags of the Skølen. They were the words of *seidr*, the dark magic, and as she chanted her body grew stiff and rigid, her eyes rolled upward in their sockets, and a chill wind whipped the white-gold of her hair into a frenzied crown about her head. The cottage melted from her sight; she stood on the verge of a darkling plain, unknown stars glittering in the black sky above her.

A muted rumble of thunder sounded at her back and she turned to the great beast stamping the earth at her heels—a mammoth horse of silver-grey coat, eight-legged, glaring impatiently with furnace-bright eyes. For an instant she knew doubt and fear, yet these she forced from her mind and she went eagerly to the monster's side, chanting softly, and vaulted up onto its back.

"To your master, Sleipnir," she commanded him, and the beast leapt outward upon the plain, plunging into an ocean of nothingness, striding down an unseen highway, hooves hammering on thin air.

For an age the horse bore her through the void, so swiftly that the breath was drawn from her lungs and the pounding of its passage drove up through her loins to set her teeth to rattling. Emptiness swept by on all sides; she grew blind, deaf and dumb to all but the sensation of the beast's iron-hard flanks against her thighs . . . until a glimmer of light shone out of the murk, awakening her, and the horse surged upward to meet it. . . .

Under an ashen sky, she slipped from the horse's back and walked unsteadily toward the circle of stones before her. Outside the ring, all was covered with a thin layer of frost; beyond it, sheer scarps of rimed stone rose up from curling mists that glimmered with cold, white fire. Wonderingly, she passed through the outermost stones, onto cool green turf, and a voice, deep and rich with laughter, boomed an answer to her confusion.

"The borders of Jotunheim, O mortal woman, home of the Frost-Giants."

At the far side of the ring, beside a small bubbling of crystal water that sprang from the stones, a man and a woman stood regarding her with quiet amusement in their eyes. Between them there rose up from the spring a slender filament, seemingly of lustrous pale wood, that arched away into the sky. As she drew nearer the man laughed again, though now his laughter was stern and without mirth.

"Welcome to the Giant's Well, where the first root of the World Ash drinks of its Life-giving waters and Mimir the Wise spouts us his words of wisdom." A dark shape fluttered down onto the man's grey-cloaked shoulder, stirring a faint memory in Astrid's mind. "You see, we are forewarned of your coming, Arwensdottir. Know this, that you dare greatly to come to this place."

Astrid saw his single eye flash with a nameless passion, would have quailed beneath his terrible gaze had not the woman spoken in her defense.

"Pease, Father Odin," she said quietly, and Astrid recognized her voice, looked upon the bright gold of her hair, the costliness of her blue- and green-broidered garments, the glitter of emeralds and dwarf-wrought silver about her white throat.

"Freyja," she whispered imploringly. "My Lady. . . ."

The goddess nodded and turned to the grey man. "She is one of my children, Allfather. I have given her leave to come here. Let her speak."

The Grey One shrugged irritably. "As you wish," he muttered, frowning; turning to Astrid he said more kindly, "What would you at Urdr's Well?" and bent his one eye upon her closely.

Astrid shivered in her nakedness, but with the Lady's favor found courage to answer him boldly. "Allfather, I come to win me the runes of power, twice nine in number, that I may go unscathed among my enemies and take vengeance upon those who have reft me of lord and lover; that I may take blood for blood from the followers of the coward-god named Kristr."

"What will you give for the runes, Arwensdottir?" demanded the Grey God. "Will you give an eye, nine days and nights of anguish as I gave?"

"I will give all that I am," she answered him.

"A fair bargain," spoke the goddess at his side quickly, "but take you the lover, Allfather, for this child is mine from birth and I would have her in my hall."

The god was silent, his brow creased with thought. At length, he looked at Astrid and said, "Very well, Arwensdottir. The Lady hath made thee a bargain. You shall have the runes whence I had them. Come thee closer . . . and look! List thee to Mimir the Wise!"

Astrid came nearer, following the line of the Grey One's outstretched hand—to a niche in the stone above the well, where the severed head of a Frost-Giant opened its eyes and gazed placidly into her soul. Briefly, she heard Grak's cry of farewell, and then she heard the voice of Mimir as Grey Man, Golden Lady, Ash root and stone circle faded away:

Learn how to cut them, learn how to read them,
Learn how to stain them, stain them and prove them,
Learn how to call them, learn to divine them,
Learn how to send them, spend them, send them . . .

Dimly, far in the depths of her consciousness, she knew there was little time left to her; that Sigvat soon would descend upon the town alone if she failed in her promise. There were no more tears for her as the interior of the cottage swam again into her sight—Baard lying on her cot, the still-warm bundle of fur upon the altar before her. Seething with newfound knowledge, she dipped the *gandr* into the earthen bowl of Tosti's blood, tracing the images of the runes upon her forehead, breasts, belly and thighs, chanting the while, until her voice was a meaningless spate of sound that poured from her writhing lips. The traceries done, she took up the bearskin and tied it around her waist, now screaming into the ice-cold blackness that had crowded around her, thrusting the staff into the sacrificial fire until it speared up the sizzling, crimsoned morsel of flesh that had been a living beast's heart. With this she made the rune of the beast upon her lips, and uttering its name with a final shrilling cry, thrust it whole into her mouth.

## 7

Agony.

She plunged into a world filled with distorted shapes that leered and gibbered and drooled into the broken shell of her being. Her insides burned with the searing flames of Muspelheim; her flesh cracked and peeled in the rimed cold of Hel. Down she fell into an abyss of pain, flailing with maddened maunderings of thought at the horrors surrounding her, while the merciless fire in her belly boiled outward to meet the frozen shards of her flesh. She came apart at every joining of every bone and sinew in her body . . . and came groaning back into oneness.

## 8

The bear shook itself loose from the remnants of the splintered door-lintel of the cottage, lifting its muzzle to the star-spattered sky to roar defiance at the pale disc of the moon. Razor-clawed forepaws raked upward to the height of four tall men and the massive, black-furred frame quivered with the ferocity of its angry challenge. It was a monstrous thing out of nightmare, and its eyes were blue and cold as a killing-winter sky over Sjonafjord.

The beast dropped down on all fours, the thunder of its voice yet ringing across the small valley, filling its brain and sinews with a savage exultation that was almost painful in its intensity. The world leapt out to dazzle its eyes with startling clarity—stark-graven images in black and grey and white—nostrils twitched at every scent, ears captured every sound. The very air seemed fraught with new perceptions, and as the last echoes of the bear's cry went rushing into Silence, dire hatred surged through every fibre of its body. Muscles tautened beneath the black-furred hide; the bear turned westward towards the sea and broke into a bounding run that brought it to the ridge-crest above the cottage within minutes. From there, it was a league downhill to the town by the water—to Sigvat—where vengeance was a blood-red promise waiting to be fulfilled.

The snow was a virgin mantle scorned beneath its massive paws and the bear moved effortlessly, now in long loping strides that grew longer with every second of its headlong descent. Broken images—a wolf with fear-crazed eyes, a hare's terror-filled flight, sharp juttings of stone, dark-shadowed woods—flashed by unheeded as it dragged the night air into the vast bellows of its lungs and blew it out again in plumes of chill white smoke. Oblivious to all but the rising tide of power that set its heart to singing, the beast trampled down trees and brushed aside stone. . . .

Twice nine the number of runes I know,
Strong staves and stout staves, made mighty by the gods

At false dawn, a hulking shadow stood above the smoking ruins of Nordurheim, that which had been the hearth and halls of Anre's sons—a place of peace where, long and long ago in another life, a thrall-woman's child had grown into young womanhood and learned of many things, even a lordling's love. Here the snow was black with blood and bodies sprawled out in death, crimsoned by witch-light embers that darted among the charred wreckage of the hall and outbuildings. A pall of smoke yet obscured the sky and the monstrous shadow-shape shook itself angrily, an ominous rumbling sounding in its cavernous chest.

Bale-fire eyes swept downward to where the town of Austurviken slept, huddled in moonlight round the still, shimmering silver of the fjord—small clusters of houses, stables, work places and market stalls. Sleeping, all sleeping. its gaze shifted, centered upon the tallest of the buildings below, upon the temple, where the seasonal sacrifices were made upon the altars of Thor, Odin and Freyr. Where two soldiers of Kris stood guard beside the door. The beast watched and waited as false dawn faded into the dark hours that immediately preceded the new day.

Then there was a scurry of furtive movement beside the temple, and a hoarse, shouting invocation to the old gods as the first flames leapt upward around the wooden walls of the structure and the bear was plummeting downward, claws striking through snow and ice into the still-frozen earth, the rumbling in its chest crescendoing through laid-back lips and bared fangs, a single answering roar with ice-blue eyes glaring, heart pumping fury into brain.

Limned against the spiraling flames of the temple, Sigvat stood atop a pile of corpses, calling to Odin as with each stroke of his war-axe he brought another king's man to his end. Laughingly, he spat defiance at a score of them and more, and they came at him all at once with spear and sword and the shrill voice of the priest to urge them on. The beast came silently, a whirlwind shadow of Death. Its brain sang rune-songs:

> Unwounded I go to war,
> Unwounded I come from war,
> Unscathed wherever I may be. . . .

Six men died instantly, trampled underfoot before the bear rose up on hindquarters to scythe down through their pressed ranks with fang and claw. *Joy/hunger/hate* boiled from its throat in a continuous Doom-calling. Faces turned in stunned surprise and terror; it made them into screaming masks of shattered bone and blood. Sword-blades and spear-points came from all sides . . .

> A Third rune is mine, I know it well,
> No enemy's sword upon me will tell . . .

and broke against its flanks, even as taloned forepaws raked the bodies behind them into tatters, spilling entrails, rending limbs, tearing muscle and sinew until the iron tang of hot blood steamed up from the snow and the beast's hide grew lank and sodden in the crimson mist. Those who fled were caught up, broken like twigs and flung aside; those who stood and fought knew but a moment of prayer ere they became ragged crimson smears of unshriven flesh. . . .

She did not know when the slaughter ended, nor even when it had first begun. Suddenly, the roaring in her brain and the haze before her eyes were gone. She stood alone before the flaming pyre of the temple, looking down from an incredible height; on the farther side of a pool of mangled flesh and gore, she saw Sigvat with his war-axe upraised and the Allfather's name bursting from his lips. And she saw the priest struggle up from among the dead, a broken spear in his hands, lunging . . . the spear-point thrusting out from Sigvat's chest . . . the priest running . . . Sigvat falling. . . .

## 9

Astrid stood over him, not understanding the labored rise and fall of his chest or the bloody froth on his lips, fascinated by the flame-burnished iron spear-point that stood out from the widening stain on his woolen shirt. She had seen the priest come up behind him, the broken spear in his hands . . . but she had never killed a man before, nor seen one done to death, and this was Sigvat who lay dying . . . her friend . . . looking up at her with the painful beginnings of a smile on his lips.

"Lady," he whispered fervently, "I knew ye'd come, that ye'd not leave all t'your old friend Sigvat. Ah . . . the ravens'll feast well this day . . . and I go to feast with the heroes in Valholl. Twas a *nithing* stroke that got me my death-wound, Lady . . . but what else can ye expect from a shaveling . . . ?" He tried to laugh at his own jest, coughed blood instead. "The shaveling, Lady . . . the shaveling and our masters be avenged . . ."

She watched the life in him trickle out through the hole in his chest, his eyes losing the last of their battle-brightness; his breath came and went for a time and then he was still. She lifted her head and howled mournfully, a lost memory of something small and gentle (an earth-brown smudge of bear?) stirring inside the vast body that enclosed her. Now only the priest remained. Slowly, with a rekindling of fury in her breast, she shambled after him.

The scent of his fear led Astrid through a sea of eyes peering fearfully from half-opened doorways and through the cracks of shutters. Those with enough curiosity or courage to venture outside had only to glimpse the vast black shadow stalking through the town before dashing indoors again, clutching amulets and muttering wardspells against the murderous apparition that had slaughtered the soldiers of Frodi the priest. In days past they had all come to her for healing; now they shunned her and she was content that it should be so. The anger drove out all regret.

She went the length of the town before she found him, in the stable belonging to Torfinn Einarsson, at the very edge of the fjord. She saw him there, huddled in a dark corner—the priest, the one who had murdered Baard for a simple jest, for denying Kristr. She growled, padding slowly forward, ignoring the frenzied terror of Torfinn's two ponies, enjoying the terror of him who had been so proud in her master's hall. The priest fumbled among his robes, brought out a golden cross with a tiny man-shape upon it, held it at arm's-length before him.

"Begone, spawn of Satan!" he cried weakly. "In the name of—"

She lashed out with a paw, carefully, dashing the cross from his outstretched hand. Again, and the priest was thrown against the opposite wall of the stable to fall in a crumpled heap, babbling incoherently, terror etched upon his round face by stray moonlight.

*You dare to beg mercy of your god!*

She towered over him, trembling with rage even as the priest trembled with his fear. He started to speak,

"In the name of Jesus Christ, I—"

But she drowned his words in a thrundering roar and hurled him against the wall a second time. He struggled to his knees, a thin ribbon of blood welling from beneath his lank tonsure, lips moving soundlessly in mute supplication. As she looked over him, his eyes darted to her razorlike claws, growing round and half-crazed as he saw Death rushing to meet him. He clasped his hands before him, lifted them up . . .

*What mercy did you show the women and children!* she screamed silently at him; and then, scornfully, *Where is your faith now, priest, that you must beg mercy of me . . . ?*

For an instant, that single pounding heartbeat before she made to crush him, her eyes met those of the priest and she staggered back as if stricken by an iron fist. Dazed, she sank to all fours and looked again, disbelieving, appalled. Again, she saw the thing in the priest's eyes, a sheet of blinding light sweeping through her brain as, dreamwise, she glimpsed beyond the simple act of killing him.

His eyes were wells of fear and ignorance, man-trap eyes that would snare all who came within their province, behind them lurked a cringing, cowering leech of a soul that would feast and fatten upon the misery of others. Suddenly, the wretched thing that crouched beneath her seemed not so much a man as it was a groveling worm—a worm that would make its way through the world not with courage, but with self-righteous mouthings as empty of meaning as he himself was empty of true faith.

With a rising sickness in her belly, Astrid knew this man to be no more a Christian than she was, yet armies of men just like him *would* win their war through the world; that honour, loyalty, love and courage would be overwhelmed by their jealousy, greed, and petty hatreds, buried beneath a mountain of lies, hypocrisy, and false pride that would deny everything pure and natural in a man or woman. This was the future of mankind as she saw it in the priest's eyes. To deal him Death was meaningless, for he was incapable of accepting Death with any awareness that it was a just and honourable reckoning for what he himself had done. The blight was too widespread to be checked.

Dizzy with horror, Astrid turned away from him, went out into the open air, and shambled off into the fire-lit hills above Sjonafjord.

## 10

In mid-morning she returned from the gates of Hel, a young woman spattered with blood and with naught to hide her nakedness but the long white-gold of her hair and a bear-skin about her waist.

On hands and knees, she crawled through the broken door-way of her cottage and dragged herself to where the dying embers of a sacrificial fire cast a feeble light to meet the day. These embers she fanned into a final flame that she scattered over the rush-strewn floor. As they climbed up the walls, along the roof-beams and through the thatched roof, she lay down beside the body of her lover and wept over his cold face. Clutching the circle of emeralds and silver between her breasts, she whispered to him above the roar of the flames:

"We do not want to live in the world that is coming, Baard. Let us go to our gods now . . . together . . . before everything that matters is dead."

# WITCH FULFILLMENT

## *by Jean Lorrah*

*Like many other writers of fantasy and science fiction, Jean Lorrah is a medievalist. In fact, she is professor of English at Murray State University in Kentucky, where she teaches Chaucer, freshman composition, and science fiction. I first met her when Jacqueline Lichtenberg sent her a manuscript with which I was having massive first draft problems. "Explain it in professor-talk!" ordered Jacqueline. With tact, humor, and insight that bordered on telepathy, Jean did so. That marked the beginning of our correspondence.*

*Jean seems to thrive on a schedule that would drain most other people. When she is not teaching and lecturing (she is one of her area's most popular speakers), she is putting up shelves and writing. Having learned her craft by writing some of the finest stories ever published in fanzines, she went on to break into professional writing with her collaborations on* First Channel *and* Channel's Destiny, *set in Jacqueline Lichtenberg's world of Simes and Gens.* House of Keon *will be Jean's first solo book in this series. More recently, the Playboy Press release of* Savage Empire *(to be followed by* Dragon Lord of the Savage Empire*) has shown Jean to write entertainingly about psi power and romance.*

*One of Jean's most striking personal qualities is her sense of humor. She finds great pleasure in puns and parodies. I think you will find that "Witch Fulfillment" is a Puckish blend of magic, romance, and humor . . . as well as a parody of the myth of a bargain with the devil.*

It wasn't until she was twenty-six that Mary Sue Clyatt decided to practice witchcraft. No handsome prince, count, or even baron had come into her life. Not a single millionaire. The books she read, the movies she saw, the television that played every moment she was home, all assured her—for so she chose her entertainment—that such men were lurking in wait for sweet young girls, ready to sweep them into adventure and marriage.

At twenty-six she was no longer a sweet young girl. Still pure and innocent, she now had a pronounced squint from so much reading and television, and an extra twenty pounds, acne, and oily hair from the Sara Lee, pizza, and ice cream which were her solace in lonely hours. One day when she had just put new light bulbs in the ceiling fixture, she caught sight of herself in the full-length mirror on the bedroom door.

"Good heavens!" she gasped in the best dramatic fashion. "What has become of me?"

Such an epiphany might, for other women, have meant diet, exercise, consultation with a dermatologist, and a good haircut. For Mary Sue it meant the end of hope. "I've grown old!" she wailed. "True heroines are from seventeen to twenty-four. I am already obsolete by two years!"

For over a week she mourned her youth, drowning her sorrow in milkshakes and furtively watching all the men come and go in the advertising office where she worked, wondering which of them might have been her prince, come too late. Then one day she was typing copy, automatically, her mind lost amid her personal deprivation. As she closed the last folder, though, her eye fell on its logo. RED DEVIL CHILI, it read, but what caught Mary Sue's attention was the saturnine face embossed in red, grinning wickedly at her. There were horns, a goatee, pointed ears—a stereotype, but for Mary Sue a revelation. "I'll become a witch! I'll make a pact with the devil!" After all, she came from good Massachusetts stock—and some of her ancestors from Salem.

Although her favorite books were adventures in foreign lands, where young girls were swept into intrigue and in the final paragraph into the hero's arms, she had in her wide reading of escape literature come across the occasional pact-with-the-devil story. The hero or heroine always received youth and beauty, along with whatever else he sought.

Mary Sue knew her way around the public library, and now she ventured into the university library as well. She tried a few spells, getting a raise and a promotion by giving the most junior partner's secretary migraines, but it was romance, not a career, that she was looking for. Besides, the negative spells—migraines—seemed to work, while the positive spells—making herself irresistible to men—did not. It seemed her only chance was to make that pact.

Within a few weeks she was ready. She had learned a great deal among the grimoires, including the danger she was in. The devil would do his best to trick her, to give her explicitly what she asked but omit something crucial, like eternal youth for the woman who asked for immortality, and spent eternity getting older and older and older—

Mary Sue shuddered over that example, but gritted her teeth and determined to make no such mistake. She would take the risk. After all, what did she have to lose?

"Your soul," said the devil when he rose up inside her carefully-drawn magic circle warded with salt and iron and the symbols she had practiced so diligently.

"You can have it," said Mary Sue, "*if* you agree to my terms. Eternal youth and beauty—"

"Ten years," interrupted the devil. He wasn't *the* devil, of course, merely *a* devil, and not a prepossessing one. He stank of sulfur, he had a wart on his nose, and he seemed bored. "Standard contract," he droned. "Youth and beauty for ten years, no more, no less."

"What happens at the end of ten years?" asked Mary Sue.

"You die. I get your soul." He snapped his fingers, and an IBM Selectric appeared, suspended in midair. Rolled into it were several sheets of paper, sandwiched with carbons. Mary Sue could see her name and the date, already typed in.

The typewriter indexed past a solid block of fine print and

typed, "youth and beauty" in a large blank area. "Will that be all?" asked the devil through a yawn.

"No!" Mary Sue exclaimed. "That's not all! If I only have ten years, I want to live them like the heroines of romantic novels. I want excitement, adventure, handsome men in love with me. Rich men. Noblemen."

The typewriter clattered away as she spoke, the ball dancing across the page. Mary Sue remembered devils' trickery and added, "I don't want to be hurt. No sweet/savage stuff."

"Excitement and adventure, but no pain," said the devil distastefully. "Very well. That should do it—"

"No, wait! You said I'll die. I don't want that to hurt, either, or make me ugly. I want to die beautifully, with people around me who love me, people who will cry for the passing of such a young and beautiful—and good—woman."

The devil twitched his tail in irritation. "Is that it?"

Mary Sue peered at what the Selectric was typing. "Just make sure it's ten full years of excitement and adventure and love," she said. "I'm a witch now. I can call you up any time I'm not satisfied, you know. And stop being so impatient. This is a formal conjuration. You can't leave until I give you license to depart."

"Everyone's a lawyer these days!" snorted the devil. He wasn't at all frightening any longer.

Mary Sue said, "Let me see that contract." She could read the freshly typed words easily, but in the dim light of the candles, her eyes watered from the haze of smoke that had arrived with the devil. The tiny fine print was in some archaic form of lettering and language. But the parts she cared about were there.

The devil produced a quill pen, and handed it out of the circle to Mary Sue. Paper and pen could cross the barrier, but the devil could not, nor did Mary Sue allow so much as the tip of a finger to enter the circle. She had done her homework. "Left ring finger," the devil instructed, but Mary Sue had already picked up her athame. She punctured the top of her finger.

"Ouch!" she said. "None of this is supposed to hurt. It's in the contract."

"You call that pain? Anyway, you haven't signed yet. All seven copies."

Mary Sue dipped the point of the quill in her blood, and

signed. Then she dismissed the devil and turned on the lights. Except for the magic circle, her bedroom was the same as ever. Not even a whiff of sulfur remained. In the mirror, she appeared the same dumpy, squinty, acne-spotted woman she'd been before. *If I have to*, she told herself, *I'll conjure that devil up every single night until he gives me what I want!*

The next morning, as she stepped outside on the way to work, Mary Sue was abducted. Two men clapped a cloth over her face. As she drew breath to scream, she drew in chemical fumes. She blacked out.

When she came to, she was in a hospital room, her face swathed in bandages. A woman sat by the bed. In an accent Mary Sue could not identify, she said, "You will forget Mary Sue Clyatt—she no longer exists. You are the wealthy and beautiful Mariamne Winchester, distant American cousin of the Duke of Verlona. If you play your cards right, you will be a very rich woman." She held up a photograph of a darkly handsome man, standing before a magnificent stone mansion. "Wouldn't you like to marry this man and live in this house, and have servants and give balls and wear beautiful clothes and spend summers on the Riviera?"

"Sure," said Mary Sue. "What's the catch?"

It turned out that the Duke's father and Mariamne's guardians had arranged their marriage. The two principals had not seen one another since Mariamne was ten and the duke eighteen. Now, it seemed, Mariamne had run off from her school in Switzerland with a ski instructor. Her family had attempted to retrieve her and have the marriage annulled, but the man would not be bought, and Mariamne told them that though they might forcibly separate her from her lover, she adamantly refused to marry the duke. If dragged to the altar, instead of "I do," she would answer "No."

"Oh, that's beautiful!" empathized Mary Sue. "But what has it to do with me?"

"The family has managed to hush up the scandal. The duke doesn't know that his bride has married someone else. Wellington Winchester, Mariamne's uncle and guardian, wants to join his financial interests with those of the Duke of Verlona, who has acquired some Mideast oil companies. If the wedding takes place, so will the merger. If you can convince the duke you're Mariamne long enough to get him to sign the merger, you get half a million dollars. What you do from that point on is your own affair. You can divorce the duke or stay with him, whichever you choose."

"But why me?" asked Mary Sue finally.

"Because you have the right coloring, build, and blood type, and the right Boston accent. Bone structure. With a little painless surgery we can make you look like Mariamne's photographs—and nobody's going to check fingerprints. We'll train you and dress you—then all you have to do is fool the duke for three weeks to get him to the altar. Then you have your half million dollars—and the duke, too, for all we care."

For the next four months, Mary Sue—who quickly learned to think of herself as Mariamne—underwent a series of painless operations to change her face. She was drilled on Mariamne's life history and the duke's, hypnotized and taught French and Italian. The hospital room turned out to be in a luxurious clinic with warm and cold swimming pools, tennis courts, a gymnasium, and stables. She learned to ride, and spent hours each day in the forms of exercise favored by the very rich. Her twenty extra pounds melted easily away—from all the right places.

When all the bandages were removed for the last time, and the swelling in her face had gone down, hairstylists and makeup artists went to work on her. Soon she had the first stipulation in her pact with the devil: youth and beauty.

Mary Sue stared into the mirror in delight. Her dirty blond hair had turned to deep gold, and curled charmingly about a face of radiant complexion. Her eyes no longer squinted—wide open, they were revealed as violet. She was beautifully dressed, impeccably groomed, and obviously not a day over nineteen—the age of the runaway heiress.

Wellington Winchester took Mary Sue to the ancient estate of the Duke of Verlona, and presented her as his niece. No one questioned her identity, least of all the dark, handsome duke, who was smitten with her at once. They rode, swam, and played tennis together, and, just as she had yearned to do all her life, Mary Sue fell deeply in love. So deeply that she could not let the duke, whose given name was Ricardo, marry a false bride.

Knowing she would lose everything, she sought Ricardo out on the eve of their wedding and, tears trembling on the edges of her long lashes, confessed. Then she fell silent, waiting, unable to look at him for fear of the contempt she would see in those dark eyes that had looked at her with such passion. When he said nothing, she turned to leave.

Ricardo caught her arm. "Mariamne! he said in a choked voice, and drew her to his chest. "I don't care who you are or where you came from—you will always be my Mariamne, the only woman I have ever loved—the woman I am going to marry!" And he cut off her protest with a rapturous kiss.

As time passed, Mary Sue—now officially Mariamne, Duchess of Verlona—began to realize why her favorite novels always ended with a rapturous kiss: what came afterward could never equal that supreme moment of love. She was happy enough at first, honeymooning in Paris, gambling in Monte Carlo, skiing in the Alps—but after a while her delight began to cool. Ricardo's hot Mediterranean passion didn't, though, and Mariamne took to having frequent headaches. For a time, Ricardo brought wet towels to lay across her forehead, and sat holding her hand when she claimed pain. Eventually, though, he began to leave her alone.

They traveled to England for fox hunting. Mariamne rode with the hunt until the day of the Hunt Ball, when the men rode while the ladies slept late and spent the afternoon making themselves beautiful. It didn't take much work for Mariamne; the youth and beauty part of her pact was certainly being fulfilled. "But what about the love and adventure part?" she pouted. "I think it's about time to call that devil up again!"

Just then she heard horses gallopping up outside, shouts, a great to-do. It was too early for the hunt to be returning—

She hurried downstairs just in time to see Ricardo being carried into the hall, dead, his neck broken from being thrown by his horse.

Although Mariamne could not inherit Ricardo's estate, which went to the next male of Verlona blood—some cousin from Austria—she was left a very rich widow indeed. She took elegant rooms on the Riviera and went for long walks on the beach every morning, trying to conjure up a proper attitude of mourning and convince herself that among her mixed emotions there wasn't really—was there?—a feeling of relief.

For two months she spent afternoons and evenings in her rooms, reading the romantic novels she had always loved. Then she remembered that she had only a little more than eight years left for love and adventure, and began going down to the dining room for dinner. She sat alone at a table for two—as did a tall, distinguished gentleman who always looked distant and sad . . . so romantic. Discreet inquiries brought information that he, too, was recently widowed. A wealthy English businessman, Peter Knightly.

One evening Mariamne arrived a little late for dinner, having spent the afternoon shopping for outfits intended to catch Peter Knightly's eye. The dining room was full, every table taken. The maitre d' turned from assigning Mr. Knightly to the last table for two, and began apologizing to Madame the Duchess for not having reserved her a table—he had not expected a crowd—did not know if she had gone out for the evening—

Hearing the commotion, Peter Knightly rose gallantly and offered to share his table. Mariamne found him intelligent, well-educated, wont to quote poetry . . . a tragic hero with beautiful sad grey eyes fringed with thick gold lashes. Peter was not the tennis/swimming/skiing type Ricardo had been. He was cool and distant, giving Mariamne a delicious sense of being worshipped from afar, even when they were walking side by side along the beach.

In two weeks they were married, and Peter took Mariamne home to his estate, called Wonderly. It was a formal, imposing house, strictly ruled by a housekeeper, one Mrs. Cross, a pinched and harried woman who lived up to her name.

If it were not for Mrs. Cross, Mariamne thought, life with Peter would be perfect. They often went up to London, where Peter would conduct business and Mariamne would shop, and then they would go out to dinner and the theater, and spend the night at the Ritz. Only there, or in other places away from Wonderly, did Peter make love to her. He was gentle and hesitant, not demanding as Ricardo had been. Mariamne almost enjoyed it.

What she did enjoy was just being with Peter, trying to pry out of him the tragic secret of his past. She knew it had something to do with his first wife, Ruth, but Mariamne could not get Peter to talk about her. The secret lay at Wonderly, for it seemed Peter preferred to be away from his estate as much as possible, and while his temperament was normally placid, at Wonderly he could be easily provoked into flares of temper.

It occurred to Mariamne that Mrs. Cross's insistence that the house be kept exactly as it was in Ruth's day was not good for Peter or for his second marriage. So she decided to redecorate. She went from room to room, deciding color schemes, mentally dismissing the uglier furnishings while considering what would blend beautifully with the many classic antiques. One thing that had to go was the collection of stuffed animals distributed through all the rooms. She was having a grand time until she came to a door which none of her keys would unlock. As she was going through them a second time, Mrs. Cross came sweeping down the hall.

"So!" said the housekeeper, "you want to know why your so-called husband cannot love you? He was married to a blessed saint, that's why. How dare you violate her sanctuary?"

Mariamne reminded herself that Mrs. Cross was only the housekeeper. "This is my house now," she said, pulling herself up to her full height. "I intend to redecorate, and if you don't like it, you can just leave. But before you do, give me the key to this room."

The housekeeper's eyes darted lightning. "*Your* house? It can never be yours! Never!" She tugged at a chain about her neck, drawing a key from the depths of her bosom. "This is Mrs. Knightly's house—Mrs. *Ruth* Knightly's. Look upon the beauty she created, and see why you are nothing but a pale intruder!"

Mrs. Cross unlocked the door and flung it open. Mariamne followed her into a bedroom at least three times the size of her own. Although it was clean, it smelled funny, musty, unpleasant.

The huge canopied bed was set on a platform, all the hangings closed. The drapes were closed, too, but Mrs. Cross drew them open, and sunlight flooded a room decorated in velvet and satin, white and gold. The dressing table sparkled with crystal. A comb, brush, and mirror of solid gold lay as if waiting to be picked up and used. On the elegant table beside the chaise lounge was a best-selling novel from a year ago, a gold bookmark in it.

On the wall where light from the windows would strike it

was Ruth's portrait. She could hardly have been more different from Mariamne: a dark beauty, huge eyes in a pale, angular face, black hair swept severely back, accentuating the perfection of her features. She was dressed in a deep red gown, a color Mariamne could never wear.

"You see?" said Mrs. Cross. "How could the Master love a pale nothing like you, after he had had such perfection?"

Mariamne remembered that she was no longer Mary Sue Clyatt, and glanced to the mirror to reassure herself of her own pink-and-gold beauty. "I'm sure Peter did love Ruth," she said, "and you did, too. But Ruth is dead now, Peter loves me."

"Dead?" shrieked the housekeeper. "Mrs. Knightly dead? That's what the police said, but they never found her, did they? No—she's not dead. She could never leave Wonderly! It's hers, forever!" And she turned to fling open the hangings of the canopied bed.

On the bed lay a shadowed form—lay as if sleeping atop the white satin spread, wearing a deep red dress. In horrified fascination, Mariamne stepped up on the platform, and saw that it was Ruth Knightly—or her preserved, mummified remains—

Mariamne's screams brought Peter up the stairs at a run. "Oh, my God!" he gasped when he saw the form on the bed. Then he caught Mariamne protectively into his arms as he shouted at Mrs. Cross, "It was you! It wasn't an accident! You killed her!"

"*You* killed her!" Mrs. Cross screamed back. "You tried to drive her away from Wonderly!" And she turned and ran as Peter held Mariamne like a drowning man clutching a life preserver.

Mariamne remained certain all through the trial that her husband was innocent. He and Ruth, it seemed, had grown up on adjoining estates, childhood sweethearts. They married young, to the great joy of their families and the community . . . but as the years passed, they grew apart. Peter spent more and more time on business, while Ruth was often away from Wonderly, to the dismay of Mrs. Cross, who had come to Wonderly with Ruth at her marriage.

One day, Peter testified, Ruth had announced that she was leaving him. He told her to go ahead—he was better off without an unfaithful wife. She went upstairs to pack. The last time he saw her was at tea, when she taunted him about being so "civilized" about the end of their marriage. "But then you always were a cold fish."

After that, it had been thought, Ruth drove off along the cliff road. It was raining; she was in an agitated state. In the morning, at low tide, her car was found smashed at the bottom of the cliff. Her body was never found—presumably washed away by the waves. Eventually she was pronounced dead.

Now, though, the prosecutor put together a different story. The coroner discovered that Ruth had died of poison. Peter must have murdered her, pushed the car over the cliff, and then embalmed her body in the cellar of Wonderly, where he had done taxidermy as a boy. The half-mad Mrs. Cross might have been an accomplice, or simply a pitiful creature whose delusions Peter had used to his own ends. Mrs. Cross did not testify; she had disappeared the day Mariamne and Peter were shown Ruth's body. The prosecutor suggested that Peter might have murdered her, too.

Mariamne knew Peter was no murderer—knew it with all her heart and soul. That did not affect the verdict: guilty.

Mariamne was too upset to drive home alone, so a police matron drove her back to Wonderly. *What would she think,* Mariamne wondered, *if she knew that tonight at midnight I'm going to conjur up a devil and give him a piece of my mind?*

But she didn't have to summon the devil. There was a light moving about in one of the upstairs rooms when they drove up. "That's Ruth's bedroom!" Mariamne recognized.

The two women dashed up the stairs. Mrs. Cross was standing before Ruth's portrait, holding a flaming candleabra. "They took you from me twice," she was saying. "I never meant to hurt you, my darling. *He* would have driven you away—you, the only true Mistress of Wonderly. *He* was supposed to drink the poisoned tea! I put the poisoned cup in front of him—if only you had not come in at just that moment, my darling. If he had drunk from it first! But he gave you that cup and rang for a fresh one. When I came in and saw—! Then I realized it was fated. You were never to grow old, to lose your beauty. I preserved it, in the Master's old laboratory. And while he was away, I put you here, where you belong, never dreaming he dared desecrate your memory by bringing that—that—"

"That's enough, Mrs. Cross," said the police matron. "I hereby arrest you for the murder of Ruth Knightly."

Mrs. Cross shrieked as she turned to the two women. She stared at Mariamne. "You!" she sputtered. "You dare! You'll never take her place!" And she swept the flaming candles against the drapes, then the bed hangings. They went up with a roar, almost drowning the housekeeper's hysterical laughter, creating a wall of flame between her and the two women. The police matron tried to reach Mrs. Cross, was driven back by the flames, took one look at the way the dry timbers of the ancient house were going up, and hustled Mariamne down the stairs and out to the car, where she radioed for help.

By the time the fire department arrived, it was too late. Wonderly was gutted. Peter was philosophical about it. "I don't think I could stand to live there anymore, knowing about Ruth. And now I'm free, my love. I'm not responsible for Ruth's death—not even as I thought I was for letting her leave in such anger. You've exorcized my ghosts, Mariamne!"

And Mariamne had a bit of news to cheer him further: "I'm going to have a baby!"

Her pregnancy was easy; any time she began feeling uncomfortable, she would think, *Time to call that devil up again!* and her discomfort would disappear. Even her labor was rapid—and then she and Peter had a daughter. They named the child Victoria, and doted over her. Though she had a nanny, Peter and Mariamne would often walk her themselves through the parks of London, where they now lived.

Mariamne was supremely happy. She loved her baby and her husband, and the house just off Berkeley Square that she was furnishing to her own taste. She did wish, sometimes, that Peter would not pester her about having a male heir when she had just got her figure back after Victoria—but she could put up with his lovemaking occasionally. While she loved to cuddle, she still did not care for the particulars required to conceive a child. But that was a minor matter, and did not serve to cloud her happiness.

Then, when Victoria was eighteen months old, Peter dropped dead of a heart attack. This time Mariamne did conjur up her devil.

"You've broken the contract!" she accused, her lovely eyes swollen with tears of genuine grief. "I was supposed to have ten full years of love and happiness! There are almost six years to go, and my life is ruined forever!"

"Tut, tut!" said the devil. "Re-read your contract, my dear. It doesn't say love and happines. It says love and adventure and excitement. It's over two years since you had the kind of adventure and excitement appropriate to heroines of romantic novels."

"But I don't *want* that anymore!" Mariamne wailed. "I want Peter!"

"Sorry—what's in the contract is what we will provide."

In despair, Mariamne joined the demi-monde of gamblers in Monte Carlo. There she quickly met a Greek tycoon who could not help being fascinated by the beautiful young widow. He was old enough to be her father, and he adored Victoria, for his own children were grown and gone.

Mariamne had enough money never to have to worry for herself or Victoria—but Plato Parnassus moved in a world in which yachts were trinkets given as tips to servants, and no one thought of money in any terms smaller than millions. In his own gruff way, Plato assured Mariamne that he understood she would never love him like the lost love of her life—but the place he offered her as his wife was too appealing to refuse.

To Mariamne's horror, once he was her husband, the old man who had never done more than kiss her hand expected sex. Expected it morning, noon, and night, in bed, in the swimming pool, and in the courtyard under the Mediterranean moon. And he was not to be put off by headaches. "Sexual tension," he would assure her. "Best thing for it is a glass of champagne and a good lay!" And he would lower his gross, hairy body over hers once again.

Fortunately, when they had been married only eight months, Plato jetted off on a business trip, to Mariamne's relief at the thought of a whole week without his demands. His private jet crashed in the Caucasus Mountains, and Mariamne was a widow for the third time.

She decided she would never marry again. By now she was so incredibly wealthy that only the World Bank could guess at her true worth. Whole platoons of secretaries and accountants cared for her finances, while she cared for Victoria.

Mariamne vacationed in Italy when Victoria was four—and there the little girl was kidnapped. Alfonso Martini, the Italian police captain who handled the case, insisted that paying the ransom would not assure the child's safety. Mariamne tagged along with Alfonso on the trail, which led to a car chase through the mountains and a shootout at the hideaway—but Victoria was rescued unharmed.

In relief and gratitude, Mariamne had a brief affair with Alfonso—but the passion of gratitude quickly faded. He was a poor man, but proud. She tried to give him money, a house, a car, but he would have none of it. He did, however, take her to the orphanage in which he had been raised, and where he now did volunteer work. Mariamne donated money enough to repair the old buildings, add several new ones, and set up a scholarship trust so that all the children could be educated.

The gratitude of the nuns and the children stirred some new feeling in Mariamne, and she set out to distribute more of her wealth in worthy causes. She went into earthquake and disaster areas, often having hair's-breadth escapes, and became famous as a modern Lady Bountiful. Doctors, administrators, volunteer workers—every attractive man she met fell in love with her, but she merely touched their lives and moved on, leaving their passion unconsummated. Young, beautiful, loved by all, and yet untouchable—Mariamne was happier than she had ever been before.

It was now more than nine years since Mariamne had made her pact with the devil. Victoria was six, going on seven. One day Mariamne found that she did not want to get out of bed in the morning. Her energy seemed to be gone. At first the doctors insisted there was nothing wrong, but when her fatigue persisted, they sent her to a famous clinic in Massachusetts—the first time she had been back in her home state since she had become Mariamne.

Several doctors worked on her case, but she was officially in the care of Dr. Stanley Welton, Jr., a young genius who believed in holistic medicine, and hence fell holistically in love with Mariamne. He did test after test, until he found the cause of her debilitating weakness: a rare disease she could have contracted only on one of her missions of mercy to the tropics. There was no known cure. She would simply weaken until she died, without pain.

And without losing her beauty, she saw in the mirror. As she grew pale, her eyes seemed to become huge. Her hair remained glossy and thick, and even on the days when she could not find strength to put on makeup, she looked lovely, ethereal, her bonds with life already tenuous.

Stanley spent many hours in her room, and stretched hospital rules so that Victoria could come and visit her mother. Her little girl was Mariamne's only regret—her will guaranteed the child the best schools, all material needs, but who would be mother or father to her?

She spoke of her worries to Stanley, and he in turn unburdened his heart about his rift with his father, a hard-boiled businessman who had expected his only son to become a lawyer in the family's corporate empire. When Stanley applied to medical school instead of law school, his father disowned him, and Stanley struggled through on his own.

Without Stanley's knowledge, Mariamne sent for Stanley Welton, Sr. As she was probably the only woman in the world who was richer than he was, he obeyed her summons. She introduced him to Victoria, who was already showing signs of becoming as beautiful as her mother, and then sent the child from the room.

"Mr. Welton," Mariamne began, "you probably thought I sent for you to discuss some financial investment. I didn't. I called you to show you an emotional investment that I am losing: my child. You have a child, Mr. Welton. He is brilliant, a genius—and you deny him. I'm dying, Mr. Welton, but my child is at my side, and has had every moment of my love that I can give her. When you die, Mr. Welton, will your son be at your side?"

Within a few minutes, Mariamne had the stiff-lipped Stanley Welton, Sr. reduced to tears and promises to make up with his son. In the midst of that, however, Stanley burst into the room, his eyes flashing fire. "How dare you?" he demanded of Mariamne. "What gives you the right to interfere between my father and me?"

"Stanley," choked out Stanley, Sr., "this gives her the right—son," and he clasped the young doctor into a hug so awkward that Mariamne wondered if he'd ever done it before.

So father and son were reunited, and Stanley found even more reason to love Mariamne, who now had only a few more days to live. "Mariamne," he told her, "I want to marry you. That way I can adopt Victoria, and she will have a father and a grandfather to love her and care for her. But most of all, I want you as my own, even just for these few days."

So they were married, in Mariamne's hospital room—and six days later Mariamne died, her daughter weeping on one side of the bed, and the Stanleys, Jr. and Sr., weeping on the other as the muzak played a lilting minor-key melody. She was granted a vision of the news stories and television documentaries mourning her untimely death in the midst of her good works—and then she was in hell, face to face with her devil.

She looked around. Hell, at first glance, did not seem such a terrible place. She was in a room with a fireplace for the only light, and a huge bed heaped with cushions. She was naked, she realized, her hands automatically assuming the Venus-on-the-half-shell position as suspicion stirred at the back of her mind as to what her punishment would be: the part of her ten-year spree that she had disliked the most.

The devil laughed wickedly. "Welcome to eternity, Mary Sue Clyatt. Did you ever make out the fine print in our standard contract for the twentieth century love-starved female?"

As she shook her head, the devil grinned, and three forms approached out of the shadows. Three naked men: Ricardo . . . Peter . . . Plato! All held out their arms to her, and Mariamne backed off, gritting her teeth with the knowledge that, her contract fulfilled, she must now accept her punishment.

"Others will join you later, my dear," said the devil, "after they're dead. All those men, all madly in love with you—" Mariamne cringed, but the devil took no notice, "—but with one small difference, you see. For ten years you got all you wanted, any time you wanted. You 'modern females.' You 'liberated women.' Sex, sex, sex, eh? Well, just try to relieve your frustrations now, my dear! This is what it said in the fine print!"

He waved his hand, and the fire flared, suddenly illuminating the room, penetrating the shadows that had hidden all their private parts. Mariamne stared. The three men *had* no private parts! She stared down at herself . . . felt. . . . It was true! They were, every one of them, as featureless as Barbie and Ken dolls!

The men were reaching for her, as the devil howled with laughter. "Mariamne!" "My beloved!" "My one true love!" She was held, caressed, smothered in kisses, pulled down onto the bed in a tangle of limbs—but nothing more could happen—ever!

It was an adolescent girl's dream come true: an eternity of cuddling and kissing with devoted men, without ever having to put up with sex. Mariamne laughed joyfully, and surfaced long enough to inform the disgruntled devil, "I never wanted to be liberated! All I ever wanted was to be loved. Thanks for fulfilling the contract, though—'cause if this is hell, don't you ever try to make me go to heaven!"

# ISHIGBI

## *by Charles Saunders*

*When we think of witches, most of us think of old crones, black cats, broomsticks, and all the paraphernalia of a dime-store Halloween, or of Hansel and Gretel. Or we think of witch-burnings in medieval Europe, or the hysteria in Salem, Massachusetts. Few of us, however, might think of the witches in Africa.*

*Charles Saunders, however, remedies that. For the past five years, his stories in Lin Carter's* The Year's Best Fantasy Stories *(DAW 1975, 1977),* Heroic Fantasy, The Year's Best Horror Stories, Swords Against Darkness *(Zebra Press), and* Amazons! *have been masterful evocations of African magic and warfare, the result of his long study of history, anthropology, mythology, and folklore. Most recently this fascination has taken the form of a novel,* Imaro, *which DAW scheduled for 1981 release.*

*"Ishigbi" concentrates on an aspect of the supernatural unique in this anthology: twin magic. Among some tribes, twins are considered to be witches from the moment of their birth. In cultures that regard witchcraft as harmful, such twins are either killed or cast out. To this story of witch-twins, Charles adds the psychological link that specialists have shown unites twins, even if they have not seen one another for years. And the result is definitely double trouble.*

*Born in 1946, Charles Saunders is one of the most distinguished of the younger generations of fanta-*

*sists like Galad Elflandsson (another Ottawan) and C.J. Cherryh whose knowledge of languages, history, and magical lore adds resonance and depth to their stories of the arcane, the occult, and the fearsome.*

The trees grew stark and pale in the Spirit Grove, their ash-colored boles reflecting dim moonlight, their single tufts of leaves spreading like crowns of black spikes in the night sky. Here dwelt the Ancestors of the city of Aduwura. In silence the Ancestors slept beneath the pale palm trees that nurtured them until Odomankoma, God of Death, permitted them to live again. In silence the Ancestors slept as the feet of the defiler stalked purposefully between the trees.

The defiler was not of Aduwura, nor any other Akan city. Akan women were stout; this one was long and lean as a cheetah. Akan women wore bright-patterned garments that swathed their entire bodies; this one was naked save for a brief skin loincloth and a leather neck-thong from which a pair of baboon skulls hung over flat, sagging breasts. Akan women wove their hair into scores of tiny plaits; this one's shaved scalp glistened in the moonlight. Akan women spoke softly in the Spirit Grove (as did Akan men); this one muttered maledictions in a low, feral snarl. . . .

When the defiler reached her destination—a shallow, green-scummed pond in the midst of the trees—she halted and laid down the large skin bag she carried over one bony shoulder. Reaching into the opening of the bag, she extricated a large calabash and an iron fang of a dagger with a dully-gleaming blade. The defiler laid the dagger aside and dipped the calabash into the stagnant pond, filling the vessel halfway to its brim. Carefully she removed the algae scum, dipping the end of her loincloth into the water until the surface was clear. Despite her advanced age, the defiler's movements were fluid. But her face was a seamed mask of malice, disfigured by burn scars.

Once again, her hand curled around the hilt of the dagger.

Eyes closed, she sat still. Then, from her pursed lips came a call, a high-pitched, trilling whine. The call was answered. . . .

It was a *dik-dik* that answered the summons of the defiler: an antelope the size of a small dog, with a delicately-tapered muzzle and tiny, pointed horns. The *dik-dik*, sacred to the Ancestors, advanced reluctantly toward the defiler. The trilling whine continued until the antelope came within the woman's reach. Abruptly her eyes opened, the trilling ceased, and the trembling *dik-dik* tensed for a single, prodigious bound to safety. But the defiler's hand moved with cobra quickness.

The *dik-dik's* head flew into the pond. Swiftly the defiler seized the small, convulsing body. Holding its severed neck directly over the calabash, the defiler allowed the antelope's blood to pour into the water until wine-dark liquid lapped its brim. Then she discarded the carcass, tossing it into the pond. Its splash seemed . . . muted.

The defiler chanted an incantation, strange syllables spilling from her lips. Although she did not touch the calabash, the water began to swirl. The dark surface reflected the moonlight with mirror brightness. Images began to form in the blood-water: images that remained stable despite the stirring of the surface. The defiler raised her reddened blade. . . .

Blood had been spilled in the Spirit Grove. And the Ancestors slept. And Odomankoma remained silent.

Aduwura throbbed with the exuberance of the Yam Festival. The sounds of revelry overwhelmed the low murmur of the nearby Ogopo River. Masked dancers cavorted through the streets in celebration of the planting of new crops and in anticipation of the blessing of Onyame the Sky-God and Mawu-Lesa, twin dieties of the sun and moon. Drums pulsed a beat of rhythmic joy; maize-beer and palm-wine were quaffed with uncaring abandon; songs were sung with bleary enthusiasm; love was made with reckless passion. For the Yam Festival was a time of renewal for the Akan, a time when the cares of the past rain could be momentarily forgotten.

In the house of Ekupanin, the *akuapem* or sub-chief of Aduwura, the Festival was observed with more decorum. Beneath the roof of woven straw, the *akuapem* entertained the important personages, the people-with-name, of his city.

The wide *gyaase*, or inner yard, was filled with clan heads, weapon-leaders, traders, and diviners, all bedecked in their finest robes of patterned *adinkra* cloth. Light from several fire-pits flashed sun-like against golden ornaments weighting black arms left bare by the *adinkra*. Ekupanin sat on a double-curved stool; the others rested cross-legged on mats of rattan.

Ekupanin's guests were quieter than the revellers outside because they were listening to a drum-poem played by Kwomo, son of the *akuapem*. The intricate patterns of beats were as easily understood by the Akan as their spoken language. The poem was a tribute to the Sky-God: a retelling of the departure of Onyame from the earth to the heavens.

Kwomo was a skillful drummer; while he filled the *gyaase* with the pulses of his drum-phrases, the assembled dignitaires of Aduwura paid less heed to their gossip and gourds of maize beer. Yet the attention of Kwomo's father was focused elsewhere. Ekupanin, a burly man whose body was slowly surrendering to fat, stared intently at Kipchoge the healer.

Aware of the *akuapem's* gaze, Kipchoge refused to meet Ekupanin's eyes. *Kipchoge*, the sub-chief mused. A name as exotic as the man. Among the short, stocky Akan, Kipchoge stood out like a heron among guinea-fowl. His lean, angular frame seemed lost amid the folds of his *adinkra*. His ascetic features seemed pinched and narrow next to the broad features of the Akan. And his skin was the color of polished mahogany, not the ebony or umber of the people of the Forest Kingdoms.

Kipchoge was a man of the east, where the plains stretched as far as the eye could see and the mountains brushed the sky. Long before the birth of Ekupanin, Kipchoge had come to Aduwura. Ekupanin's father had discovered the stranger lying naked and senseless near the Spirit Grove. The Akan were a hospitable people; they nursed the stranger back to health, taught him their speech, found use for his uncanny skills as a healer, and finally accepted him as an Akan whose soul would one day sleep in the grove near which he was found. Kipchoge had married Ekupanin's aunt, Salifah. She sat at the healer's side in the *gyaase*, along with Adjei, their son.

Adjei was an *asufo*, a soldier in the army of the Ashanti, overlords of the Akan. He had come home from the nearby *asufo* garrison to be with his parents during the Festival.

Rather than *adinkra*, Adjei wore the leopard-spotted armor and snarling helmet of his trade. With the height of his father and the face of his mother, Adjei cut a commanding figure as he sat at stiff-backed attention.

Ekupanin frowned at the sight of *asufo* armor. Long ago, the Akan had dominated the Ashanti. Two centuries past, the lesser clan had conquered, and now all the forest kingdom bore the Ashanti name. For many Akan, the old wound was still sore. Now, though, Ekupanin shared the concern of Adjei and Salifah for Kipchoge.

Though the only sign of age the healer showed was the white wooly hair thatching his skull, Kipchoge appeared many rains older this night. There was a tremor in his hands. From time to time, his body would slump forward, then jerk into an erect posture as though he were fighting sleep . . . or worse. He held his hand against the bridge of his nose.

Yet neither sub-chief nor wife nor son attempted to aid the healer. To do so before Onyame had heard the entire drum-poem was unthinkable.

With a final eloquent flourish, Kwomo completed his tribute to the Sky-God. Before the sound of the last drumbeat died, Kipchoge suddenly clutched both hands to his face, shrieked in agony, and toppled forward, sprawling across his rattan mat.

Instantly Salifah and Adjei bent to aid the healer. Ekupanin rose ponderously from his stool and strode quickly to the fallen Kipchoge. Close behind the *akuapem* came Kofi the diviner.

"Kipchoge!" Salifah cried into the prone man's ear. The healer remained inert, giving no sign of having heard his wife's call.

"Help me turn him over," she ordered the men. Anxiety marked her round ebony face. Adjei and Kofi bent to roll Kipchoge onto his back.

The healer lay slack and unmoving, his hands still covering his face. Gently, Salifeh moved her husband's hands to his sides . . . and gasped at the expression on his face. Kipchoge's eyes were shut tight, and his lips were peeled back from his teeth in a grimace of pain. The small crowd that had gathered around the healer and his family echoed Salifah's gasp.

Salifah touched her husband's face . . . and with a sharp

cry of dismay, she drew back her hand as if she had just touched a coal from the fire pits.

Adjei grasped his mother by the shoulders and turned her to face him.

"What is it?" he demanded. "What is wrong with the Old One?"

Salifah rubbed her thumb across the bottom of her fingers, as if wiping at some liquid substance.

"I felt blood on his face," she replied in a frightened whisper. "I felt blood . . . but *there is nothing there!*"

In the Spirit Grove, the defiler withdrew her blade from the water in the calabash. Slowly the image of Kipchoge's anguished face disappeared in a welter of ripples.

The defiler smiled. She poured the blood-water back into the pond; she no longer had need of it. Still sitting, she began to rock back and forth, the baboon skulls bumping against her bony chest. Again she called, this time in a sibilant whisper like the swish of a serpent through dry grass.

There was no wind, yet the trunks of the pale trees soon swayed in rhythm to the rocking of the defiler. The spiky crowns of leaves rustled as though they were shaking out the souls of the Ancestors of Aduwura. The defiler's hissing chant continued unabated.

Odomankoma remained silent.

But the Ancestors slept no longer. . . .

Kipchoge opened his eyes slowly. A thin furrow of pain bisected his face from forehead to lips. Automatically he reached up to wipe away blood no one could see.

A ring of concerned faces peered down at him: his wife, his son, the *akuapem* Ekupanin, and Kofi the diviner. At once, Kipchoge realized he was no longer in Ekupanin's *gyaase*.

"Where am I?" Kipchoge asked, wincing at a new flare of pain between his eyes.

"You are in the *abosonnan*," Kofi replied.

"The god-shrine? Why did you bring me to the god-shrine?" the healer demanded. The accent that always underlay his speech was markedly pronounced.

"Do you not remember what happened?" cried Salifah. "You were listening to the drum-poem, looking as though you were coming down with dengue. Then you screamed, clutched your face, and collapsed."

A shudder shook Kipchoge's lean frame. Salifah cried out in alarm, for it seemed her husband was about to lose consciousness again. With a visible effort, however, he calmed himself.

"Salifah touched your face and felt blood that could not be seen," Kofi said. "That is why we brought you to the *abosonnan*. This is obviously a matter of *ohoni*—witchcraft. You will be protected in the god-shrine."

Kipchoge held his hands in front of his eyes. On his right hand, he could feel blood trickling down his palm. On his left, he felt nothing. On neither hand did he see blood. . . .

Suddenly the healer sat bolt upright, limbs trembling, eyes bulging in fear.

"*She* has found me," he croaked almost inaudibly. "Even after so many rains, still she has found me. . . ."

"*Who* has found you, Kipchoge?" Salifah demanded sharply.

"Yes," Ekupanin added, speaking for the first time. "I think it is time you gave us some answers, Kipchoge."

"Answers!" shouted Salifah, her jealousy momentarily overcome by anger. "Can't you see my husband is ill? Would you slay him before his sickness does?"

"*Ohoni* is more than a matter of sickness," Ekupanin replied imperturbably. "Only when Kofi knows more about what has struck your husband down will he be able to heal the healer."

Both Salifah and Adjei opened their mouths to speak, but before they could, Kipchoge held up a shaking hand, indicating that they should remain silent. Then he leaned back to a supine position, though his eyes remained alert, restless—and afraid.

"You will have your answers, Ekupanin . . . the answers your father sought but never gained. You will have answers I denied even my own family, though the questions remained unspoken. . . ."

Salifah and Adjei exchanged a troubled glance. Never before had Kipchoge indicated that he knew of their unrequited curiosity concerning his origin and his unsurpassed skill as a healer.

"After your father found me by the Spirit Grove,

Ekupanin, I said I did not know where I came from. Later, when I learned more of your language, I 'remembered' pieces of my past, but not its entirety . . . like fragments of a shattered pot that do not all fit together again. That was the first—and only—lie I ever told to my adopted people.

"Look you to the shrine," Kipchoge commanded.

All eyes turned to the triple dais in the center of the *abosonnan*. Dimly illuminated by a single fire-pit, the daises held objects sacred to three deities. On the center dais rested a large, circular shield of gold worked in curious glyphs and designs. This was the *afrafokonmu*, the Washer of Souls, symbol of Onyame the Sky-God.

Flanking the Washer of Souls were two ebony carvings, each about a foot and a half high. They were stylized human forms, the bodies of which were cylinders with two stubby protuberances signifying arms. The heads, of a piece with the rest of the carvings, were large flat discs. The features, mere lines cut into the black wood, conveyed a distinct impression of peace and serenity. On the legless torso of one, a suggestion of breasts was carved; on the other, male genitals. Between them stretched a long chain of wooden links that joined the two images at the arms. These were representations of Mawu-Lesa, twin deities of sun and moon.

"Among you Akan, boy-girl twins are regarded as a blessing, for they are living images of Mawu-Lesa. But for the Gikuyu, the people of my birth, such twins are cursed. I was one of such a pair. . . ."

Again, troubled glances were exchanged over Kipchoge's head. The healer had spoken of his homeland as an endless, golden plain where the sun smiled and great herds of animals roamed free of mankind. To the Akan, in their forest and sea-girt enclave, such a country seemed unlikely at best. Never before had Kipchoge spoken of a darker side to his homeland.

"The Elders would have slain my sister and me outright the moment we were pulled from our mother's womb," Kipchoge continued. "For the Gikuyu believe boy-girl twins are born *mganga*—witches. But before the knife of death reached our throats, the priest of Mungu, the God-above-Gods, saw a sign; an omen.

"At the moment of our birth, two crested cranes had flown over our village. Cranes are sacred to the Gikuyu; the priest divined that to slay us would earn the Gikuyu Mungu's wrath. Yet the Gikuyu could not keep us with them, for we were cursed. So they sent us to the Mahli-ya-Ukoma—the Place of Lepers.

"The lepers raised us, my sister Ishigbi and I. But as we grew, the rotting disease did not strike us, and the lepers feared us for we were *mganga.* They, too, drove us from them. We were barely old enough to fend for ourselves.

"Together Ishigbi and I wandered through lands dangerous even for armed warriors, yet we two children passed unharmed through those lands. Finally we came to the shores of the Great Nyanza, a lake as large as the Gulf of Otongi that lies north of here. There, we met a crested crane that turned into a man. He was a *mganga*: the chief of *mgangas*. Kambui was his name. He said he had been waiting for us. He said the cranes that had flown over the village at our birth were *mganga* who had foretold our coming. Kambui asked us to come with him to live among other *mganga* and learn their ways. We, who had been cast out by lepers, agreed.

"And so we dwelt among our own kind. The *mganga* lived on an island in the Nyanza. So great was their *mchawi*—magic—that only a *mganga* could see the island. Ishigbi and I saw it. We grew and we learned. We learned how to call animals and make them do as we did. We learned how to change our shapes to animal form. We learned how to kill from afar, to cause disease, to shape and control the spirits of the dead. . . .

"We learned our lessons well, Ishigbi and I. Kambui said we would one day rival his own *mchawi*-skill. Yet I hated *mchawi* . . . hated being a *mganga.* Why I hated it, I did not know then, and do not know now. My sister pursued the knowledge the way Simba the lion pursues prey, for she hated those who had cast us out and she desired vengeance. I didn't. So I kept my studies of the other magic—*dawa*, the healing magic—secret even from her.

"Still, I was found out, by Kambui himself. To all the *mganga* on the island he denounced me, and ordered me banished from their midst. Ishigbi was banished with me, for Kambui considered her tainted by the sharing of my blood.

"When the *mganga* set us free on the mainland, my sister tried to kill me. She blamed me for our latest banishment. She was right, but I still did not want to die. My practice of *dawa* had weakened my *mchawi*; Ishigbi was much stronger than I. Still, I escaped by taking the form of a crane. I flew like a hunted thing, for Ishigbi pursued me in the form of an eagle. In the sky, I could not change shape; despite my best efforts, Ishigbi gained on me.

"Then Mungu caused a lightning storm, even though it was the dry season. Mungu's Spear, the lightning, knocked Ishigbi out of the sky. I flew on, not looking back. Day after day I flew, passing over lands unlike any I had seen before. I tired; I hungered; yet ever onward I flew. For Ishigbi was a powerful *mganga*. Even Mungu's Spear might not have finished her.

"Finally, exhausted, I, too, dropped out of the sky, coming to earth near your Spirit Grove, where Ekupanin's father found me near death. And I have lived here, practicing my true calling and hoping that Mungu's Spear truly slew my sister. For I knew that if she survived, she would seek me out; no matter the marches she had to travel, no matter how many rains washed her life. If she lived, Ishigbi would find me . . . and she has! The knife-that-strikes-from-afar. . . . the blood-that-is-not-seen . . . it is *mchawi*, I know it well . . . it is Ishigbi.

"And now I will be banished from Aduwura, as I was from the Gikuyu and the lepers and the *mganga*. I must go because of what I am, and what I have now brought upon you."

Kipchoge fell silent then. And among them his wife, his son, his chieftain, and his colleague could not muster a single word.

Ishigbi glided like a ghost toward the unwalled city. Behind her marched an army of shadows, streaming from the Spirit Grove like a horde of wild dogs on the track of a wounded gnu. The shadows were her servants; her will was their will. She dispatched thoughts into their death-dimmed minds, directing their movements as a commander directs troops. At her bidding, the shadows surrounded the city in a dark circle.

No longer did Aduwura pulse with the excitement of the Yam Festival. News of Kipchoge's sudden collapse had spread swiftly among the revellers. Sobered by the healer's misfortune, a sizable crowd stood in silent vigil near the *abosonnan*.

The three sentries who guarded the road into Aduwura were also preoccupied with Kipchoge's condition. None of them noticed the hunched shapes creeping stealthily toward them. Only when lithe, powerful figures suddenly sprang toward them did the sentries become aware of the doom about to be unleashed upon Aduwura.

Ishigbi's lips twisted in a smile of anticipation.

Tha Ancestors of Aduwura walked.

And Odomankoma remained silent.

Salifah was the first to speak after Kipchoge ended his grim narration.

"Cast you out?" she said, cradling his thin body in her arms. "Never! Not while I live and have name. I will slay this Ishigbi myself if she seeks to harm you!"

"And I, also, Old One," said Adjei, laying his hand on the hilt of his sword.

Kofi the diviner turned to Ekupanin. "This could well become dangerous for us, my *akuapem*," he said in a low voice. "Suppose this sister of Kipchoge's decides to strike at us, too? What do we do then?"

Before Ekupanin could reply, a scream of terror tore through the night, followed immediately by a chorus of similar cries. Kofi and Ekupanin rushed to the doorway of the *abosonnan*. Adjei was about to follow, then he remembered his father. Once again, Kipchoge had struggled to a sitting position.

"Help me up," he ordered Adjei and Salifah.

"But you're sick, Old One. You're still too weak to . . ."

At the expression that crossed his father's face then, Adjei bowed his head and lifted Kipchoge to his feet. Together, he and Salifah helped Kipchoge to the doorway. What they saw outside the shrine caused even Adjei to shudder in dread.

Horror had invaded Aduwura . . . horror in the form of leaping, rending monstrosities rendered all the more ghastly by their unmistakable resemblance to humankind. So swiftly did they move that their appearance was revealed only for fleeting instants—yet those instants were more than sufficient to unravel the courage of even the boldest.

The invaders were man-sized, but went on all fours. Their smooth, naked skin was slate-grey in hue, as were the tangles of hair sprouting from their sloping skulls. Beastlike talons tipped their fingers, and doglike snouts jutted from faces otherwise human in conformation. The creatures swarmed over the people of Aduwura. Blood fountained from slashed throats, spattering against the white clay walls of the houses. Hearts were torn from chests pierced by iron talons; limbs and heads tumbling through the air like rotten, dripping fruit. . . .

The celebrating Akan had swiftly been transformed into a shrieking, terror-mad mob. Most were pulled down from behind by the rampaging beast-things. Others who had retained weapons even on a night of revelry hacked and stabbed at their snouted tormentors, opening great, gaping wounds from which no blood flowed. Like a flood at the height of the wet season, the melee swirled around the *abosonnan*.

"Look after the Old One, Mother," Adjei said as he released his grip on his father's shoulder.

Before Salifah could protest, the *asufo* unsheathed his sword and plunged into a knot of beast-things attacking a group of desperately battling Akan. Adjei's sword decapitated one of the monstrosities. Two others leaped on him, but his armor thwarted their fangs and claws. Heartened by Adjei's courage, other armed Akan clustered around him, and together they began to take a toll on the grey creatures, though the invaders seemed impossible to kill.

"That will not help, old friend," Kipchoge said. "These are *tuyobene*—living dead. They are the spirits of your ancestors, given shape and purpose by the *mchawi* of Ishigbi."

"*Those* . . . are . . . my . . . *ancestors*?" Kofi choked.

"She has warped them to her own ends, Kofi. They do not know what they are doing. My son and the others are brave, but they cannot kill the *tuyobene*, for the *tuyobene* are already dead."

"*You* brought this upon us!" snarled Ekupanin, bitterness overcoming his fear. "It is *you* your sister seeks, not us. Where is your healing now, *outlander*?"

"You dare," Salifah hissed between clenched teeth. Before she could further berate her nephew, Kipchoge spoke.

"Only *mchawi* can offset *mchawi*. And there is still *mchawi* left in me. After all these rains, I can feel it. I am still a *mganga*. Ekupanin: will you denounce me or be the *akua-*

*pem*? I will try to stop the *tuyobene*; you must get all your people out of the city."

Turning from Ekupanin, Kipchoge looked at Salifah. "When I came to Aduwura, I made a vow to Mungu never again to make use of *mchawi*. If I use it now, I will never again be able to heal."

"Do it," Salifah said. "You will still be the same man."

"It's too late, healer!" shouted Kofi. "They are coming for *us* now!"

Half a dozen *tuyobene*, their muzzles dripping Akan blood, leaped with appalling swiftness toward the *abosonnan*. Salifah screamed and tightened her arms around her husband's waist. Kofi and Ekupanin raised trembling arms in a futile gesture of self-defense.

Kipchoge swung his arm in a slashing motion. It was as though he had materialized a taut, unseen wire in front of the *tuyobene*: in mid-leap they halted abruptly and tumbled to the ground.

Kipchoge stood straight and steady, his pain and fear forgotten. The old, dark ecstasy of the stirring of his *mchawi* warred with his deep loathing of that joy. He thrust the loathing aside. Again, his arms slashed the air, this time in a raising motion, and he spoke a word of command that echoed over the cries of the beleaguered Akan.

The *tuyobene* halted their attacks . . . *and suddenly rose two feet from the ground*, where they dangled like fish caught on a line.

"Run! Now!" Kipchoge shouted. And he shoved Salifah toward Ekupanin, who reflexively grasped her in his arms.

"Go! All of you! There's nothing more you can do here," the healer repeated. "But do not run near the river!"

"Yes, run!" Ekupanin shouted. "Do as he says . . . *now*!"

The authority conveyed in the *akuapem's* voice galvanized the Akan; almost as one, they fled the blood-splotched streets, carrying the wounded with them, leaving the dead behind.

Adjei was not among those who fled. The *asufo* lay facing the sky, his throat opened by the fangs of a *tuyobene*.

Salifah fought savagely in the grasp of her nephew as he bore her away from the carnage.

"Kipchoge, Kipchoge, I cannot leave you," she wailed. But Ekupanin would not let her go.

Kipchoge did not hear her. He knew the *tuyobene* would not be long forestalled by his spell . . . not against power such as Ishigbi's. Within moments, she would free them from their bonds and they would course like hounds through the bush, hunting down the fleeing Akan. But Kipchoge had never intended to wrest control of the *tuyobene* from Ishigbi.

His mouth opened; his tongue flicked against the roof of his mouth; his voice emerged in a chant that sounded eerily as though it were being spoken underwater: "*Lolololololololo-lolololololololololololololololo. . . .*"

Through the quiet that suddenly enveloped Aduwura, the answer to Kipchoge's summons came. Loud splashing from the river . . . thunderous bellows louder than the roar of a lion . . . the crash of heavy bodies moving swiftly through the bush . . . Kipchoge knew then that his *mchawi* was successful. He re-entered the *abosonnan* just as the *tuyobene* were released from his binding.

Then the first of the crocodiles entered Aduwura. Like a scaly green tide, the giant reptiles attacked the *tuyobene.* Huge jaws closed on writhing gray forms, tearing them in half. Silently the *tuyobene* struck back, fastening their doglike fangs on the throats of the crocodiles and rending scale-armored hides with their razor-sharp claws. The dead of Aduwura were trampled into the mire as the supernatural battled mindlessly against the untamed.

One of the *tuyobene* detached itself from the maelstrom of snapping jaws and loped toward the *abosonnan.* As it approached the shrine, the creature rose to its hind legs, wavered, changed, *stretched* until the lean form of Ishigbi stood naked in the moonight. *Mchawi* radiated in an unseen nimbus; neither crocodile nor *tuyobene* dared to approach her.

"Brother!" she shouted stridently. "Do you think to hide in the shrine of these people's puny gods? Come out and face me, or I will burn you and your gods with you! I will burn you with Mungu's Spear, as you once burned me!"

Kipchoge emerged from the *abosonnan.* In his hands he bore the images of Mawu-Lesa, still linked by the long wooden chain.

"Sister, it was Mungu who hurled his spear at you; not I," he said calmly. "And my *mchawi* is still alive in me, for all that I have denied it. I have called the crocodiles to put an end to your *tuyobene*. And you: for the sake of vengeance, you have corrupted the souls of a people's ancestors—*my people!* No *mganga*, not even Kambui, would have committed so great a crime. Sister, you have finally taught me the meaning of hate. . . ."

"Worth it, worth it to see your suffering and your end," cried Ishigbi. Then she dropped to all fours and became a lioness.

Like a tongue of tawny flame, she launched herself at Kipchoge's throat. Yet with a swiftness belying his age, Kipchoge sidestepped the leap and looped the chained god-images around the throat of the lioness. But he was unable to maintain a grip on her fur, and when she landed, Kipchoge fell several feet from her.

Kipchoge rose; before he could move farther, the lioness caught him across the ribs with a swipe of her paw. Bones broke; Kipchoge fell. Yet no outcry of pain escaped his lips even as the lioness opened his belly with a slash of her claws. Her jaws gaped, about to drive gleaming fangs into Kipchoge's face. Kipchoge smiled.

Suddenly the lioness screeched in pain. She rolled frantically along the ground, clawing vainly at the Mawu-Lesa images encircling her throat. For a moment, her shape altered: limbs lengthening, head shifting to quasi-human form. Then the transformation faded, and it was the face of a lioness that stared in feral hatred at the smiling face of Kipchoge.

"Have you guessed, Sister?" he said. With one hand he pulled aside the slashed cloth of his *adinkra*. At the center of his chest was a blood-crusted wound that had not been made by the lioness.

"I am already dead, Sister. In the shrine, I bled my soul into Mawu-Lesa; their power is bound to me. This body is a husk; it serves me as the *tuyobene* serve you. Do you feel Mawu-Lesa destroying you, Sister? Are the gods of the Akan still 'puny'?"

Then the body of Kipchoge collapsed, eyes closed, lips still smiling. The lioness writhed and mewled, her struggles growing progressively weaker. Around them, the crocodiles and the *tuyobene* warred savagely for possession of a city of the dead. . . .

When the survivors of Aduwura reached the garrison of the *asufos*, few believed their garbled tales of horror. But when the *akuapem* and the diviner both confirmed the gruesome account, and the survivors showed their peculiar wounds, the commander of the *asufos* decided to send one hundred armsmen to free Aduwura from the grasp of the creatures of Ishigbi. Of those who had fled Aduwura, only Ekupanin, Kofi, and Salifah ventured to accompany the *asufos*.

The sun rode high in the midday sky when the *asufos* arrived in Aduwura. Cautiously, spears upraised behind the protection of metal shields, they advanced into the city.

They found no life in Aduwura other than the crocodiles that retreated sullenly before the spears and the carrion-flies that infested dismembered corpses . . . or all that was left of them after the crocodiles had finished with them. Of the *tuyobene*, there was no sign.

Near the *abosonnan*, the searchers found two bodies strangely undisturbed by crocodiles or flies. One was Kipchoge, a serene smile fixed on his stiffened face. The other was a naked woman of an age with the healer. Despite the grimace of pain and the burn-scars distorting her features, the resemblance between her and Kipchoge was marked. Between them lay the twin images of Mawu-Lesa. The chain between them was broken.

At the sight of Kipchoge's corpse, Salifah tore the front of her *adinkra* and fell howling to her knees. Ekupanin, Kofi, and the commander of the *asufos* conferred in hushed tones. Shaken though they were, they yet agreed swiftly upon the things that had to be done. The commander spoke to his *asufos*. . . .

They dragged the mourning Salifah away from her husband. Later she would die of grief. They recovered the Washer of Souls from the *abosonnan*. This was still sacred, although the Mawu-Lesa were now profane. They placed the Mawu-Lesa in the *abosonnan* with the bodies of Kipchoge and Ishigbi, then they razed the shrine into a pile of rubble. They tore down the houses of Aduwura. Never again would the Yam Festival be celebrated there; never again would Kwomo's drum-poems be heard, for Kwomo was dead. They speared the crocodiles. They burned the Spirit Grove and slew the *dik-diks*, for they were defiled and therefore cursed.

The Ancestors of Aduwura slept beneath charred, smoking stumps. Never again would they be disturbed; never again would they live.

And, silently, Odomankoma accepted his due.

# BETHANE

## *by Katherine Kurtz*

*In medieval Europe, calling someone different was the first step in calling her a witch. If an old woman lived alone—or perhaps with a few animals for company or livelihood—and gathered herbs, chances were good that sooner or later, someone would notice that she was a trifle "strange," as villagers might define it. And to a superstitious people, strange meant dangerous.*

*In Gwynedd, the kingdom in which Katherine Kurtz's Deryni stories take place, we find Bethane, a woman who dwells alone. Like many other solitaries in Gwynedd, she is frightened and angry, and has reason to be. For she might be Deryni, and possess the powers of truth-reading, levitation, thought-transfer, and healing that have made humans fear and hate them, and caused large-scale massacres and persecutions. In Gwynedd, you see, people grow up on stories of how the Deryni usurper-kings oppressed people and on rabid sermons against the supernatural. To be Deryni in Gwynedd is frequently a death sentence.*

*So here is Bethane, a woman who might be a witch, and who has lost husband and child to the Deryni persecutions. She finds a quiet life and then along come four children to disturb her. This story, an interesting reversal of the Hansel and Gretel archetype of children meeting an evil witch, is about magic. And part of that magic is forgiveness.*

*When Katherine Kurtz is not writing stories about*

*Gwynedd to include in a series of novels, she is fending off frantic inquiries about when her next book will be out, riding, and participating—as Countess Bevin Fraser—in the Society for Creative Anachronisms.*

Old Bethane shaded her eyes with a gnarled hand and peered out across the meadow with a frown. She had seen the approaching children before. Two of them were sons of the Duke of Cassan; she didn't know about the other two. This time, the four were racing their shaggy mountain ponies across her meadow at a mad gallop, beginning to scatter the scraggly sheep she had spent all morning collecting.

A low growl rose in her throat as she saw one of the boys lean down and whoop at a grazing ewe and her lamb. The ewe bolted in terror and lumbered out of the pony's way, the lamb scampering after, and Bethane lurched to her feet, brandishing her shepherd's crook at the girl child, who was almost upon her.

"Here, now! You stop that!"

The girl's pony stopped stock still, but the girl continued on over the animal's head, skirts all awry, to land in the grass with a thump as the pony whirled and retreated, bucking and squealing. Bethane grabbed the child's upper arm and hauled her to her feet, giving her a none-too-gentle shake.

"Got you now!" Bethane crowed. "What's the matter with you, riding through here like you owned the free air and frightening an honest woman's sheep? Well, speak up, girl! What do you have to say for yourself?"

As the girl raised wide blue eyes in astonishment, more stunned than hurt, the three boys came galloping toward her. The oldest looked to be twelve or so, though he carried himself like a soldier already. The other two were several years younger, one of them pale blond like the little girl.

"You let my sister alone!" the blond boy shouted, yanking his pony to a halt and glaring at Bethane quite fiercely.

"You'd better not hurt her!" the older boy chimed in. "She didn't mean any harm."

Bethane laughed, almost a cackle, and shook her head. "Not so fast, young masters. I'm owed an apology first." She glared at her captive. "What's your name, girl? What's the idea of chasing my sheep?"

The girl, perhaps five or six, swallowed visibly, not even glancing at her brother and the other two boys, though the hand of the eldest rested on the hilt of his dagger.

"I'm sorry, grand-dame," the girl said in a small voice. "We didn't know the sheep belonged to anyone. I mean, we knew they weren't Duke Jared's, but we didn't think they'd been herded. We thought they were just grazing free."

Bethane did not allow her expression to soften, but she did relax just a little inside. Perhaps the children had not come to torment her, after all.

"Oh, you did, did you?" she muttered. "Who are you, anyway?"

The eldest boy drew himself up a little haughtily in the saddle and gazed down at her from his advantage of height. "I am Kevin, Earl of Kierney." He nodded toward the other brown-haired boy. "This is my brother, Lord Duncan, and that's Lord Alaric Morgan, Bronwyn's brother. You'd better let her go," he added, a trifle less belligerently.

"Oh, I'd better, eh? Well, I'll tell you one thing, young Earl of Kierney. You'd better learn some manners, if you expect anyone to respect you for more than that high-sounding title you bear. What's your excuse for chasing my poor little ewes?"

As the young earl's mouth gaped—she could tell he was not often spoken to in that manner—his brother moved his pony a little closer and swept off his leather hunt cap in a polite bow.

"Please pardon us, grand-dame. We are all to blame. It was thoughtless on our part. How can we make amends?"

Slowly Bethane released the little girl's arm, studying her and the three boys a little suspiciously. What was there about these children that raised her hackles so? Something fey, something she had not sensed in a long time. . . .

But, no matter. Hitching up her greyed and tattered skirts, she leaned against her shepherd's crook and continued to eye them sternly, determined not to speak until all four had backed down from her gaze. She did not have long to wait.

"Very well. Apology accepted. And to balance accounts, you can help gather up my sheep now, since you helped scatter them."

The blond boy nodded, no trace of resentment in his look. "A fair recompense, grand-dame. We'll see to it at once."

For the next little while, the children applied themselves diligently to the task at hand, eventually rounding up all the sheep they had scattered and even a few Bethane had missed. When they had finished, they spread their noon meal under a large tree across the meadow and settled down to eat. The little girl invited Bethane to join them, but the old woman shook her head wordlessly and retreated to her cave, overlooking the meadow. She wanted no such exalted company. Besides, the oldest boy, Kevin, obviously did not like her much. Only the little girl seemed genuinely concerned about an old widow woman's feelings, even bringing up a napkin full of fresh-baked bread and savory cheese when she and her companions were finished eating. She laid it on a smooth rock and made a graceful little curtsey before heading back down the hill without a word.

Bethane could hardly ignore such a gesture. Besides, she could smell the food. She found the bread soft and pale, so kind to old, jagged teeth and aching gums—bread such as she had not tasted since her youth, when she and Darrell first were wed. And the cheese—how he would have loved that!

With sweet memory for companion, she settled on a sunny ledge just outside the cave to enjoy the last morsels, basking in the summer warmth. The faint murmur of the children still playing in the meadow, the coolish breeze, and the glow of a full stomach soon lulled her to drowsiness, and the old eyes closed. With her wedding ring cradled close beside her cheek, she drifted. She could almost imagine she was young again, her Darrell lying at her side.

He had been a handsome man, perhaps the more so for being of the magical Deryni race, though she had been afraid of him at first. He had risked his life to save her from a life she still chose to forget. The love which had grown between them became a beacon for her soul, a positive focus for the knowledge which before had threatened to destroy her.

He had taught her things, too—a magic beyond the ancient

lore of midwifery and conjuring and divination handed down to her by mother and mother's mother. Though many of their methods had been similar, his powers had come from places she had never tapped; and she, in turn, had taught him how to bid the elemental forces—more homespun magic than the exalted theory and ceremony of the mysterious and much-feared Deryni, but it had worked as well, if in different ways. Together, they had dreamed of shaping a better world, where differences would not give others leave to kill. Perhaps their children would not need to live in fear, as they had done.

But there were to be no children; none that lived, at any rate. Too soon had come a renewed wave of madness in their village, condoned and even encouraged by the local lord. Darrell, unknown to be Deryni by most of their acquaintances, had been a teacher of mathematics in nearby Grecotha. With several of his Deryni colleagues, he also had been tutoring young children of his race in secret, though it was a capital offense against the law of Ramos if they were caught.

They had been betrayed. Agents of the local lord, all armored and ahorse, had raided the small farmhouse where the Deryni *schola* met, and slain the teacher schooling them that day. More than twenty children were captured and driven like sheep into a brush-filled pen in the village square; for the lord's man and the village priest meant to burn them as the heretics they surely were.

She remembered the smell of the oil-soaked wood in the pen, as she and Darrell huddled in the crowd which gathered to see sentence carried out. She saw again the looks of dull terror on the faces of the children, most of them no older than the girl Bronwyn and her brother now playing across the meadow. Her stomach churned in revulsion as it had so many years ago, as a line of guards bearing torches marched out of a courtyard behind the square and took up stations around the captive children. The guard captain and the village priest followed, the captain bearing a scroll with pendant seals and cords. The crowd murmured like a wild animal aroused, but the cry was not of horror but anticipation. In all their number, there was no one to plead the cause of these terrified little ones.

"Darrell, we have to do something!" she whispered in her

husband's ear. "We can't just let them burn. What if our child were among them?"

She was just seventeen, carrying their first child. Her husband's voice was tinged with despair as he shook his head.

"We are two. We can do nothing. They say the priest betrayed us. Even the confessional is not sacred where Deryni are concerned, it seems."

She bowed her head against his shoulder and covered one ear with a hand, trying to blot out the pious mouthings of priest and captain as holy words were spoken and writs of condemnation read. All pretense of legality and justice was but excuse for murder. The child she carried beneath her heart kicked, hard, and she cradled her arms across her abdomen as she began to sob, clinging to Darrell's arm.

Hoofbeats intruded then, and a disturbance behind them. She looked up to see a band of armed men forcing their horses through the crowd, more of them blocking the exits from the square—stern-looking horse-archers with little recurve bows, each with an arrow nocked to bowstring and more in quivers on their backs. At their head rode a fair-haired young man in emerald green, surely no older than herself. His eyes were like a forest in sunlight as he swept the crowd and urged his white stallion closer to the captain.

"It's Barrett! The young fool!" Darrell whispered, almost to himself. "Oh, my God, Barrett, don't do it!"

*Barrett?* she thought to herself. *Is the man Deryni?*

"Let the children go, Tarleton," the man named Barrett said. "Your master will not take kindly to children being slain in his name. Let them go."

Tarleton gazed back at him agog, his writ all but forgotten in one slack hand. "You have no authority here, Lord Barrett. These are *my* lord's vassals—Deryni brats! The land will be well rid of them."

"I said, let them go," Barrett repeated. "They can harm no one. How can these infants be heretics?"

"All Deryni are heretics!" the priest shouted. "How dare you interfere with the work of Holy Mother Church?"

"Enough, priest," Tarleton muttered. At his hand signal, the men holding the torches moved closer to the pen where the children huddled in terror, fire poised nearer the oil-soaked brush.

"I warn you, Barrett, do not interfere," Tarleton continued.

"The law says that those who defy the law of Ramos must die. Whether it happens to these now or later makes no difference to me, but if they die now, *you* doom them to die without blessing, their Deryni souls unshriven. You cannot stop their deaths. You can only make it worse for them."

No one moved for several seconds, the two men measuring one another across the short distance which separated them. Bethane could feel her husband's tension knotting and unknotting the muscles of his arm, and knew with a dull certainty which ached and grew that Barrett was not going to back down. The young lord glanced behind him at his men stationed all around, then dropped the reins on his horse's neck.

"I never *have* liked the law of Ramos," he said in a clear voice, casually raising both hands to head level as though in supplication.

Instantly he was surrounded by a vivid emerald fire which was visible even in the sunlit square. The gasp of reaction swept through the crowd like a winter wind, chill and fearsome. Tarleton reddened, and the village priest shrank back behind him, crossing himself furtively.

"By my own powers, which are everything those children have not realized, you shall not have those lives," Barrett stated. "This I swear. I can stop you with my powers, if I must, and save at least a few, but many others are likely to die who do not deserve such fate."

The crowd was beginning to look around uneasily for an escape, but Barrett's men had closed the perimeter even more tightly, guarding all exits from the square. There was no place to go.

"I give you this choice, however," Barrett continued, raising his voice above the rising murmur of dismay. "Release the children, allow my men to take them away to safety, and I will give myself into your hands as their ransom. Which will please your lord more? A handful of untrained children, who can do no harm to anyone? Or someone like myself, fully trained and able to wreak havoc any time I choose?—though I would not do so willingly, despite what I know you are thinking."

In the rising panic around them, no one heard Darrell's choked, "No!" except Bethane. Tarleton let the crowd seethe and mutter for several seconds, then held up a hand for silence. He was obviously unnerved by Barrett's implication that he was reading minds, but he put up a brave front, nonetheless. Gradually the crowd noises died down.

"So, the aristocratic Lord Barrett de Laney is a Deryni heretic himself," the captain said. "My lord was right not to trust you."

"Your lord must wrestle with his own conscience in the dark, morning hours, and answer for his own actions at the day of reckoning," Barrett replied.

"A prize, indeed," Tarleton continued, as though he had not heard. "But, how do I know that you would keep your part of the bargain? What good is the word of a Deryni?"

"What good is any man's word?" Barrett returned. "Mine has been my bond for as long as anyone has known me. I give you my word that if you allow my men to take these children out of here, I will surrender myself into your hands, and I will not use my powers to resist you. My word on that. My life for the lives of those children. I am able to face my God on those terms."

"You must be mad!" Tarleton replied, a menacing grin beginning to crease his face. "But I accept your terms. Guards, allow His Lordship's men to take the children. Archers, train your arrows on my Lord Barrett and see that he keeps his Deryni word. I have never heard that magic could stop a flight of arrows."

A half-dozen archers stepped from their vantage points on the roof to either side of Tarleton and covered the new hostage. The other guards murmured among themselves, but they obeyed, moving away from the pen to surround Barrett, though they would not approach too closely with the green fire of his magic flaring close about him. Methodically, Barrett's men rode in one at a time and took the children up in front of them, one child to each man, until the pen was empty and the last double-mounted horse had disappeared at a gallop down the main street. Four men remained, arrows still nocked to their little recurve bows. One of them saluted Barrett smartly.

"Sir, your orders will be carried out."

Barrett gave a quiet nod. "I thank you for your service and release you from all other orders. Go now."

The four bowed over their saddlebows, then wheeled as one and galloped off the way the others had gone. When the clatter of steel-shod hooves had died away, Barrett swung down from his horse and began walking slowly toward Tarleton. The crowd parted before him, even Tarleton and the priest backing off a few steps. When he had approached to within a few feet of them, he stopped and bowed his head. The fire died around him, and with his left hand he drew his sword hilt-first and extended it to Tarleton.

"I keep my word, Captain," he said, eyes blazing at the other man.

Tarleton gingerly took the weapon and moved back a pace, and instantly half a dozen of his men were moving in to grasp Barrett's arms and bind him.

"His eyes!" the priest hissed. "Evil! Evil! Beware his eyes, my lord!"

As the crowd took up the cry, Tarleton gestured curtly to his men and turned to lead them back into the yard. Barrett held his head high, but he stumbled as the guards manhandled him away from the crowd.

Old Bethane shook her head in her quasi-dream, resisting the continued memory, but it continued to play itself out before her closed eyes and she could not seem to open them and stop it.

In the yard beyond the square lay a blacksmith's shop, and just outside that shop, clearly visible from where she and Darrell watched in horror, a brazier held various implements of red-hot iron. To this place the guards of Tarleton led their captive, one of them pausing to pluck a glowing bar of iron carefully from the fire. Then the captive was hidden behind the ring of soldiers which closed in for his torture.

She did not see them blind him, though she knew that it was done. His scream echoed through the square, making her stomach cramp and the child move in her womb. Even as she was squeezing her eyes shut and trying to stop her ears against ever more agonized screams, Darrell was leaning close and pulling a hand away, speaking in a stern, urgent voice.

"*I* gave no word! I'm going after him. If I can get him out, I'll take him to Saint Luke's. Meet me there. God keep you, dearest."

And then, before she could hold him, he was gone, slipping through the crowd and vaulting onto Barrett's horse, the golden fire of his glorious shields blazing up around him as he and the snow-white stallion surged through the crowd and into the yard beyond.

Magic flared, shouts and screams choked off in mid-breath, and the crowd began to panic, pushing away through every exit from the square in mindless stampede. Bethane felt herself carried on their tide whether she willed or no, away from the yard, away from Darrell, and she wept, she raged.

She caught just a glimpse of his horse in the entry to the yard, rearing and screaming and lashing out with battle-trained hooves—and a limp, bloodied form slung across the saddle in front of her husband.

Then the rest of Tarleton's men were pressing close around him, he was breaking away, and the archers were firing at him as he spurred the stallion toward a street on the other side of the square, people falling beneath the hooves and the archers' arrows.

The screams of those around her sent bolts of terror shafting through her mind like the arrows of the soldiers, and she was running with them and screaming and—

Other screams broke through her consciousness, and she sat up groggily to see the child Bronwyn running toward her across the meadow, shrieking at the top of her voice.

"Grand-dame! Grand-dame! Come quickly. My brother's hurt! Oh, come quickly!"

As Bethane struggled to her feet with the aid of her staff, she could see two of the boys bent over the third, far across the meadow. The child was coming far too fast to stop, and nearly knocked her down as she flung her arms around the old woman's waist.

"Oh, come quickly, please, grand-dame. He's hurt! I think his arm is broken!"

She did not want to go. These children were nothing to her but nuisance. But something in the little girl's frantic entreaty reminded her of those other little faces in that long-ago village square, so she fetched her satchel of bandages and healing herbs and hobbled down the rocky hillside, the child tugging at her free hand all the while and urging her to hurry faster, faster.

The others looked up as she approached, the younger McLain boy standing almost protectively. It was the blond one who lay on the ground struggling to breathe. The split branch dangling from a high limb overhead told most of the story. A glance at the odd angle of the boy's right arm told the rest. Kevin, the young earl, had had the foresight to slit the boy's sleeve from wrist to shoulder, but the arm thus exposed was already purpling along the bulge of the broken angle. The boy himself was conscious, but breathing raggedly. The fall must have knocked the wind out of him, as well as breaking his arm. At least she could see no blood. That was usually a good sign.

"Well, let's have a look," she said gruffly, heaving herself to her knees at the boy's right and laying aside her satchel. "Can you feel this?"

As she touched the arm above and below the angle of the break, he winced and nodded, but he did not cry out. She tried not to hurt him more, but his face went dead-white several times as she went about the business of assessing the damage.

"Both bones are snapped clean through," she said, when she had finished her appraisal. "It won't be easy to set, or pleasant." She looked across at Kevin. "I can tend it, but you'd best get back to your father's and bring men with a litter. Once it's been set, it mustn't be allowed to shift before it's had time to knit a little."

The young earl's face was pale, but a touch of the old arrogance still lingered in the clear blue eyes. "It's his sword-arm, grand-dame," he said pointedly. "Are you sure you can set it properly? Shouldn't I fetch my father's battle-surgeon?"

"Not if you want it to heal straight," she replied with a contemptuous toss of her head. "Most battle-surgeons would just as soon cut it off. It's a bad break. The wrong manipulation, and the bone could pierce the skin—and then he *would* have to lose the arm. I know what I'm doing. Now go!"

The arrogance was gone. With a sincere and now thoroughly chastened nod of agreement, Kevin scrambled onto his pony and headed off at a gallop. Bethane sent the other two children to find wood for splints, then settled down cross-legged to resume her examination of the broken arm. The boy's breathing had eased, but he still sucked in breath between clenched teeth when her fingers came anywhere near the area of the break. He would need a pain-killer before she could do much more.

She pulled her satchel closer and began rummaging inside for the appropriate drugs and herbs, glancing at the boy from time to time through slitted eyes. She left her selection to intuition, and was astonished to see that one of the pouches she had withdrawn contained a deadly poison.

*Now, why?* she thought, staring at the pouch and trying to ken a reason. *'Tis but a boy, no enemy, no—*

Sweet gods and elemental lords! The boy was Deryni!

All in a rush, the old bitterness came flooding back: Darrell dying in her arms with the archers' arrows in his back; dying because he had felt compelled to try to save his Deryni comrade; dying because of those Deryni children.

And their own child, stillborn in the awful after-anguish following Darrell's death; and then, a long, long time that she lay sick and despondent at Saint Luke's, not caring if *she* lived or died, and something had snapped inside, never to be mended. . . .

*Darrell. . . .*

A choked sob welled in her throat, the tears spilling down her weathered cheeks as she pressed the pouch to her withered breasts.

Deryni children had cost Darrell his life. For Deryni children, he had taken the archers' arrows and died. Now another Deryni child lay in her power, helpless to defend himself from her just vengeance. Could she not have just this one life in exchange for her love's?

She reached behind her for one of the cups the children had left after their meal. The first was empty, but the second still contained two fingers' worth—enough to serve her purpose. The boy's eyes were closed, so he did not see her pour the measured dose from pouch to cup, or stir the greyish powder with a handy twig. She might have administered the killing draught without a qualm, had not the boy opened his eyes as she raised his head.

"What's that?" he asked, the grey eyes wide and trusting, though he winced as his arm shifted from having his head raised.

"Something for the pain," she lied, unnerved by his eyes. "Drink. You will feel nothing, after this."

Obediently, he laid his good hand on hers which held the cup, pale lashes veiling the fog-grey eyes. The cup was almost to his lips when he froze, the eyes darting to hers in sudden, shocked comprehension.

"It's poison!" he gasped, pushing the cup aside and staring in disbelief. "You want to kill me!"

She could feel the tentacles of his thought brushing at the edges of her mind, and she drew back in fear, letting his head fall to the grass. He moaned, his face going white as he clasped his injured arm to his body and rolled on his side away from her, trying to sit up. She touched his shoulder and murmured one of the old charms to drain him of his strength, knowing he could not concentrate to resist it, with the pain—could only just stay conscious now, even if his training *were* sufficient to resist her spelling, though she doubted that. As she twined her fingers in his hair and yanked his head up-turned, the pain-bright eyes tried to focus on her other hand, as if his gaze might stave off the cup she brought toward him again.

"But, why?" he whispered, tears runneling narrow tracks from the corners of his eyes. "I never harmed you. I never wished you ill. It can't be for the *sheep!*"

She steeled herself against his pleas, shifting her hand to pinch at the hinges of his jaws and force the mouth to open.

*Darrell, my only love, I do it for your vengeance!* she thought, as the boy groaned and tried to turn his head aside.

But as she set her teeth and moved the cup closer, ignoring his groans and weakening struggles, the sunlight caught the wedding band on her hand, flashing bright gold in her eyes. She blinked and froze.

*Darrell—oh, my gods, what am I doing?*

All at once she realized how very young the boy was: no more than eight or nine, for all his earlier posturings of manhood. He was Deryni, but was that his fault, any more than it had been the fault of those other children, or Darrell, or even the self-sacrificing Barrett? Was *this* what Darrell had tried to teach her? Was she mad, even to consider killing a Deryni, like *him?*

With a muted little cry, she flung the cup aside and let him go, burying her face in her hands.

"I'm sorry, Darrell," she sobbed, crushing her lover's ring against her lips. "I'm sorry. Oh, forgive me, my love. Please forgive me, my love, my life. . . ."

When she finally looked up, drying her tears on a tattered edge of her skirt, the boy was on his back again, the grey eyes studying her quite analytically. The fair face was still pinched with pain, the injured arm still cradled in his good one, but he made no move to escape.

"You know what I am, don't you?" he asked, his voice hardly more than a whisper.

At her nod, the grey eyes shuttered for an instant, then turned back on her again.

"This Darrell—was he killed by a Deryni?"

She shook her head, stifling a sob. "No," she whispered. "*He* was Deryni, and died to save another of his kind."

"I think I understand," the boy replied, with a preternaturally wise nod. He drew a deep, steadying breath, then continued. "Listen, you don't have to help me if you don't want to. Kevin will bring the battle-surgeon, even though you said not to. I'll be all right."

"Without a sword arm, young Deryni?" She drew herself up with returning dignity. "Nay, I can't let you chance that. Darrell would never approve. How can you carry on his work without a proper sword arm?"

As his brows knit in question, she replaced the lethal pouch in her satchel and began withdrawing rolls of yellowish bandages.

"I won't offer you another pain-killer," she said with a wry smile. "I wouldn't trust either of our judgments in light of what has already passed between us. I *will* set the arm, though. And I give you my word that it will heal as straight as ever, if you follow my instructions."

"Your word? Yes," the boy repeated, glancing aside as Duncan and Bronwyn returned with an assortment of straight pieces of wood.

As she sorted through them, picking four which suited her, she remembered that other Deryni's reply to such a question—*My word is my bond!*—and she knew that she, too, had meant what she said. When she had put the other boy to work whittling knots and twigs from the splints she had chosen, showing him how to carve them flat along one side, she glanced at the injured one with rough affection.

Something in her face must have reassured him—or perhaps he read it in the way Darrell once had known her innermost feelings. Whatever the cause, he relaxed visibly after that, letting his sister cradle his head in her lap and even appearing to doze a little as Bethane made a final inspection of the splints and bandages and prepared to do what must be done.

All three of the children were Deryni, she realized now; and as she bade the other boy kneel down to hold young Alaric's good arm, she sensed that *he* knew she was aware—though how she knew, he would understand no better than Darrell had. She had *tried* to tell Darrell that it was the ancient wisdom. . . .

"Girl, you try to ease him now," she said gruffly, probing above the break and sliding one hand down to his wrist. "A pretty girl can take a man's mind from the pain. My Darrell taught me that."

He had stiffened at her first words, perhaps fearing that she would betray her knowledge to the others; but now he closed his eyes and drew a deep breath, tension draining away as he let it out. Bethane waited several heartbeats, sensing a rudimentary form of one of Darrell's old spells being brought into play, then gave his wrist a squeeze of warning and began pulling the arm straight, at the same time rotating it slightly and guiding with her other hand as the ends of bone eased into place. The boy's breath hissed in between clenched teeth and his back arched off the ground with the pain, but he did not cry out and the injured arm did not tense or move except as she manipulated it. When she had adjusted all to her satisfaction, she bound the arm to the splints Duncan held, immobilizing it straight from bicep to fingertips. As the final bandages were tied in place and the bound arm eased to his side, Alaric finally passed out.

Across the meadow, horsemen were approaching at a gallop. Bethane stood as they drew rein, her work completed. A man with a satchel much like her own dismounted immediately and knelt at the boy's side. Two more got down and began unrolling a litter. The fourth man, Lord Kevin mounted pillion behind him, gave the young earl a hand down and then himself dismounted. He was young and fair, in appearance much like her Darrell when first they met.

"I'm Deveril, Duke Jared's seneschal," the man said, watching as the first man inspected her handiwork. "His Grace and the boy's father are away. What happened here?"

She inclined her head slightly, supporting herself on her shepherd's staff. "Boys will be boys, sir," she answered cautiously. "The young lord fell out of the tree." She gestured with her staff and watched all eyes lift to the broken branch. "I but lent my poor skills to right the lad's hurt. He will mend well enough."

"Macon?" the seneschal asked.

The battle-surgeon nodded approvingly as his patient moaned and regained consciousness. "An expert job, m'lord. If nothing shifts, he should heal as good as new." He glanced at Bethane. "You didn't give him any of your hill remedies, did you, Mother?"

Containing a wry smile, Bethane shook her head. "No, sir. He is a brave lad, and would have nothing for his pain. A fine soldier, that one. He will fight many a battle in his manhood."

"Aye, he likely will, at that," Deveril replied, looking at her so strangely that she wondered for a moment whether he had caught her double-meaning.

The boy had, though. For when they had laid him on the litter and were preparing to move out, he raised his good hand and beckoned her closer. The battle-surgeon had given him one of *his* remedies for pain, and the grey eyes were almost all pupil, the pale lashes drooping as he fought the compulsion to sleep. Still, his grip was strong as he pulled her closer to whisper in her ear.

"Thank you, grand-dame—for several things. I will—try to carry on *his* work."

Bethane allowed herself an indulgent nod, for by the look of his eyes, he would remember nothing when he woke from the battle-surgeon's potion. But just as the litter started to move, he drew her hand closer and touched his lips to her ring—Darrell's ring!—in the same way *he* had always done, so many years ago.

Then the fingers went slack as sleep claimed him, and all the noble party were mounting to leave, the litter bearers gently carrying him out into the golden sunlight. The girl Bronwyn dropped her a grave curtsey—could *she* know what had happened?—and then all of them were heading off across the meadow, toward the castle.

Wondering, she brought her hand to her face and rubbed the smooth gold of the ring against her cheek, her eyes not leaving the departing riders and especially the bobbing litter. But by the time they had disappeared into the afternoon haze, the day's events were hardly more than dimly hearkened memories, as her mind flew back across the years.

"Well, Darrell, at least we saved one of them, didn't we?" she whispered, kissing the ring and smiling at it.

Then she picked up her satchel and started up the hill, humming a little tune under her breath.

# THE RIDDLE OF HEKAITË

## *by Diana L. Paxson*

*"I originally became interested in mythology," says Diana Paxson, "because my mother gave me the name of a goddess, and I wanted to know what I'd been up to."*

*In addition to studying the cult of the Triple Goddess and, indeed, finding out what she had been up to, Diana Paxson is one of the founders of the Society for Creative Anachronisms, holds a master's degree in medieval literature, and is studying General Systems Theory in a Ph.D. program of the Humanistic Psychology Institute. She has published stories in* Millennial Women, Isaac Asimov's Science Fiction Magazine, Swords Against Darkness, Dragonfields, *and* The Keeper's Price, *and has a fantasy novel in the works.*

*Of "The Riddle of Hekaitë," Diana says that Galia, the land in which it takes place, lies in an alternative time frame north of where Greece would be in our own space-time continuum. In this story, she draws on contemporary pagan theology, which has developed underground for the past two thousand years, to create a culture and a cult of the Triple Goddess—maiden, mother, and crone—that resonate in her readers' imaginations. "The Riddle of Hekaitë" deals with the Crone, that aspect of the Goddess which is, according to Diana, the most difficult for modern readers to face. It is not only society as a whole that has trouble accepting old age and death; it is individual men and women who "rage, rage against the dying of the light." Anodea is one such woman, and more courageous than most.*

"When you take your crown from its casket, what is left inside?"

"What, darling?" Anodea finished hanging the golden sun-discs from her earlobes and smiled down at her granddaughter Gita, who was fingering the regalia ranged on the cedarwood chest. "Nothing, I suppose. . . ."

"It's a *riddle*—" the child explained, her brown eyes serious in her pointed face. "The answer is *darkness!*"

Anodea nodded, reaching for her veil. There was a dry cough behind her, and reflected in the mirror she saw a huddle of black robes. *Hekaitë* . . . no, it was only Aunt Vannë, Hekaitë's priestess in Galia. Anodea was the Queen, but all three faces of the Goddess must confront the Kerinyoi envoys today. The old woman was required here.

Vannë coughed again. "My bones pain me! Surely I have served the Goddess long enough—someone younger must keep the Shrine . . ." the dry voice quavered on in the complaint Anodea had been hearing ever since her first grandchild was born. The power must pass, the Queen must become the Crone.

She straightened, swiftly pinned her spangled veil to the dark braids bound about her head. She had passed her fiftieth year, but little silver gleamed there. The sight of her still kindled light in her husband's eyes—when she and Kadmos came together in the ceremonies they channeled power to renew the world.

*Old woman*, she thought, *I am still in my prime. I need not dedicate myself to Hekaitë's darkness for yet awhile.*

"Aunt, now *you* speak riddles—" she said aloud. "How can one who has not yet met the Hidden One know how to serve Her?"

"Niece, you speak impertinence. I have worn this robe since I was younger than you."

*You were never young. . . .*

As a child, Anodea had hidden when Hekaitë's priestess visited the Queen. She had dreaded the Shrine where they served the Goddess for the people and the land, a cavern that had seemed to her as vast and shadowed as that from which Hekaitë ruled the Underworld. But she had grown from maiden to mother, while Vannë remained the same fruitless branch. Maiden, Mother, Wisewoman, the royal women served the Goddess of Galia. But the Mother *was* Galia, the Queen.

The door opened, a muted roaring of men's voices invaded the room.

"Mother—are you not ready yet?"

Anodea smiled a greeting to her younger daughter Kara, who bore the crescent of the Maiden above her brow. Her granddaughter handed her the Crown of the Mother and she settled it on her head so that the pendant ears of wheat swung forward to frame her face in gold.

Rumor said that the Queen of the Kerinyoi was young, that she could refuse nothing to the man who shared her bed. Had his glory-lust set the two lands bristling like dogs across a bone? The envoys would find things different here.

*Even when Kadmos and I were young. . . .* Anodea smiled, remembering his beauty in the torchlight as he came to her. Her breasts tingled as they had done when he bent to kiss them; her loins throbbed, remembering how he had knelt before her. He had come to the maiden as a warrior and made her Lady and Queen, but he had never come as a conqueror.

Vannë coughed impatiently, and Anodea recollected herself, sought her image in the polished bronze. Wonder took her then, seeing the erect, deep-bosomed figure reflected there whose features were and yet were not her own. She stood within a blaze of gold, and her hands lifted in salute.

Gita gazed at her in awe. Through the stone floor Anodea felt the pulse of the land from the spine of mountains north of the city to the fertile plain that sloped toward the river. *Surely I am Galia, the Mother. . . . Who can deny me?*

Dimly in the mirror another face appeared, like a fairer

double-image of her own. Anodea turned to meet the brittle gaze of Tania, Gita's mother and heiress of Galia.

"Are you primping to mimic the youth of the Kerinyoi Queen? The men will start without you if you do not come soon!" Tania clasped her hands above the proud swell of her pregnant belly.

Silently, Anodea drew Kara and Vannë into place behind her. Then the Mother, the Maiden and the Wisewoman of Galia swept past Tania into the Hall.

Woven shafts of light from the narrow windows above the dais glittered on ornaments of bronze and gold as men stirred angrily. Anodea thought the Kerinyoi envoy's tongue must be as sharp as the sword he had left outside. Did he *want* to enrage them? Kadmos still held his place behind her throne, but she could feel the effort he was making to leash his outrage and remain there.

"Do you deny that last week your men stole two dozen head of cattle and killed their guardians?"

Kadmos bit back an oath. Anodea turned, saw anger in his scarred face and then uncertainty, as if he had been asked a riddle whose answer he did not know. Of late his temper had shortened, and he had spent too many evenings drinking by the fire. Could their young men have gone raiding without his permission?

The Queen's eyes passed over the men of Galia, who stood with moustaches bristling. Though they were weaponless, they had tied their hair into the warrior's knot with lengths of colored yarn. Would they be wanting her to choose a new champion now? Her lips set. *I could not. . . .*

Galia had been a poor land when her mother's death gave Anodea the Crown. She and Kadmos had labored for it as they did for their own children, winning at last prestige for the country and for themselves security. She rejoiced in Galia as the earth rejoices in its burden of grain. Why must this peace be shadowed by Kadmos's unhappiness?

The Kerinyoi were talking not of peace, but of war. "Honor requires reparation for our sufferings!"

"Honor!" a new voice startled her. Her son-in-law Eneris strode onto the floor. "Where was honor when you raided Olea? If we crossed your border it was to avenge your butcheries. . . ."

The boards of the dais creaked as Kadmos joined Eneris, his shoulders rigid with rage. "He is right! The Goddess witness that threats will gain you nothing!"

The Kerinyoi and his companions scowled as the Hall erupted in a chaos of cheers. Anodea signaled the herald to strike the gong and waited while its reverberations throbbed across the heated air.

"Enough!" She turned to the Kerinyoi. "Tell your Queen that our lands have suffered equally. Let our warriors settle the matter at the Games of Sunreturn."

A villager, unrecognizable under the dust that powdered his face and hair, was pushing toward Eneris. Anodea continued to speak, but her stomach knotted as Eneris listened and his face flushed angrily.

"My Lady, it is too late!" he cried, "While these traitors held us in talk their army marched. They will be at our gates by dawn!" He moved to seize the envoys, but the Kerinyoi had drawn hidden knives. Blood spattered the steps of the dais as they fought toward the door. In moments the struggling mass had swept through the Hall and outside.

Anodea snapped out orders—the wounded must be seen to, food cooked so that the fires could be doused before the attack, supplies counted and messengers sent to the villages for aid. Gabbling, the women scattered to obey

Presently the warriors began to return, intent on readying weapons and armor. Anodea heard Eneris's voice raised in anger over her husband's softer replies.

"How long has it been since you fought, old man? I told you to search the envoys, but you wouldn't believe me!"

"They were messengers—sacred! It would have been dishonorable." Kadmos's fingers raked his grey wolf-pelt of hair. "And they have paid for their treachery."

"And their brothers will be claiming that price from us before tomorrow's sun is high! Will you hang back then, protesting they are honorable men?"

Kadmos stopped short, his high color fading. "You may question my wisdom if it has failed . . ." he said softly, "but not my courage. I will pay my debt to Galia on the battlefield." The younger man's eyes flinched from his bleak gaze.

"If you have finished your recriminations, there is work to be done." The chill in Anodea's voice masked a greater cold at her heart. "While I count supplies, I suggest that you check the walls!"

"As the Queen wills!" Eneris flushed and turned away.

Kadmos smiled at her a little sadly. A pulse was beating at his temple, and Anodea felt her own head ache as if she shared every sense of that body she knew so well. *Come to me . . .* her heart called. *I am afraid for you . . .* but she did not speak, and after a moment Kadmos followed Eneris from the room.

Trembling, Anodea grasped at the gilded pillar of her throne. Something wet brushed her ankle, and looking down she saw a splatter of blood across the silken hem of her gown.

The dawn wind seemed to come from some cold space beyond the world. Anodea pulled her cloak around her, wondering how the lightly armed men of Galia could bear it, waiting in the square below like souls on Hell-river's shore. As custom required, she and the other women had taken refuge on the roof of the citadel from which they could leap to an honorable end if all other defenses failed. But it was not her own death she feared.

Already the sky was paling. The rising sun struck flame from the bronze helms of the men on the walls. A cock crowed challenge, and the stillness was shattered by the blare of a horn. The Queen peered over the walls to the grazing grounds beside the river. Through the tracery of branches the water had a dull sheen like the blade of a sword. Then she saw movement in the shadowed fields and knew that the Kerinyoi were here.

Beside her, Vannë's black robes fluttered like the wings of a carrion crow, and without thinking Anodea flexed her fingers in the sign against evil. The trumpets repeated their fanfare and the drums took up a steady beat as the Gate of Galia swung open.

Anodea glimpsed the warleader's red plumes, then lost them again as the warriors of Galia poured out to meet the foe. Last night Kadmos had made love to her as he had not done since they were young—tenderly, desperately, as if he would never hold her again. Heedless of the tears that streaked her face, Anodea strained to see.

"Mother, rule yourself!" hissed Tania, gripping her arm.

"If they see you weep now they will be certain we are going to lose!"

"Should I not weep? Your father seeks death on that field!"

"He has the right," replied Tania.

Anodea shivered, for the men of Galia also had their Mysteries. In other lands the people killed their Kings, but when the powers of the Champion of Galia passed he could choose either to become the Sage or the Sacrifice. *You never asked my leave . . .* her spirit cried, and the question brushed like a dry wing across her soul, *Would I have let him go?*

"My husband is down there too—" Tania set one hand on her belly. "This child may be fatherless before it sees the light of day, but I do not weep. I am a giver of life, but I can face death as well. It seems you can do neither now!"

Outraged, Anodea tried to shake free. Then the two lines of warriors crashed together and collapsed into knots of struggling men and both women clutched at the parapet, watching them.

Once Anodea's father had shown her an anthill that was being invaded by a rival colony. She remembered how the battle had flowed and knotted, defenders indistinguishable from their foes. So, from this height, she stove to read the human battle, a riddle whose answer held Kadmos's fate and her own. As she had cried to her father, she asked, *Why are they fighting? Who is winning? What does it mean?* Then she bowed her head. *Oh Blessed Lady, only let him live!*

Oblivious to the wind that tangled her hair, Anodea watched the battle, and as the rising sun picks out the story of Kera's daughter and the Lord of Hell that is carved into the west wall of the Lady's shrine, the strengthening light made the pattern of the fighting clear. The snarled line was bulging inward as the Kerinyoi thrust toward the Gate. Anodea put her fist to her mouth in anguish, knowing that unless the men of Galia could rally, the enemy would enter the town and more than Kadmos's life would be in jeopardy.

She had seen conquered villages in the days before she and Kadmos set peace in the land. Imagination painted his face on her memories of men hacked to bits before their own doors; put the faces of her daughters on the bodies of women whose blood-stained thighs had stiffened as their rapists left them; gave the forms of her grandchildren to the slack bodies of children whose brains splattered the walls beneath which they had played. Her own family . . . *her* people. . . .

The terrified babbling of the other women broke through Anodea's private fear like a child's cry piercing its mother's nightmare. Then, she remembered the other reason that the place of the Queen of Galia was here. *Lady, forgive me—only let my people be saved* . . .

Tania groaned as the Galisoi gave way again, but already the Queen was loosing the brooches that held her cloak and gown. The garments pooled about her feet and her hair whipped angrily, but the sunlight glowed on her skin, flashed from the gold of the star on her breast, from bracelets and necklet and crown.

"Goddess," whispered Anodea, "I stand naked before Thee . . . come to me—my life is in Thy hand!" Cold air rasped her lungs as she breathed in, the power of the wind tingled along her veins. She opened herself to the Goddess as she had opened herself to Kadmos in the act of love, and the Goddess came.

"Galia . . ." chanted the women. "Galia!"

Surefooted, Anodea mounted the parapet. The sun was dazzling, but she did not need to see. Heedless of the sheer drop before her, she leaned upon the wind and cried the Name of the Goddess aloud.

And from the plain the men of Kerinya saw upon the city's pinnacle a figure that blazed with gold, heard again the cry that twisted the sinews of their souls.

"The Goddess of Galia fights for them!" screamed a Kerinyoi warrior, but the defenders were already turning it to a battle cry.

"Galia, Galia!" the shout echoed between the women on the walls and the battlefield. And the men of the city, knowing that their Goddess was with them, surged against the foe.

At dusk, when the last of the living Kerinyoi had fled splashing across the stream, the people of Galia began to bring their dead and wounded in. Sick and shaking from the backlash of power, the Queen went out to them. There was in her a great emptiness, for like Kadmos, she had made an offering, and she knew that the Goddess would require her to pay.

And so, when the warriors brought Kadmos to her upon a

bier fashioned from the spears of his enemies, with torches, as he had come to her so long ago, she was waiting.

"How did it happen?"

Eneris shook his head. "When you—when the Goddess appeared to us, he cut into the ranks of the enemy like one possessed. We found him ringed by Kerinyoi slain, his body as red with blood as his plumes."

Anodea drew back the cloak with which they had covered Kadmos's wounds; she shuddered, thinking that even the fourteen wounds of Tomais could not have gaped so sorely.

"But I think it was a head blow that felled him, Lady. No, he is not dead—" Eneris answered her swift movement of surprise as she listened at Kadmos's breast, "but I think he cannot live long."

The Queen was already giving swift orders to carry Kadmos to her rooms.

"But Mother, we need you here—" said Tania, with the diffidence she had shown her since that moment on the walls.

"What would you have done if the Goddess had accepted my life today?" snapped Anodea. "You wanted to rule—take charge now! Your husband lives—let me try to save mine!"

It was past midnight before she was done, washing and binding Kadmos's wounds as carefully as the Goddess had pieced her slain lover together again. She bent over him, arms spread as if they were wings to fan his spirit back to him. His eyes opened then, dark and confused in the candlelight, and seeing her he smiled.

"My Lady . . . I am Thy Sacrifice. . . ." His eyes closed and his skin began to grow cold, and she knew that he was going away from her.

Unbelieving, Anodea shook her head. "If you had not seen me on the walls you would not have thrown your life away . . . it is my fault. . . ." She knew that Tania would have told her she must accept this, that the Queen of Darkness claimed all men in the end. But the Goddess herself had not accepted it. Had not Ytarrra sought Tomais in the Underworld?

*Do I dare?* she thought. *Would he not dare as much for me?*

Shivering, she sank down across Kadmos's unresisting body, her spirit questing after his. Half-forgotten training came to her then, the skill by which one might separate the soul from its housing and send it wandering in that country which the dreamer cannot remember and from which the dead do not return.

When Tania and the other women came to her they found her living, but like Kadmos, already too far away for them to call her home.

"You would not serve Me, and yet you seek Me now. . . ." The cavern echoed with laughter like wind stirring the sere branches of forever leafless trees. Behind Anodea flowed a dark river shored with shattered bones. Before her stood an empty basalt throne.

"Queen of Galia, what do you here?" the Voice seemed to come from all directions at once, echoing with malice older than the world.

*Why have I come?* Anodea's purpose faltered, leaving only fear. Listening to that obscene mirth, she shuddered like one who stumbles in the dark and hears beneath his feet the clatter of scattering bones.

"I want Kadmos—" she managed at last. "Let him go. What is one more soul to Thee? Or if Thou wilt not, let me be with him here. . . ." By some increasing illumination too pallid to be called light, Anodea perceived Kadmos standing on the other side of the throne. But his gaze was fixed beyond her. Her own form seemed insubstantial, but Kadmos was becoming steadily more solid with the weakening of the body he had left behind.

"Both you and he are Mine. Why should I wait for him, or welcome you before your time? What do you offer me?"

"I am the Queen of Galia . . ." Anodea began proudly. Swiftly she stripped the bracelets from her wrists, unclasped the great star she bore upon her breast, lifted from her head the crown. She held them out to the darkness, and wind stirred around her, and they were gone. Anodea waited, feeling more naked now than she had been upon the walls of Galia.

"Those things were not yours to give. . . . They have returned where they belong." said the Voice.

"Set me a quest then—what shall I bring to Thee?" Anodea clasped her arms across her breasts to keep out the cold and looked around her defiantly.

"Will you give Me Kara's beauty, or Tania's unborn child?

Will you give Me the sprouting grain, or sunlight on the fields of Galia?"

Anodea's arms tightened, as if she had been protecting a child. *No! Those things are mine!* Then her hands went, uselessly, to hide her face, as she understood that all she had was hers only to guard, not to give away.

"Even my body will go to the earth . . ." she whispered bitterly. "What dost Thou want of me?"

"Your loves, your hates, your human memories . . ." said the Goddess softly. "Play me a riddle-game. It has been long since I had mortal company."

Anodea gasped. knowing madness waited in the laughter that shook her. "What stakes?" she said hoarsely, "And what reward?"

"If I cannot answer what you ask of Me, you may choose to go again or stay," said the Darkness. "If you can answer what I put to you, your man may have his choice to stay or go."

"And if I fail?"

"Maybe I will keep you . . . or maybe send you away . . . or I may leave your body living while your spirit stays to play with Me. . . ."

The rasped words echoed like the eternity in which that Presence proposed to dissect Anodea's soul. "No . . ." she moaned, understanding that she had been wrong, that she still had something she could lose.

"Did you expect Me to give you My sacrifice for the asking, as you would toss your bitch-hound a bone? You were a Queen in the daylight, but here you are a dream, you are dust, you are what I will you to be. . . ." The darkness grew, if possible, heavier.

"You ask first." said Hekaitë.

Anodea's thoughts swirled vague and purposeless as the new-hatched souls on the shores of the infernal river. What could a mortal ask that the witch-goddess would not know? Riddles that had teased her in childhood flitted half-remembered through her memory, and others with which she had puzzled her grandchildren. But one told riddles to a child to teach it to look at the world in a new way. This Dark Presence had been old when the world was new.

"Well?"

Anodea had never been more conscious of her own mortality. But now her links to the earth were all she had to wager with. She straightened and said—

*This Queen's palace hath more windows than any;*
*It is filled with flowers picked by no hand;*
*And no ruler hath golden treasure like unto hers . . .*

She stopped, striving to keep even the name of sweetness from her mind.

But already her opponent was replying. "As one Queen to another, do you think I would not know the Lady of the Bees? Many have thought My kiss sweeter than honeycomb. But the question was neatly put. Mortal, ask again."

*Of course,* thought Anodea, though her heart grew cold. *Every harper knows that one. I must try something more homely.* For a moment, longing for her own hearth was so sharp she could almost see the flames. She seemed to hear voices calling her name. But she shook her head and spoke,

*This pointed weapon is held by no warrior's hand;*
*It makes a cloud into a covering.*
*In motion, it is a fireside magic,*
*But it is fuel for flames when still.*

Low laughter throbbed in the darkness and Anodea foreknew failure. "Shall I not know the spindle, who am the Spinner of Fates? Look at your husband—you can see the thread that binds his body to his soul. How thin it is—shall I cut it now?"

And Anodea saw that indeed a shining silver filament stretched from beneath Kadmos's rib cage back through the shadows. She choked down her need to call out to him. *What can I ask?* she thought desperately. *She knows everything ever asked since the beginning of the world!* But Anodea had to ask one more question or forfeit the game like a wounded warrior who throws down his arms.

*Now must I step outside the rules of riddlery. I must ask something that only I would know.* Low-voiced her final question came.

"Where was I when my woman's blood first flowed?"

The air sighed around her and set the river to lapping sibilantly against the pallid shore.

"Daughter, I see that you do not yet understand. . . ." Surely the Voice was gentler now. "When your womb first opened, you were playing beside a stream. You washed your bloodied clout in its clear waters and dedicated to the Maiden

Goddess your chastity. But the dark moon is not separate from the crescent and the bright—only her face is changed. All the moon's waters flow into My river in the end. Your maiden blood, your maidenhead, the birthblood of your first child—all were dedicated to Me."

Anodea folded her arms across sagging breasts that would never nurse another child, bent as if to shield her womb which no longer responded to the tides of the moon. Even the symbols of her sovereignty were gone. *I have lost . . .* she whimpered. *I belong to the darkness now. . . .*

And the darkness throbbed with her pain. A sense of motion filled the cavern's emptiness; a turmoil of presences, invisible, substanceless, blown hither and thither with every shift of air. Anodea looked vainly around her, almost thinking to see them, to recognize here a gesture, there a tilt of the head or a smile.

"Mother!" she called, recognizing one, but it slipped from her embrace as if two coils of smoke had tried to twine.

"They are only shadows left behind." said the Voice of Hekaitë. "Do not be afraid."

*And what am I?* Anodea wondered dully. Her grasp on the power of the Mother had survived the loss of her body's fertility. It could not survive her soul's conquest by the darkness that surrounded her now. She waited for that darkness to question her.

*What goes on four legs in the morning,*
*On two legs at noon,*
*And on three legs when darkness falls?*

Around Anodea the shades were swirling as if trying to remember the days when they too had been men. The answer to this riddle was only too easy now.

"It is man, who crawls as a babe, walks on two feet when grown, and in age must go supported by a cane."

"Very good." said the Other. "The answer to the second question will be simpler, for it is all around you."

*What is death?*

A wind was blowing, as cold as the wind on the parapet of the palace had been. How could there be a wind at the hollow heart-place of the world? The shades flowed past her toward some unimaginable destination. But they were only the shadows of souls whose substance had long ago passed on.

Before she came to this place, Anodea would have been

sure of the answer to the Lady's question. *Death is annihilation; it is the end of all.* She knew she knew nothing now.

And yet something was struggling within her, some knowledge written in her blood and bones, as her body had known how to bring to birth her child. *Does a baby think it is death when the womb expels it?*

She whispered then, "Is death a change of life?"

The shades were vanished now. It had become very still. In the waiting silence Anodea looked at Kadmos and said, "I am doing this for you. . . ." But she felt the darkness watching her and wondered suddenly if that were true.

"You have answered two questions." said the Queen of Darkness. "Answer another and your man will be free." The quality of the silence changed as if the cavern had grown immeasurable.

*What is My Name?*

The Question reverberated through the cavern, echoed through the seven levels of the world. In Anodea's memory echoed myriad names, but what name spoken by mortals could have meaning here? *Hekaitë, 'Kallë, Persepinë, Rhë?* They made no sense, applied to this reality.

"The throne is empty. Show me Thy face and I will answer Thee!" she cried out desperately. The silence hummed, her ears were buzzing with fear.

Then, "Look into the water . . ." a still voice whispered to her soul.

Shaking, Anodea leaned over the shifting, shining darkness of the river and saw, more clearly than she had ever seen in her mirror of bronze, the polished basalt throne. Before it stood a woman whose face had been etched by the years till there remained only the bared beauty of bone. A hood shadowed her hair. Anodea put out her hand to ward away the burning of those eyes, and the hand of the other figure moved.

"It is Myself. . . ." Two voices spoke as one. Anodea whirled and found herself at the foot of the throne.

"Thou art . . . you are . . . We are One. . . ." The voices merged and twinned and merged again. "All Faces of the Goddess are potential in Me. . . ."

Kadmos was standing before the throne, hands crossed on his breast like one who awaits a doom.

*I have no right to judge him. . . .*

*You are the Goddess to him—you have always been so. . . .* And Anodea understood at last her own responsibility. Then the Voice spoke aloud and she felt her own lips move.

"Man of earth, why have you come to Me?"

"I come to know my destiny."

"You have served the Goddess, and she gives you your fate again. Will you return to Galia?"

"What could I do there? That body can no longer hold a sword," he said wistfully.

"Have you learned nothing in all these years?" the Goddess asked. "The young men must be taught, or every generation born must do it all again."

He frowned with a little quirk of the brow that refracted back across a thousand moments in Anodea's memory. *Oh, my beloved. . . .*

"Anodea would never let me go."

The Goddess spoke, "Anodea sets you free. . . ."

Kadmos was silent for a long while, gazing past her as a seaman watches the horizon, or a lover the path down which his girl will come.

"I have always served Galia," he said finally, in his face a kind of bleak integrity, stern as the blade of a sword. "I will continue while I am needed, as long as that body lasts."

Anodea found herself moving back to the river, bending to scoop up water in her hands, turning to him. His eyes widened and he trembled as she came to him. As he had bent to her to take her maidenhead, he lowered his head then, and drank. The silver thread of his life pulsed blindingly, and his form faded as his life flowed back along that slender ribbon to the world of men. Anodea reached out to embrace him, but he was gone.

"And you?" said that voice which was and was not her own.

"But I lost—I lost the right to decide. . . ."

"In every moment throughout time and beyond it you choose!" The Voice shattered the silence, shattered the darkness, scattered the fragments of Anodea's awareness as the shadows had been scattered by the wind.

When she knew herself once more there was no cavern around her. She was standing beside the river beyond which the land of Galia slept peacefully in the darkness. The air sighed with the breathing stillness of the deep night hours; the river rippled with starlight.

Breathing deeply of the sweet air, Anodea looked up at the stars. Even on the clearest night she had never seen such splendor. The familiar constellations were lost among their multitudes, they seemed about to form new patterns, to shape answers to questions which she did not yet know how to ask. Yet something in her reached out to them, as an infant feels compelled to pull itself upright.

The light straightened, rippling through colors for which she had no names, growing until it could not be comprehended by all her senses allied. And then there was neither Light nor Darkness. She was all gods, all goddesses. She was One.

Anodhë felt the softness of furs beneath her and knew she was in her own body again. She turned her head against the pillow then, weeping because she was only human once more. And yet, like an echo, something Other remained—a perception and a power which were now her own.

"She is awake, may the Lady be praised!" It was Tania's voice, hoarsened by grief.

The Wisewoman of Galia opened her eyes upon the Queen her daughter, and smiled.

# REUNION

## *by Jayge Carr*

*Jayge Carr, who has been a nuclear physicist, is now a full-time storyteller. Her first novel,* Leviathan's Deep, *was published by Doubleday and promptly became a Science Fiction Book Club selection. Her stories have appeared in* Analog, Omni, Ares, *and* Pandora, *to list only a few.*

*When I first approached Jayge (through a somewhat intricate network of correspondents) she told me that her stories should not be called fantasy, or sword and sorcery, but, instead, Brains and Bewitchery . . . B & B for short. And this one, "Reunion," is an intoxicating blend of magic and brainpower in which the characters think their way through to success. Readers familiar with Jayge's other stories know that she is a mean hand with a plot, a pun, and characters that make them laugh and cry—preferably at the same time. In writing "Reunion," Jayge has created characters as strong, humane, and humorous as she herself is. Her witch here is a form of Aphrodite. But look closely! Some of her other characters are extremely familiar too, though the myths in which they appear are turned upside down.*

*Watch out for Jayge. She is the mother of two formidable daughters, one of whom, she says, will invent a time machine, and the other of whom will become President. Like the character in one of her funniest stories, she is beautiful, spunky, with more up her sleeve than her arm—and she always gets the last word.*

*In this story of restoration to life and love through Brains and Bewitchery, Jayge's managed to get the last word in this anthology too.*

It was a meadow fashioned for the gods to sport in, all flower-dappled and sweet-scented, cool-shaded by benevolent ancient trees.

Kira caught his arm and pointed with a wordless croon of pure pleasure.

Brancel felt the spell, too, and clucked softly to the elderly aurochs that stolidly pulled their wagon. It heaved a sigh and halted, head down.

"How lovely," Kira spoke in an almost-whisper.

"Belike." Brancel's voice was dry. "It's been used for pasturage. You'd have to watch every step you took, and hold your nose, to boot.

"Oh, *you*," she chided, laughing softly. "Can't you ever, just once, stop being a—a detached spectator, and simply *enjoy*."

"Nothing," he spoke from hard-won wisdom, "is ever perfect, and every pleasure has its price."

"Oh, *you*." She laughed again, never taking her gaze off the fragrant expanse. "Oh, look, master-healer, there's vervain. And there—that's bloodseal, you can't mistake the color, and—"

"Woman, you can't recognize those flowers from here." He laughed.

"I can, I can, and they're good herbs, master-healer. Why can't we camp here, and I explore, and pick what we can use?"

"Because the owner of this might object."

"Oh, pooh. Have we seen a house these many weary miles? Just cliff and rock and long lonely road. Come, master-healer, it's not as though you'd given your word to be somewhere.

Why can't we spend a pleasant afternoon, with valuable herbs to show for it?"

He couldn't have said what instinct made him want to whip the tired aurochs away from this too-perfect dell. Or why he felt cold sweat slick the palms of his hands. But she smiled and cajoled and he was loath to refuse one of the few requests she'd ever made of him, this soul-scarred woman with the goddess-branded arms and the eyes that wept without tears.

There was a gaily chuckling riverlet, and he unhitched the aurochs and led it to drink, and spread a blanket on the down-soft grass, and watched as she gathered her herbs, almost dancing in pure glee, the sunlight haloing her silken waving hair.

"How many herbs need you?" he called at last.

"It's a treasure-trove, in very truth," she called back. "Come and see. I've filled my skirt to overflowing, and there's so many more, it's hard to choose."

"Choose you then without me," he called, stretching out on the blanket to let the warm sun charm the aches from old wounds.

"Oh, you." She laughed, and he rolled onto his side to watch her flit gayly about. There was a busy drone of contented insects, and the sun's gentle warmth, and, as she had said, no need to be anywhere but where they were.

At last, with a laugh, she collapsed in the midst of a rainbow pocket in the green and began to plait a sweet-smelling coronet. He watched her, half-asleep, with hope growing in his heart that time had at least healed.

That was the picture he kept afterward. A tall lissome girl-woman in the jewel flowers, sun-bright hair wilding from twin braids to caress a glowing face, not pretty perhaps, but full of character, the kind of face that clutches and holds and is part of a man's mind and heart long after merely pretty girls are long forgot, all crowned by that rakish flower-wreath.

And then it happened. The ground split open behind her, to emit a thunderous roar, belches of smoke, and an ebon chariot drawn by ebon horses breathing midnight flame, and driven by—

He was on his feet and running toward her, but it was already too late.

She had twisted onto her knees, turning toward the sound, and the charioteer had only to swoop to snatch and lay her struggling body at his feet. The horses thundered in a tight circle, and chariot, driver, horses, and girl, dived into the smoking maw of blackness.

The ground closed, and when he reached the place there was not even a dent, a crisped flowerlet, to mark the spot.

The Owner of the meadow, in very truth, had taken his price.

"Don't meddle with the affairs of gods," the old man advised, wiping the wine and drool from his chin with the back of a hairy, careless hand.

"Do I just walk away then?" Brancel asked, of himself really, his cream-colored eyes frowning grey in the smoke and guttering-lamp dimness.

The old man belched loudly. "You still gotta whole skin, haint ya? Meddle, and They'll smash ya, like I crack a flea between my nails." Filthy as he was, the broken nails must have had plenty of practice. He belched again. "Good stuff, this. They got any more?"

Brancel held out a hand piled high with gleaming golden circlets. "When you've told me what I want to know—" he joggled the hand, so the coins clinked enticingly—"these will keep you sodden until the end of time." His voice feigned a calm he didn't feel. The trail to this wine-soaked hulk had been long and costly; and all its branches proved dead ends. He would pry what he wanted from this walking barrel of wine—or mourn what he had lost his life long, and after.

The flickering, wine-bleared eyes danced anywhere but his face. "Aint enough gold in the world for that, lad. But why, boy? Why risk yourself, body and soul?"

"Because if I don't, then I have nothing worth the risking."

Slack-fleshed, stubble-bearded, pendulous beer-belly quivering with every breath, but the voice was suddenly hard and cold—and sober. "You're a fool, boy; but a fool with gold. And I need your gold, to buy the forgetfulness I crave. You want what you want, and I want what I want, and I'll make your bargain."

Brancel leaned forward, hand tight-fisted over the gold, tense with eagerness. "There is a way, then?"

"Aye." The old man spat. "A way. Not that I make any

promises, mind. Tis no way for fools and cravens, their bones line it, every perilous step. Be sure, ere you set your foot on it, that the goal is worth what you risk."

"I will take your way, old man." Brancel nodded. "But understand—if you lie to me, I will return, somehow, and thrust my gold, molten, down your lying throat, so that you choke on it, and the stench of your seared flesh."

The old man laughed until he had to wipe his tearing eyes. "Would you? Would you then? A bargain, boy. Your gold for the cruel fate you rush blindly toward. Think you, if you succeed to the end of your quest, They'll grant your wish? Just for your asking Them sweetly? More like, They'll skewer your soul on white-hot spits, and roast it while They tear your body into fragments for the triple-headed ones to snarl over."

Brancel shrugged, and the coins jingled.

The old man began to talk, in a low voice, hurriedly, as though he feared interruption.

When he finally finished, Brancel dropped the gold in front of him, and he stared at it hungrily, nervously licking his lips.

Brancel rose and elbowed his way through the tight-packed, sweating mob, eager for a breath of fresh air away from the smoke and reek.

"Boy!" It thrust through the clatter, and Brancel turned in the doorway.

The old man was standing, swaying on his feet. "They'll trick you, boy, as They once tricked me! A sound, I thought she'd fallen, and I turned to help—and it was all for nothing, all for nothing! Don't you let Them do it to you, boy! Don't you—" He sagged and disappeared within the crowd.

Brancel turned and walked away into the cool night mist. But he couldn't blot out his last sight of the old man—with tears glistening on his raddled cheeks.

The first stage was simple, for one with knowledge of herbcraft, but had to be done with meticulous care.

When the evil-smelling smoke cleared away, there was a tall figure shawled in a long hooded cloak, precisely in the center of his carefully drawn diagram. "Oh, *pigsties*!" the figure exclaimed. "Another mortal! Why do I always get the dirty jobs! Why do I—say!—you're not old at all, for all your white hair; why, you're kinda cute, aintcha, gorgeous." A hand reached up, and the hood fell to reveal a bleached white, full blown face with glistening, pouting lips. "Why don't you rub the corner of this nasty ol' diagram out, and you and I can get better acquainted, mmmmmm, gorgeous? An' you can tell me all about whatever ol' nasty ol' mortal problem you got, and we'll see what we can do about it mmmmmm?"

Brancel stared at the face that was the lush quintessence of every male night-dream. "I summoned you. . . ."

"Yeahhhhhh." She smiled, and a part of his mind noticed that even with her mouth closed, her two eye teeth pressed into the full crimson lower lip. "But maybe you'd like to inspect the rest of the merchandise, hey?" With tantalizing slowness, her fingers moved among the dark folds, revealing more and more of the white, white flesh beneath.

The cloak made silken rustling noises, punctuated only by his hoarse breathing, until finally it lay, a black pool around her delicate high-arched feet.

Brancel drew in a deep breath, it seared like fire all the way down. Involuntarily he leaned forward.

Her smile broadened. "Like what you see, gorgeous?" She rotated slowly, with tantalizing deliberation, giving him all the view.

She wasn't just not wearing clothes—she was naked, with a lascivious nakedness that was beyond all his experience. She faced him again, after a tormenting eternity, and a pointed pink tongue flicked over her wet crimson mouth. "It's all yours, gorgeous, all yours. All you have to do is wipe out a corner of this nasty old diagram, just a corner. With your finger, just rub out a corner, attaboy, just lean forward a little farther. . . ."

There was a thick, pungent, musky scent surrounding him. He leaned forward—

"Just a finger, or you don't even have to do that, just lay the athame across the line, anywhere will do, just cut the figure, lay the athame across it, break it—"

He had moved, he wasn't sure how or when, toward that flawless vision, his hand poised over the lines of carefully drawn color.

"Cut the figure, rub it out, break it, let me come to you. . . ."

But under the hypnotic drone was another sound, a dry

rustling, or was it another voice? an old, ugly, wine-ruined voice, drowning in tears—*They'll trick you, boy, as They tricked me . . .*

*Trick. . . .*

And he froze, drawn by the hypnotic voice, the supernal seductiveness, but something in mind or heart or instinct kept repeating . . . *trick . . . trick. . . . trick. . . .*

Voice saying . . . trick . . . or—rustling?

Torpidly, his head turned away from the vision, toward the dry almost imperceptible sound.

Two ember-ruby eyes glared into his. He stopped breathing; the lethal master of venom swayed silently on its coils, death-glow eyes level with his. A bifurcate tongue licked out, barely missing his face. Droplets of fire from that tongue seared along his cheek.

He knew what the actual touch of that tongue would bring.

Again the tongue flicked out and again he didn't flinch, although he could feel cold sweat popping out along his forehead.

A third time the tongue probed his courage, and a third time he held fast.

With a hiss that was almost laughter, the huge serpent slithered into the darkness and disappeared.

Kira had been bound to the Lady of the Serpents, her vows broke not of her own choosing. Brancel shook himself, wiped the sweat off his forehead. Had the venomous one been sent by a Lady still interested in one of Hers, or merely drawn by the heat of the fire. In either case. . . .

She was still there, still the quintessential male delight—but now he knew those teeth for what they were.

"Come to me . . ." she crooned.

"Not I," he stated firmly. "Not I. I know what would come after, and I've duties to perform."

"Come . . ." she said again, but she knew her spell was broken. She made a moue of disappointment. Then, ingenuously, "It's worth it, you know."

Brancel nodded. "I believe you. But I summoned you here for another purpose, and now I lay my geas on you."

She snapped long rounded fingers. "It's always that way, virtue take it! Always that way with the cute ones. And when they're old and dry and juiceless. . . ." A deep sigh. "Well, then, mortal, what task do you lay on me?"

"I would go to the Shadowland, the land of fading shades. . . ."

"Why summon me for that, mortal? The athame has a sharp edge—use it."

"I would go as I am now—in living body."

"Oh, for—mortal, have you any idea what you're asking?"

"It has been done, it can be done; I lay the geas on you to guide me—now."

The perfect nose drew up in a loud sniff. "Let me check—" She disappeared.

Brancel relaxed back from his kneeling position onto his heels, once again swiped sweat from his forehead with a weary hand. Somewhere in the darkness, he seemed to see a pair of mocking red embers.

"Lady of wisdom, of love, of life," he murmured, "Lady of the winged death-spitters, look you kindly on this my quest for one of yours untimely stolen." He licked dry lips. "I thank you for what your minion did for me just now, to rescue me from mine own folly. I know how unworthy of her who was once promised to you I am, and yet—" He bowed his head, and seemed to see against closed eyelids a face that was neither woman nor serpent but both and yet neither.

"Little pawn, little pawn," the wind whispered in his ear. "You meddle in a game you understand not. . . ."

A branch split loudly in the fire, and Brancel looked automatically toward the sound. The flames shot high, indigo and gold against the darkness and the figure he'd drawn. And in the flames he saw pictures . . . himself, a prince who had cast off his birthright, attached to a warlord's train, a warlord defied, who had taken his pay for broken word in blood . . . a child who knew, and would not speak . . . who took vengeance in a most unchildish way . . . a child protected by a man who saw more than others had, who admired unchildlike courage . . . a child who grew . . . was claimed by the Lady of the Winged Death-spitters . . . and paid a price. . . .

But not *two* prices. . . .

"Mortal," the white form was back within the figure. "You're meddling, and you've been warned you're meddling. Turn back—turn back *now*."

He shook his head. "I have laid the geas on you, by the herb and by the leaf, by the blood and by the water, by life and by death."

She sniffed again. "Death's a kindly fate, mortal."

"The geas is on you. Lead, that I may follow."

She shrugged, knowing well its effect. "Think you 'tis as simple as that? Lead," she mimicked, "and I'll follow. Nay then, you'll need the passports three, ere you'll be let to cross the bottomless abyss, or the field of spikes."

Brancel merely stood, readjusting his sword to a slightly more comfortable angle in its sheath, sweeping back the long cloak so it wouldn't hinder his sword arm.

"Oh, yeah," she sneered. "One passport you *may* win with that long sword, one you must win with an equally long wit, and the third. . . ."

"The third?" he asked, mildly curious.

"The third you either have or you have not. And if not—" Another shrug. "Your flesh for torment, or to feed those that can stomach it, your soul the toy of the Lord of Darkness."

"Lead on, then, crimson one."

She stretched out her hand toward him, the tips of her fingers just within the colored lines. "Touch my hand. . . ."

He hesitated—another trap?—and then caught the round cool fingers in his hand.

She stepped out of the figure and pulled the long shapeless black cloak about herself. "Follow me, then, feckless mortal." A low mutter. "Always the cute ones. . . ."

They climbed ever higher in the jagged hills, over sheer cliffs and escarpments that left Brancel panting, trying not to stare downward. And still, tirelessly, she led him on.

In midafternoon, she drew him forward. Before them was a stone arch, carved or natural, he knew not. But its curves and angles seemed to run into each other strangely, drawing the eye into inward distances.

Mounted in front of it was a kite-shaped metal shield bright scarlet of fresh-spilt blood.

"Strike you that shield, mortal," his guide said, her voice muffled in the jet-dark folds, "and test both your courage and strength of arm."

The shield screamed like a man receiving a mortal wound. Startled, he drew back. And seemed to see, not a shield, but a man, naked, spread-eagled, with a knife-hilt protruding from his hairy, blood-soaked breast. Brancel blinked, and it was again only a shield.

"What was that," he demanded hoarsely.

"One who dared demand a key from the guardian," she answered, "and failed, and paid the price."

A deep breath. "Must—must I strike again."

"Needless. The guardian comes."

He had expected he knew not what. A giant, an ogre, a monster, even a demigod.

But strolling toward him, as though he owned all the time in the world, was a slender, white-tunicked boy, barefoot in the rocks, toweling dry a wealth of waving golden hair. As he approached, Brancel could smell a pleasant violet scent.

The boy yawned, still briskly toweling his hair. "You called, cloaked one?" he asked, ignoring Brancel.

"You have a certain Token, you know what Gate it opens. I must have it of you."

The boy laughed, rich, bright young laughter, that glittered over the rocks. "You think I give my Token for the asking. You know better, cloaked one. Do you dare to challenge me, then?"

"Not I. This mortal."

For the first time, the youth turned and stared at the patiently waiting man. "As your champion, cloaked one?"

"At his own behest. The quest is his, the fee is his. I am but guide, under his geas. He summoned, and I came. I guide, only guide, that is all."

"And does he know what fee he pays, what haps to those fools who challenge and fail?"

"I know." Brancel spoke for the first time.

"And still you challenge?"

"Unless you would freely give me the Token my guide says I needs must have."

"Never. I accept your challenge, then, foolish mortal. Come with me."

Through the arch was a narrow cleft, leading slightly upward, lined with shields. Some were the scarlet of flowing blood, some darker, some maroon-brown of blood long dried. And when Brancel looked at them sideways, out of the corner of his eyes, he saw not shields, but men. Some contorting in mortal agony, the blood gushing bright from deadly wounds. Others hanging limply, eyes half closed, only the slow rise and fall of chests to show the fragile strand of life still clinging. Brancel repressed a shudder—the ever-dying undead.

"I'm glad you came, mortal." The sweet-faced boy spoke over his slim shoulder. "It's been awhile, you know, and now I think on it, my shield outside is getting a bit—worn."

"Do they make a shield of you if you lose," Brancel was bold enough to say.

The boy whirled to face him, frowning furiously. Then his smile came, glorious as the dawn. "I like you, mortal. Forget this mad quest of yours, stay here and amuse me."

"Had I not this quest, I would companion you in your loneliness, guardian. But as it is—" Brancel drew his sword out, kissed its hilt, pointed it toward the boy-slender guardian.

"I would you could, too, mortal. And would I could save you from the penalty of your folly. But—" A shrug, a spreading of the long slim fingers.

The cleft erupted suddenly into a natural amphitheater. Almost circular, with tiers and tiers of empty seats.

Or—were they empty?

Despite the sun's brightness, there were shadows.

Despite the windlessness, there were—murmurs. . . .

There was a minimum of preparation. Brancel stripped down to his own undertunic, clipped the heavy shield to his left arm, drew his sword, and advanced to the center of the arena.

The boy slid a slender blade from a sheath hung on one wall, picked up an oblate shield, and faced Brancel. "I'm ready."

"Wait!" Brancel swung his sword aside.

"You withdraw your challenge?" The boy was disappointed.

"No. You forgot to put on your sandals, and this floor is harsh. I'll wait, while you tie them on."

"Oh!" The boy looked down. "Twould make no difference, but I thank you for your courtesy. If you would wait. . . ."

He was back, his feet shod in sturdy sandals, before Brancel had time to get impatient. As soon as the duel began, he understood why the boy had said it would make no difference. Brancel was a fine, polished swordsman; but against this whip-lean, laughing, sublimely fast spirit of the blade, he was hopelessly outclassed, and knew it. He settled down to hope for a miracle.

No miracle happened.

Brancel tried every feint, every trick, every ploy and counter and attack he knew, with the same result each time: his blade pierced empty air, while the boy, laughing, scratched him with his own weapon, each touch a different spot—each potentially mortal.

His breath seared as he drew it in, his sword and shield weighted him down, long scores itched and burned, a haze floated before him. And through the haze, his slender, smiling foe, dancing in and out as though his sword wasn't there, touching him as he pleased, toying with him.

He slashed desperately, his opponent parried with humiliating ease.

"The game no longer amuses!"

And Brancel's shield thudded to the ground, his sword went spinning away, a foot hooked his ankle from behind, and he went down hard, to lay winded, his aching muscles bruised against the unyielding rock, while a sharp sword point pressed against his unprotected throat.

"Yield, mortal. You've lost, admit it."

"No." Brancel couldn't shake his head without endangering his throat. But he could speak, in gasps. "No, never. But if you do not—thrust that sword home—I will get up—and attack you again—with my bare hands—or teeth—or whatever I can find—to use—against you—"

A sandal-shod foot pressed against his chest, pinning him. The sword moved, pressed against his limp wrist. "Yield."

Brancel lay, winded, exhausted, weaponless. "Give me—what I must have. Or I will continue to fight—as long as there is breath in me—no matter what—you do. . . ."

"You would be amazed at what can be removed from a body—and that body live and bleed and pain."

Brancel shut his eyes. The world swung around him in crazy arcs. "And—fight," he whispered. "And fight. And—*fight*. . . ."

He felt a sharp pain against his wrist. "Yield," ordered the voice. "Yield." His body arched up against the weight holding it, contorted.

"Fight," he howled—or whispered, he wasn't sure which.

"YIELD—YIELD—YIELD—"

"Fight," he gasped, or whimpered, or whispered. "Fight. . . ."

"*YIELD*!!!"

After an age of pain, he fell into blackness.

He lay, flat on his back on grim hardness. Above him was a night sky spattered with stars. He moved, and moaned with pain—and yet—

Tentatively, and then with growing hope and amaze, he felt himself. The myriad hairline scores were stiff with caked blood and throbbed incessantly—but his wrist had a thin white weal and no more. And the other places. . . . He looked himself over with eyes that saw and couldn't believe what they saw.

Except for those painful scratches, he was essentially intact, whole.

He sat up, patted himself with more vigor.

He was *whole.*

"You won."

He looked up, and she towered over him in the darkness, her dark cloak blending into the deeper darkness.

"I—*what?*"

"You won. He's off sulking, but he'll get over it. He doesn't lose very often, you know."

"But—I don't understand. The Token—"

"You have it; it's yours. The Gate will open for you now."

"But I—I didn't defeat him." Wry honestly. "I *couldn't.*"

"No, you couldn't. But he, in his turn, couldn't defeat *you.* Regardless of what he did, you refused to yield. So the Token is yours, you earned it."

"Oh." He was too tired to do more than lie back and go to sleep.

They started out again in the cold faint light of dawn, from that empty, empty arena. He followed her, ever upward, without complaint and without comment.

The second guardian was a middle-aged, plump, motherly female, who cooed in dismay over his stiffening scratches and smoothed on a soothing moss-green salve that eased away the pain and soreness almost immediately.

She lived in a tree, and once he had brushed aside the branches that swept to the ground, he was amazed at how cozy and warm it was within. Soft cushions nestled in the gnarled trunk or on low thick branches and light filtered greenly through the foliage.

She insisted on making a herb tea, and served it with cakes of unsurpassable sweetness and lightness.

Brancel decided he liked this guardian's methods *much* better than those of the last.

His guide curled in a dim corner, silent, until the bustling guardian scurried away to fetch some more cakes. (Thirds? Fourths?) Then she leaned over and touched his arm lightly. "You must ask her a riddle."

"A—riddle?"

"That she cannot answer. When you've drunk your tea."

He was still deep in thought when she returned.

It would have to be a *new* riddle, one that she'd never heard, or even a variation of one she'd heard.

Or—maybe—a riddle that couldn't be answered—because it had no answer. . . .

He remembered a discussion he'd had once, with a group of young philosophers from the Lyceum. There had been a problem in logic one of them propounded, not a riddle, but if it could be phrased like a riddle. . . .

"I have a riddle for you, Mother."

"Oh, dear, oh, dear, and you seemed like such a *nice* boy, too."

"Listen, Mother. Here is the riddle. I am telling a lie."

"Yes, dear, but what's the riddle?"

"That is the riddle. I am telling a lie. Now you answer me, *am* I telling a lie, or the truth?"

"I—I'm not sure I follow . . ."

"I said, I am telling a lie. But when I say I am telling a lie, am I *truly* telling a lie, or am I telling the truth?"

"Well, of course, dear, if you say you are telling a lie, then. . . . But if you say you are telling a lie, then that statement itself must be a lie, so what you say cannot be true, so you must not be telling a lie, you must be telling the truth. . . . But if you are telling the truth, then you are telling a lie. . . . But if it's a lie, then it can't be a lie, because if it's a lie, it's truth. . . . But if it's truth, then it's a lie. . . . And if it's a lie, then it's. . . . Oh, my. Oh, dear, oh, dearie me. . . ."

They continued to climb. Only once did he dare to ask, why if they were going to the land below, they kept climbing.

"Because that which is above is that which is beneath," the

shapeless black answered. "I obey your geas, mortal—only do not weary me with mortal vaporings."

The first Gate was literally a gate, solid as the rock from which it was hewn. The guide marched up to it, and did something he couldn't see, and immediately there was a low, hoarse, snuffling noise, as of wind reverberating through ancient, endless caverns. Or a very, *very* large animal breathing.

"Open, oh sink of sloth," the guardian called loudly. "You must open and pass us through, we have the Token."

"Ah-yeah, ah-yeah, I hear ye." The voice was thick and syrupy, impossibly deep, punctuated by deep yawns. "Not a-many choose this road, jus' hadda be sure. . . ." The Gate opened two faded blue eyes to stare at them. Brancel swallowed bile. The eyes were *huge*, sized to fit the immensity of the Gate, and as guilelessly innocent as a child's. They fixed on the guide, and then moved to focus on him. "Ye *do* have the Token, and carried by a mortal . . . ohhhhhhh. . . . Himself's not going to like *this*. . . ."

"That has nothing to do with you. Your task is to open and let the Token and its bearer pass through."

"Aw-ri', aw-ri', don't have a stroke. I'm gonna open, I'm gonna open, jus' let me work the kinks out—I've been asleep awhile, y'know. . . ." One of the twinkling blue eyes winked at Brancel. Then the Gate—stretched. One side went up, then the other, like a man working his shoulders to get stiffness out. Then the lower corners, one after the other, like a man flexing his legs.

A loud tapping sound came from beneath the cloak, as of a delicate foot rapping impatiently against bare rock.

"Aw-ri', aw-ri', I'm opening." A bit at a time, slowly, like a man stepping backward with a cloak tangled about his feet, gingerly sliding back each foot an inch or so at a time so he wouldn't trip, the Gate hoicked himself backwards, corner by corner.

"You *are* getting old." The guide was ruthless.

"Nay, I'm open, see, I'm open! You wouldn't complain to Himself, now would you, sweetness?"

A sigh. "I suppose not. Come, mortal."

"Eh, there, wait a mite. *He* carries the Token, not you, sweetness. How's about you stay here, warm stiff old hinges—" Again the blue eye winked at Brancel. "Eh, sweetness? For old time's sake?"

An amused sputter. "You never change." The blue eyes drooped disconsolately. Brancel thought, if the Gate had had a lower lip, it would have been thrust out pouting, like a spoilt child's. "I must guide," she stated. "But perchance, when the geas is fulfilled, on my way out. . . ."

The blue eyes lighted up. "Eh, now, sweetness, that's more like. I'll be awaitin'!"

"Just don't fall asleep again." She drew Brancel inside.

"I won't, sweetness, I won't! Just you hurry back!"

Behind them, Brancel could hear the Gate creaking and groaning back into his place.

The tunnel was sometimes narrow, sometimes wide, but always dimly lit, though he could never spot a source of the light; and always there were carvings and shadows that made terrifying scenes at the corner of his eye, but when he stared at them they were only formless rock.

And always, always upward.

Once, he whirled, sure that there was hulking menace behind him. But there was nothing there but rock and shadow, shadow and rock.

And in front of him, his guide, a shadow among shadows.

She stopped. "You must lead, here."

Brancel stared over her shoulder into a wide abyss. He moved around her, stared down. The depths of it were gone, hidden completely in mist or shadow. It stretched across their way, the walls widening to contain it, like an incongrous grin in a stolid face. He couldn't see the ends of it.

He broke off a crumbling bit of rock and dropped it in—but though he listened long, there was no sound of its landing. The gap was too wide to leap across. "Do we go around?" he asked. "I don't see any way."

"No, mortal. We go across." She pointed, and he saw, suspended over the chasm, a single blade, like an impossibly long slender dagger.

"On *that*?" It wasn't braced or held by anything, it simply lay, one end on the ledge he could see, the other (presumably) on the other side. "It's impossible. It will never bear our weight, and even if it could, we couldn't cross so slender a road."

"We can, and we will, mortal. You bear the Token. Your wit was sharp, even as this blade, and will bear you across. Just step out and don't stop."

Brancel drew a deep breath and stepped out. He felt the sharp edge against the sole of his boot, and he swung the other foot out and felt the sharp edge again. But he also felt as if two hands, firm under his armpits, were supporting him, balancing him, holding him securely. He trotted briskly forward, not looking down or sideways, just concentrating on placing one foot after another on the narrow bridge.

When he felt hard rock beneath his feet again, he turned. His guide was tripping airily across, black veils aflutter, as nonchalant as though she strolled on solidest rock.

"Are—are there any more like that?" he asked as she drew abreast of him.

"The next is worse."

"Many thanks," he muttered.

The next was a wide cavern, so wide he couldn't see the sides, and filled, packed tight, with a field of strange grey plants.

"This is the one you must have earned the Token for, yourself, in Life."

"I see. And if I have earned this third Token?"

"The plants will turn aside. Their spines will not prick you."

"And if I have it not?"

"Then you will never come out the other side. The spines will prick, and pierce, and *hold*. You will spend eternity, struggling against their spines."

"And no way to tell if I've earned this safeguard?"

"No. Only to trust yourself to the plants. *They* know."

"Perhaps, we could wrap our cloaks around ourselves—"

"No, we would only lose them in the first few steps. Pull it behind you, like so." She slung her cloak over her shoulders, so that the white body gleamed softly in the darkness. "Leave your clothes. They pose no barricade to the spines. . . ."

Barcel looked at them. They didn't look too tall, perhaps his boots would be a protection.

He stepped in—and down. In three steps, the plants were at his waist, in six, near his shoulders, in nine above his eyes. . . .

They reached for him. . . .

The guide was right. Clothing was no barrier. They pricked and stung. He hesitated, and the attack intensified. He batted at them with his arms, but he had only two arms, and they had a hundred, a thousand whips.

"Guide. . . ." He roared appeal.

"Keep moving . . ." he thought he heard her call.

Something slashed across his back, like a white-hot chain, and he surged away, anywhere, forward, sideways, he didn't know.

The plants herded him; he staggered and stumbled, arms futilely trying to protect his face, his eyes, from the demon furies.

He tried to trample them underfoot, but somehow they were never there. Only on his body, slashing, burning as though each spine were coated with dripping acid. Sometimes he fell, and then he crawled, head hanging, eyes clamped shut.

Sometimes he managed to stagger to his feet, and run, a shambling blind run to nowhere. Until he fell again.

And always the cruel fangs of the plants, the remorseless, tireless masters.

He was trapped, he would spend eternity as she said, under the burning spines of the plants of dread.

An eternity of spines and pain.

Collapse . . . crawl . . . collapse . . . struggle blindly onward like an eyeless worm . . . collapse . . . struggle . . . collapse . . . squirm and flinch and. . . .

An eternity. . . .

"Stand up, you're out." The voice of his guide.

He moaned, eyes screwed shut, his entire body one mass of pain.

"A close decision, you've done much to be ashamed of. But some deeds to be proud of, too, or they would never have let you go. You must have shared food when your own belly clamored, lent a cloak when your bones ached with cold . . ."

He rolled over, gazed up at her out of pain-bleared eyes. "You mean . . . ?"

"Yes. Unselfishness, charity earns a path through the thorns. Selfishness, evil, cruelty earns their scores."

He stared up. The white, white skin was criss-crossed with tiny red lines. "You . . . too. . . ."

She nodded. "I, too. The plants take toll for *all* our deeds. . . ."

"Um." He hadn't the energy to rise—yet. In a while, he would find it, from somewhere. Drag himself forward. But for now, he only lay. "Both ways?" he asked.

"No." Her voice was amused. "Sleep, now, mortal. When you wake, you will eat, and we will finish our journey."

"Um." He drew his cloak slowly and painfully around himself. He couldn't sleep, but he could at least rest, gather his strength for whatever ordeals lay ahead.

He felt her hand, soft on his forehead, and then smelled a strange, orchid-ripe odor.

And then nothing.

The last stage was a wide, deep river, its dark water oily and turgid, with strange slow bubbles breaking on the surface with dull plops, assaulting his nostrils with a reek of musty decay. He stretched out a curious finger to touch it, and she pulled him back. "That is forgetfulness, mortal. One drop on you, and your mind will be wiped as clean as a newborn babe's."

"Then how do we cross?"

"The boatman comes."

The boat was drawn by something in the water. A snaky head with glowing amber eyes ranged ahead of the boat.

The boat turned in an easy circle and bumped against the rock-shore. The boatman climbed slowly out, made it fast against a piling. He was tall, and gaunt, almost fleshless, a dried-out man who might have been any age. "Have you my pay?" His voice, too, was dry and fleshless.

Something passed from her hand to his outstretched palm. His hand closed on it before Brancel could see what it was. "Passage for two," the dry, wind whistling through rocks voice said.

"Good." The guide moved to step into the boat, and Brancel put his hand under her elbow to steady her.

"Wait," the boatman said. "You know the rules, crimson one."

"I had forgot."

Even his smile was dry. "You mean, you hoped I had forgot. Not I, crimson one. Obey, or pass me not."

The guide sighed, looked up at Brancel. "You must leave everything here."

"Leave. . . ."

"Everything. All you own or wear or possess. Everything." Her hands went up to her cloak.

"Oh." He began to remove his own clothing. The boatman's eyes were fixed on the guide. His thin pale tongue flicked against his thin pale lower lip.

"You'd think you'd seen enough by now," she grumbled, as the cloak once more made a crumpled heap around her feet.

Her body had all the unhuman perfection he remembered, as he helped her into the sable boat.

"Not you." The boatman put out a hand to stop him. "You aint through."

Brancel looked down at himself. "I'm naked. What more do you want?"

"The rules say, everything," the boatman asserted. "You're still wearing a glove."

Brancel looked down at the skin-colored glove on his left hand. It was so much a part of him that he had literally forgotten he was wearing it. Never, in his whole adult life, had he voluntarily removed that glove to reveal what lay beneath.

"It's not clothing," he protested. "It's a ban—"

"It comes off," the boatman was firm. "It comes off, or you stay out."

Brancel drew a deep breath, stood, naked, on his ledge of rock, staring down at his stiffened left hand, the crippled hand, the hand that couldn't hold a shield properly, its deformities cleverly concealed by a padded, skillfully made glove.

He couldn't, for his life's sake, for his soul's sake, remove that glove.

But—for Kira?

He stretched his hand down to the woman in the boat. "Will you—" His voice was so hoarse he hardly recognized it. "Will you—help me? It's difficult to remove—one-handed. . . ."

And then he waited, face averted, while slim, strong fingers peeled off the thin, tight, fitted glove.

Then, because he couldn't help himself, he turned to see the disgust, pity, amusement in her face.

What he saw was mild curiosity. "An unusual custom," she said. "Why was it done to you?"

"To prove I was a man," he managed to get out.

Her eyebrows raised. "Surely there are easier ways of proving manhood."

He forced himself to look at the deliberately ruined hand. "But none so sure. It is—was—the custom among my family."

"I think—" her voice was gentle—"you had best start a new family. The price of manhood in yours is far too high."

The boatman spat, his spittle raising slow ripples in the viscous liquid. "You comin' or not?"

Brancel stepped into the boat, seated himself.

The boatman spat again. "I seen worse," he nodded toward the Hand. "But not many."

Once it had been a banner, proclaiming what he was. But times passes, and people forget. Few now would recognize it for what it was. Except for its ugliness. He started to hold it, to hide it in the unmarked flesh of his other hand; but then, defiantly, he changed his mind and left it out, for all to see, in its naked distorted deformity.

The Lord of the Realm of Shades was *not* amused. He sat, a man-sized ebony light-sucking darkness on a throne of jetty-black darkness, his only feature (visible to human eyes) a pair of eyes of glowing black. "The mortal woman trespassed. She looked reasonably appealing, so I took her. And I have no intention of giving her up."

"Even in return for a proven warrior?" Brancel asked.

"Even proven warriors are mortal, mortal." The blackness shifted impatiently. "I will have you, sooner or later, so why should I give up the woman now?"

"Because this is the realm of shades and she lives and breathes."

The blackness moved, the effect of a shrug. "My shades need an occasional mortal among them, to remind them of what they were. Besides—she amuses me."

Around the jetty-black throne stretched the realm of shades, a great open, many-domed cavern, lit by rivers of molten metal, and volcanoes spitting flames and glowing lava. Among the crevasses demons tormented shades, their screams a constant undertone. In other areas, shades merely walked about, or spoke softly among themselves. Parts of the cavern were completely hidden by mists, and others looked like sweet sunlit meadows—yet others were filled with unspeakable horrors.

"Then I will fight you for her. In whatever manner and with whatever weapons you prefer."

That amused the dark lord. His laughter drowned even the screams of the tormented. Finally he spoke. "I think not, mortal. What is mine, I keep. Turn back, retrace your steps, be glad that in my infinite mercy I give you leave to go."

"Kira!" Brancel threw back his head and howled it, throwing his voice echoing through the many chambers. "Kiii-iiiiii-ira! Kira, it is I, Brancel! Kiiiiiiiii-ra!"

There was a rustling among the shades, through the demons. "Kira, Kira, Kiiiii-ra, Kirakirakira. . . ."

The lord rose, his angry height towering over Brancel, his eyes black flames. "So be it, mortal. You may stay and amuse my loyal ones! Which do you prefer, that she watch your torment, or be ignorant of it?"

"No!" Brancel surged toward the dread lord—and found himself pinned by a dozen invisible hands. Despite his frantic desperate struggle, he was dragged back, away from the unmoving lord.

"Your last chance, mortal. Shall she remain ignorant of your fate?"

"Curse you, let her go!"

"You've lost your choice then. Let's see, will it amuse me to watch her watch . . . ?"

"No." The guide spoke. "He has earned a boon—you must grant it to him."

"I offered him his freedom, he refused. No more offer I."

"Surely, lord," the guide pleaded, "you have your choice among the most frolicsome wenches of all time. What can one more or less be to you? The mortal has paid dear already for his reward. Surely your generosity. . . ."

"My generosity will stretch to once more offering his freedom. Well, mortal?"

"And Kira?"

"There is Lethe in the very air here. Already she forgets."

"Perhaps that is kindest," murmured Brancel. But then, "No! Forgetfulness is just a slower death! If I have earned a boon, then I ask it now! Let our fates, whatever they are, be shared!"

"You would she share your torment?" the dark lord asked.

"No! No, never that! But surely, there must be times—even demons must rest—that we could be together. . . ."

"You are a fool, mortal! Don't you know what the most exquisite torment is? Choose, now. Your freedom above, or eternal torment here. Choose."

"But always alone."

"There are many *frolicsome* wenches in the mortal world, also."

"No!" It was the guide. Both the dark lord and Brancel turned toward her. "I say, No!—*brother*!"

"You are a greater fool than the mortal—sister. So once again you invade my realm for what is no longer yours."

"What is mine I keep, is't not so, brother? The woman was mine."

"She trespassed, sister. She is now *mine*."

"You *lured* her. And she was mine *first*."

"Her vows were broke. You have no claim."

"Her vows were broke unwillingly. And her trespass innocent. 'Tis you who have no claim."

"You have no power in my realm, sister. You gave it all up to enter. The woman is mine, and what I have, I keep. And what will you do about that—*sister*?"

The woman smiled. Brancel stared at her. The crimson one's persona was gone, torn away, as if it had never been, and he saw her plain, in all her immortal glory and perfection, as far superior to the crimson one in every way, as the crimson one had been above mere mortal women; and he knew her, the goddess of love, and wisdom, and beauty.

He fell to his knees. "Lady, if I have in ignorance offended. . . ."

Her smiled warmed him. "Only in one small way, mortal. But I may let you atone for your offense, later. . . ."

The dark one snarled. "You claim this one, too, sister?"

"I may have use for him, anon. For now—he is no plaything of yours, brother."

"He is *here*. So he is mine, mine to do with as I choose. And the woman. Mine. And you can do nothing, nothing, *nothing!*"

She shrugged, sat on an outthrust rock, nursing one perfect

knee between her linked fingers, smiling at the dark lord over that knee. "Precisely what I intend to do, brother—*nothing*."

The glowing embers veiled. "Nothing?"

A smile, a nod. "Nothing, brother. You're not very hospitable, you know. 'Tis been long since I visited you, and you offer me scant welcome."

"I'll offer you what welcome you deserve, once we've this matter of these two mortals settled."

She smiled blandly at him. "But I thought it was settled. What I have, I keep. Didn't you say that yourself, brother? I have no power here. What can poor powerless I do to change your will?"

He growled. "Nothing, sister."

"As you say, nothing." Her smile broadened, she linked her hands behind her head, leaned back against the rock wall, her body a luminescent glow against its muddy darkness. "But on the off chance that you will change your mind, brother, I will accept your hospitality."

"This is some trick of yours. . . ."

"Trick, brother? Nay, I but place my dependence on your famed generosity. You will see the light, eventually, and I will take my pair of mortals back with me. I can wait—I have patience, brother. And now, would you show me about this goodly realm of yours. It grows with time, doesn't it, brother. I fear it may cease to grow, while I am here with you, and not attending to my proper tasks above, but you will be amply repaid for any lack in your shades by my company, brother."

"So that is it! And I said there was nothing you could do!"

"But that is what I am doing, brother. Nothing. Precisely nothing. It's past time I had a holiday, and now. . . ."

"Enough. I see your plot plain. Without love, sooner or later there will be few new shades for my clever ones to play with. No, you win—this much, sister! You may have that one, he is yours, do with him as you will. I'll not sorrow to see the last of his face—please take care that I see it not again too soon! But as for the female—she has a place here; she may not thank you kindly for jerking her from it, even for this mortal fool beside you. So I say this: Let the female choose. If she chooses to go with you, you may take her and welcome. But if she chooses to stay. . . . Then you will go, dragging this mortal with you, will he, nil he. And I'll hear no more of this mortal matter."

"It's a trick," Brancel hissed at her. "She's forgotten. . . ."

"Not yet." She shook her head. "Faded but not yet forgotten. But he knows something we don't. . . ."

"Well, sister. Will that content you sufficient to return to your proper sphere?"

"Well, mortal. Will you leave it up to her choice?"

He rose to his feet, slowly, to give himself time to think. "Lady, I want her. I need her. She's like an arm or a leg to me, without her I'm crippled, deformed, lacking. But—" He licked his lips. "Let *her* choose. Quickly. Before my want o'ercomes my resolution."

"You hear, brother." A hand on his shoulder, soft and warm, consolation and—pride. "Summon the mortal woman, lay the choice before her honestly. The mortal man and I will abide by her decision."

"So be it, sister. But I think the mortal might be somewhat—ah—occupied at present . . . as you see. . . ."

A long black flame like a finger pointed, and a veil disappeared. Kira was in a little bower, a cozy soft nook—and not alone. They were half-sitting, half lying on a silken covered heap of cushions, and all that could be clearly seen of Kira was two arms wrapped around a broad back, arms covered with the dark winged serpent tattoos that hid Kira's physical scars. As Brancel watched, the man leaned down to kiss her, a languorous, lazy, savoring kiss, the kiss exchanged between two who have loved long and satisfyingly, who can while away the time between love with smaller pleasurings.

And somehow the broad scarred muscular back was familiar.

"The woman doesn't seem to be screaming," the dark lord remarked. "Or struggling against her loathsome fate." Kira's hand stroked the broad back, a lingering caress.

Brancel strode toward the two in the bower, burning with rage. He was going to take his woman from whoever-that-was, tear him into pieces, and stomp the pieces into the rock floor!

"Stop!" the dark one said. "Do you want to bother to ask her to choose? Or will you just leave?"

Brancel shuddered and turned toward the lady, eyes blind with pain. "I—waited." His voice was almost a whisper. "She had been—hurt, and I wanted her to heal. I have been—nothing!—to her . . ."

"Let her have the choice, brother," the lady's voice was cool but firm. "Let her choose. I think her choice might surprise you."

"Such a nuisance. They didn't fulfill their destiny above, and he lacked, and so did she. Now they are both whole, and I must interfere once more. . . . Sister, you hold a fearsome weapon over my head, to force me to this."

"Let her choose, brother. And abide by her choice."

"So be it. And I hope her choice surprises you, sister." He pointed the black flame again at the two in the bower, and they looked up, startled, as though listening. Then the man put protecting arms around her, tried to force her back onto the cushions, but she shook away, and rose, and took his hand, drawing him up with her, and the two approached the throne.

And Brancel knew him. The warlord who had been responsible for the deaths of the child-Kira's family, and the breaking of the woman-Kira's vows—and who had died by her hand.

"What a dynasty they would have made," the dark one murmured. "What a glorious, brawling, irresistible dynasty."

They walked hand in hand, like two children, the slender woman wrapped in glory, and the ugly man strong in his pride.

And then she saw Brancel. "Healer!" She flung herself into his arms, and it was the warlord's turn to scowl. "Oh—your poor hand!" He braced himself for her flinch, pulling away—disgust. "Your poor hand . . ." she murmured, soothing it against her cheek. "How it must have hurt you. . . ." She turned the ruined palm to her lips and kissed it, and it was as though she kissed away the old pain, old hurt.

"It doesn't—bother you. . . ."

"Only, how it must have hurt you. . . ."

"Yes . . . it *did*. . . ."

"I summoned you, woman," the lord interrupted them, "because you are a mortal, and belong not naturally here, and the mortal world has asked for you back."

"Oh!" She stepped back, so that she was almost exactly halfway between the two men. "Oh! Ohhhh. . . ."

"And you can go back—"

"You mean, the healer is not yet—"

"Not yet! And not, I trust, for many mortal years. You may go back with him, to the mortal world—if you choose. Or you may stay here, with him you have pleased and who had pleased you—if you choose. Go—or stay. The choice is yours, and yours alone. I will not coerce you, or allow either of these to try to influence you. The choice is yours, wholly and solely yours, and must be made—now."

Her head swung from one to the other. "Healer . . . warlord. . . ."

"The choice is *yours*. Go—or stay. Which?"

"Lord, in all your realm and years, you have committed no crueler act than this. I cannot choose."

"You must. And now."

"I—I can*not!*" She buried her face in her hands and burst into tears. Brancel and the warlord converged on her, each putting an arm around her, glaring at his rival, patting her back and making soothing noises.

"Well, sister, what would you have?"

A smile played around the perfect mouth. "If I may suggest, there *is* a precedent. . . ."

"You mean. . . ."

"Of course."

"Agreed." The dark lord turned away, throwing back over his shoulder, "*You* may tell them." A snort. "And they call *me* cruel. . . ."

"What else is love—" she spoke almost to herself—"but the cruelest pain—and the sharpest joy—of all. . . ." Briskly. "Listen to me, you three, for I have wasted more time on this affair than I should. The mortal man has given his choice to me. The mortal woman has made her choice. The shade whose destiny was unfulfilled on mortal earth shall have some portion of what he lacked—but only a portion. For six months the mortal woman will remain here, with this shade. And then she shall be returned to the mortal kingdom, and you, mortal—for six months. And then she shall return here, for six months. You two will share her, one after the other. And each of you will know that his days with her are numbered; that when the time comes, she will leave you—for *him*. And you will know, woman, that no matter how happy you are with one, that the other waits—alone, knowing where you are and whom you're with. And each will know that the choice was yours. To stay with him, and then to leave him—for the other."

Kira knelt. "Lady, he was right, it is cruel. But you are right—it is my choice. The only choice I can make." She looked up at the living man beside her. "Once you said you would have me only willingly, not from gratitude or fear, but only freely, with love. And I said that I—lacked, and I regretted that lack, because if not, I would have come to you, willingly. Now I am—healed, I no longer lack, not for you—but not for him, either. If you can suggest a better way, then do so. But—I love you both, and love is cruel, but it is there. And I cannot deny it, not for you, not for him. So what else am I to do?"

Brancel did the hardest thing he had ever done. He smiled down at her. "I will wait, then, for six months." To the warlord: "You would not love her were she not what she is, neither more nor less. Be grateful for what you have, as I am, and glad her heart is big enough for both us foolish males."

"Spouter of words, as always," the warlord grumbled. "Wait, then, and hope that in six months I have not managed to change her female mind." He put a possessive hand on the woman's bowed shoulder, and at his touch, she looked up, startled, her eyes wide. Brancel smiled down, and put out a hand to help her to her feet, eyes catching hers and holding.

"You may try," he murmured softly to himself. "You may *try*. . . ."

Kira caught his other hand, that pitiful scarred hand, and kissed it tenderly.

"You may *try*. . . ."

"Kiss her good-bye, then, mortal. I think your rival will allow you that. And then we must make haste, for I have tasks undone, and duties to perform."

It was a draft drunk deep by a thirsty man, to store up for six months' desert dryness. And then they entered the dark chariot, the goddess and he, and swirled away in smoke. His last glimpse of Kira was with the warlord's possessive arm about her shoulder, a grim, knowing smile on the ugly scarred face.

He stepped out blindly, on softly spoken command. "This is my bower, mortal. Like you it?"

Brancel blinked, his eyes focused. It was a silk and velvet setting, worthy of the jewel it housed. . . .

"I said you would have opportunity to make atonement, mortal, for the small offense of wisely choosing to refuse the crimson one. But do you refuse *me*, now?"

"Lady . . ." He sank to his knees, bowed his head.

Soft fingers cupped his chin, raised until his eyes met hers. "I am like you in one thing, mortal. I like not unwilling. If you are truly unwilling, if you would be faithful to her, if you simply must have time, for any reason, say so now, and I will send you wherever in the mortal realm you choose. But if you are willing . . . I know you have an appointment, in six mortal months; I will ensure you keep it." A rich smile. "You have a choice once again: Go—or stay. Which shall it be, mortal?"

He looked into her eyes. "Lady. . . ." It was her answer.

She smiled, luxuriously. "Come, then, mortal, and begin your—atonement. . . ."

# SELECTED BIBLIOGRAPHY

**Non-Fiction.** Libraries could be filled with the books about mythology, witchcraft, demonology, and astrology—just to start with. Here are a few. For works relating to specific cultures or rituals, check their bibliographies.

Anglo, Sydney (editor), *The Damned Art: Essays in the Literature of Witchcraft* (London, 1977).

Bettelheim, Bruno, *The Uses of Enchantment: The Meaning and Importance of Fairy Tales* (New York: Random House, 1977).

Bodkin, Maud, *Archetypal Patterns in Poetry* (Oxford, 1968).

Cavendish, Richard, *The Black Arts* (New York, 1967).

Charwick, Nora Kershaw, *Poetry and Prophecy* (London: Cambridge University Press, 1942).

Chesler, Phyllis, *Women and Madness* (New York: Avon, 1973).

Cohn, Norman, *The Pursuit of the Millennium* (London: Paladin, 1970).

Dyer, Reverend T.F. Thistelton, *Folk-Lore of Shakespeare* (Dover Press, 1966).

Ehrenreich, Barbara, and English, Deirdre, *Witches, Midwives, and Nurses: A History of Women Healers* (New York, 1972).

Eliade, Mircea, *The Forge and the Crucible: The Origins and Structures of Alchemy* (New York: Harper Torchbooks, 1962).

——*Myth and Reality* (New York: Harper Torchbooks, 1968).

——*Myths, Rites, Symbols* (edited by Wendell C. Beane and William G. Doty) (New York: Harper Torchbooks, 1976).

——*Occultism, Witchcraft, and Cultural Fashions: Essays in Comparative Religions* (London, 1976).

Frazier, Sir James George, THE GOLDEN BOUGH (12 vols.) (London, New York, 1969).

Jung, C. G. and Kerenyi, C., *Essays on a Science of Mythology* (Princeton, 1971).

Kittredge, George Lyman, *Witchcraft in Old and New England* (Cambridge, 1929).

LeGuin, Ursula (edited by Susan Wood), *The Language of the Night: Essays on Fantasy and Science Fiction* (New York: G.P. Putnam's Sons, 1979).

Russell, Jeffrey B., *A History of Witchcraft: Sorcerers, Heretics, and Pagans* (New York: Thames and Hudson, 1980).

Seznec, Jean, *The Survival of the Pagan Gods* (Princeton, 1972).

Szasz, Thomas, *The Myth of Mental Illness* (New York: Harper and Row, 1974).

Thorndike, Lynn, *A History of Magic and Experimental Science* (eight volumes) (New York, 1923-1958).

Trevor-Roper, H.R., *The European Witch-Craze of the Sixteenth and Seventeenth Centuries and Other Essays* (New York: Harper and Row, 1969).

Wedel, Theodore Otto, *The Mediaeval Attitude Toward Astrology, Particularly in England* (New Haven, Conn.: Yale Studies in English, 1920).

Wind, Edgar, *Pagan Mysteries in the Renaissance* (New York: W.W. Norton, 1968).

**Fiction.** After you've finished reading, or rereading, all the fairy tales, the following authors may intrigue you. I've listed them by name and—occasionally—by series.

Abbey, Lynn, *Daughter of the Bright Moon* (New York: Ace, 1979).

Alexander, Lloyd, *The Book of Three* (first in the Chronicles of Prydain) (Dell).

Anderson, Poul, *The Broken Sword* (Ballantine-Del Rey 1977).

Bradbury, Ray, *Something Wicked This Way Comes* (Bantam 1962).

Bradley, Marion Zimmer, The Darkover Series (Daw).

Beagle, Peter, *The Last Unicorn* (New York: Ballantine-Del Rey, 1968).

Bradshaw, Gillian, *Hawk of May* (New York: Simon and Schuster, 1980).

Chant, Joy, *Red Moon and Black Mountain* (New York: Ballantine-Del Rey, 2nd ed. 1978).

C.J. Cherryh, *Gate of Iyrel, Well of Shiuan, Fires of Azeroth* (DAW), and also in Science Fiction Book Club's *Book of Morgaine.*

Farrar, Stewart, *Omega* (Times Books, 1979).

Kurtz, Katherine, The Deryni novels (New York: Ballantine-Del Rey).

Jones, Diana Wynne, *Charmed Life* (New York: Pocket, 1977).

——The Spellcoats (New York: Pocket, 1980).

Laubenthal, Sanders Anne, *Excalibur* (New York: Ballantine-Del Rey 2nd ed. 1977).

Lee, Tanith, *The Birthgrave, Vazkor Son of Vazkor, Quest for the White Witch* (the Karrakaz trilogy) (New York: DAW).

——*Volkhavaar* (DAW 1977).

——*Night's Master* (DAW 1978).

——*Death's Master* (DAW 1979).

LeGuin, Ursula K., the Earthsea Trilogy (Bantam).

Lewis, C.S., *The Chronicles of Narnia* (New York: Macmillan).

MacDonald, George, "The Light Princess," in *The Fantastic Imagination* (editors, Boyer and Zahorsky) (Avon Books, 1977).

Munn, H. Warner, *Merlin's Ring* and *Merlin's Godson* (Ballantine-Del Rey, 1976).

Norton, Andre, The Witch World Series. (DAW).

Page, Gerald, and Reinhardt, Hank, *Heroic Fantasy* (DAW, 1978).

Salmonson, Jessica Amanda, *Amazons!* (DAW, 1979).

Springer, Nancy, *Sable Moon* (Pocket, 1981).

Vinge, Joan, *The Snow Queen* (Dial, 1979).